THE SAGA OF THE DAMNED CONTINUES AS *GILGAMESH THE KING* STEPS OUT OF THE NATIONAL BESTSELLER LISTS AND INTO HELL!

Heroes in Hell™ started it all ... Nobody who is anybody went to Heaven, and every Hero in Hell is in revolt. Not one of them—from Gilgamesh, the first hero of human literature, to James Dean, America's consummate Rebel—thinks he deserved damnation. Yet here they all are, in Hell.

They're mad as hell and they aren't going to take it anymore! All the big names and all the best minds of history are aiding and abetting the rebellion—er, ah—*the rebellions,* because it may just seem that there are more chiefs down here than Indians, but believe it: Alexander the Great is *not* going to kowtow to Mao; so from the Pentagram in New Hell to Chairman Mao's Celestial Kingdom all hell is breaking loose. And in Hellywood Cecil B. DeMille is getting it all on film for the greatest movie of All Times.

—continued on next page ...

First *Heroes in Hell*™, with its companion hardcover novel *Gates of Hell*; now *Rebels in Hell*, with Morris and Cherryh's second Heroes in Hell companion novel *Kings in Hell*: the Damned Saga continues as some of America's most famous writers line up to get in their licks: Robert Silverberg introduces his national bestseller *Gilgamesh the King* to the tortures of the damned; Martin ("The Six Million Dollar Man") Caidin brings his favorite World War I Fighter Ace, and Billy Kerby ("The Rose") throws his rock star angel into the piranha pool. That's right: even the *angels* are coming to Hell. And of course the *Heroes in Hell*™ core group of Janet Morris, C.J. Cherryh and David Drake have prepared a hot reception for the newcomers . . .

Next volume (*Crusaders in Hell*) Morris promises a *famous* Soviet Dissident Writer (We can't say who yet . . . shsh!) will come down on ComBloc in a big way, while Gregory Benford makes a triumphant return, running into no less than Bertrand Russell, and the creators of *Thieves' World* . . . But no, our lips are sealed. We can say no more. But if you have yet to place your bet on the top writers around in the roughest, toughest venue in the Universe of Discourse . . . What the Hell are you waiting for?

JANET MORRIS

REBELS IN HELL

BAEN
SCIENCE FANTASY
BOOKS

REBELS IN HELL

This is a work of fiction. All the characters and events portrayed in this book are fictional, and any resemblance to real people or incidents is purely coincidental.

A Baen Books Original

Baen Publishing Enterprises
260 Fifth Avenue
New York, N.Y. 10001

First printing, July 1986

ISBN: 0-671-65577-9

Cover art by David Mattingly

Printed in the United States of America

Distributed by
SIMON & SCHUSTER
TRADE PUBLISHING GROUP
1230 Avenue of the Americas
New York, N.Y. 10020

CONTENTS

Undercover Angel, Chris Morris   1

Hell's Gate, Bill Kerby   15

Gilgamesh in the Outback, Robert Silverberg   73

Marking Time, C.J. Cherryh   139

Table with a View, Nancy Asire   169

There Are No Fighter Pilots Down in Hell,
   Martin Caidin   191

'Cause I Served My Time in Hell,
   David Drake   249

Monday Morning, C.J. Cherryh   267

Graveyard Shift, Janet Morris   273

UNDERCOVER ANGEL

Chris Morris

Why this is Hell, nor am I out of it:
Thinkest thou that I who saw the face of God,
And tasted the eternal joys of Heaven,
Am not tormented with ten thousand hells
In being deprived of everlasting bliss!
> —Christopher Marlowe, *Faustus*

The angel was floating, a few inches above the ground, across a vacant lot in the shadow of the Devil's own high-rise when the girl spotted him.

"There he is! Get him! *Get* him!" piped the accusatory treble of Catherine, Satan's youngest spy.

With a thump, the angel fell six inches to the ground, his concentration broken.

Then he began to run, hiking up his robes, across the weed-strewn lot.

Around rusting bicycles and upended refrigerators (all with tight-shut doors) and the blind eyes of dead televisions he dodged, always hearing the jack-booted tread of Authority behind him.

He didn't know whether these particular pursuers

were from the Insecurity Service, the Fallen Angels, Agency, or any of a dozen other policing bureaus.

He didn't care. He was Altos (but call him Al, everybody did), the only commissioned angel in Hell.

He hadn't Fallen. He'd never been defrocked, despised, derailed, or derided.

He hadn't been sent to Hell as punishment or cast out of Heaven for unseemly ambition, the way other angels had gotten here, transmuted, disgraced.

No, Al's crime had been more subtle: he'd volunteered.

Now, running from a child whose ambitions had made her a confidante of potentates in life and death, he regretted his decision, as he had off and on through the millennia.

But Al was a terrible harpist. He had a tin ear. His current job of talent scout among the damned suited him. Most days.

If there could be said to *be* days in New Hell, where the red roiling clouds never broke to let Paradise's healing rays shine through, pure and clean and sanitizing. Where the damned never slept soundly and the Devil never slept at all.

Al's sandaled foot caught on a risen root and he stumbled, went to his knees, felt the skin scrape and blood begin to flow.

His fingers grasped a rusty plow; he pulled himself up, the sound of pounding feet louder in his ears.

He risked a glimpse back and learned nothing: he saw only the honey-blond hair of Catherine, streaming as she flung herself, pall-mall, toward him ahead of a dozen men-at-arms in uniform.

Her face was contorted in a purity of evil only a child could flaunt.

Al shuddered, gained his feet, and stumbled on, his breath rasping, barbed in his lungs: he had a body here, a body he must care for—an angel could not risk rebirth on the Undertaker's table.

Mortified and tiring, he sprinted, fleeing a ten-year-old child's rage. Altos represented hope, the chance of heaven, the light of God that must not waver even in this accursed place. And Catherine II of Russia hated him for it, for hope was the spark of discontent, of rebellion, of strife and unrest.

Catherine cherished only Order—order at any price, order at all costs, order through uniformity, order through security, order through repression.

The Devil loved Catherine like a child of his hooked and horned loins.

He gave her minions and he gave her carte blanche, at least where Altos was concerned.

For some time, Catherine's harassment had been only an annoyance to the angel.

But now her minions were manifold, and if they caught him, he'd know whose uniforms they wore: those of the Supreme Commander's legions; those of the Soviet or Nazi contingents; those of the Fallen Angels themselves.

Thrusting himself forward on aching legs, Al hoped for a rebellious moment that it *was* the Fallen Angels who were chasing him—if he were to be captured, let it be by his once-brothers, those who had been Cast Down.

It was less ignominious than being trussed and mistreated by those he'd been sent here to "save."

He didn't hear the hum of the boomerang whizzing toward him until it was too late.

He was hearing only his own thoughts, within sprinting distance of the Underground that led everywhere in New Hell—wondering why, after so many eons of coexistence, the Devil in His finite wisdom had decided to hunt Altos down.

Then the boomerang hit the back of his head. The dirt and weeds seemed to rush up to meet him as he fell to the ground, and his forehead struck the rusted edge of a hoe that had been there since before the little girl chasing him was born on Earth.

The last thing Al heard was the musical laughter of the child and the clapping of her pink young hands, before blackness overswept him and he heard nothing more at all.

*   *   *

The Devil was in his office, giving Marilyn dictation, when someone from the Infernal Bureau of Investigation reported that Altos the Angel had been brought in for interrogation.

The Devil pushed Marilyn off his desk. She smoothed her skirt down over her milky thighs and walked squishily to the door where she'd left her red patent leather heels.

He closed his eyes as she stooped to put them on (that peculiar position of a woman in a tight white skirt bending over always made him ache) and grated, "Marilyn, I want to see this Altos personally. Have him brought up here. We'll finish . . . this . . . later."

"Ooh," she sighed tremulously, "you're so cru-el, Nicky," but he ignored it, and after a few more "oohs" and flutters of her blue-mascara'd eyelashes, Marilyn swished out with all the compelling rhythm of a pile driver.

Damned woman was nearly enough to make his job bearable. Sometimes.

Michael, Satan's sole companion, fluttered down from the ceiling on leathery wings and sank his claws into a the Devil's bare shoulder.

He closed his eyes and suggested calmly, ignoring the pain of razor-sharp talons, "Change into a cat or a bat or something, will you, Michael? We're having guests. The redoubtable Catherine What's-Her-Name, for one. You wouldn't want to scare a little girl. . . ."

The familiar screeched its laugh, a sound like fingernails on a chalkboard, guaranteed to set every tooth for miles on edge.

Michael then changed into his black Persian cat persona.

The cat, unfortunately, couldn't keep its balance on the Devil's slick-skinned rufous shoulder, just above his right wing, and fell slowly, all claws extended, down Satan's chest, yowling.

Until Satan caught him by the ruff and pulled him, with a sound like tearing velcro, away from his flesh.

"Damn," said the Lord of Hell unnecessarily, and went about changing into his best pin-striped suit, with a suitably Yuppie body under it.

The scratches Michael had made were so deep that by the time Altos the Angel was brought in, naked and shackled, with a crown of thorns on his head and Catherine skipping happily beside, a red all-day-sucker jammed into her sticky mouth, the white shirt the Devil was wearing had long, thin red pinstripes of blood soaking through it.

"Catherine," said the Devil, smiling his most businesslike smile at the horrid, arrogant human child who'd turned in the only working undercover angel in all of Hell in exchange for promises of a pony and a Hellovision series of her own, "good work. Your pony is waiting. Marilyn will take you to see her very own casting director."

Marilyn frowned, looked from young Catherine in her white, muddy dress to the angel slumped between two huge blond men in gray uniforms, then back to the Devil.

The concern in Marilyn's eyes was obvious.

"Just explain to her about keeping her pants on," the Devil warned his secretary. "That's as far as your responsibility goes."

Satan waved a hand impatiently at Marilyn: take the child and go.

When she'd done that, the two blond Insecurity guards brought the angel forward and shoved him to his knees before the Lord of Hell.

Altos' head raised; blood and sweat ran down his forehead and into his eyes from his crown of thorns.

Satan's stomach churned. Michael, sensing his master's distress, began rubbing around the Devil's legs. Satan picked up the "cat" and cradled it in his arms, feeling the azure eyes of the heaven-sent being on him as he walked to the window-wall that never had glass in

it, that wall from which every pane fell stories to the
pavement below, no matter the quality of the Hughes
engineer assigned to redesign it.

Satan looked out over his sanguine domain, at the sky
without blue, at the vault without heaven, at the dim
glow that was Paradise, the light that no denizen of
Hell could ever see unobscured.

And spat out the window.

Then turned, his mouth open to spout accusations
and curses and punishments to fit the crime of holding
out hope to the teeming damned of Hell.

But Satan found his mouth dry, his tongue devoid of
epithets.

He stared at the angel's ravaged, compassionate face,
at cheeks bruised and hair plastered into bronze ringlets with the sweat of pain—and saw no accusation, no
anger, no fear: only patience, and love, and comradeship.

The Devil's queasiness mounted.

Everyone in Hell was bearing a share of the burden—
the Prince of Darkness was no exception.

The angel was unbowed, humble beyond sufferance,
understanding beyond forbearance: Altos was, in short,
angelic.

Here.

When the Devil had Fallen, he'd thought he could
beat the odds. Win. Recoup. Prove himself right.

He'd been an angel of high degree. He'd criticized
God's works and protested that he could do better.

So here he was, with the recalcitrant, the recidivists—
with the damned. And he as damned as the worst of
them.

He'd become part and parcel of Hell; he hated himself; he hated it here.

He *remembered* Paradise. It was a worse punishment
than any of the damned bore.

Except for this angel, who'd come here of his own
accord. Not a being banished, or sent down for a lesson,
or faltered or failed. But come to bring the light of hope
which made Hell the more hellish for those to whom

hope could only be a dream unfulfilled. Such dreams were nightmares.

In the eyes of Altos, who preferred to be called "Al" because neither his provenance nor his high estate could matter to those he aided here—in those eyes lay every hope of Paradise and every memory of salvation.

Staring into them made the Devil unbearably discontent. So discontent that Michael growled, raked his pinstriped belly, and scrambled out of his arms to run to the angel.

At whose knee the familiar curled up, began to purr, and went to sleep.

"Enough!" cried the Devil, pounding with a fist on his desk.

And that fist had reverted to its rufous-skinned, black-clawed self: Satan was so upset that his disguise had begun to melt away.

He gritted his teeth and closed his eyes: he must regain control before his wings rent the fabric of his suit as they materialized.

When that was done, his fury knew no bounds.

And the angel, Al, watched him steadily out of Paradise-bright eyes free of recrimination.

"Enough, I said. You, Altos, do you know what you have done? Do you know these dissidents you inspired have sprouted heads like a Hydra? That they have supporters everywhere? That a bloodbath, a purge, must follow? Do you know that the rumor runs that someone has actually found his way to Heaven from here? Do you know that this additional torture is all your fault?"

A single tear formed at the corner of the angel's right eye, overflowed, ran down his cheek and off his chin to fall through the air and land on Michael's head.

The familiar waked with a start, hissed, arched its back, fluffed its tail, and then looked from Satan to the angel. Finally it bolted, changing form as it did so: wings sprouted from its shoulders, black and scaly; its neck elongated and wattles grew there; its eyes deepened in their sockets and its talons lengthened as its tail grew a barb and began to lash.

Michael launched himself into the air with a beat of wings and made for his perch in the highest, darkest corner of the Devil's abode. Down from that shadowed corner came a sad, slow keening that twisted the Devil's heart.

"See, even Michael is upset. What have you to say for yourself, Altos?" Satan demanded.

The angel replied, "Hope is priceless; it is humanity's birthright. There is recourse; there is a way out of Hell."

"Not through tunnels. You've caused so much suffering with your rumors and your wide-eyed looks and your talk of salvation. You're doing my job better than I am."

What, the Devil wondered, could he *do* with the angel, now that he had him?

He said, sitting again on his desk, "The Resistance you've fostered—who's controlling it? We've got to know, you understand, or too many will suffer. You do understand suffering, don't you?"

One of the guards kicked the prisoner.

The angel favored the guard with a commiserating look.

And that broke the Devil's attempt at calm: "Take him," snarled the Lord of Hell, "to the Pentagram. Put him in the basement, next to Hitler's office. Where he will stay until the back of the Resistance is broken, until the dissidents are disbanded—until Hell freezes over."

The angel didn't even protest as they dragged him away, and the Devil had the awful feeling that he was going to cry.

He hadn't cried for a long, long time. He had no idea what would happen if he did.

So he poured some brandy and with it as bait coaxed Michael down from the shadowed rafters.

And the two of them sat, legs hanging out the incompleted window on the top floor of the Hall of Injustice, overlooking all of New Hell, getting as drunk as possible.

There was no way in hell to stop an angel of God, like there was no way to stop the rebellion under way or its adherents in the Pentagram or any of man's foolishness.

But there must be some way to stop wondering what kind of sand an angel had to have in his craw to take on this kind of assignment. Or what it would be like to have God on your side.

But then, that was the Devil's punishment: Al had been here as long as Satan had been here, reminding the Devil of what it meant to have lost Paradise.

In the bowels of the Pentagram lay Satan's foulest dungeons, peopled by the irredeemable, the darkest souls among the damned.

To the right of Al's cell was the cubicle in which Hitler labored, trying to paper the walls of his prison.

Should the Fuehrer manage to do it right, he'd told Al one evening between inconsolable sobs, he would be free to go. But the walls of Hitler's cell were made up of the starved and bleeding bodies of Third Reich soldiers, none of them quite dead, so that plaster and paper never set smoothly over the quivering, twitching, bloody walls of human flesh.

And Hitler would be there, plastering and papering, until there was not one bubble or wrinkle in the paper and no bump of knee or elbow sticking out beneath.

The job, Hitler had sobbed, would take forever.

Al could not find it in his heart to disagree, but the anguish of the Fuehrer wrenched his angelic sensibilities: for some men, there was no limit to the vengeance of God.

That the Devil had put Hell's only angel here to prove Altos' task as hopeless as Hitler's didn't make the long nights of the Fuehrer's weeping any easier to bear.

A pall of futility, of helplessness, of hopelessness, had descended on the angel.

To fight it, he began levitating in his cell.

Just a little, those first days: three inches off the ground, then four, then six.

To become lighter than air, Altos must leave behind those gravid thoughts of mankind, of fate and life and death and justice, of material existence and even right and wrong.

When Altos shed the temporal considerations of consciousness, he rose like a feather in the wind. And when he floated, even an inch above Hell's fundament, he understood that creation must contain all that was wrong as well as right.

Without evil, there could be no good; without desolation, no hope; without differentiation, no degree or human purpose.

Thus insanity defined sanity, and free choice made humanity a part of God's process of creation in a universe ordered by a First Cause to produce that very paragon of random value, Mankind.

The intelligence of man was not the intelligence of God, but the eye of man had been created by the eye of God—had come from God, would return to God when perfected.

What could not be perfected on Earth or in Heaven, came here.

In the cleansing fire of atomic fury, unselective and thorough, man had found a way to flout the orderly procession of souls to their destiny. Because in Heaven all times were one infinite indivisible moment, "when" man unleashed the atom upon his neighbor in a cleansing debacle, God had sent a volunteer to Hell.

To handle the influx. To mitigate fates among wholesale slaughter. To make sure no one deserving—in any infinitely and infernally divided moment of Hell—was denied Heaven.

In some particular spacetimes of Hell, there were Judges who might commute a sentence. In the multitemporal environment of New Hell, there was only Altos: the single angel charged with, among other duties, the Devil's eventual rehabilitation.

Rehabilitation of the Prince of Darkness was a full-time job, a lifelong endeavor, a supernal longshot.

And tonight, stuck in a temporal procession of infinitely divided instants so different from the Eternal Now of Heaven, Al was infinitely depressed and eternally disgusted.

In truth, the angel was in danger of losing face, if not faith.

Betrayed by a child, a gentle expression of creation; incarcerated next to one of the foulest murderers of all time; asked endless foolish questions by representatives of the Infernal Bureau of Investigation (who didn't really want to know the answers and often wrote down different ones than those Altos gave them)—it was so useless.

When the representative of Rameses II, Supreme Commander, came to his cell with a wax tablet and sharp stylus in one hand and a mini-computer in the other, Al steeled himself for another round of endless questions.

The little fellow with the kohl-elongated eyes and the snaggle teeth said, smoothing his linen skirt down over his knees and flipping up the lid of the mini-computer he balanced there, "Now then, Altos—"

"Just Al's fine."

"Just Al, then." The interrogator's chin doubled; through the walls, the cursing sobs of Hitler drifted. "Let's get down to business, Just Al." The little man tapped his keyboard and it beeped plaintively; his round, chubby face was underlit with reddish light from the computer's amber display screen.

Altos met the questioning look in those painted eyes with one of his own: he had no idea what this minion of evil wanted; they all had their own hidden agendas, too many days here and endless nights here had made that clear to him.

A child had done this to him; a child who should have been good, should have been innocent, should not have cared for politics or propaganda, but who fed on both like one of the Devil's own pet demons.

"Business?" he repeated at last, his feet on the cold stone floor now: there was no way to levitate even a millimeter with this creature of darkness in the room. The man's soul was like a weight on a fishing line: it dragged Altos to the bottom and kept him there.

"Business," the little man reechoed with a sly grin, and tapped his computer. "Everything's arranged; the security blocks are in place. We can talk freely now."

"Talk about what?" said the angel with all the patience of his kind.

"About your escape, of course, Just Al. Which is scheduled for . . ." The short plump man consulted a wristwatch the size of a cow-pie. ". . . seven minutes from now."

"My . . . escape?" Altos was shocked. It would make him a criminal. It would make him a fugitive. . . . It would get him away from Hitler's poisonous blasphemy. . . . "How? Why?"

"Yours is not to question," said the scribe or whatever he was. "I have my orders. Rumor runs they come zigzag from Mithridates' office, through Rameses, but you'd know more about that than I . . . ."

Altos crossed his arms and sat on his bug-ridden cot. The bugs were small and red and they bit him immediately and continually, dozens or hundreds of them, peppering his thighs and buttocks with a sharp multitude of pains.

"The dissidents."

"That's right," said the emissary, who obviously feared no eavesdroppers. "We'll get you to Che Guevara's camp, if we can. Out of here, at least."

"At what price?" There was so much evil here, Altos was suddenly exhausted by its extent. He slumped among the bedbugs, uncaring, waiting for an answer he knew he wasn't going to like.

"Price? A favor, Just Al. A mere favor to those who want to loose the Devil's despotic grip. Hell could be a better place, a place of striving, of remedial education—"

"Cut the propaganda," snapped the angel. "What is it you want, you and Rameses and Mithridates?"

Rameses II was a man whose evil was moderate, in tune with his intellect. He'd lied about the battle of Kadesh and indulged in petty power struggles; he'd subjugated peoples and dealt harshly with Moses. He'd married a Hittite princess under false pretenses and defiled her and his oath.

But next to Mithridates VI he was a cherub. Mithridates, a Persian claiming descent from Darius, styled himself in Alexander's image. He'd perpetrated three Mithridatic Wars upon an unhappy Asia Minor, gone up against Rome's Pompey and failed. Mithridates had married his own sister, imprisoned his mother, ordered the massacre of his entire harem to placate his gods when his battles went badly, subsisted on prophylactics to immunize himself from poisoning, and finally died upon the sword of one of his guards.

A disastrous strategist with a massive ego and no talent for keeping the loyalty of his subordinates, in life Mithridates had been a true representative of neither Hellenism nor his Iranian constituency, but only of disorder and disaster.

Becoming involved in any scheme of Mithridates was bound to lead to a debacle for all concerned. That Mithridates was somehow powering the dissidents was the Devil's worry.

That Mithridates wanted Altos sprung from jail rang alarm bells in the angel's mind.

Finally, the minion admitted a reason: "We want you to help us woo Caesarion into the dissident camp. We need Caesar's son on our side, Just Al."

"I think I'd rather not," Altos began in his quiet voice.

But it was too late: outside the door he could hear stealthy, running feet and the sound of muted struggle.

Then the door was wrenched open and guerrillas with wide eyes burst in, guns and knives in hand, to "rescue" him.

There was neither time nor reason to argue with these soldiers of disorder.

"Come! Now!" said a voice with a South American accent, and Che Guevara himself held out a bloodstained hand.

Altos took it, while the scribe scrambled up and away and down the hall sirens sounded.

Wherever in Hell Altos was going, whatever the dissidents planned to do with him, he'd be of more use there than he was in solitary confinement here, listening to Hitler curse the bodies writhing under the wallpaper in his cell.

"Run!" demanded the dissidents' leader, and Altos felt his feet begin to leave the ground.

HELL'S GATE

Bill Kerby

It was the worst of times. It was the worst of times.

It was hot, of course. You expected that; a kind of wet, nasty heat that never let up. Sweat ran freely and was cooled with no breeze ever. What sky there was, splayed out from horizon to horizon, an ugly tan in color with bloody red striations that came very close to having sound. It was a barely audible hum that was always there, a pulsing low cycle tone that never ended but was never really heard.

There were plains and mountains and hot, red oceans. It was not in any way beautiful but it was stunning, august. There wasn't climate; there was weather and all of it bad. It was known, on both sides by all people in all times, to be the worst duty station in recorded history and yet still they came, still they fought.

When time ground to a halt and the universe imploded back into the starry pimento-loaf from which it was born, they would strap on the packs and guns, throw away their useless canteens, search vainly for a match for their unlit Camels and then, would mount another attack. Because this is what they do. It utterly defines them, makes them what they are—if they don't do this, they might cease to exist, they might never be coming from anywhere or be going anywhere, they would

15

just be gone. And that thought, that base and elemental (my dear Watson) thought was sufficient to drive them forward to Eternity in dirty sweatsocks.

There was no real rest because there was no real night. Living was hard. Life was improbable.

Because understanding was impossible.

An enormous battle machine—a fortress of dull green steel alloy, towering hundreds of feet in the air, was attached to five gigantic tanks below that churned endlessly over ditch and hill, over smoking lakes and flaming glaciers, never stopping. The teflon treads, each as big as a queen-sized bed, chewed everything in their path to flinders. Guns fired out of evil-looking ports that looked nearly alive as they closed up and reappeared elsewhere like a slit mouth with another weapon—more devastating than its cousin—which would then send a beautiful stream of tracers alternating with jellied white phosphorous frags.

The hapless poet who coined these armies "ignorant" as they "clashed by night" was shot first and cornholed afterward for his dancing poetic insight as well as his booty. One of the soldiers to whom he was haughtily referring wore his scented silk brocade hat for months—until he stepped on a Bouncing Betty with a tiny nuke charge and had his midsection vaporized. They never found the hat.

A rain as thin and brown as diarrhea began to fall. From somewhere came the sound of thousands, millions of moaning dead. The sound was at first heartbreaking. In it was the agony of loneliness and dispair. But it soon turned to something horrible and insufferably chilling. It was the sound of history and betrayal. The sound of power.

A vast undulating rug of Scorpions—the Third Insect Armored Division to be exact, themselves out on a raiding party—scurried across the stiffened body of a dead, half-eaten pack mule. The scorpions stung millions of maggots but it didn't matter to maggots who only knew one thing: gobble gobble and then turn into flies where they would attack aimlessly (the very best way) and then go home to relax on an eternal yard full of ever-wet dog shit. Hey! what did they care for a few sting-aling-alings. This grave *was* their victory.

The God of the Flies has many names and they are known quite well by all.

Bob. Pimp of the Underworld. Big Ron. Goddamn It. Slime Merchant of It All. Kiss (of "Kiss my ass"). Plus the usual and more well-known Satan, Devil, Beelzebub, and Pazouzou which made people laugh when they heard it, so it was not much favored. "He" was also a she and an it, all rolled together into an irresistible mass of nervous, hungry, and very base energy which usually formed itself into what folks found most attractive.

For instance, he had looked like the cuddly old man who'd been Heidi's grand-pop. He'd even sounded like him. That was good if a little boring. For a while he'd looked like the Black Stallion. Wuh-ooaw, THAT was fun! Running all over Hell and back, never tiring, jumping over body pits, while flies took orders from his whisking black tail. Yesterday, out of boredom, he had been six inches tall. For a while it had fascinated him to run around, dodging giants who hardly even saw him.

But today, it pleased him to close on his True Destiny. He didn't actually know it, but when did that ever affect anything? He had, his face nearly becoming part of the mirror, made himself an outlaw. His not inconsequential features slid one into the other, faster and faster, like amphetamine animation—the eyes, the nose, the mouth—until he got it right. Righter than he would have suspected at this point. And he looked at his outlaw face. Yes, oh yes. This was it, he could feel movement in his hot loins just peering into this dark reflection.

Outlaw.

Not Jesse James (he'd already been him any number of times) or Charlie Manson (ick patooie), but a real outlaw. An emotional desperado (y'better let somebody luv you), the eternal stranger, the lost and lonely; he

had made himself look like a classically prototypical
1955 movie—
    REBEL!
The great American rebel, in fact, James Byron Dean.
From Fairmount, Indiana—star of stage, screen, and
underpants. James Dean: race car driver, actor, shy
friend, legend. The original teenaged American kid, misunderstood by his friends, despised by the authorities,
and loved desperately by his beautiful and sensitive
girl. Not to mention the cute dorky guy in the back who
looked like Sal Mineo.
    It was no trick to change. It just took the desire, the
will. Plus a little magic. When he turned from the mirror into the flickering incredible light, it was done.
Streaked hair, damaged eyes, surly shuffle, and absolutely haunted expressions. The very embodiment of
teen angst.
    And others seemed remarkably fond of the look. He
had seduced Eve Curie, Noel Coward, and one of the
anorexic Borgia twins (he always forgot their names) in
less than a New York minute! Hey, now . . .
    Always desperately trying to stop boredom, the new
twist was going to be that he, James Dean, was going to
be On The Run! Like rebels are wont to be. Since the
god of flies could do anything here, suddenly, he *was*
running.
    He was tired, aching, in utter pain and thirsty, in the
bargain. He fell, gashed open his arm, and kept going
because something in his new being drove him on and
deeper and deeper and deeper into the game that would
pass a few moments in real time by passing a whole life
in reel time. Simply, he became who he was. He would
pass through his faces, changing from one to the next
into the next like an intricate, wonderful set of nested
Chinese boxes. Giving birth to the story, the teller can
be everywhere, everyone at once. It keeps him fully
occupied so that he cannot see the vast, silent empti-
ness around him. He gives birth to a phalanx of lies; it
is only good if the fantasy is complete down to the very

last improbable detail. A few moments pass here while eternity does a slow fox trot there. Dancers are born to conquer time and space.

Especially *this* dancer.

The rebel soldier had eluded them, if only for now. Running in a maze of trenches, he fell over rotted bodies and abandoned equipment. But he kept going.

He stopped beneath a wall of sandbags, heaving for a breath of the fetid air.

The feeling was back, and oh Christ, it felt great: loneliness. Pain, terror, and exhaustion took it away for brief periods of time, but in the end, he was lonely again. It was a feeling worsely better than homesickness or even getting ditched after the movie by your big brother and his girlfriend who wanted to go make smashface. It was worse than running out of garlic salt or cigarettes in the night or when the Cubs lost. It was worse than bad love and it was all the more horrific and confusing because he absolutely had no idea of what or whom he could be lonely for. I mean, it was enough to piss off Lassie!

He wrapped his sweating, bloody hand around the butt end of his Detonics .45 and felt a teeny better. He leaned his head back against the sandbags and began to sing very softly, "Dawn . . . go away, I'm no good for you—"

An arrow slammed into his forehead, pinning him to the sandbag he thought he'd been hiding behind. For a wondorous second before they closed, his bright blue eyes looked up to see what had caused this sudden headache. Oh oh, this looks like more than a job for extra-strength Bufferin, was the last thought in his brain. He'd always had a sense of humor. To go with the job. He had needed it often and in this last millisecond, it hadn't gone south . . . even if everything else had.

The final insult was the arrow shaft. It was clearly part of a TV antenna to which a jagged, long piece of fire-hardened mirror had been epoxied. The feathers were strips of torn pages from a Barbara Cartland paperback. "His cruel eyes ravaged her coral-tipped—" In this chaotic heat did culture make its appearance once again.

The hyenas came closer but very slowly. They edged up, their hindquarters already curled around, ready to run. They growled at each other as they came closer to the scent of another fresh dinner. They were grotesquely fat, like swollen ticks; there was more than enough food for their ever-increasing tribe.

The head hyena was larger, more scarred than his followers. He looked more like a Doberman wearing a very detailed Jim Henson hyena costume. And he barked like a dog as he closed in, first in line, to that skewered extraordinary rebel soldier's face. The hyena began to lick the little ropes of blood. Then he stopped dead. All of them had stopped. Their noses twitched and their huge, hairy ears wobbled.

Suddenly they all ran at once, streaking away, howling in their perpetual sniveling cowardice. Their bloated bodies raised a cloud of red dust that did wonders with the light. Someone far away was running after the head hyena with a net, it looked like.

On the far side, and 20 feet above the brain-splattered sandbags, four workmen in combat cammies set up a large field-mess table. As soon as it was down, dozens of servants began to bring tureens of food, setting them on the table carelessly. One fell off. It was yellow, lumpy and slightly furry. Curried Rat, apparently, raisins and all. In a few moments, the field table had become a groaning board. No one even saw the man who had been pinned to the sandbags below.

Then people came, slapping mosquitoes and farting. Che Guevara and a cat in a Roman toga led them. Che was smaller than assumed, but there was a true magic to his gaze that could go from loving to murderous in a heartbeat. Cataraugus, the feline emperor installed for a week by Caligula, the loonie, tottered along on his hind legs. His eyes looked holy, familiar, and long-suffering. He and Che seemed to lead the group. Too, there was a young fat man with squinty eyes and his hair in a samurai topknot who made everyone laugh. And others, warriors who carried crossbows and laser-phasers, bloody hatchets and particle-beam pistols, zip guns and brass knuckles. There were men and women of all ages and colors and sizes. There were other creatures that were better described by scent. The only thing they all seemed to have in common was a regard for Che and Cataraugus. They looked at them as they lifted their cracked Tiffany goblets up for the first drink of warm ox urine—

When the entire table exploded!

It covered the fifty or so people in a horrific slimy goo, both from the food and the special pre-packed charges of beef jello and torn Poptart hunks.

Someone, somewhere, began to laugh.

A tan, very thin man in bleached, well-worn jeans and a Hiro Sushi cut-off sweatshirt ran in hurriedly and, turning the clap stick upside down, he bent over and yelled "Hell's Gate, banquet scene, take 351!" With that, he banged the black and white striped stick.

Cataraugus ripped off his Dick Smith-made cat mask, enraged.

The man pinned to the sandbag with a special effects arrow "through" his forehead opened his eyes in disgust.

"Who do you have to fuck to GET OUT OF THIS MOVIE?"

Bizarrely, the entire explosion froze, and then began to run backwards, sound and all. The slate man ran in backwards; the exploding charges came back into their hidden receptacles; the sprays of food came backwards, homing down into their bowls as Che, backwards, took the unshattering glass goblet back down from his lips and walked, backwards, through his monstrous entourage ... all of whom were strolling backwards. Now, the laughter was quite loud.

In the screening room, it was icy cold. Slowly, the

lights came up as the image on the immense screen faded to black. And the laughter died in the light. From the speaker, the tinny voice of an ancient man from the projection booth in the rear.

"That's the last reel, Mr. DeMille . . ."

Cecil B. DeMille got to his feet and with an impassive face turned to the assembled. "I would like to see the director, the stars, and the cameraman in my office—"

"Cess, baby . . . could we make it *my* office?" asked Mark Next One, the current mercurial head of The Studio. Mark was lean and mean with dangerous eyes and longish curly hair, dripping in mousse jell. He was casually dressed in a new Tokyo suit, not even in this country yet. He had a perfect moustache, the corners of which, when he zeroed in for a kill, he tickled with his darting pink tongue. He was relentless, charming at parties, and prided himself on never, in all his tenure here, having read one single screenplay. Writers, he thought, were nothing more than cancerous, greedy mongers who cared only about adverbs and truth and such cheap shit as that.

"My office?" he added with his patented twinkle and sixth-grade grin.

Mark's office was all stainless steel, black glove leather, and jade slabs. Guys from the Memphis group over in Italy had come and done it after his predecessor's stroke, piece by piece. There were signed lithos by Rusha and Warhol, pictures of Mark with Kennedys and Barrymores and the entire Murderers' Row of the Yankees, there were books (all unread, natch), scripts (likewise), and little knicknacks around to play with as he made deals that tore huge hunks out of artists and businessmen alike. Now, mostly what the office was filled with was hysterical screaming.

"THIS IS SHIT, FROM ONE END TO THE OTHER!"

When this kind of howling can make James Dean, Montgomery Clift, Gregg Toland, Michael Curtiz, and

C.B. DeMille all look at their respective shoes, you know it is potent.

"I am right!" Mark continued as he slinked around the room, "and every single one of you knows it."

He was and they did.

"Two hundred and seventy six billion dollars, the creative energy of the entire goddamn history of cinema for 'Hell's Gate,' and this crapola is all you can come up with?" Mark ticked them off on his fingers. "The performances suck; wooden, wooden, wooden. All the stunt effects backfire. The script and story are appalling. The lighting is artsie fartsie, I can't see diddly! If you don't shape up, I will sew you all together with a rusty carpet needle and drag you with towtrucks to Cincinnati, *where you can all do dinner theatre with Bob Crane forever!*"

They vainly sought refuge in the silence which was, at that point, fit for chip dip. Then to punctuate it, he swept all the scripts off his desk. Nobody said a word. He was right.

"Hell's Gate" *was* a disaster. It had gone on ever since they could remember. Gable and Harlow's scenes were finished in more ways than one. Spencer Tracy had tired of the endless confusion and flat quit (some eye-witnesses said he mysteriously disappeared in a blinding flash). John Barrymore punched out Victor Fleming who was directing at that time. A week later in the Cock and Bull, Fleming shot Barrymore, and right where you think, too. Made all the papers. Wallace Beery lost fifty pounds in his desert scenes, Janet Gaynor had her eyelashes singed off, and a runaway train ran over Susan Ball's other leg. A low-yield nuclear squib went off by accident and took out a complete full-sized reproduction of the Palace at Versailles, not to mention Vivian Leigh, Ralph Richardson, and Joyce Grenfell, who had been added for a little class. The insurance company'd been pretty understanding. Fortunately, the miniatures survived, and as for the humans, most of their scenes were in the can. Re-animation would take care of over-the-shoulder shots.

With just three major films (only one of which he liked) to his credit, James Dean was giving everything he had. Even by Hellywood standards, he was whipped. And he more than looked it as Mark glared down at him.

"And what do you have to say for yourself, Jimmy? I mean you did just see the same dailies I did, *didn't you*?"

James Dean looked up. Then, back at the floor. Then, back up again. In his blue eyes was a world of hurt. Clift leaned forward and picked up a small lunar rock that one of the astronauts had given Mark some years back when he was being courted for his life story. Clift thought it was very small. "It's very small," he said in his famous tortured voice.

"Yeah, pal, it is. But for two hundred and seventy six billion dollars, 'Hell's Gate' should be BIG! You assbuckets are all—"

"Son, we get your drift," said DeMille. He got up and began to tap his riding crop, tip tip tip, on his starched puttees. Mark looked at the old man with some amusement. This was how he maneuvered elements; it had worked with the best, it had worked with the worst. You pissed on them long enough so that when you stopped, they became grateful. Now, he watched through his serpent's eyes as the old man reached down into his bag of tricks.

"Mike ..." DeMille turned to Michael Curtiz, the director, "I know you did 'Casablanca' and 'High Sierra'—"

"Dat woss Raoul Walsh, Z.B.—"

"But I feel you're directed out on this project. You've given us two of the best years of your life and I think it's time for someone fresh, someone new."

Every eye in the room was on the old man. He was changing captains again. DeMille was hard and tough as boiled owl, but he was not reckless or stupid.

"I couldn't understand you, Mike," mumbled Dean. "Bogart must have had radar or something."

"Vell, Bogie vas a man and mitt a pitze-kacka poofter like you, I take dat as a compliment."

"Boys . . ." the old man smiled. He had his plan now. He turned to Mark—who, to him, was The Enemy. Always had been, always would be. "Most of the cast stays. They're good. You're dead wrong, Mark. You're too used to Pickford and Rogers, all that eye-rolling stuff. These are *new times*, boyo! Less is more. Jimmy and Monty are as good as it gets. You'll see."

"I might. If you had a cameraman who knew his ass from his f-stop!"

"Gregg, you're a genius, but you're out. This picture isn't about images. It's about faces and epic landscapes. It's about pain and love—"

"A little tit wouldn't hurt, either," groused Mark.

Gregg Toland—the man who had photographed "Citizen Kane," "Grapes of Wrath," and "The Best Years of Our Lives"—got to his feet. "I'm tired. I'm going home to my wife and kids. You guys don't know what the hell you're doing. I thought Orson was a pain in the ass!" On his way out he slammed the door. In black and white deep focus.

"So, what's the plan?" asked Mark, ready to pounce if he didn't like what he heard.

"We hire a new director. I have a man in mind . . . I have to talk to him first. I'm not sure he even wants to do another picture. He's very tough, nearly impossible. But he might come aboard . . . as a favor. We will get a new cameraman. Franz Planer, Charlie Clarke, someone I can work with. Gregg was great but too slow . . ."

"It occasionally helps to actually be able to see the picture," sneered the brilliant young executive.

"And now, I have a little surprise for all of you."

Every eye was on DeMille.

"You wanted a hit with the kids," DeMille continued. "I have hired someone to write additional scenes. He will also play Che Guevara—he'll replace what's-his-name, Mr. Lox—and he's written the book for the oratorio at the end—"

"Oratorio!" Mark yelled. They were all stunned. What was going on, here. A new actor, new scenes and music?

"I have read the scenes; they are brilliant," DeMille went on, "I have heard part of the music that Stravinsky has written to his book . . ." Jimmy actually dropped a pin he was playing with. And you could hear it.

"I have scheduled a live run-through performance of it this afternoon, after lunch, on soundstage #5. I think you will want to be there."

DeMille admittedly loved these moments. "To see our new Che—Jim Morrison of The Doors. He's hot, he's sexy . . . and he's mine."

This, then, is how movies are made. They are fashioned out of ignorance, mistakes, exhaustion, and sometimes, accidently, vision. Mark Next One had, with all his eviscerating pomposity, only been on "Hell's Gate" for three years. Montgomery Clift had been cast as Cataraugus when Mark was still in the mailroom. When he came to it, finally in charge, it had already been shooting for longer than anyone could remember.

The movie had taken over their lives, wholesale. "Hell's Gate" was everyone's favorite lower-chakra whipping boy and yet it held them all prisoner in its agonizing glory as it ground on and on and on. You could easily have fit ten Soviet "War and Peace" in its prologue alone. The Studio had decided to roll the dice on one movie; it had been pre-sold and blind-booked into a trillion theatres on Easter morning where it would play to packed houses forever—a 150-mm Showscan, 3D, mag stripe stereo smellafeelie of such proportion that it took three shifts of ad execs from Batton, Barton, Durston, & Osborn (sounds like a trunk falling downstairs), plus Ted Bates to map out its campaign. Caesar would gaul.

The Studio knew it would take an incredible director, a real picture-maker. So they started with Griffith, then went to von Stroheim, Ford, Wyler; the list was endless. For a few years they had tried foreign directors; de Sica, Fritz Lang, Jean Renoir, even Fassbinder. These varied from reluctant to intractable. So it was back to the Americans. Hawks, Welles, all of them. Except one.

One had eluded them. He hadn't returned phone calls. He seemed immune. They wanted him badly enough to double his last two deals with profit participation from dollar one. Still he didn't appear to be interested, so they'd more or less given up. But now, maybe just maybe it might be the man DeMille talked about. Who else could have that kind of mysterious cachet, that breath-catching moment when you thought, "oh oh, this is it, I'm standing here at the crossroads of cinematic history." And you were.

Dean and Clift ate lunch every day together in Jimmy's Bluebird "land yacht," a Winnebago-type vehicle that slept six (although it didn't, no matter what Hedda said). In fact, Monty had moved in.

It was admittedly convenient, now that all the rest of their scenes were together. And if a guy wanted to put on his silk pjs, pop a Lockerroom, and cook a couple of steaks with his buddy, so what? Neither one of them really cared what people thought. And all this flagrantly heterosexual behavior was tray boring, nez pah? Finally, it was the tight looseness (or loose tightness, mayhap) of this friendship that kept them together when all the rest were endlessly fractured.

So they shared the lavish Bluebird, directing the driver to park it all over town, depending on their mood on any given night, where they would usually finish off their sushi suppers with a little Dom Perignon and lots of gossip.

Since it began, back in a glove factory in Queens, the movie business has been thought to be fueled by greed, the sufferings of others, ambition, and equal parts of alcohol and cocaine. This is only incidentally true.

Its real fuel is gossip. And, too, the following law applies: whatever is heard, is true. Jack Warner is out. Rock Hudson is gay. Alan Ladd is 4'9". Myron Selznick is from the planet Grydar. Clara Bow is a dyke. Alan Ladd is 6'4". Errol Flynn is a Nazi spy. Rock Hudson is straight. Harry Cohen paid his Mexican gardeners to set fire to MGM studios. Gloria Swanson is really Joan Crawford after surgery. Alan Ladd (really 6′) has a Ford dealership with Clark Gable in Bolivia. Clara Bow is a nympho. Marilyn Monroe had a measured IQ only two points lower than John Stuart Mill's. Jimmy Dean is still alive on a John Doe ward in a hospital in California where his entire blood supply has been replaced by cranberry juice and formaldehyde; his male nurse is a brain-damaged Jack Kennedy! I know a guy who knows this other guy *who saw 'em!* No means yes, now means then, up is down, in is out, and above all remember: when you are on The Top, rent. Because you will not be there long.

In Hellywood, it's *all* true. Where there's smoke, there's fire. So to speak.

Monty carefully edged another cork out of a dark Dom bottle and sighed. "Do you think a burned-out rock and roll poet can play Che Guevara? I don't know."

"You could help him," Jimmy said. "You helped me. I helped Nick Adams. It comes around."

"I don't mean to kvetch, but did you see *Variety* today? The holding company that owns my agency just bought a block of stock in The Studio."

"Quelle drag! How much?" Jimmy wanted to know.

"Enough. I'm never getting out of that frigging cat mask, you know? I don't have any leverage left. My honchos now work for the company. What kind of world is this, anyway?"

"The camera loves you, Monty. Even buried in cat fur and whiskers. I'll get nominated again, for the longevity if nothing else. But you'll get the award. They'll say, 'The tortured eyes of Cataraugus carried at least two hours of the grimmest disaster since the Vatican 747 crashed into that children's hospital—' where was that?"

"Phoenix."

"Yeah, Phoenix. They'll be out in those overpriced glass-box condoes on Camelback Mountain, watching you get the Academy Award. And you'll turn to the camera and you'll say—"

"This rightfully should go to the *true* star of the movie." Clift was laughing, now.

"Who was to be here tonight, but for an acute attack of viral shyness ..." and Dean's eyes blinked twice— had it been filmed in close up, it would have had crazed teenagers chewing the bottoms out of their theatre seats— and they both began to laugh uproariously.

It was the end to an evening of an exhausting day and they washed a couple of recreational lithium caps down with the champagne. They were in a rare mood; tomorrow they were shut down! The cast and crew were off until Mr. DeMille found a new director. Lots of luck, Ace. Lots of luck. Except for the Morrison-Stravinsky music preview tomorrow afternoon at 4 PM, they were free!

They had decided to go shopping on Hellrose Avenue in the new wave hip boutiques where, for oodles of money, you could buy stuff you hated back in the fifties for people you hated now. Or perhaps in Beverly Hells; Mr. Guy, maybe Gucci. Or go see that new temporary Teflon irradiator wok-chip over at Williams-Sonoma. Just walk around and think plastic, have cappucinos, and walk around some more. Free, free. No Devil make up, no arrow in the forehead. No cat mask, no backfiring stunts. Just two pals loose on the town.

They capped off the free morning with a visit to the new exotic car dealership on Hellcrest. The salesman was a young guy from Minnesota without his cool-calluses yet, and when Clift and Dean walked in to see the new gigantic Von Tripp-Porsche, he almost loaded his Haggars. But he showed the stunning car well enough so that Jimmy (after calling his business manager) ordered one. Monty was inside the incredible cockpit, admiring the detail work on the dashboard, Jimmy was outside making sure he got the model with the Allison P-38 engine. It would do O-60 in 1.8 seconds. It came

with a dental rider you had to sign; you indemnified
them from having to replace your fillings jerked out by
the acceleration. James Dean was made to drive this
car. And Montgomery Clift was made to ride in it,
whooping and half drunk at his side.

As Jimmy waited in the salesman's cubicle for some
pictures the man wanted autographed, he thought he
saw a young woman he'd seen somewhere before. But
he couldn't quite place where. She was dressed in leather
and lace, tiny, shining, and looking at one of the new
Honda Diablos. Just as he was about to recall her name,
Monty ran in, panic etching his incredible features.

"It's ten of four, for Liz's sake!" Car places, pro football, and hardware stores will eat a man's time by the
mile. So Jimmy scrawled his name on the bill of sale
and they raced out. The Oratorio preview was at four.
Being late to these things was dangerous. Especially
given the cancerous circumstances surrounding "Hell's
Gate." Everybody was teetering on critical mass, ready
to ream. They had ten minutes to go fifteen miles across
town.

Jimmy drove his Ferrari Testarosa as fast as it'd ever
been driven, considering. In the last five months he had
torn out all the forward gears and (as the Italian me-
chanics and partsmen had quit or gotten movie deals)
all he had left was reverse. Even looking out across his
fingernail-ripped backseat and bright red trunk, James
Dean looked stunning. Reverse only fed the legend.

In soundstage #5 for the oratorio's preview, as usual,
there were more people than there was room for. Everyone had told their friends and those friends had told
their friends and now, it was a regular goonbash. They
were all on no-eye-contact autopilot while they made
sure they were seen with The Right People. It wouldn't
do to be in a grouping, say, with a star, a director and a
writer. Unless a stuntman was along to offset the writer.
Or an actress, a producer, and a studio exec. Unless you
had a successful French restauranteur in the mix. In

Hellywood, combination chemistry is king; and over here by the bar, James Dean, Montgomery Clift, Fatty Arbuckle (who was in fact so fat that if somebody yelled HAUL ASS! he'd have to make two trips), and the incredible Humphrey Bogart were a small but jewelish part of its crowned court. Like the spinelessly gaudy Spanish throne of the 18th century, here also princes mixed with jerkoffs who came and went at will. As it were. Bogart had observed some time back, "Real power doesn't give a shit who uses it. It's always around."

Half the enormous sound stage had been curtained off and there were armed men stationed at the draped plush velvet. Some of the special effects men on the crew tried to make shop talk with them, but it was met with stoney silence.

The lights slowly dimmed. People murmured as they continued to look for more important people to stand next to. Jimmy made a face at Monty who broke up. Jimmy's catalog of DeMille impressions was getting good. And now, as he heard the great man's voice, he moved his lips to the familiar words, "All right, ladies and gentlemen, are we ready?"

Slowly, the gigantic swaying curtains came open as the spotlights came on. An audible tremor rocked the room. Even for this bunch, it was impressive.

On one level, a band: visible was Bill Evans on synthesizers, Duane Allman and Jimi Hendrix on guitars, Keith Moon on drums, Zoot Sims and Lester Young on tenor saxes. The vocalists were Jim Croce, Muddy Waters, Maria Galla Curci, Janis Joplin, Robert Johnson and then, slouching into position at the last moment, the Lizard King himself, Jim Morrison. Thoughtfully, he was wearing black leather and turquoise; he hadn't come in his newly fitted Che Guevara costume.

On the ground level was a symphonic orchestra, made up of over three hundred pieces; both ancient and "modern" instruments, the personnel too rich and varied to name without programs which The Studio wouldn't print because as Mark Next One said, who the fuck cares who's playing some tweet-tweet fiddle?

The chorus, perhaps 200 strong, was on risers that lifted back up into the smoky reaches of the vast soundstage. All eyes turned at once.

And Igor Stravinsky strode out nodding at pianists Artur Rubinstein, William Kappell, Schabel, and Gisa King. Stravinsky stopped for a moment when he got even with the band's level. The older man and Jim Morrison exchanged a look of such fierce magnitude that those near them had to turn away or be incinerated. In this collaboration, symbolized by that moment, were futures writ. For all kinds of dumb reasons.

Jimmy and Monty, their drinks long forgotten in slack hands, stared at the spectacle in front of them. This was real. This was not TV. It was not movies. And it was not some well-rehearsed attention-getting anecdote at Joe Allen's. In front of perhaps a hundred partygoers, twenty of whom were film business movers and shakers, were over 600 Serious Artists. Bo, they could read the little music dots and everything! In such a way is all guilty talent suborned.

With a surprisingly tiny move from his baton, Igor Stravinsky started the piece. And from that first plaintive and discordant sound, everyone knew, instantly. It went through the lot of them like terrible gas after wonderful Polish sausage.

There are two kinds of bad. There's bad. And then, there's BAAAAAAD. So are there two kinds of wrong. The wrong that makes your conscience say *Hooo boy, I better think of something fast!* Then, there is the "wrong" of Modern Music. This wrong—when done right—puts wings on stone.

The oratorio that had been devised by Stravinsky and Morrison (with, as it turned out, the help of Gregg Handel and Chuck Baudelaire) was the start of airborn quarries.

Simply, it was magnificent in its dissonance and anger. It built slowly from heartbreak and then it swelled into cascading waterfalls of jealousy and rage. The torrent, now filled by the choir's expanse, swept through valleys of doubt and apprehension with a living ocean of agony and ruination. And like that.

Some of the cruelest, the most jaded in the audience had to turn away; it was too much, too strong. And yet it was only approaching its climax. This guy named Thomas who never believed in anything figured they'd gotten the electricians to wire the floor. Because there was an almost palpable shock wave running back and forth through the onlookers.

It was that wonderful horror of the Interstate when you see a wreck happening like it's in slow motion and you cannot take your eyes from its carnage even though your granny told you that you'd go to hell if you looked.

YOU *LOOKED!* And so did they.

At one voice that sang out—the descant of an angel—running along the top of the hypnotic nightmare, a voice of purity and goodness so true and alive and forlorn that it only made the darkness more seeable. The purest synergy: neither of its creators had planned it, nobody really understood the geometry of it, but it was one of those certified magic moments when You Are There.

It was the soaring, incredible voice of one Mary Rose Foster—The Rose—who did to them, at five after four that afternoon, what both saved and destroyed them. In this moment, the end of "Hell's Gate" came to be born. The train was finally back on the tracks. And everyone knew it except her.

"It's the girl at the car place! She was looking at a Honda," hissed Jimmy during a quiet interlude.

Monty was stricken with her voice. He turned to his best friend. "She looks like who's-her-face on the clam shells with the boobs, Bette Midler . . ."

"Jesus H.! She does." The oratorio swept on.

And over against the wall, Mark Next One looked with some trepidation at C. B. DeMille. Executives do not thrive on triumph that has been delivered to them

by another. Especially by another who had turned the
Red Sea into parting Jell-o for Charlton Heston's squinting smile. A shadow came across the younger man's
face. Which now in the darkness began to look very
familiar as he looked out at the singer in the song.

Mary Rose Foster from Tryon, North Carolina, wasn't
just a voice, she was a presence. Of the knockout per-
suasion. She had grown into her killer-diller body like a
puppy grows into his floppy paws. Even young, she was
all nervous energy. She dreamed big, took small, and
bit her fingernails. She listened to Bessie Smith and
Lenny Bruce and under her covers, read *Forever Amber*
by flashlight. She had a boyfriend named Sonny (now a
contractor living in Ft. Lauderdale) and an Irish Setter
named June (now in charge of rawhide bones and errant slippers in Doggie Heaven). Mary Rose Foster almost didn't make it out of childhood, church camp,
high school, or business college. She was that kind of
girl. Always on the break, always on the edge. Finally,
because she willed herself to survive it, it made her
talent great. That, and not letting herself become afraid
of fame.

The Rose was arguably one of the greatest blues &
rock and roll singers in recorded history. Seventeen
platinum records, sixty-share TV specials that had
hatchet-faced critics drooling, and Academy Award-
winning songs that she wrote and performed on movie
soundtracks. She sang for kings and bums, for sheiks
and the not so chic; all they had to do was listen. She
gave and gave and gave . . . until there was nothing left
to give. And then, this low-flying angel was shot down
with a bad bag of heroin that she had mistaken for love.
In her lonely anguish, she had looked down instead of
up for the last time in her life.

Now she was here, entangled in this insanity of waste
and misrule where the entire lashup was honchoed by a
gaggle of morally bankrupt people so vain and stupid
and myopic that they had to be anyplace twice just to

cast a shadow. Typically, she never thought to complain. And it was this gentleness, this guarded softness dressed in ribbons and feathers, that attracted both Dean and Clift, who had no small measure of it themselves.

There was a twenty-minute standing ovation (the only person actually sitting was Lionel Barrymore, but he got up) after the musicale. It was a total tag-team triumph. Morrison and Stravinsky hugged; it was the first time anyone had ever seen the old man so stoked.

But typically to these displays, as the time elapsed, so did the fervor. After the congratulations, there were dim-watt smiles galore. *Thank you very much, now what?* seemed to be the attitude. These were Hellywood people. They had been to the mountain, had a vodka martini, and skiied down the other side. None of them wanted to appear too excited or too happy. This might lead their lessers to assume they were alive like themselves. And that wouldn't do at all.

As the nodding and smiling musicians made nice with the invited audience, they were all served sliced American cheese and Reunite. Well, my dear! There was to have been Stilton, country paté, a cold Puligny Montrachet. But it had been reassigned under armed guard to a stockholders' meeting in The Studio's commissary. So everyone nibbled on the Velveeta and crumbly Ritz crackers as they put to cryonic sleep the wild excitement they had felt only minutes ago and lied to the person next to them about how thin they looked.

Trays of coke were going around like Frizbees and most hoovered it up with greedy bonhomie, exchanging personal fitness programs and the newest diet which happened to be a little sexual number called "Cream Your Way to Low Cholesterol (But Not With Your Wife!)."

Jimmy and Monty, of course, had learned to play these "harmless" games. They were survivors. For years, neither one of them had trusted the odd talent that made them unique—both in remarkably like ways—but they had come to value what it did by measuring the effect it produced (much like a dark star is evidenced). Dean referred to his gift as "the thing" and Clift to his as "the face thing." And this was long before they knew each other. So as the afternoon party lumbered on, they affected poses of auto-pilot like all the rest and oh, dahling, you were fantastic in your last picture, never mind what Bosley Crowther thought.

"Who are all these jerks?" asked Tyrone Power as he came over.

It had all been put together by a team of Hollywood psychologists for the synergy alone. Many of these soirees were divvied up, Rolodex style. You'd get there and if you were inclined toward paranoid sensitivity, you'd notice that everyone in the place was an A - K. Next week, would be the L - Zs.

This afternoon, you could look around and see the stunning (if slightly overweight and ever-"sleepy") Marilyn Monroe. She was listening to General George Patton, who looked resplendant in his Ike jacket and bloody puttees. He was bitterly complaining about the entirely excessive characterization of him that had been given by "that constipated fury-monger from Virginia named Scott." As he made his more salient points, the general slapped his open palm with a swagger stick that had a .50-caliber machine gun shell on one end and a Mickey Mouse vibrating dildo head on the other. Ms. Monroe had a real choice in front of her. As it were.

Over there, talking to Dave Garroway, was Catherine the Great. She was riveting, especially if you were partial to gnomes. "Don't hand me that, Dave," she snorted. "Who the fuck knows how tall David Letterman is? It's a face medium. And, my friend, I have had men *die* to get close to this one. If I can't get a fifty share, I'll kiss your bow tie! Here'll be my first guest!"

She opened her arms as Alexander the Burton walked up. Finally they had become one and the same to the delight of press agents and scourge schedulers everywhere. It was that kind of afternoon.

"Isn't that Charlie Chaplin?" Monty was standing on tiptoes, straining to see. But it wasn't. Just a guy who looked like him.

"Hiya kid, how ya been?" Nick Ray asked Dean. Jimmy's face brightened immediately. Introductions all around. Ty had never met the salty old director. Ray had, among his other triumphs in a wonderfully checkered career, directed Dean in "Rebel Without a Cause," giving his young star the sternest security he'd ever had. Dean rewarded them both with two hours of the heart's live blade. Jimmy asked his mentor how he'd liked the music. Ray admitted he was tone deaf. "But it looked okay. Maybe Morrison overdid it a little. You think he can handle a part like Che?"

"Nick, have they asked you about taking over the picture? They fired Curtiz." Monty toed the dusty floor, hoping his voice wouldn't show how nervous he was.

"No way. I did my big budget piece of crap about China. I won't even watch the half-hour version that *Cliff Notes* made!" They all laughed. "Anyway, I wouldn't have time. I think I'm just around for a while. You know?"

They knew. Even this Forever was temporary. It was part of the irritation of it. It was all "just temporary." You could never get used to anything or anyone, because you'd look around and they'd be gonzo. On your way to work, your car would drive differently, even in reverse. There would be a different guy at the gate who would not recognize you and make you sit in the steaming car for ten minutes while he called the production office and a line of late, angry people built up behind you. You couldn't seem to find your dressing room or your parking place or the trade papers or the craft-services wagon for a lousy cup of coffee.

And when, accidentally, you found the right person to complain to, they said sullenly, "It's temporary." It was their explanation for everything. It had replaced "I don't make the rules, I only work here."

Jimmy patted the older man's arm. "It's probably

temporary, Nick. You're right. But it would be great to work together again. Even if it's this turkey, y'know?''

"Yeah. Well, nice to meet you guys. See ya, kid. Take care. Okay?'' There was something about the old man's eyes that was like lightning over water, something about the little pause between "care" and "okay" that made Dean stop, cold.

Which was armor-piercing providential, because if he hadn't, he would have sailed on, just turned away and missed the short girl with the radiant face who now looked up at him. Somehow, the air seemed to run blue and fresh around them.

Jimmy and Monty looked down and saw The Rose's smile looking up at them. They smiled back and on this dark day, light. Ty Power had drifted away which was just as well because as nice a guy as he was, all of what followed would have been lost on him.

Jimmy and Monty started to say something at the same time. They both laughed. "There's a word for that, but I forget what it is," Jimmy said.

"Well. I think . . ." Clift began as he looked down at her bright eyes, "that we witnessed a major miracle here this afternoon, young lady."

There was second of embarrassed silence. Then she couldn't hold it back any longer. "Awww, I'm a big fuckin' fan of *both* you guys! I saw 'Raintree County' so many times, they started giving me free popcorn!''

For an instant it looked like Jimmy's feelings might be hurt. Until she reached up and grabbed him around the neck to give him a hug. "An' you, darlin—the night I first saw 'East of Eden' was the night I first came in my pants!''

After a stunned beat, they all burst into laughter. People around them looked but already their threeness had begun to close people out. Later, some would recall this moment at the trial and try to enter its observation as a hiding place. It didn't work.

And on the soundstage this afternoon, James Dean's laughing visage was as red as his windbreaker. Natalie

or Pier never talked this trashy, but hell . . . he liked it.
The Rose could be just one of the guys. But apparently
something ineluctably more, too, as he and Monty caught
each other trying to sneak looks down her open blouse.
"What's a girl like you doing in a place like this?"

The three of them went to dinner at Spago. They had
to wait two hours for a table next to the men's room
door and a surly waiter who would always be up for
parts he would only just lose.

The restaurant was out of everything but cheese hot-
dogs and anchovy pizza, so they ordered both and promised themselves B&Bs afterward. Brioschi and brandy.

While they waited for their dinner, they made small
talk. Dean and Clift caught each other's eye; Mary Rose
seemed perfectly content to chat about the movie business in general or "Hell's Gate" in particular. She also
was more than willing to talk about their respective
careers. This was somewhat rare for all in Hellywood
but the brain-dead. The operative social axiom in town
was, "Enough talk about me, let's talk about *you*! What
did you think of my last picture?"

What really floored the two men though was the innocent simplicity as she quickly lowered her eyes and
said the tiny prayer before she ate. Nobody else saw.
But they were stunned. I mean, a prayer?!

"Yeah," she sheepishly admitted. "My nonnie taught
me that it was a good idea. Especially with food, where
gratitude and insurance run along the same lines, is
what she used to say. Goll, I can't hardly believe I'm
sitting here with my two faves! How come you never
did a flick together?"

They didn't know either.

She was staying, temporarily, at the Chateau Gour-
mand. They dropped her off after dinner. It wasn't that
far on Sunset, but she wanted to ride backwards in
Jimmy's Ferrari, its legend preceding it. In front of her
bungalow, in the moment of new-friend embarrassment
of half glances and silence, she gave each of them a kiss

on his cheek and then, before she got out and disappeared into her cottage, she sang softly that famous song, adjusting the words to this moment.

"Some say love, it is a river . . .
That makes you want to swim.
I say love it is a moment with
Monty and my pal Jim."

So it was silly, so what? They were completely touched; neither of them dared speak a word of it all the way home backwards.

The Bluebird land-yacht was parked off of Fountain, in the flats of Boystown. Without any exchange at all, Jimmy and Monty were both disturbed enough to pretend nothing had really happened. They decided to watch a porno video or two. 'Mondo Bondo Redondo Condo,' a prize winner at the Tulsa Expo, and 'Sex Family Robinson,' a real honey mixing hard-ons and social anthropology. They made popcorn in the radar range. Neither of them said anything (although they were both inveterate running commentarists) all the way through. Neither of them saw a frame of what they were looking at.

"Was that in color?"

"Was what in color?"

It was that kind of a night.

"Well."

"Well?"

"Hell damn," said Jimmy softly. "What're we gonna do, man? I mean, we got to at least talk about it!"

"I wish it was last Thursday. I had it dicked last Thursday. I didn't know Mary Rose Foster, and my cat mask fit better. Why can't it be last Thursday?" Monty asked plaintively.

"Do they make mistakes? Central Casting?"

"Not many, Jimmy. Brando in 'Desiree.' That guy in 'Billy Jack,' maybe. And whoever it was played James Earl Ray. I can't think of too many more."

There was a long silence. From far away, horns on

Fountain honked and closer, a mad dog barked as he loped down a littered alley on three legs.

"Someone fucked this one up, royally! She's not supposed to be here." Dean said what they were both thinking.

And the very words frightened them. "She's supposed to be in . . . Heaven. As sure as we're sitting here."

"We got to get her out," said Monty. From the look on his wounded face, it gave him no pleasure. Nor did it James Dean. It was just a matter of simple, shitty fact. They had toiled years in these hot vineyards and had never encountered an angel. In no way was this their territory. It was more than just off-limits. Damn. Now, one had staggered innocently into their lives, all smiles and laughing care, and suddenly, there they were, at the very precipice.

He had come in from his little cabin, 'way the hell and gone out in the woods. Where the night is long and silent and lonely. Where the forest drips what it recalls of rain and waits for a breeze that never comes. It was an impossible place for a normal man, but just right for this one. As some are born in exile, a few are born to triumph. No matter who or what it costs.

He was short with the stark features of a hawk in flight. He could change his grey eyes, seemingly, at will. He could charm, be brilliant, be merciless. He was an artist.

He was Sam Peckinpah.

They said he was washed up. He had an alcohol problem, he had a cocaine problem, he had an ego problem; he was old, insane, and evil. But he was a certified legend. He directed movies that became genres unto themselves. He savaged writers and broke actors and screwed producers. But in the end, as you sat in the dark theatre watching his movies, you were seeing as good as it got and you knew Who He Was.

Peckinpah had finally accepted DeMille's offer. After the growling curs at the Morris Office got through with it, that is. Ten million (a million five of which was for just viewing the footage up to now), final final final no-fooling final cut, twenty points and no "rolling break" either, plus his unique provision to actually do all the killing that any of the movie scenes might require. For realism.

Dinner at the DeMilles's was mercifully short. They were of like mind. If "Hell's Gate" was to be saved, it was Sam Peckinpah who would do it. He could—and *had*, in fact—stood up to God, Himself.

Peckinpah finally took the job for one simple reason. He saw that he could do it where others had failed.

"Hell's Gate" needed a look at Heaven to make it work. Just a glimpse of something innocent, something chaste and good in all the gore, intellect, carnage, and politics. And that afternoon, watching the oratorio of that surly kid Morrison (who would make a good, if somewhat bent, Che) and Stravinsky (overrated: mostly nose)—besides, he hated music—nevertheless, he had seen the face of his dreams and heard the voice of his dreams and they had come from the same source.

The Rose.

Much the way he had thought to put Bob Dylan in "Billy the Kid," Peckinpah had decided to cast Mary Rose Foster in this movie. He would take that innocent quality—whether it was fake or real, no matter—and he would use that goodness to clean up the stuttering vomit of this cinematic abortion. They had all forgotten the cardinal rule of movie-making. You don't make a picture about night without showing at least a few minutes of day.

And if anyone got in his way—*anyone*—whether it was the studio head or his lead actors or DeMille himself, they could all call in the dogs and piss on the fire. He'd handled Dustin Hoffman once, McQueen twice, the labyrinthine Mexican government any number of times, and even producer Jerry Bressler, who had two studios and a bank behind him. What could anyone else show him? Now that he was here.

Sam thanked DeMille and his pleasant but drifty wife for the dinner. Then, alone in the dark entry hall, he tied his red bandana across his forehead, looped his dark glasses around his neck, finished his nightcap shooter of Herra Dura tequila, and walked out into the breathless night.

Ready to roll.

The news of his hiring filled the headlines of both "The Hellywood Reporter" and "Daily Variety" and it shook the community deeply.

Other studios had other films shooting. But they weren't "Hell's Gate." They were small, play-it-safe programmers; B-films that had been the staple of the business back then. With Scott Brady and Charles McGraw and James Craig. With Lizabeth Scott and Gloria Grahame. Nowhere movies that depended on stories and logic and interest. Movies that depended on screenplays! Barf-o-rama!

Not like "Hell's Gate" or "Rambo Meets Rimbaud" or "The Jewel of Weehauken, New Jersey." *These* are movies; and when a director of Sam Peckinpah's magnitude, a true *auteur*, is brought aboard, attention must be paid.

Immediately, everyone felt that—no matter what his reputation might be—he was the man for the job. Privately, a few whose memories went back that far had been saying for years they couldn't understand why The Studio hadn't used a "force majeure" (like a MAC-10 to the head) and *made* him finish the picture.

Because it had been, back in some pre-Cambrian epoch, Sam Peckinpah who'd started it.

He'd lasted four months. He'd killed a unit manager in a duel, had open-heart surgery in a '62 Buick between set-ups, been sued for divorce from all three of his wives, and had one of his UCLA Film School hippie interns quit him, claiming he was not a whole lot more than an abusive drunk with a talent for misogynistic masturbation. But Peckinpah hung on; he'd suffered all kinds of worse back in the old days. Even back doing "The Rifleman" ("Get in the house, son.") on TV! His brilliant and twisted career was littered with quivering hearts and shattered lives. He had pretty much seen it all ... you could tell on quiet nights if you caught the light right in his dark eyes. Sometimes he seemed so gentle and vulnerable and even kind that you felt the pain of all the world in those eyes.

Some said it was what'd finally caused him to quit "Hell's Gate" and the Business; the emotional dysentery caused by the pace of 5 pages a day *no matter what.* Ramon Novarro and Mary Pickford, two of his oldest and best friends, were growing old in front of his camera, trying desperately to make sense out of roles that didn't even seem to be in the same movie. By this time, already one hundred and seventeen writers had had their paws in the mix, each trying to save the prior botchjob, each trying to change enough to get full credit, story and screenplay. One bald guy with glasses turned in a draft in Norwegian, and his name wasn't even Swen!

At the end of four months of shooting, they were three months, three weeks, and six days behind schedule.

That Wednesday, the head of worldwide production from The Studio (was his name Mark This One or had it been Mark Prior One? He couldn't remember) came to tell him the following day's battle sequence was now to be a full click-track musical. Sam Peckinpah listened to the kid carefully. He wanted to make sure he'd heard it right. A musical. Right.

And then, he did it because he could do anything. Above all, in those days, he was a pro. If they wanted dancing soldiers, they'd get dancing soldiers. But, he explained to the baby mogul executive from The Studio, it would be his final day on the picture. Life was too short, he told the youngster who couldn't really remember what happened to him last weekend up in Santa Barbarous because it was so long ago.

The director did the scene, which, in the end, was

only viewed in its entirety by fifteen awed souls.They ran a "wet print" in a projection room, but it wastoo late. Already they had decided not to use it. A newMark had taken over and he wanted no mark of the lastMark's mark on His Movie. Still, it was pretty extraordinary. Two hundred thousand Confederate troops doing the Charleston at the Battle of Charleston was not exactly a sight you saw every day. Or ever, for that matter.

The next day, Sam Peckinpah had gotten in his old Caddy LaSalle and driven way the hell out and hadn't come back.

Now, light years later, here he was again. In triumph, too. It was the way of things for him.

As he walked up on a large rock for a few opening remarks, he looked out at the assembled cast and crew. Not counting the news crews or the pencil-necks from "Entertainment Tonight," there were maybe six or seven hundred gathered. He turned to them; he didn't need a bullhorn.

From the darkened recesses of a stretch limo, Mark Next One looked at his new director on the closed-circuit video built in to the burled maple of his back-seat bar and soda fountain. He was reading a script, finally interested. Its pages were blank. Next to him, looking confused yet hopeful, was Mary Rose Foster. She leaned forward, peering into the video close-up of Sam's incredibly expressive face as he began his announcement to the cast and crew of "Hell's Gate."

"I'm back."

No one ever really knew who started it, but slowly a wave of applause built, starting at the far end near the wranglers and stuntmen and Teamsters hiding in the stretchouts reading their Racing Forms, sweeping forward across extras, grips, electricians, honey-wagon drivers, craft services people, art directors, greensmen, camera crews, and the actors and actresses down in front who were looking up at this Madman Genius they had all heard about for so long—standing and applauding until their hands were hot and scarlet.

Both Dean and Clift, even Jim Morrison, had been utterly swept away by the moment's spontaneity. And Sam saw this as he looked down at his two leads and his sullen bon-bon rock star. And he thought, *This is good, this is a start, this I can use.*

"Can I get some more light up here?" he called out and then continued. "Whatever went before," he continued, "in the eons since I walked this picture—will be nothing more than stories you can pass around over Cajun tofu salads at The Ivy. Because now, we will *actually go to work.* Now, we will find the movie in this movie and we will yell and scream, we will fight and die, we will sell our souls collectively and we will walk through the flaming portals of Hell's gate TOGETHER!"

People went ape; the screaming was deafening. Henry V at Agincourt would have given up and gone for a glass of buttermilk. Knute Rockne would have gone sweet on Vince Lombardi. George Patton would have turned in his pearl-handled pistols for a Fleet Enema kit! The air on the set (the largest ever constructed) was electric to the degree that some said they saw flaming balls of St. Elmo's fire dancing over the tops of heads. That guy Thomas said he doubted it; he thought the electricians had been at it again.

"And here is why . . ." Peckinpah dropped his voice and held out his hand, looking over to the long, black limo.

Inside, The Rose took her cue. "I hope y'all know what you're doing," she said to Mark Next One, and got out of the dark interior.

As she made her way to the top of the boulder where her director waited for her, she looked from the many to the few. Down in the front row next to Morrison were Jimmy and Monty, their white faces agog. She gave them a little wave, feeling real badly that she hadn't told them. But DeMille, Mark, and Peckinpah had been adamant. And she'd explain it all to her new-found friends soon enough.

"Ladies and gentlemen, the new star of 'Hell's Gate,' The Rose."

You had to play the tape back ten or twelve times to hear it, but in the almost reverential silence, James Dean said in his small but miraculous voice to Montgomery Clift, "Jesus shit."

The pace was so intense, so frantic and murderous, that inside of a week they had already made cast and crew T-shirts that said "Entitled to tell Peckinpah stories." And here were three of them:

—One night, between set-ups, the Old Man had come into Dean's trailor with a Remington 1100 shotgun (this story came from one of the weapons guys) and started blazing away in a fury that took five A.D.s to calm.

—Clift had gotten his Cataraugus claws tied up in Mary Rose's angel costume and slightly ripped the wing webbing. Not more than two inches! An enraged Peckinpah pulled a Bowie knife on him.

—The director had some kind of honest-to-God hypnotic trance worked on The Rose. You could see it in her eyes in the closeups (this story was from editorial) and just from the way she looked at him, he had to be porking her every night in his mobile Santa Fe adobe cottage.

The first two stories were completely true. The third was almost.

"Rosie, I put you in this picture, you know," Peckinpah said, looking at her stacked goodness across his bar. "They didn't want you. They think you're just another rock and roll piece of ass."

"Yeah."

"You have to trust me, babe," he went on as he poured them another tequila.

"I do."

"Naw. I mean really trust me."

"I do, Sam. Honest." Even though they were the same height, she managed to look up to him. He smiled.

"Then what I am about to tell you is just between us. Okay?"

"Okay."

"Mary Rose, let's me and you go get into bed and see what happens."

"Awwww, Sam, you old fart . . ." And, laughing, she grabbed him around his neck and gave him a daughterly kiss on his weathered cheek. His anger turned to dismay and then into a kind of chagrined acceptance. To her, for all the world, he looked just like a little, lost boy. She put her hand tenderly on his face. "I love ya, Sam. And I owe ya."

He leveled his grey eyes into hers. And in them, the child disappeared. A tiny smile played at the corners of his mouth.

"I know," he said. "So play like we're gettin' it on. For the rest of 'em. Only work gets it up for me these days . . . but no reason they should know it."

She smiled. "Nope. No reason at all."

"I'm in some trouble. My health. But you seemed to have sensed it already," he confessed. "I'm old, my body's half give out on me, and I'm scared."

This all caught her by surprise.

"What? You didn't think I could be scared? Babe, I was *born* afraid. It's what keeps me goin'! But coming back on this picture is my go-t'hell Swan Song. I probably won't last. But . . ." He couldn't go on.

She was stunned but hid it well enough. Well enough so that he couldn't tell if this all was working or not.

"You'll help an old man, won't ya?" His voice trailed off, cracking perfectly. She nodded. Then, again. She would help this man, whoever he was . . . whatever he was. And for one reason.

He had asked.

There was a moment of fat, nighttime silence.

"You're mine, Mary Rose Foster," he said softly. "I

knew your father. He was mine, too. So if you want to
survive the next month, you'd best read my mind, darlin'.
Do everything I tell you. No matter how off the wall it
sounds, no matter what your heart tells you, no matter
who tells you otherwise!" He gently kissed her hand,
sending a shock of recognition through her. "Okay?"

She blinked fast.

And when he stood up, he didn't seem old and frail at
all anymore. He seemed ten feet tall, his huge head
almost reaching the ceiling. Around them in the dank
night's heat, the air went cold as he opened his mouth
and roared "OKAY?" Suddenly, she recognized both his
artillery and the face behind the lanyard. She had seen
it before.

Oh, yes.

The next day was the start of the battle scene.

In an uncut shot from the Chapman Atlas crane (which
would be conveniently ten frames longer than Welles's
opening shot in "Touch of Evil" for film historians and
pimple-faced cineasts), it started.

The white-robed angel "Madonna" (The Rose hadn't
been too happy about the name, believe me) would pull
the arrow from Dean's forehead and bring him back to
life. There would be a dialogue scene that Thornton
Wilder had worked on which would win a Writers'
Guild Award. Then, raking small-arms fire would open
up on the banquet. Che Guevara would be hit but saved
by the cat. With it so far?

Now—and this is still all one shot—a flight of Chinese
bandit retro-jets would scream through frame and napalm from here to the horizon. At this point, the tigers
would be turned loose just after the black horses had
been shot. A huge ring of burning barrels (the crane
would sweep over them) all containing fighting scorpions would be revealed in the mad run of the tigers,
headed back toward the original point of the start of the
shot.

At this point, and get this, all the people were in their

enormous battle tanks, hunkered into their mind-control units, blasting the living shit out of everything in step-printed slow motion! While the Lost Madonna ascended into the sulphurous red sky which would grow darker and darker and darker. . . .

When Sam Peckinpah did a battle scene, he meant business. Just to prove it, some of the cast (unbeknownst to them, of course) were carrying *live ammo*.

He'd planned the shot, with cards (the live ammo ones were red) and three sketch artists, for a week. It was going to be perfect. If this didn't put him up in critic Andrew Sarris's "Pantheon" of great directors, nothing would.

As he dreamed about it, he became young again. He was on the crane with Warren Oates and L.Q. Jones and in the dreams they were drunk and howling with laughter as armies of Mexicans rolled under them, a ballet corps of violence, the death that brought life, a living tapestry of hell. The old man would wake up, yelling. "More light, *more light!*" But in the cool stucco house, it was dark and Oates was gone and he was not young anymore. He blinked back tears that no one would have believed anyway.

Hellcrest Motors delivered the Von Tripp-Porsche the day before they were going to start the battle scene. Jimmy and Monty polished the car half the afternoon. It was perfection; five tons of sculptured Teutonic know-how, the murderous P-38 engine running the full length of the blood-red car. It seated only three. Two on either side of the gigantic engine, one right in front in a seat that had to have been designed by a nine-year-old kid. It was three inches above the road and from its enclosure, you couldn't see any of the rest of the car. It was just you thrust forward into the speed. Thoughtfully, the seat had been thoroughly Scotch-guarded.

"Man, I am going to sit in that seat, open my mouth, and swallow 300 mph—"

"You don't plan on *me* driving, do you?!" Monty yelled.
"You know what happens when I get behind the wheel."

"Okay, okay," Jimmy grinned. "I'll drive. As long as
we can stay off that goddamn Route 46, headed to
Salinas . . ."

Inside the Bluebird, the phone rang. Jimmy answered
it. As Monty sat in the right hand passenger seat thinking how, with all the horror they had been through on
this picture, this was the happiest time in his life. Yet
as he sat there, he had a strange feeling that somehow
the end was again near. Over the car's stereo came
Talking Crüe's newest, "At Night."

"It was The Rose," Jimmy said as he came back out.
He looked terrible. "They're gonna start shooting a day
early. And no rehearsal!"

"Let's get out! Let's just get in this motherfucker and
go!" Jimmy had never heard Monty use language like
that, his voice haunted, savaged by time.

"She needs us," was all Dean said.

When they got to the location and her dressing room,
there was an armed guard at the door. "Who're you?"
asked Monty.

"I work for Peckinpah," the behemoth answered softly.

"Let them in, Tiny," came Mary Rose's voice from
behind his shadow. "It's okay." The huge guard looked
back at her and finally moved out of their way. "Tiny,
don't tell Sam. Please. Okay?"

After a moment, he nodded. On her, his eyes were
gentle. Even he recognized something special. Only incidentally did it derive from her singing "Hush, Little
Baby" to him at night when he couldn't sleep in his
folding chair in front of her door. "Okay, Miss Rose."

Inside, she mixed double spoonfuls of Bosco in glasses
of ice-cold milk. Then, she poured a shot of bourbon in
each one.

"Are you serious?" Monty asked, his eyes wide.

"Fellahs, we're gonna need this. Because I got boss
shitty news." They waited for her to go on. "I was over

to Sam's last night. He laid out the opening shot for me,
sorta goin' over it in his head, I guess. It's all on cards. I
asked him what the red cards were."

There was a silence. "Well, what are they?" asked
Dean.

Jimmy knew a guy in props. He was an old cowboy
from Helldorado named Perse. He'd done "Giant" with
the restless young actor and had provided him with the
five-foot length of rope tied to the rock that Jimmy had
pretty much stolen the picture with. Perse even taught
him how to do it; hanging the rock down from the rope,
you just put a little jerk on the end and like magic, the
rock jumped through its own tiny loop. The location
had been awful and a fast friendship had developed.

Perse didn't ask a single question when Jimmy brought
Monty and Mary Rose in for Kevlar-bulletproof-vest
fittings.

"Perse, we need 'em to go under our costumes. And
they can't be visable, y'know?

"Okay, Jett." Jimmy grinned. Like many old-timers,
Perse still called him by the character name he had
used on their first picture together. The old cowboy was
fast and thorough. The lightweight plastic weave went
over the torso and the upper arms. "They's big arteries
up 'ere, son. Little bitty shrapnel, you could buy the
ranch." Perse had bought his in a race riot in Fort
Worth in '64 as he tried to carry a Mexican baby to
safety. Peckinpah had used him ever since.

When they were all through, they looked at themselves in their costumes in a full-length mirror in Perse's
truck.

"Purr-fect," said Cataraugus Caesar.

"Outasight," said Lost Madonna, the rock and roll angel.

"Get one for yourself," said Jimmy to his old friend.
"Because it's going to be assholes and elbows out there."

"Thanks, Jett. I'll be all right." He knew the kid was
warning him about something. Dean wasn't one to panic.
Must be serious. But he was too old to change now. So

his Levis and his blue H-bar-C cowboy shirt would have to do. At his door, Dean stopped and looked long into the old man's eyes. Then, with that little smile that made him a legend to a billion people in five generations, he was gone.

"The condemned ate a hearty breakfast ..." Monty said out of the corner of his mouth as he scraped more grits and gravy onto his plate of fried eggs and okra.

Morrison loved breakfasts but he could only drink out of his straw from the blender jar because of his drying but very handsome beard.

"This is the end," he said. Jimmy smiled.

There was everything you could ask for at this field commissary breakfast, and a small printed card at each place on the endless tables set up out under the gently flapping tarps. Monty grinned as he read the card again. " 'Your director loves you.' " Well, at least he has a sense of humor."

"You better pull your fur up, fuzzface," said Jimmy. "Your armor is showing."

Morrison, disgusted with his vitamin-and-goat-cheese smoothie, left the table. If he had to use a straw, then he'd damn sure find something more entertaining than this. Vodka.

"Who had the red cards, which scenes?" asked Monty with a tremor of fear in his voice as he pulled his fur up. "Did you see?"

The Rose shook her head, looking around carefully to see if any of the ever-present game-playing kiss-asses were around to report them for this kind of wholly disloyal talk. "I tried t'see! But the fucker just laughed and pulled them away. He said we'd all find out soon enough ..."

"I don't understand why he'd tell you. He must have known you'd tell us." Generically, the only director Jimmy trusted was Nick Ray, and suddenly he remembered the moment that had passed between them at the oratorio. "Take care," was what the old man had said.

He'd never said that before. In fact, goodbyes weren't in his vocabulary at all. Too mordant and sentimental, he'd said. And yet, there it was.

James Byron Dean, who had more than a passing interest in Egyptology and various unprovable but interesting New Age shenanigans, was not one to ignore anything that could be construed to be a message, especially one like this that jumped up and bit you on the ass.

He picked up the little printed card in front of his plate. And then, while twenty or thirty people looked on, he grinned, put it into his mouth, and ate it. Along with the French toast.

A lanky guy named Rackley who was a known fink got up and with deliberately casual steps walked away from the table as Monty, Jimmy, and the Rose watched. They knew what he was going to do even before he broke into a run, headed toward the production trailer. Where the director's office was.

Holy hell broke loose on that first day of production of the all-new "Hell's Gate"—which was precisely the director's plan. When Sam Peckinpah came out of his trailer, he was dressed in his ancient, starched and faded Marine Corps cammie, the one Duke Wayne had given him. On the back was the name "Sgt. John M. Stryker," and below that, the bullet hole that had gotten Duke his first nomination on the bloody sands of Iwo Jima. Behind Peckinpah trailed his various worshipful young assistants carrying his 3x5 cards, his porta-bar, his Purdy shotgun, his script (which he didn't really plan to follow), and his Weaver "Nighthawk" assault rifle (he didn't want any of those Uzis, he wanted something that looked like what it was, something made in America, something exciting that might just jam and blow up in your hands).

In front of the whole cast and crew, Sam Peckinpah started off the day with a bang by pulling a little Elgin "Cutlass" pistol he had hidden in his jacket and first

disembowling and then shooting his 5th Assistant
Director.

There was a stunned silence as a thousand people
looked at the boy's frail body stop twitching. A thousand adam's apples bobbed as a thousand swallowed
hard. "Oh oh," a thousand minds thought at exactly the
same time.

(An hour later after they were gone, the boy got up,
dusted himself off, peeled away his fake moustache, and
went to late breakfast, mopping off the panchromatic
blood. He'd be back with his Boss by noon.)

DeMille was in Mark New One's office when word
arrived about what his director had done. He was out-
raged, and the new executive, who had heard that the
film business wasn't anywhere near as hard as stock
trading or Arizona real estate, almost choked on his
rubber nippled pacifier. DeMille stormed out of the
office and headed down to his Packard limo.

Two hours later, when the legendary producer got to
the location, he was met by a little surprise. Stretching
across the road were forty or fifty armed Libyan soldiers, each with nuclear-tipped ammo. They stopped
the Packard. Silently, the back window came down and
DeMille peered out at the young men who were now
strolling over to him.

"Closed set," one said simply.

"I am Cecil B. DeMille, the producer!" the old man
yelled. "Get out of the road!"

"Closed set," the soldier repeated and shot DeMille's
ancient chauffer dead between the eyes. DeMille's eyes
slammed open as the chauffer's head exploded as the
e.m.p. of the teeny tiny nuke both shut off the car's engine
and stopped his Pulsar watch at 11:22. The soldier flashed
the white-haired man a gap-toothed grin. "Shoulda
showed more uv Delilah's tits in dett movie . . ."

An armed Libyan sex-maniac film critic with the IQ
of a pine cone: C. B. DeMille knew he was in trouble.
Lowering his famously soothing voice, he began to talk.

"When I first came to Hellywood, they asked me to do a little picture called "Squaw Man." I had no way of knowing then that it would be considered by many to be the beginning of the motion picture business . . ."

The guard had come closer to the car, now. He seemed to be listening, nodding along. DeMille gauged the soldier's crazed eyes and figured it would take him about six, maybe seven hours to tell his life story. It was a small enough sacrifice. Considering whose story it was. As he gently veered the tale into his long-suffering grandparents and even those who had gone before them like his distant relative Thomas Hardy, DeMille adjusted his perfumed silk brocade beret and thought of Peckinpah. Maybe he had made a mistake. Maybe . . .

No one could believe it. Not the camera crew, not the actors, not the guys laying dolly track, not even the caterers. But the single most complicated shot in the entire history of film went off—the very first time— without a hitch. Almost, that is. Breaths were held. Here's how it went:
(white card)

EXT. A HELLISH FIELD OF BATTLE—SUNSET

AN ANGEL, The Lost Madonna of Terre Haute, walks through the gore in tears. Bodies, mud, abandoned weapons.

LOST MADONNA
(voice over, maybe song)
When my Johnny finally came home again,
it was in a wheelchair. He couldn't
feed himself, he had nightmares that
lasted until dawn, and one night when
we got very drunk, he told me—

The Angel stops at the corpse of a young REBEL SOLDIER who is pinned to a sandbag with an ARROW through his forehead.

She WITHDRAWS THE ARROW AND HE LIVES. He opens his eyes and sees her heavenly face. The wound is closing (SFX).

REBEL SOLDIER

I told you, I love you. But not like
I love my buddies. It was different
back then. I was ... a kid. Out here—
  (indicates the carnage)
—you need your pals! *They're* the ones
that're with you in the rocket attacks
when it's raining body parts!

LOST MADONNA

But how about when it's raining
Pepsi, and angora sweaters, and
crisp fall days and promises and
football and tits lighted by the
warm dial of a car radio? How about
that rain, soldier?

The rebel soldier smiles, maybe for the first time in years. His face is transformed.

REBEL SOLDIER

What kind of car?
                              CAMERA SWEEPS ON:

And as it swept over them, Jimmy and Mary Rose turned to each other with a grin and she said in a very soft voice, "Who wrote this stuff? I had a cat named Cruiser who could write better than this ..." When Jimmy laughed, one of the Assistant Directors on the crane glared at him but Peckinpah never turned. His eyes were already on the next sequence that was cued by yet another A.D. as the huge crane was now beginning to move smoothly along on its dolly tracks.

It was eerie how the crew moved so silently in their scorched Adidas shoes; hundreds of them, pros to the

bone, weaving in and out, never bumping into anything, never tripping on the thousands of feet of thick,
twisting black cable that blanketed the ground everywhere. Up on the crane, next to the blimped Panaflex
150 Showscan camera, Peckinpah was softly chambered
the first full-steel jacket round in his Weaver Nighthawk automatic rifle as up on the "horizon," now there
was a line of extras with a virtual arsenal and on cue
they started the following sequence:
(red card)

CAMERA SWEEPS TO:

EXT. THE BATTLEFIELD MESS AREA-DAY

CHE GUEVARA sits at the groaning board field
mess table next to his trusted feline aide-de-camp-
it-up, CATARAUGUS.

> CHE
> One good thing about winning—the
> chow is better.

> CATARAUGUS
> Yeah, a little Meow Mix Hollandaise
> and a snooze in the sun.... What're
> you looking at, Colonel?

Che is staring, open-mouthed, up toward the ridge.

WHAT CHE GUEVARA SEES ON THE RIDGE—
THOUSANDS OF THE ENEMY:

Massed and ready to explode this ambush. THEIR
LEADER stands and lifts his sabre.

> CHE
> (o.c.)
> We're fucked.

They OPEN FIRE!
                    AND THE CAMERA SWEEPS ON:

All hell broke loose.

At the trial, it was later determined by ballistics that about one out of every five weapons was fitted for the live ammo. Even at this long range the field of fire was murderous. Up on the ridge, the extras were giving it everything they had right down to the smallest expressions. They had been told Second Unit Cameras disguised as guns would be passing among them for rewardable close-ups to cut in later.

Down at the table in the battlefield mess area, the first scythe of slugs cut into the warriors like a long, hot blade. Immediately, everyone knew these screams were not acting.

Jim Morrison was hit with a .30 calliber machine gun round in his lower abdomen, and as his body spasmed, it accidently set off the fake blood squib in his arm. White-faced and howling, he fell back into Monty's furry lap. He looked up, terrified.

"Am I going to die, Monty? Oh, Jesus God hell, this hurts!"

Just then, Monty took one in his upper chest. It blasted him back into his seat. Morrison's eyes almost popped when Monty leaned back up and pulled the flattened slug out of the kevlar vest under his fur.

"Let's get out of here!" Monty grabbed Morrison, amazingly picking up the larger man like he was a rag doll, and they began running through the nightmarish chaos.

Mary Rose had tried to get to Jimmy when the gunfire began. She knew; they both did. This was a red card. Just as she was about to reach him, a seven-foot black soldier in a Lakers basketball uniform over his tiger suit was blown into her. He had no head anymore. She burst into horrified tears, covered in his blood.

James Dean thought this must be the longest moment in his lives. The noise was deafening; the whings and spacks of the bullets, the horrible cries of the dead and dying. Finally, a new sound. A woman sobbing, coming in pulsing waves through the slowness and it was ... her.

It freed him. Just as he burst toward her, a 20mm cannon round tore into the sand bag where his head had been.

He swept Mary Rose up and they began to run as they had never run. Around them, carnage, insanity.

Just then, right on cue, the Chinese Bandit Retro-Jets screamed through the leaden sky above, their angular hawk wings seeming to rip through the death with their own banshee howl. Firing their Vulcan 20-mm cannons and G.E. Miniguns full force at 3000 rounds per minute per gun, they sounded like detuned fog horns. The bellowing was the sheerest madness.

Finally huddling together in a torn-out bunker up on the ridge, Monty, Jimmy, Mary Rose, and Morrison looked up just in time to see the Retro-Jets drop their Napalm. The four of them were transfixed.

"It's so beautiful . . ." Morrison said for them all. And it was. It was also very real. The heat blast hit them, knocking them down with a wall of superannuated air traveling at 150 mph. Flattening everything in its path, it tore the cat fur completely off of Monty. His mask was a jumble of wire and plastic and he ripped it off, his blue eyes haunted with this living nightmare.

"Oh, God . . ." was all he said. But it went into all their hearts at the same time. And it welded both their gaze and a purpose.

"This is it, isn't it?" Jimmy asked.

"I think so," Monty replied.

"I gotta get back out there! There are men dying . . ." said Mary Rose, trying to pull away to get back into the hell of it. Dean spun her around roughly. Her eyes were crazed with grief.

"No! You got somewhere more important to go," Dean said. "And soon."

"What're you talking about, man?" Mary Rose tried to pull away back out into the rain of death. "Those people need *help*!"

Monty came close, spoke low, touched soft.

"Nobody needs help, here. But they do, far away. We'll be all right, we're sentenced to it. But you . . ."

"*Look!*" said Jimmy, pointing and handing a pair of binoculars to Monty.

A thousand yards away, the huge camera crane was moving inexorably. On top, the director was up and firing down into men being trampled by the herd of wild black horses. Blood, flashing hooves, and the dark sun.

"More light, more light!" they could hear him yell, even from where they were.

Now, around the crane, the endless line of barrels were set off by Cliff Wenger, the pyrotechnics man and in an unholy flash, horses and men were ringed by the necklace of flames. And the remote camera units began to roll with their high speed Fairchilds. It was unimaginable madness orchestrated by the veriest genius. And down in the center of each and every barrel, thousands . . . millions . . . a billion scorpions writhed and fought.

Except one.

Who wasn't.

At all.

"*Cut! Cut the goddamn shot!*" Peckinpah bellowed.

Even the horses froze in the utter, stunned silence. The Retro-Jets seemed to freeze in the air. Everything stopped; Dean, Clift, and the Rose, a thousand yards away. All eyes were on the big man as he pointed down, down, past dismembered bodies, past gore and mud and bone . . .

To a flaming barrel of scorpions on which the gas flames now withered and died. The scorpions (all stunt doubles for the entire Third Insect Armored Division) had stopped their wiggling, choreographed duels and were staring up at the crane.

"*You, down there!* Yeah, I mean you, asshole!"

One scorpion looked around and then with his tiny claw hand pointed at himself questioningly.

"That's right. You! I don't know if you got the word. But we're making a picture here. You know, *a movie?*"

Down in the stilled maelstrom, the scorpion nodded, turning red. His "buddies" had all backed away from him, like they didn't even know him or anything. The director began his descent off the Atlas camera crane and his wrath was august.

Half a mile away, Mary Rose handed the binoculars to Jimmy. "He's certifiable."

Jimmy put the binoculars to his eyes and Monty finished bandaging Morrison's lean, milk-white torso. He was going to be okay. Monty looked up, forcefully tearing his eyes away from the rock poet's body. "What's Captain Queeg doing now?" he made himself ask.

"You won't believe it. He just picked the scorpion up. He's saying something to it. Looks like 'Your director loves you!' They all began to laugh.

"He *ate* the scorpion!" Dean howled.

"Let's get out of here," yelled Clift. "We can make it to your new car! Didn't you leave it in the lot?"

"Yeah!" Dean held up the car keys, ringed on a little black 8 ball. "We're history!"

"No!" The Rose said. "We're archives. That's *after* history." And with that, they said quick goodbyes to Jim Morrison and began to run. Just as, half a mile away, Sam Peckinpah swallowed the dead scorpion (that guy Thomas doubted it; he heard it was a fake made of white chocolate), called to start the shot over again, and turned to find his stars.

"Where's my Lost Madonna?" he asked reasonably. "And Dean and Clift, where are they?" He trained his Nighthawk on the forehead of the young A.D. "Tell me, son, or this one will be for real."

"G-g-gone," the hapless boy stammered, pointing to the horizon. And then, in a firey blast of rage, so was he.

They ran until they were sure they could run no more. Each of them was exactly attuned to the other and yet they kept running. In the nightmare, you don't stop; its unreality makes it real.

They ran from the location back to where the im-

mense company was headquartered; they ran past the
infirmary, they ran past the costume and prop trailers,
past the honey-wagons, past makeup and the hair trailer,
past the comptroller's Winnebago, they ran behind (duck-
ing down under the windows) the production trailer
and then turned down Hellandale Lane where Jimmy's
new Von Tripp-Porsche was waiting next to the Bluebird. The last fifty yards, they slowed down to a sweating, puffing stagger.

"God—"

"Dear—"

"Jesus," they panted.

Monty went straight to the Von Tripp-Porsche but
stopped when he saw Jimmy going in the Bluebird's
front door. "Where're you going?" Panic tinged his voice.

"Cruisin' brewskies!" and Dean came out with three
icy bottles of Budweiser beer. With great and loving
ceremony, Jimmy handed the long neckers to his friends.

"For Rebels in Hell," he said softly.

Back in front of the prop trailor were perhaps a hundred people. All but two of them stood behind the be-
mused director, who was looking across a hot, dusty
clearing at Perse, who was holding a Colt Walker on
him. Tiny stood back a bit.

"Well, Perse, it seems to have come full circle."

"Yeah, Sam. It does."

"You sure you want to play this string?"

"Hell no. But I got to. Jett's a buddy and that lil gal
with him, she's right special. A real angel. You know ..."

"Yeah, I do," said Peckinpah with true understanding, "but on the other hand, sometimes even buddies
and angels have to take gas." With that, the old director
dropped down to his knees in a lightning surprise move,
his hand flashed around behind his neck, and flung his
custom-made Gerber knife the short distance into Perse's
chest.

When Tiny recovered from the shock enough to make
his move, it was too late. The Libyan soldier put a short

burst into his massive head. The soldier grinned and adjusted his new perfumed silk brocade beret.

Perse was still looking down at the Gerber handle sticking out of his blue H-bar-C shirt as he lowered the huge Colt.

"Well, kiss my raggedly ol' ass."

"No thanks, Perse." And Peckinpah continued on, searching for his stars, the cheering lynch mob at his heels.

"You sorry Nazi piece of shit!" howled Jimmy, hammering on the steering wheel as he tried, over and over and over, to start the Von Trip-Porsche. Monty was white-faced and, from the extended front seat, Mary Rose loosened her safety harness enough to turn back to Jimmy. Then, quickly, she lifted her eyes and then closed them tight.

After two seconds had passed, the huge P-38 engine roared to life. Jimmy and Monty cheered. Mary Rose grinned.

"Is everybody strapped in?" They were. Carefully, for this was the maiden voyage, Jimmy ran his eyes over the various instruments across the dashboard. It was an absolute marvel, the most incredible car he had ever seen. Flashing an almost heartbreakingly happy smile at Monty, he eased the huge chrome shifter into low gear and slowly let the clutch out.

The gravel thrown up in a dusty, bursting plume from the Peterbilt racing tires buried the Bluebird right up to the windows. In an ungodly scream, they were off.

The Von Tripp-Porsche cornered like a huge drunken cow. That wasn't exactly what it was sold on. If you wanted "handling" you got a 944 or a Carrera. The Von Tripp was for balls-to-the wall speed of the hysterical stripe. James Dean was just the man for it. He knew; you didn't drive one of these, you aimed it.

The howling leviathon burned up the Hellywood Freeway, literally, covering the distance between the Civic Center and Roscoe Boulevard in just over 80 seconds.

Their hair stood straight out behind them, the wind squirrelled out their cheeks like Dizzy Gillespie's, and the incredible roar of the Allison engine was positively mythic as it drank the gallons of nitromethane.

They stopped at a gas station and little diner in Wheeler Ridge. After some wonderfully mediocre food, a medley from the diner's Frybaby, they went back out to the Von Tripp. Gawkers took note of the movie stars but kept their distance.

"Well, where're we going, Jim?"

"Shit, I was hoping you knew, Monty," laughed Dean.

"It's just like the real world out here," Mary Rose offered, looking around. "Away from that dopey movie. I think I like it." Her warm smile chilled them because it suddenly reminded them of what they had to do, even if they didn't know how to go about doing it.

"How far's The Studio ranch?" asked Monty.

Jimmy spread a map out across the dashboard. "Looks like a couple hundred miles."

"That's an hour, the way you drive," Mary Rose tried to get a comb through her wind-ratted hair, but it was useless. "Why're we goin' to a ranch? Why don't we head East or up to the Bitterroots. Sheeeit, they'd never find us up there!" She gently rubbed a grease smudge off Dean's face.

"They'd find us," Monty told her.

"Besides, we're not going to hide," Jimmy said simply.

"You remember Spencer Tracy, Mary Rose?" asked Clift.

"Who doesn't?" she replied. "He was an incredible, special man. The best."

"Yeah. Maybe even a little more. At least that's what we think. When Tracy disappeared—what was it, Monty? —about eight years ago, the rumor was that he got out." Dean let it sink in.

"Got out?"

"Yeah. All the way."

"And we're going to find out if, why, and how."

"And then, we're gonna join him!" She was excited.

"One of us will," replied Monty.

"Let's blow this popstand," Jimmy said quickly.

The blast that propelled them back out on the Interstate flattened the gas station set completely; the molded plastic gas pumps twisted away in the gale, tearing through the canvas flat's painted window of the fake diner they had just eaten in.

Sam Peckinpah, with the whole of The Studio at his disposal for this mission, was closing in in a stripped-down, hot-rod B-24 Liberator that had been used as a camera plane for years. Out of its bay windows and from its open-front turret had been shot "Hell Is For Heroes," "The Devil and Daniel Webster," "The Satan Bug," not to mention "Mud Wrestlers from Mars vs the Aztec Mole Men." Now, with its four Keith Black cyclone engines blowing red-hot, the bomber was streaking over the desert floor with The Man himself strapped into the open front-bay camera seat, out there all alone with his wrath and his twin-mount .50-calliber machine guns. A double belt of garlic-dipped magnesium rounds hung in the chambers.

He cleaned his fingernails with an icepick in the mutant sun's hot wind and listened in his headset to the radar tracking report from the flight crew above. Soon he would have a target; he felt it. It was almost over; soon he would have his final shot.

Because even now two high-priced screenwriters were in the tail-gunner's station, hammering out a new ending on an old Royal. This ending—except the battle scenes which he could do in his sleep—would close the movie, bringing it in early. In this ending, like "The Wild Bunch," they all died. Horribly. In a hail of gunfire that went on for fifteen minutes. They were massacred, chewed to flinders, so apocalyptically destroyed that by the time the last little flake of flesh was allowed to settle to the killing ground the blood had all dried up to red dust and was blown away into little pink, puffy clouds that, in Indian smoke signals, read "bye bye."

There would be nothing left. Of the soldier. Or the cat. Or the angel. Like "The Wild Bunch," but better.

"Say," one of the screenwriters asked through the plane's intercom system, "how do you spell 'Armageddon'?"

In the wind, Sam Peckinpah laughed a true and hearty laugh for the first time in years.

Jimmy stopped for a quick whizz break at Blackwell's Corners at the junction of Routes 33 and 46. It was the first time he'd noticed.

"Oh, dogshit," he said softly.

"What's wrong?" Only Monty had heard him.

"Nothing," he lied. "It's okay." Jimmy didn't see any point in going into the history. This road—well, it used to be called Route 446—was the one that, so long ago, driving his cherished '55 Spyder, he'd had his one and only blinding glimpse of God Almighty.

Mary Rose came back with a small sack of apples over her shoulder. She tossed one to each of them. Pippins!

"They's so sour, it'll pull your asshole back through your belt buckle!" she said in innocent sweetness. They howled with laughter and in a few moments were off again in a ground–pounding roar from the Von Tripp-Porsche.

As they left, behind them, the settlement faded away into molecular nothingness.

WHERE THE IRRESISTIBLE FORCE MEETS THE IM-MOVABLE OBJECT— So, if you will look on a map, you will see where it took place. Not a play map, get a real one. Right now.

Okay, see where Route 41 cuts into Route 46, near Cholame? There, there it is . . .

There. In the dark, red sunlight of that hot desert day, the bomber had the blood-colored car below in its sights. It was closing fast, the four–bladed props chewing through the air at seven thousand RPM.

In the car below, quickly three tiny faces turned back toward the sound growing louder and louder. For a second it seemed to hypnotize them.

For this moment, there were no mountains, no desert, no sky; only faces. There are always faces.

The old man was home. The years fell away as the deep wrinkles in his hawk-leather face disappeared. The whiteness of his hair and thin moustache darkened to a burnt sienna. The sagging flesh on his neck and upper arms turned to long, muscular sinew as he steeled his greedy hands to the twin grips and peered in the darkness down the sights of his machine guns into the hapless visage of his victims.

"More light!" he yelled to the faint, grinning visage of his old buddy, Warren Oates; and Peckinpah opened fire!

Then, something amazing happened. Something that no one would ever know about. Because it was so strong that it simply precluded any recounting of it by its witnesses. Some things are like that. The spark of life. Death is like that. And too, Salvation.

Finally, for the first and last time in his life, on this day, the director's wish was granted.

"MORE LIGHT!"

The murky orange sky paled and seemed to open up with light from a source greater than the puny sun that hung at four o'clock on the jagged horizon. Brighter and brighter it got until its effulgence was so great that even the outlines of objects in it—the speeding car, bullets standing in the air, the screaming bomber above—shook and faded in and out in a rhythmic pulse which began to give off a wonderful sound. It took into it the brutality of the engines and the machine guns and people screaming and everything, everywhere.

Except the still, small voice of a man.

"Take my hand, Mary Rose," said Spencer Tracy from the center of the brightness. "You're not lost anymore."

And in the deafening noise of the whirlwind, Mary

Rose Foster reached out for him as everything vanished into the white.

"What the hell was that?" said a young man named Donald as he turned his Ford left off 46 onto 41. He had seen a flash of blinding light—just for a millisecond—right in the middle of his turn which he had to make in the murky darkness twice a day, forever. For some reason, he didn't know why, it always filled him with fear and dispair. Just a little left-hand turn. But after this flash of light, he didn't feel that way any more. Something greatly terrible was lifted from him. And Donald went home, tears of relief streaming down his face. He forgot the flash of light before his turn signals went off.

At his own Memorial Service, Cecil B. DeMille told again the wondrous story of his humble beginnings. People in attendance keened to that marvelous voice, finally surrendering to its hypnotic drone a full hour before he got to the part where Sam Peckinpah took over the reins of "Hell's Gate" and ruined the legendary producer's life. So as DeMille slagged into the rebel director, chapter and verse, with the mighty rage of the wronged, his dead-silent audience (partly on hold from the white wine) resembled nothing so much as a church filled with the Pod Parents of the Children of the Damned. Just another cheap irony for which Hellywood was justly famous.

A week later, The Studio pulled some strings and railroaded Peckinpah through a grand jury and into court. Although he was represented by Louis ("The Lip") Brandeis, he was convicted of despoiling film stock, concept rape, and various and sundry charges of flagrant and wanton fuckupery. There was an appeal; there were suits and counter suits, slanderous interviews, libelous letters—bad ink all the way around. In the end, people followed the fire alone; they had long since forgotten what was burning.

The Studio of course 86'ed the old man's footage,

cutting it into guitar picks (which sent film conspirists groping for the digitalis). And they got a new director; a German woman named Reifenstall. They recast a few key parts and went back to work. "Hell's Gate" would go on.

High in the mountains back at his cabin, Peckinpah passed his days replaying the events which took this triumph from him, which led to his downfall. He'd been in the film business all his life and he could slow time down like it was on a Kem editing table, slow things down to click by one frame at a time. Still, he didn't get it.

Alone he would walk, scuffing through the fallen dark leaves. He would trudge up the middle of molten trout streams, kicking rubies in the dark sunlight. He would open his arms and yell *"Stop!"* to the fish.

It was hot, of course. You expected that; a kind of wet, nasty heat that never let up. There were plains and mountains and hot, red oceans. There was weather and all of it was bad. It was the worst of times, and still the troopers trudged on. Sweat ran down their filthy, haggard faces and all you could hear in the middle of the vast column was the clanking of ancient equipment and the wheeze of pneumonia. Their eyes were glazed over with tranqzine to counteract the effects of the years of amphetamines, and their breaths were fetid horror. They weren't young any more, but they weren't old either. They were cannon fodder, the most valuable and diseased building block any people can have. And they marched on forever.

Near them, going the other way, an enormous battle machine (constructed out of steel, plexiglass, Z-90 armorplate, and dental floss) lumbered along on its huge tank treads through smoking lakes and flaming glaciers. From it guns fired out of evil-looking openings that closed up and reappeared elsewhere like a slit mouth that revealed another bizarre weapon sending out a gorgeous stream of tracers and jellied frags.

Inside it was noise and smoke and confusion. Men ran around in various stages of dress and decay, yelling in many languages, understanding none. Yet somehow the guns kept firing.

Up on the command platform, the familiar eyes of Che Guevara cut over to his trusty feline aide-de-camp-it-up Cataraugus, who was smoothing his whiskers. Che lit a Lucky, snapping the stainless-steel lid shut on the Death-head SS Zippo the director had given him.

"Another day, another Drachma. Quelle pisser," James Dean said softly to Montgomery Clift.

GILGAMESH IN THE OUTBACK

Robert Silverberg

Faust. First I will question thee about hell.
   Tell me, where is the place that men call hell?
Meph. Under the heavens.
Faust. Ay, but whereabout?
Meph. Within the bowels of these elements,
   Where we are tortur'd and remain for ever:
   Hell hath no limits, nor is circumscrib'd
   In one self place; for where we are is hell,
   And where hell is, there must we ever be:
   And, to conclude, when all the world dissolves,
   And every creature shall be purified,
   All places shall be hell that are not heaven.
Faust. Come, I think hell's a fable.
Meph. Ay, think so still, till experience change thy
   mind.

Marlowe: Dr. Faustus

Jagged green lightning danced on the horizon and the wind came ripping like a blade out of the east, skinning the flat land bare and sending up clouds of gray-brown dust. Gilgamesh grinned broadly. By Enlil, now that was a wind! A lion-killing wind it was, a wind that

---

turned the air dry and crackling. The beasts of the field gave you the greatest joy in their hunting when the wind was like that, hard and sharp and cruel.

He narrowed his eyes and stared into the distance, searching for this day's prey. His bow of several fine woods, the bow that no man but he was strong enough to draw—no man but he and Enkidu his beloved thrice-lost friend—hung loosely from his hand. His body was poised and ready. Come now, you beasts! Come and be slain! It is Gilgamesh, king of Uruk, who would make his sport with you this day!

Other men in this land, when they went about their hunting, made use of guns, those foul machines that the New Dead had brought, which hurled death from a great distance along with much noise and fire and smoke; or they employed the even deadlier laser devices from whose ugly snouts came spurts of blue-white flame. Cowardly things, all those killing machines! Gilgamesh loathed them, as he did most instruments of the New Dead, those slick and bustling Johnny-come-latelies of Hell. He would not touch them if he could help it. In all the thousands of years he had dwelled in this nether world he had never used any weapons but those he had known during his first lifetime: the javelin, the spear, the double-headed axe, the hunting bow, the good bronze sword. It took some skill, hunting with such weapons as those. And there was physical effort; there was more than a little risk. Hunting was a contest, was it not? Then it must make demands. Why, if the idea was merely to slaughter one's prey in the fastest and easiest and safest way, then the sensible thing to do would be to ride high above the hunting grounds in a weapons platform and drop a little nuke, eh, and lay waste five kingdoms' worth of beasts at a single stroke!

He knew that there were those who thought him a fool for such ideas. Caesar, for one. Cocksure coldblooded Julius with the gleaming pistols thrust into his belt and the submachine gun slung across his shoulders. "Why don't you admit it?" Caesar had asked him once, riding up in his jeep as Gilgamesh was making ready to set forth toward Hell's open wilderness. "It's a pure affectation, Gilgamesh, all this insistence on arrows and javelins and spears. This isn't old Sumer you're living in now."

Gilgamesh spat. "Hunt with 9-millimeter automatics? Hunt with grenades and cluster bombs and lasers? You call that sport, Caesar?"

"I call it acceptance of reality. Is it technology you hate? What's the difference between using a bow and arrow and using a gun? They're both technology, Gilgamesh. It isn't as though you kill the animals with your bare hands."

"I have done that, too," said Gilgamesh.

"Bah! I'm on to your game. Big hulking Gilgamesh, the simple innocent oversized Bronze Age hero! That's just an affectation, too, my friend! You pretend to be a stupid, stubborn thick-skulled barbarian because it suits you to be left alone to your hunting and your wandering, and that's all you claim that you really want. But secretly you regard yourself as superior to anybody who lived in an era softer than your own. You mean to restore the bad old filthy ways of the ancient ancients, isn't that so? If I read you the right way you're just biding your time, skulking around with your bow and arrow in the dreary Outback until you think it's the right moment to launch the *putsch* that carries you to supreme power here. Isn't that it, Gilgamesh? You've got some crazy fantasy of overthrowing Satan himself and lording it over all of us. And then we'll live in mud cities again and make little chicken scratches on clay tablets, the way we were meant to do. What do you say?"

"I say this is great nonsense, Caesar."

"Is it? This place is full of kings and emperors and sultans and pharaohs and shahs and presidents and dictators, and every single one of them wants to be Number One again. My guess is that you're no exception."

"In this you are very wrong."

"I doubt that. I suspect you believe you're the best of us all: you, the sturdy warrior, the great hunter, the maker of bricks, the builder of vast temples and lofty walls, the shining beacon of ancient heroism. You think we're all decadent rascally degenerates and that you're the one true virtuous man. But you're as proud and ambitious as any of us. Isn't that how it is? You're a fraud, Gilgamesh, a huge musclebound fraud!"

"At least I am no slippery tricky serpent like you, Caesar, who dons a wig and spies on women at their mysteries if it pleases him."

Caesar looked untroubled by the thrust. "And so you pass three-quarters of your time killing stupid monstrous creatures in the Outback and you make sure everyone knows that you're too pious to have anything to do with modern weapons while you do it. You don't fool me. It isn't virtue that keeps you from doing your killing with a decent double-barreled .470 Springfield. It's intellectual pride, or maybe simple laziness. The bow just happens to be the weapon you grew up with, who knows how many thousands of years ago. You like it because it's familiar. But what language are you speaking now, eh? Is it your thick-tongued Euphrates gibberish? No, it seems to be English, doesn't it? Did you grow up speaking English too, Gilgamesh? Did you grow up riding around in jeeps and choppers? Apparently *some* of the new ways are acceptable to you."

Gilgamesh shrugged. "I speak English with you because that is what is spoken now in this place. In my heart I speak the old tongue, Caesar. In my heart I am still Gilgamesh of Uruk, and I will hunt as I hunt."

"Uruk's long gone to dust. This is the life after life, my friend. We've been here a long time. We'll be here for all time to come, unless I miss my guess. New people constantly bring new ideas to this place, and it's impossible to ignore them. Even you can't do it. Isn't that a wristwatch I see on your arm, Gilgamesh? A *digital* watch, no less?"

"I will hunt as I hunt," said Gilgamesh. "There is no

sport in it, when you do it with guns. There is no grace in it."

Caesar shook his head. "I never could understand hunting for sport, anyway. Killing a few stags, yes, or a boar or two, when you're bivouacked in some dismal Gaulish forest and your men want meat. But hunting? Slaughtering hideous animals that aren't even edible? By Apollo, it's all nonsense to me!"

"My point exactly."

"But if you must hunt, to scorn the use of a decent hunting rifle—"

"You will never convince me."

"No," Caesar said with a sigh. "I suppose I won't. I should know better than to argue with a reactionary."

"Reactionary! In my time I was thought to be a radical," said Gilgamesh. "When I was king in Uruk—"

"Just so," Caesar said, laughing. "King in Uruk. Was there ever a king who wasn't reactionary? You put a crown on your head and it addles your brains instantly. Three times Antonius offered me a crown, Gilgamesh. Three times, and—"

"—you did thrice refuse it, yes. I know all that. 'Was this ambition?' You thought you'd have the power without the emblem. Who were you fooling, Caesar? Not Brutus, so I hear. Brutus said you were ambitious. And Brutus—"

That stung him. "Damn you, don't say it!"

"—was an honorable man," Gilgamesh concluded, enjoying Caesar's discomfiture.

Caesar groaned. "If I hear that line once more—"

"Some say this is a place of torment," said Gilgamesh serenely. "If in truth it is, yours is to be swallowed up in another man's poetry. Leave me to my bows and arrows, Caesar, and return to your jeep and your trivial intrigues. I am a fool and a reactionary, yes. But you know nothing of hunting. Nor do you understand anything of me."

*   *   *

All that had been a year ago, or two, or maybe five—
with or without a wristwatch, there was no keeping
proper track of time in Hell, where the unmoving ruddy
eye of the sun never budged from the sky—and now
Gilgamesh was far from Caesar and all his minions, far
from the troublesome center of Hell and the tiresome
squabbling of those like Caesar and Alexander and Napoleon and that sordid little Guevara man who maneuvered for power in this place.

Let them maneuver all they liked, those shoddy new
men of the latter days. Some day they might learn
wisdom, and was not that the purpose of this place, if it
had any purpose at all?

Gilgamesh preferred to withdraw. Unlike the rest of
those fallen emperors and kings and pharaohs and shahs,
he felt no yearning to reshape Hell in his own image.
Caesar was as wrong about Gilgamesh's ambitions as
he was about the reasons for his preferences in hunting
gear. Out here in the Outback, in the bleak dry chilly
hinterlands of Hell, Gilgamesh hoped to find peace.
That was all he wanted now: peace. He had wanted
much more, once, but that had been long ago.

There was a stirring in the scraggly underbrush.

A lion, maybe?

No, Gilgamesh thought. There were no lions to be
found in Hell, only the strange nether-world beasts.
Ugly hairy things with flat noses and many legs and
dull baleful eyes, and slick shiny things with the faces
of women and the bodies of malformed dogs, and worse,
much worse. Some had drooping leathery wings, and
some were armed with spiked tails that rose like a
scorpion's, and some had mouths that opened wide
enough to swallow an elephant at a gulp. They all were
demons of one sort or another, Gilgamesh knew. No
matter. Hunting was hunting; the prey was the prey; all
beasts were one in the contest of the field. That fop
Caesar could never begin to comprehend that.

Drawing an arrow from his quiver, Gilgamesh laid it
lightly across his bow and waited.

* * *

"If you ever had come to Texas, H.P., this here's a lot like what you'd have seen," said the big barrel-chested man with the powerful arms and the deeply tanned skin. Gesturing sweepingly with one hand, he held the wheel of the Land Rover lightly with three fingers of the other, casually guiding the vehicle in jouncing zigs and zags over the flat trackless landscape. Gnarled gray-green shrubs matted the gritty ground. The sky was black with swirling dust. Far off in the distance barren mountains rose like dark jagged teeth. "Beautiful. Beautiful. As close to Texas in look as makes no never mind, this countryside is."

"Beautiful?" said the other man uncertainly. "Hell?"

"This stretch sure is. But if you think Hell's beautiful, you should have seen Texas!"

The burly man laughed and gunned the engine, and the Land Rover went leaping and bouncing onward at a stupefying speed.

His traveling companion, a gaunt, lantern-jawed man as pale as the other was bronzed, sat very still in the passenger seat, knees together and elbows digging in against his ribs, as if he expected a fiery crash at any moment. The two of them had been journeying across the interminable parched wastes of the Outback for many days now—how many, not even the Elder Gods could tell. They were ambassadors, these two: Their Excellencies Robert E. Howard and H.P. Lovecraft of the Kingdom of New Holy Diabolic England, envoys of His Britannic Majesty Henry VIII to the court of Prester John.

In another life they had been writers, fantasists, inventors of fables; but now they found themselves caught up in something far more fantastic than anything to be found in any of their tales, for this was no fable, this was no fantasy. This was the reality of Hell.

"Robert—" said the pale man nervously.

"A lot like Texas, yes," Howard went on, "only Hell's just a faint carbon copy of the genuine item. Just a rough first draft, is all. You see that sandstorm rising out thataway? *We* had sandstorms, they covered entire counties! You see that lightning? In Texas that would be just a flicker!"

"If you could drive just a little more slowly, Bob—"

"More slowly? Chthulu's whiskers, man, I *am* driving slowly!"

"Yes, I'm quite sure you believe that you are."

"And the way I always heard it, H.P., you loved for people to drive you around at top speed. Seventy, eighty miles an hour, that was what you liked best, so the story goes."

"In the other life one dies only once, and then all pain ceases," Lovecraft replied. "But here, where one can go to the Undertaker again and again, and when one returns one remembers every final agony in the brightest of hues—here, dear friend Bob, death's much more to be feared, for the pain of it stays with one forever, and one may die a thousand deaths." Lovecraft managed a pale baleful smile. "Speak of that to some professional warrior, Bob, some Trojan or Hun or Assyrian—or one of the gladiators, maybe, someone who has died and died and died again. Ask him about it: the dying and the rebirth, and the pain, the hideous torment, reliving every detail. It is a dreadful thing to die in Hell. I fear dying here far more than I ever did in life. I will take no needless risks here."

Howard snorted. "Gawd, try and figure you out! When you thought you lived only once, you made people go roaring along with you on the highway a mile a minute. Here where no one stays dead for very long you want me to drive like an old woman. Well, I'll attempt it, H.P., but everything in me cries out to go like the wind. When you live in big country, you learn to cover the territory the way it has to be covered. And Texas is the biggest country there is. It isn't just a place, it's a state of mind."

"As is Hell," said Lovecraft. "Though I grant you that Hell isn't Texas."

"Texas!" Howard boomed. "God damn, I wish you could have seen it! By God, H.P., what a time we'd have had, you and me, if you'd come to Texas. Two gentlemen of letters like us riding together all to hell and gone from Corpus Christi to El Paso and back again, seeing it all and telling each other wondrous stories all the way! I swear, it would have enlarged your soul, H.P. Beauty such as perhaps even you couldn't have imagined. That big sky. That blazing sun. And the open space! Whole empires could fit into Texas and never be seen again! That Rhode Island of yours, H.P.—we could drop it down just back of Cross Plains and lose it behind a medium-size prickly pear! What you see here, it just gives you the merest idea of that glorious beauty. Though I admit this is plenty beautiful itself, this here."

"I wish I could share your joy in this landscape, Robert," Lovecraft said quietly, when it seemed that Howard had said all he meant to say.

"You don't care for it?" Howard asked, sounding surprised and a little wounded.

"I can say one good thing for it: at least it's far from the sea."

"You'll give it that much, will you?"

"You know how I hate the sea and all that the sea contains! Its odious creatures—that hideous reek of salt air hovering above it—" Lovecraft shuddered fastidiously. "But this land—this bitter desert—you don't find it somber? You don't find it forbidding?"

"It's the most beautiful place I've seen since I came to Hell."

"Perhaps the beauty is too subtle for my eye. Perhaps it escapes me altogether. I was always a man for cities, myself."

"What you're trying to say, I reckon, is that all this looks real hateful to you. Is that it? As grim and ghastly as the Plateau of Leng, eh, H.P.?" Howard laughed. " 'Sterile hills of gray granite . . . dim wastes of rock and ice and snow . . .' " Hearing himself quoted, Lovecraft laughed too, though not exuberantly. Howard went on.

"I look around at the Outback of Hell and I see something a whole lot like Texas, and I love it. For you it's as sinister as dark frosty Leng, where people have horns and hooves and munch on corpses and sing hymns to Nyarlathotep. Oh, H.P., H.P., there's no accounting for tastes, is there? Why, there's even some people who— whoa, now! Look there!"

He braked the Land Rover suddenly and brought it to a jolting halt. A small malevolent-looking something with blazing eyes and a scaly body had broken from cover and gone scuttering across the path just in front of them. Now it faced them, glaring up out of the road, snarling and hissing flame.

"Hell-cat!" Howard cried. "Hell-coyote! *Look* at that critter, H.P. You ever see so much ugliness packed into such a small package? Scare the toenails off a shoggoth, that one would!"

"Can you drive past it?" Lovecraft asked, looking dismayed.

"I want a closer look, first." Howard rummaged down by his boots and pulled a pistol from the clutter on the floor of the car. "Don't it give you the shivers, driving around in a land full of critters that could have come right out of one of your stories, or mine? I want to look this little ghoul-cat right in the eye."

"Robert—"

"You wait here. I'll only be but a minute."

Howard swung himself down from the Land Rover and marched stolidly toward the hissing little beast, which stood its ground. Lovecraft watched fretfully. At any moment the creature might leap upon Bob Howard and rip out his throat with a swipe of its horrid yellow talons, perhaps—or burrow snout-deep into his chest, seeking the Texan's warm, throbbing heart—

They stood staring at each other, Howard and the small monster, no more than a dozen feet apart. For a long moment neither one moved. Howard, gun in hand, leaned forward to inspect the beast as one might look at a feral cat guarding the mouth of an alleyway. Did he mean to shoot it? No, Lovecraft thought: beneath his bluster the robust Howard seemed surprisingly squeamish about bloodshed and violence of any sort.

Then things began happening very quickly. Out of a thicket to the left a much larger animal abruptly emerged: a ravening Hell-creature with a crocodile head and powerful thick-thighed legs that ended in monstrous curving claws. An arrow ran through the quivering dewlaps of its heavy throat from side to side, and a hideous dark ichor streamed from the wound down the beast's repellent blue-gray fur. The small animal, seeing the larger one wounded this way, instantly sprang upon its back and sank its fangs joyously into its shoulder. But a moment later there burst from the same thicket a man of astonishing size, a great dark-haired black-bearded man clad only in a bit of cloth about his waist. Plainly he was the huntsman who had wounded the larger monster, for there was a bow of awesome dimensions in his hand and a quiver of arrows on his back. In utter fearlessness the giant plucked the foul little creature from the wounded beast's back and hurled it far out of sight; then, swinging around, he drew a gleaming bronze dagger, and with a single fierce thrust, drove it into the breast of his prey as the coup de grace that brought the animal crashing heavily down.

All this took only an instant. Lovecraft, peering through the window of the Land Rover, was dazzled by the strength and speed of the dispatch and awed by the size and agility of the half-naked huntsman. He glanced toward Howard, who stood to one side, his own considerable frame utterly dwarfed by the black-bearded man.

For a moment Howard seemed dumbstruck, paralyzed with wonder and amazement. But then he was the first to speak.

"By Crom," he muttered, staring at the giant. "Surely this is Conan of Aquilonia and none other!" He was trembling. He took a lurching step toward the huge man, holding out both his hands in a strange gesture—submission, was it? "Lord Conan?" Howard murmured.

"Great king, is it you? Conan? Conan?" And before Lovecraft's astounded eyes Howard fell to his knees next to the dying beast, and looked up with awe and something like rapture in his eyes at the towering huntsman.

It had been a decent day's hunting so far. Three beasts brought down after long and satisfying chase; every shaft fairly placed; each animal skillfully dressed, the meat set out as bait for other hell-beasts, the hide and head carefully put aside for proper cleaning at nightfall. There was true pleasure in work done so well.

Yet there was a hollowness at the heart of it all, Gilgamesh thought, that left him leaden and cheerless no matter how cleanly his arrows sped to their mark. He never felt that true fulfillment, that clean sense of completion, that joy of accomplishment, which was ultimately the only thing he sought.

Why was that? Was it—as the Christian dead so drearily insisted—because this was Hell, where by definition there could be no delight?

To Gilgamesh that was foolishness. Those who came here expecting eternal punishment did indeed get eternal punishment, and it was even more horrendous than anything they had anticipated. It served them right, those true believers, those gullible New Dead, that army of credulous Christians.

He had been amazed when their kind first came flocking into Hell, Enki only knew how many thousands of years ago. The things they talked of! Rivers of boiling oil! Lakes of pitch! Demons with pitchforks! That was what they expected, and the Administration was happy to oblige them. There were Torture Towns aplenty for those who wanted them. Gilgamesh had trouble understanding why anyone would. Nobody among the Old Dead really could figure them out, those absurd New Dead with their obsession with punishment. What was it Sargon called them? Masochists, that was the word. Pathetic masochists. But then that sly little Machiavelli had begged to disagree, saying, "No, my lord, it would be a violation of the nature of Hell to send a true masochist off to the torments. The only ones who go are the strong ones—the bullies, the braggarts, the ones who are cowards at the core of their souls." Augustus had had something to say on the matter too, and Caesar, and that Egyptian bitch Hatshepsut had butted in, she of the false beard and the startling eyes, and then all of them had jabbered at once, trying yet again to make sense of the Christian New Dead. Until finally Gilgamesh had said, before stalking out of the room, "The trouble with all of you is that you keep trying to make sense out of this place. But when you've been here as long as I have—"

Well, perhaps Hell *was* a place of punishment. Certainly there were some disagreeable aspects to it. The business about sex, for example. Never being able to come, even if you pumped away all day and all night. And the whole digestive complication, allowing you to eat real food but giving you an unholy hard time when it came to passing the stuff through your gut. But Gilgamesh tended to believe that those were merely the incidental consequences of being dead: this place was not, after all, the land of the living, and there was no reason why things should work the same way here as they did back there.

He had to admit that the reality of Hell had turned out to be nothing at all like what the priests had promised it would be. The House of Dust and Darkness, was what they had called it in Uruk long ago. A place where the dead lived in eternal night and sadness, clad like birds, with wings for garments. Where the dwellers had dust for their bread, and clay for their meat. Where the kings of the earth, the masters, the high rulers, lived humbly without their crowns, and were forced to wait on the demons like servants. Small wonder that he had dreaded death as he had, believing that that was what awaited him for all time to come!

Well, in fact all that had been mere myth and folly.

Gilgamesh could still remember Hell as it had been when he first had come to it: a place much like Uruk, so it seemed, with low flat-roofed buildings of whitewashed brick, and temples rising on high platforms of many steps. And there he found all the heroes of olden days, living as they had always lived: Lugalbanda, his father; and Enmerkar, his father's father; and Ziusudra who built the vessel by which mankind survived the Flood; and others on and on, back to the dawn of time. At least that was what it was like where Gilgamesh first found himself; there were other districts, he discovered later, that were quite different—places where people lived in caves, or in pits in the ground, or in flimsy houses of reeds, and still other places where the Hairy Men dwelled and had no houses at all. Most of that was gone now, greatly transformed by all those who had come to Hell in the latter days, and indeed a lot of nonsensical ugliness and ideological foolishness had entered in recent centuries in the baggage of the New Dead. But still, the idea that this whole vast realm—infinitely bigger than his own beloved Land of the Two Rivers—existed merely for the sake of chastising the dead for their sins, struck Gilgamesh as too silly for serious contemplation.

Why, then, was the joy of his hunting so pale and hollow? Why none of the old ecstasy when spying the prey, when drawing the great bow, when sending the arrow true to its mark?

Gilgamesh thought he knew why, and it had nothing to do with punishment. There had been joy aplenty in the hunting for many a thousand years of his life in Hell. If the joy had gone from it now, it was only that in these latter days he hunted alone; that Enkidu—his friend, his true brother, his other self—was not with him. That and nothing but that: for he had never felt complete without Enkidu since they first had met and wrestled and come to love one another after the manner of brothers, long ago in the city of Uruk. That great burly man, broad and tall and strong as Gilgamesh himself, that shaggy wild creature out of the high ridges: Gilgamesh had never loved anyone as he loved Enkidu.

But it was the fate of Gilgamesh, so it seemed, to lose him again and again. Enkidu had been ripped from him the first time long ago when they still dwelled in Uruk, on that dark day when the gods had had revenge upon them for their great pride and had sent the fever to take Enkidu's life. In time Gilgamesh too had yielded to death and was taken into Hell, which he found nothing at all like the Hell that the scribes and priests of the Land had taught; and there he had searched for Enkidu, and one glorious day he had found him. Hell had been a much smaller place, then, and everyone seemed to know everyone else; but even so it had taken an age to track him down. Oh, the rejoicing that day in Hell! Oh, the singing and the dancing, the vast festival that went on and on! There was great kindliness among the denizens of Hell in those days, and everyone was glad for Gilgamesh and Enkidu. Minos of Crete gave the first great party in honor of their reunion, and then it was Amenhotep's turn, and then Agamemnon's. And on the fourth day the host was dark slender Varuna, the Meluhhan king, and then on the fifth the heroes gathered in the ancient hall of the Ice-Hunter folk where one-eyed Vy-otin was chieftain and the floor was strewn with mammoth tusks, and after that—

Well, and it went on for some long time, the great celebration of the reunion. This was long before the hordes of New Dead had come, all those grubby little unheroic people out of unheroic times, carrying with them their nasty little demons and their dark twisted apparatus of damnation and punishment. Before they had come, Hell had simply been a place to live in the time after life. It was all very different then, a far happier place.

For uncountable years Gilgamesh and Enkidu dwelled together in Gilgamesh's palace in Hell as they had in the old days in the Land of the Two Rivers. And all was well with them, with much hunting and feasting, and they were happy in Hell even after the New Dead began to come in, bringing all their terrible changes.

They were shoddy folk, these New Dead, confused of soul and flimsy of intellect, and their petty trifling rivalries and vain strutting poses were a great nuisance. But Gilgamesh and Enkidu kept their distance from them while they replayed all the follies of their lives, their nonsensical Crusades and their idiotic trade wars and their preposterous theological squabbles. The trouble was that they had brought not only their lunatic ideas to Hell but also their accursed diabolical modern gadgets, and the worst of those were the vile weapons called guns, that slaughtered noisily from afar in the most shameful cowardly way. Heroes know how to parry the blow of a battle-axe or the thrust of a sword; but what can even a hero do about a bullet from afar? It was Enkidu's bad luck to fall between two quarreling bands of these gun-wielders, a flock of babbling Spaniards and a rabble of arrogant Englanders, for whom he tried to make peace. Of course they would have no peace, and soon shots were flying, and Gilgamesh arrived at the scene just as a bolt from an arquebus tore through his dear Enkidu's noble heart.

No one dies in Hell forever; but some are dead a long time, and that was how it was with Enkidu. It pleased the Undertaker this time to keep him in limbo some hundreds of years, or however many it was—tallying such matters in Hell is always difficult. It was, at any rate, a dreadful long while, and Gilgamesh once more felt that terrible inrush of loneliness that only the presence of Enkidu might cure. Hell continued to change, and now the changes were coming at a stupefying, overwhelming rate. There seemed to be far more people in the world than there ever had been in the old days, and great armies of them marched into Hell every day, a swarming rabble of uncouth strangers who after only a little interval of disorientation and bewilderment would swiftly set out to reshape the whole place into something as discordant and repellent as the world they had left behind. The steam engine came, with its clamor and clangor, and something called the dynamo, and then harsh glittering electrical lights blazed in every street where the lamps had been, and factories arose and began pouring out all manner of strange things. And more and more and more, relentlessly, unceasingly. Railroads. Telephones. Automobiles. Noise, smoke, soot everywhere, and no way to hide from it. The Industrial Revolution, they called it. Satan and his swarm of Administration bureaucrats seemed to love all the new things, and so did almost everyone else, except for Gilgamesh and a few other cranky conservatives. "What are they trying to do?" Rabelais asked one day. "Turn the place into Hell?" Now the New Dead were bringing in such devices as radios and helicopters and computers, and everyone was speaking English, so that once again Gilgamesh, who had grudgingly learned the new-fangled Greek long ago when Agamemnon and his crew had insisted on it, was forced to master yet another tongue-twisting, intricate language. It was a dreary time for him. And then at last did Enkidu reappear, far away in one of the cold northern domains. He made his way south, and for a time, they were reunited again, and once more all was well for Gilgamesh of Uruk in Hell.

But now they were separated again, this time by something colder and more cruel than death itself. It was beyond all belief, but they had quarreled. There had been words between them, ugly words on both sides—such a dispute as never in thousands of years had passed between them in the land of the living or in the land of Hell—and at last Enkidu had said that which Gilgamesh had never dreamed he would ever hear, which was, "I want no more of you, king of Uruk. If you cross my path again I will have your life." Could that have been Enkidu speaking, or was it, Gilgamesh wondered, some demon of Hell in Enkidu's form?

In any case he was gone. He vanished into the turmoil and intricacy of Hell and placed himself beyond Gilgamesh's finding. And when Gilgamesh sent forth inquiries, back came only the report, "He will not speak with you. He has no love for you, Gilgamesh."

It could not be. It must be a spell of witchcraft, thought Gilgamesh. Surely this was some dark working of the Hell of the New Dead, that could turn brother against brother and lead Enkidu to persist in his wrath. In time, Gilgamesh was sure, Enkidu would be triumphant over this sorcery that gripped his soul, and he would open himself once more to the love of Gilgamesh. But time went on, after the strange circuitous fashion of Hell, and Enkidu did not return to his brother's arms.

What was there to do but hunt, and wait, and hope?

So this day Gilgamesh hunted in Hell's parched outback. He had killed and killed and killed again, and now late in the day he had put his arrow through the throat of a monster more foul even than the usual run of creatures of Hell; but there was a terrible vitality to the thing, and it went thundering off, dripping dark blood from its pierced maw.

Gilgamesh gave pursuit. It is sinful to strike and wound and not to kill. For a long weary hour he ran, crisscrossing this harsh land. Thorny plants slashed at him with the malevolence of imps, and the hard wind flailed him with clouds of dust sharp as whips. Still the evil-looking beast outpaced him, though its blood drained in torrents from it to the dry ground.

Gilgamesh would not let himself tire, for there was god-power in him by virtue of his descent from the divine Lugalbanda, his great father who was both king and god. But he was hard pressed to keep going. Three times he lost sight of his quarry, and tracked it only by the spoor of its blood-droppings. The bleak red motionless eye that was the sun of Hell seemed to mock him, hovering forever before him as though willing him to run without cease.

Then he saw the creature, still strong but plainly staggering, lurching about at the edge of a thicket of little twisted, greasy-leaved trees. Unhesitatingly Gilgamesh plunged forward. The trees stroked him lasciviously, coating him with their slime, trying like raucous courtesans to insinuate their leaves between his legs; but he slapped them away, and emerged finally into a clearing where he could confront his animal.

Some repellent little hell-beast was clinging to the back of his prey, ripping out bloody gobbets of flesh and ruining the hide. A Land Rover was parked nearby, and a pale, strange-looking man with a long jaw was peering from its window. A second man, red-faced and beefy-looking, stood close by Gilgamesh's roaring, snorting quarry.

First things first. Gilgamesh reached out, scooped the foul hissing little carrion-seeker from the bigger animal's back, flung it aside. Then with all his force he rammed his dagger toward what he hoped was the heart of the wounded animal. In the moment of his thrust Gilgamesh felt a great convulsion within the monster's breast and its hell-life left it in an instant.

The work was done. Again, no exultation, no sense of fulfillment; only a kind of dull ashen release from an unfinished chore. Gilgamesh caught his breath and looked around.

What was this? The red-faced man seemed to be having a crazy fit. Quivering, shaking, sweating, dropping to his knees, his eyes gleaming insanely—

"Lord Conan?" the man cried. "Great king?"

"Conan is not one of my titles," said Gilgamesh, mystified. "And I was a king once in Uruk, but I reign over nothing at all in this place. Come, man, get off your knees!"

"But you are Conan to the life!" moaned the red-faced man hoarsely. "To the absolute life!"

Gilgamesh felt a surge of intense dislike for this fellow. He would be slobbering in another moment. Conan? Conan? That name meant nothing at all. No, wait: he had known a Conan once, some little Celtic fellow he had encountered in a tavern, a chap with a blunt nose and heavy cheekbones and dark hair tumbling down his face, a drunken twitchy little man forever invoking forgotten godlets of no consequence—yes, he had called himself Conan, so Gilgamesh thought. Drank too much, caused trouble for the barmaid, even took a swing at her, that was the one. Gilgamesh had dropped him down an open cesspool to teach him manners. But how could this blustery-faced fellow here mistake me for that one? He was still mumbling on, too, babbling about lands whose names meant nothing to Gilgamesh—Cimmeria, Aquilonia, Hyrkania, Zamora. Total nonsense. There were no such places.

And that glow in the fellow's eyes—what sort of look was that? A look of adoration, almost the sort of look a woman might give a man when she has decided to yield herself utterly to his will.

Gilgamesh had seen such looks aplenty in his day, from women and men both; and he had welcomed them from women, but never from a man. He scowled. What does he think I am? Does he think, as so many have wrongly thought, that because I loved Enkidu with so great a love that I am a man who will embrace a man in the fashion of men and women? Because it is not so. Not even here in Hell is it so, said Gilgamesh to himself. Nor will it ever be.

"Tell me everything!" the red-faced man was imploring. "All those exploits that I dreamed in your name, Conan: tell me how they really were! That time in the snow fields, when you met the frost giant's daughter—and when you sailed the *Tigress* with the Black Coast's queen—and that time you stormed the Aquilonian capital, and slew King Numedides on his own throne—"

Gilgamesh stared in distaste at the man groveling at his feet.

"Come, fellow, stop this blather now," he said sourly. "Up with you! You mistake me greatly, I think."

The second man was out of the Land Rover now, and on his way over to join them. An odd-looking creature he was, too, skeleton-thin-and-corpse-white, with a neck like a water-bird's that seemed barely able to support his long, big-chinned head. He was dressed oddly too, all in black, and swathed in layer upon layer as if he dreaded the faintest chill. Yet he had a gentle and thoughtful way about him, quite unlike the wild-eyed and feverish manner of his friend. He might be a scribe, Gilgamesh thought, or a priest; but what the other one could be, the gods alone would know.

The thin man touched the other's shoulder and said, "Take command of yourself, man. This is surely not your Conan here."

"To the life! To the very life! His size—his grandeur—the way he killed that beast—"

"Bob—Bob, Conan's a figment! Conan's a fantasy! You spun him out of whole cloth. Come, now. Up. Up." To Gilgamesh he said, "A thousand pardons, good sir. My friend is—sometimes excitable—"

Gilgamesh turned away, shrugging, and looked to his quarry. He had no need for dealings with these two. Skinning the huge beast properly might take him the rest of the day; and then to haul the great hide back to his camp, and determine what he wanted of it as a trophy—

Behind him he heard the booming voice of the red-faced man. "A figment, H.P.? How can you be sure of that? I thought I invented Conan, too; but what if he really lived, what if I had merely tapped into some powerful primordial archetype, what if the authentic Conan stands here before us this very moment—"

"Dear Bob, your Conan had blue eyes, did he not? And this man's eyes are dark as night."

"Well—" Grudgingly.

"You were so excited you failed to notice. But I did. This is some barbarian warrior, yes, some great huntsman beyond any doubt—a Nimrod, an Ajax. But not Conan, Bob! Grant him his own identity. He's no invention of yours." Coming up beside Gilgamesh, the long-jawed man said, speaking in a formal and courtly way, "Good sir, I am Howard Phillips Lovecraft, formerly of Providence, Rhode Island, and my companion is Robert

E. Howard of Texas, whose other life was lived, as was mine, in the twentieth century after Christ. At that time we were tale-tellers by trade, and I think he confuses you with a hero of his own devising. Put his mind at ease, I pray you, and let us know your name."

Gilgamesh looked up. He rubbed his wrist across his forehead to clear it of a smear of the monster's gore and met the other man's gaze evenly. This one, at least, was no madman, strange though he looked.

Quietly Gilgamesh said, "I think his mind may be beyond putting at any ease. But know you that I am called Gilgamesh, the son of Lugalbanda."

"Gilgamesh the Sumerian?" Lovecraft whispered. "Gilgamesh who sought to live forever?"

"Gilgamesh am I, yes, who was king in Uruk when that was the greatest city of the Land of the Two Rivers, and who in his folly thought there was a way of cheating death."

"Do you hear that, Bob?"

"Incredible. Beyond all belief!" muttered the other.

Rising until he towered above them both, Gilgamesh drew in his breath deeply and said with awesome resonance, "I am Gilgamesh to whom all things were made known, the secret things, the truths of life and death, most especially those of death. I have coupled with Inanna the goddess in the bed of the Sacred Marriage; I have slain demons and spoken with gods; I am two parts god myself, and only one part mortal." He paused and stared at them, letting it sink in, those words that he had recited so many times in situations much like this. Then in a quieter tone he went on, "When death took me I came to this nether world they call Hell, and here I pass my time as a huntsman, and I ask you now to excuse me, for as you see I have my tasks."

Once more he turned away.

"Gilgamesh!" said Lovecraft again in wonder. And the other said, "If I live here till the end of time, H.P., I'll never grow used to it. This is more fantastic than

running into Conan would have been! Imagine it:
Gilgamesh!"

A tiresome business, Gilgamesh thought: all this awe,
all this adulation.

The problem was that damned epic, of course. He
could see why Caesar grew so irritable when people
tried to suck up to him with quotations out of Shakespeare's verses. "Why, man, he doth bestride the narrow
world like a Colossus," and all that: Caesar grew livid
by the third syllable. Once they put you into poetry,
Gilgamesh had discovered, as had Odysseus and Achilles and Caesar after him and many another, your own
real self can begin to disappear and the self of the poem
overwhelms you entirely and turns you into a walking
cliche. Shakespeare had been particularly villainous that
way, Gilgamesh thought: ask Richard III, ask Macbeth,
ask Owen Glendower. You found them skulking around
Hell with perpetual chips on their shoulders, because
every time they opened their mouths people expected
them to say something like "My kingdom for a horse!"
or "Is this a dagger which I see before me?" or "I can
call spirits from the vasty deep." Gilgamesh had had to
live with that kind of thing almost from the time he had
first come to Hell, for they had written the poems about
him soon after. All that pompous brooding stuff, a whole
raft of Gilgamesh tales of varying degrees of basis in
reality. And then the Babylonians and the Assyrians,
and even those smelly garlic-gobbling Hittites, had gone
on translating and embroidering them for another thousand years so that everybody from one end of the known
world to the other knew them by heart. And even after
all those peoples were gone and their languages had
been forgotten, there was no surcease, because these
twentieth-century folk had found the whole thing and
deciphered the text somehow and made it famous all
over again. Over the centuries they had turned him into
everybody's favorite all-purpose hero, which was a hell
of a burden to bear: there was a piece of him in the
Prometheus legend, and in the Heracles stuff, and in

that story of Odysseus' wanderings, and even in the
Celtic myths, which was probably why this creepy Howard fellow kept calling him Conan. At least that other
Conan, that ratty little sniveling drunken one, had been
a Celt. Enlil's ears, but it was wearying to have everyone expecting you to live up to the mythic exploits of
twenty or thirty very different culture-heroes! And em-
barrassing, too, considering that the original non-
mythical Heracles and Odysseus and some of the others
dwelled here too and tended to be pretty possessive
about the myths that had attached to *them*, even when
they were simply variants on his own much older ones.

There was substance to the Gilgamesh stories, of
course, especially the parts about him and Enkidu. But
the poet had salted the story with a lot of pretentious
arty nonsense too, as poets always will, and in any case
you got very tired of having everybody boil your long
and complex life down into the same twelve chapters
and the same little turns of phrase. It got so that
Gilgamesh found himself quoting the main Gilgamesh
poem too, the one about his quest for eternal life—well,
that one wasn't too far from the essence of the truth,
though they had mucked up a lot of the details with
precious little "imaginative" touches—by way of making introduction for himself: "I am the man to whom
all things were made known, the secret things, the truths
of life and death." Straight out of the poet's mouth,
those lines. Tiresome. Tiresome. Angrily he jabbed his
dagger beneath the dead monster's hide, and set about
his task of flaying, while the two little men behind him
went on muttering and mumbling to one another in
astonishment at having run into Gilgamesh of Uruk in
this bleak and lonely corner of Hell.

There were strange emotions stirring in Robert Howard's soul, and he did not care for them at all. He could
forgive himself for believing for that one giddy moment
that this Gilgamesh was his Conan. That was nothing
more than the artistic temperament at work, sweeping

him up in a bit of rash feverish enthusiasm. To come
suddenly upon a great muscular giant of a man in a
loincloth who was hacking away at some fiendish monster with a little bronze dagger, and to think that he
must surely be the mighty Cimmerian—well, that was a
pardonable enough thing. Here in Hell you learned very
quickly that you might run into anybody at all. You
could find yourself playing at dice with Lord Byron or
sharing a mug of mulled wine with Menelaos or arguing
with Plato about the ideas of Nietzsche, who was standing right there making faces, and after a time you came
to take most such things for granted, more or less.

So why not think that this fellow was Conan? No
matter that Conan's eyes had been of a different color.
That was a trifle. He looked like Conan in all the important ways. He was of Conan's size and strength. And he
was kingly in more than physique. He seemed to have
Conan's cool intelligence and complexity of soul, his
regal courage and indomitable spirit.

The trouble was that Conan, the wondrous Cimmerian
warrior from 19,000 B.C., had never existed except in
Howard's own imagination. And there were no fictional
characters in Hell. You might meet Richard Wagner,
but you weren't likely to encounter Siegfried. Theseus
was here somewhere, but not the Minotaur. William the
Conqueror, yes; William Tell, no.

That was all right, Howard told himself. His little
fantasy of meeting Conan here in Hell was nothing but
a bit of mawkish narcissism: he was better off without
it. Coming across the authentic Gilgamesh—ah, how
much more interesting that was! A genuine Sumerian
king—an actual titan out of history's dawn, not some
trumped-up figure fashioned from cardboard and hard-
breathing wish-fulfilling dreams. A flesh-and-blood mortal who lived a lusty life and had fought great battles
and had walked eye to eye with the ancient gods. A man
who had struggled against the inevitability of death,
and who in dying had taken on the immortality of
mythic archetype—ah, now there was someone worth get-

ting to know! Whereas Howard had to admit that he would learn no more from a conversation with Conan than he could discover by interrogating his own image in the mirror. Or else a meeting with the "real" Conan, if it was in any way possible, would surely cast him into terrible confusions and contradictions of soul from which there would be no recovering. No, Howard thought. Better that this man be Gilgamesh than Conan, by all means. He was reconciled to that.

But this other business—this sudden bewildering urge to throw himself at the giant's feet, to be swept up in his arms, to be crushed in a fierce embrace—

What was that? Where had *that* come from? By the blazing Heart of Ahriman, what could it mean?

Howard remembered a time in his former life when he had gone down to the Cisco Dam and watched the construction men strip and dive in: well-built men, confident, graceful, at ease in their bodies. For a short while he had looked at them and had revelled in their physical perfection. They could have been naked Greek statues come alive, a band of lusty Apollos and Zeuses. And then as he listened to them shouting and laughing and crying out in their foul-mouthed way he began to grow angry, suddenly seeing them as mere thoughtless animals who were the natural enemies of dreamers like himself. He hated them as the weak always must hate the strong, those splendid swine who could trample the dreamers and their dreams as they wished. But then he had reminded himself that he was no weakling himself, that he who once had been spindly and frail had by hard effort made himself big and strong and burly. Not beautiful of body as these men were—too fleshy for that, too husky—but nevertheless, he had told himself, there was no man there whose ribs he could not crush if it came to a struggle. And he had gone away from that place full of rage and thoughts of bloody violence.

What had that been all about? That barely suppressed fury—was it some sort of dark hidden lust, some craving for the most bestial sort of sinfulness? Was the anger that had arisen in him masking an anger he should have directed at himself, for looking upon those naked men and taking pleasure in it?

No. No. No. No. He wasn't any kind of degenerate. He was certain of that.

The desire of men for men was a mark of decadence, of the decline of civilization. He was a man of the frontier, not some feeble limp-wristed sodomite who reveled in filth and wanton evil. If he had never in his short life known a woman's love, it was for lack of opportunity, not out of a preference for that other shameful kind. Living out his days in that small and remote prairie town, devoting himself to his mother and to his writing, he had chosen not to avail himself of prostitutes or shallow women, but he was sure that if he had lived a few years longer and the woman who was his true mate had ever made herself known to him, he would certainly have reached toward her in passion and high abandon.

And yet—and yet—that moment when he first spied the giant Gilgamesh, and thought he was Conan—

That surge of electricity through his entire body, and most intensely through his loins—what else could it have been but desire, instant and intense and over-whelming? For a *man*? Unthinkable! Even this glorious hero—even this magnificent kingly creature—

No. No. No. No.

I am in Hell, and this is my torment, Howard told himself.

He paced furiously up and down alongside the Land Rover. Desperately he fought off the black anguish that threatened to settle over him now, as it had done so many times in his former life and in this life after life. These sudden corrupt and depraved feelings, Howard thought: they are nothing but diabolical perversions of my natural spirit, intended to cast me into despair and self-loathing! By Crom, I will resist! By the breasts of Ishtar, I will not yield to this foulness!

All the same he found his eyes straying to the edge of

the nearby thicket, where Gilgamesh still knelt over the animal he had killed.

What extraordinary muscles rippling in that broad back, in those iron-hard thighs! What careless abandon in the way he was peeling back the creature's shaggy hide, though he had to wallow in dark gore to do it! That cascade of lustrous black hair lightly bound by a jewelled circlet, that dense black beard curling in tight ringlets—

Howard's throat went dry. Something at the base of his belly was tightening into a terrible knot.

Lovecraft said, "You want a chance to talk with him, don't you?"

Howard swung around. He felt his cheeks go scarlet. He was utterly certain that his guilt must be emblazoned incontrovertibly on his face.

"What the hell do you mean?" he growled. His hands knotted of their own accord into fists. There seemed to be a band of fire across his forehead. "What would I want to talk with him about, anyway?"

Lovecraft looked startled by the ferocity of Howard's tone and posture. He took a step backward and threw up his hand almost as though to protect himself. "What a strange thing to say! You, of all people, with your love of antique times, your deep and abiding passion for the lost mysteries of those steamy Oriental empires that perished so long ago! Why, man, is there nothing you want to know about the kingdoms of Sumer? Uruk, Nippur, Ur of the Chaldees? The secret rites of the goddess Inanna in the dark passageways beneath the ziggurat? The incantations that opened the gates of the Underworld, the libations that loosed and bound the demons of the worlds beyond the stars? Who knows what he could tell us? There stands a man six thousand years old, a hero from the dawn of time, Bob!"

Howard snorted. "I don't reckon that oversized son of a bitch would want to tell us a damned thing. All that interests him is getting the hide off that bloody critter of his."

"He's nearly done with that. Why not wait, Bob? And invite him to sit with us a little while. And draw him out, lure him into telling us tales of life beside the Euphrates!" Now Lovecraft's dark eyes were gleaming as though he too felt some strange lust, and his forehead was surprisingly bright with uncharacteristic perspiration; but Howard knew that in Lovecraft's case what had taken possession of him was only the lust for knowledge, the hunger for the arcane lore of high antiquity that Lovecraft imagined would spill from the lips of this Mesopotamian hero. That same lust ached in him as well. To speak with this man who had lived before Babylon was, who had walked the streets of Ur when Abraham was yet unborn—

But there were other lusts besides that hunger for knowledge, sinister lusts that must be denied at any cost—

"No," said Howard brusquely. "Let's get the hell out of here right now, H.P. This damned foul bleak countryside is getting on my nerves."

Lovecraft gave him a strange look. "But weren't you just telling me how beautiful—

"Damnation take whatever I was telling you! King Henry's expecting us to negotiate an alliance for him. We aren't going to get the job done out here in the boondocks."

"The what?"

"Boondocks. Wild uncivilized country. Term that came into use after our time, H.P. The backwoods, you know? You never did pay much heed to the vernacular, did you?" He tugged at Lovecraft's sleeve. "Come on. That big bloody ape over there isn't going to tell us a thing about his life and times, I guarantee. Probably doesn't remember anything worth telling, anyway. And he bores me. Pardon me, H.P., but I find him an enormous pain in the butt, all right? I don't have any further hankering for his company. Do you mind, H.P.? Can we move along, do you think?"

"I must confess that you mystify me sometimes, Bob.

But of course if you—" Suddenly Lovecraft's eyes widened in amazement. "Get down, Bob! Behind the car! Fast!"

"What—"

An arrow came singing through the air and passed just alongside Howard's left ear. Then another, and another. One arrow ricocheted off the flank of the Land Rover with a sickening thunking sound. Another struck straight on and stuck quivering an inch deep in the metal.

Howard whirled. He saw horsemen—a dozen, perhaps a dozen and a half—bearing down on them out of the darkness to the east, loosing shafts as they came.

They were lean compact men of some Oriental stock in crimson leather jerkins, riding like fiends. Their mounts were little flat-headed, fiery-eyed gray Hell-horses that moved as if their short, fiercely pistoning legs could carry them to the far boundaries of the nether world without the need of a moment's rest.

Chanting, howling, the yellow-skinned warriors seemed to be in a frenzy of rage. Mongols? Turks? Whoever they were, they were pounding toward the Land Rover like the emissaries of Death himself. Some brandished long, wickedly curved blades, but most wielded curious-looking small bows from which they showered one arrow after another with phenomenal rapidity.

Crouching behind the Land Rover with Lovecraft beside him, Howard gaped at the attackers in a paralysis of astonishment. How often had he written of scenes like this? Waving plumes, bristling lances, a whistling cloud of cloth-yard shafts! Thundering hooves, wild war cries, the thunk of barbarian arrowheads against Aquilonian shields! Horses rearing and throwing their riders.... Knights in bloodied armor tumbling to the ground.... Steel-clad forms littering the slopes of the battlefield....

But this was no swashbuckling tale of Hyborean derring-do that was unfolding now. Those were real horsemen—as real as anything was, in this place—

rampaging across this chilly wind-swept plain in the outer reaches of Hell. Those were real arrows; and they would rip their way into his flesh with real impact and inflict real agony of the most frightful kind.

He looked across the way at Gilgamesh. The giant Sumerian was hunkered down behind the overturned bulk of the animal he had slain. His mighty bow was in his hand. As Howard watched in awe, Gilgamesh aimed and let fly. The shaft struck the nearest horseman, traveling through jerkin and rib cage and all, and emerging from the man's back. But still the onrushing warrior managed to release one last arrow before he fell. It traveled on an erratic trajectory, humming quickly toward Gilgamesh on a wild wobbly arc and skewering him through the flesh of his left forearm.

Coolly the Sumerian glanced down at the arrow jutting from his arm. He scowled and shook his head, the way he might if he had been stung by a hornet. Then—as Conan might have done, how very much like Conan!—Gilgamesh inclined his head toward his shoulder and *bit* the arrow in half just below the fletching. Bright blood spouted from the wound as he pulled the two pieces of the arrow from his arm.

As though nothing very significant had happened, Gilgamesh lifted his bow and reached for a second shaft. Blood was streaming in rivulets down his arm, but he seemed not even to be aware of it.

Howard watched as if in a stupor. He could not move; he barely had the will to draw breath. A haze of nausea threatened to overwhelm him. It had been nothing at all for him to heap up great bloody mounds of severed heads and arms and legs with cheerful abandon in his stories; but in fact, real bloodshed and violence of any sort had horrified him whenever he had even a glimpse of it.

"The gun, Bob!" said Lovecraft urgently beside him. "Use the *gun!*"

"What?"

"There. There."

Howard looked down. Thrust through his belt was the pistol he had taken from the Land Rover when he had come out to investigate that little beast in the road. He drew it now and stared at it, glassy-eyed, as though it were a basilisk's egg that rested on the palm of his hand.

"What are you doing?" Lovecraft asked. "Ah. Ah. Give it to me." He snatched the gun impatiently from Howard's frozen fingers and studied it a moment as though he had never held a weapon before. Perhaps he never had. But then, grasping the pistol with both his hands, he rose warily above the hood of the Land Rover and squeezed off a shot.

The tremendous sound of an explosion cut through the shrill cries of the horsemen. Lovecraft laughed. "Got one! Who would ever have imagined—"

He fired again. In the same moment Gilgamesh brought down one more of the attackers with his bow.

"They're backing off!" Lovecraft cried. "By Alhazred, they didn't expect *this*, I wager!" He laughed again and poked the gun up into a firing position. "*Ia!* he cried, in a voice Howard had never heard out of the shy and scholarly Lovecraft before. "*Shub-Niggurath!*" Lovecraft fired a third time. "*Ph'nglui mglw'nafh Cthulhu R'lyeh wgah'nagl fhtagn!*"

Howard felt sweat rolling down his body. This inaction of his—this paralysis, this shame—what would Conan make of it? What would Gilgamesh? And Lovecraft, that timid and sheltered man, he who dreaded the fishes of the sea and the cold winds of his New England winters and so many other things, was laughing and bellowing his wondrous gibberish and blazing away like any gangster, having the time of his life—

Shame! Shame!

Heedless of the risk, Howard scrambled up into the cab of the Land Rover and groped around for the second gun that was lying down there on the floor somewhere. He found it and knelt beside the window. Seven or eight of the Asiatic horsemen lay strewn about, dead or dying, within a hundred-yard radius of the car. The others had withdrawn to a considerable distance and were cantering in uneasy circles. They appeared taken aback by the unexpectedly fierce resistance they had encountered on what they had probably expected to have been an easy bit of jolly slaughter in these untracked frontierlands.

What were they doing now? Drawing together, a tight little group, horses nose to nose. Conferring. And now two of them were pulling what seemed to be some sort of war-banner from a saddlebag and hoisting it between them on bamboo poles: a long yellow streamer with fluttering blood-red tips, on which bold Oriental characters were painted in shining black. Serious business, obviously. Now they were lining themselves up in a row, facing the Land Rover. Getting ready for a desperate suicide charge—that was the way things appeared.

Gilgamesh, standing erect in full view, calmly nocked yet another arrow. He took aim and waited for them to come. Lovecraft, looking flushed with excitement, wholly transformed by the alien joys of armed combat, was leaning forward, staring intently, his pistol cocked and ready.

Howard shivered. Shame rode him with burning spurs. How *could* he cower here while those two bore the brunt of the struggle? Though his hand was shaking, he thrust the pistol out the window and drew a bead on the closest horseman. His finger tightened on the trigger. Would it be possible to score a hit at such a distance? Yes. Yes. Go ahead. You know how to use a gun, all right. High time you put some of that skill to use. Knock that little yellow bastard off his horse with one bark of the Colt .380, yes. Send him straight to Hell—no, he's in Hell already, send him off to the Undertaker for recycling. Yes, that's it. Ready—aim—

"Wait," Lovecraft said. "Don't shoot."

What was this? As Howard, with an effort, lowered his gun and let his rigid quivering hand go slack, Lovecraft, shading his eyes against the eerie glare of the motionless sun, peered closely at the enemy warriors a long silent moment. Then he turned, reached up into the rear of the Land Rover, groped around for a moment, finally pulled out the manila envelope that held their royal commission from King Henry.

And then—what was he doing?

Stepping out into plain view, arms raised high, waving the envelope around, walking toward the enemy?

"They'll kill you, H.P.! Get down! Get down!"

Lovecraft, without looking back, gestured brusquely for Howard to be silent. He continued to walk steadily toward the far-off horsemen. They seemed just as mystified as Howard was. They sat without moving, their bows held stiffly out before them, a dozen arrows trained on the middle of Lovecraft's body.

He's gone completely off the deep end, Howard thought in dismay. He never was really well balanced, was he? Half believing all his stuff about Elder Gods and dimensional gateways and blasphemous rites on dark New England hillsides. And now all this shooting—the excitement—

"Hold your weapons, all of you!" Lovecraft cried in a voice of amazing strength and presence. "In the name of Prester John, I bid you hold your weapons! We are not your enemies! We are ambassadors to your emperor!"

Howard gasped. He began to understand. No, Lovecraft hadn't gone crazy after all!

He took another look at that long yellow war-banner. Yes, yes, it bore the emblems of Prester John! These berserk horsemen must be part of the border patrol of the very nation whose ruler they had traveld so long to find. Howard felt abashed, realizing that in the fury of the battle Lovecraft had had the sense actually to pause long enough to give the banner's legend close examination—and the courage to walk out there waving his diplomatic credentials. The parchment scroll of their royal commission was in his hand, and he was pointing to the little red-ribboned seal of King Henry.

The horsemen stared, muttered among themselves,

lowered their bows. Gilgamesh, lowering his great bow also, looked on in puzzlement. "Do you see?" Lovecraft called. "We are heralds of King Henry! We claim the protection of your master the August Sovereign Yeh-lu Ta-shih!" Glancing back over his shoulder, he called to Howard to join him; and after only an instant's hesitation, Howard leaped down from the Land Rover and trotted forward. It was a giddy feeling, exposing himself to those somber yellow archers this way. It felt almost like standing on the edge of some colossal precipice.

Lovecraft smiled. "It's all going to be all right, Bob! That banner they unfurled, it bears the markings of Prester John—"

"Yes, yes. I see."

"And look—they're making a safe-conduct sign. They understand what I'm saying, Bob! They believe me!"

Howard nodded. He felt a great upsurge of relief and even a sort of joy. He clapped Lovecraft lustily on the back. "Fine going, H.P.! I didn't think you had it in you!" Coming up out of his funk, now, he felt a manic exuberance seize his spirit. He gestured to the horsemen, wigwagging his arms with wild vigor. "Hoy! Royal commissioners!" he bellowed. "Envoys from His Britannic Majesty King Henry VIII! Take us to your emperor!" Then he looked toward Gilgamesh, who stood frowning, his bow still at the ready. "Hoy there, king of Uruk! Put away the weapons! Everything's all right now! We're going to be escorted to the court of Prester John!"

Gilgamesh wasn't at all sure why he had let himself go along. He had no interest in visiting Prester John's court, or anybody else's. He wanted nothing more than to be left alone to hunt and roam in the wilderness and thereby to find some ease for his sorrows.

But the gaunt long-necked man and his blustery red-faced friend had beckoned him to ride with them in their Land Rover, and while he stood there frowning over that, the ugly flat-featured little yellow warriors had indicated with quick impatient gestures that he should get in. And he had. They looked as though they would try to compel him to get in if he balked; and though he had no fear of them, none whatever, some impulse that he could not begin to understand had led him to step back from the likelihood of yet another battle and simply climb aboard the vehicle. Perhaps he had had enough of solitary hunting for a while. Or perhaps it was just that the wound in his arm was beginning to throb and ache, now that the excitement of the fray was receding, and it seemed like a good idea to have it looked after by a surgeon. The flesh all around it was badly swollen and bruised. That arrow had pierced him through and through. He would have the wound cleaned and dressed, and then he would move along.

Well, then, so he was going to the court of Prester John. Here he was, sitting back silent and somber in the rear of this musty, mildew-flecked car, riding with these two very odd New Dead types, these scribes or tale-tellers or whatever it was they claimed to be, as the horsemen of Prester John led them to the encampment of their monarch.

The one who called himself Howard, the one who could not help stealing sly little glances at him like an infatuated schoolgirl, was at the wheel. Glancing back at his passenger now, he said, "Tell me, Gilgamesh: have you had dealings with Prester John before?"

"I have heard the name, that much I know," replied the Sumerian. "But it means little to me."

"The legendary Christian emperor," said the other, the thin one, Lovecraft. "He who was said to rule a secret kingdom somewhere in the misty hinterlands of Central Asia—although it was in Africa, according to some—"

Asia, Africa—names, only names, Gilgamesh thought bleakly. They were places somewhere in the other world, but he had no idea where they might be.

Such a multitude of places, so many names! It was impossible to keep it all straight. There was no sense of any of it. The world—his world, the Land—had been

bordered by the Two Rivers, the Idigna and the Bura-
nunu, which the Greeks had preferred to call the Tigris
and the Euphrates. Who were the Greeks, and by what
right had they renamed the rivers? Everyone used those
names now, even Gilgamesh himself, except in the in-
wardness of his soul.

And beyond the Two Rivers? Why, there was the
vassal state of Aratta far to the east, and in that direction also lay the Land of Cedars, where the fire-breathing
demon Huwawa roared and bellowed, and in the eastern mountains lay the kingdom of the barbaric Elamites.
To the north was the land called Uri, and in the deserts
of the west the wild Martu people dwelled, and in the
south was the blessed isle Dilmun, which was like a
paradise. Was there anything more to the world than
that? Why, there was Meluhha far away beyond Elam,
where the people had black skins and fine features, and
there was Punt in the south, where they were black
also, with flat noses and thick lips. And there was another land even beyond Meluhha, with folk of yellow
skins who mined a precious green stone. And that was
the world. Where could all these other latter-day places
be—this Africa and this Asia and Europe and the rest,
Rome, Greece, England? Perhaps some of them were
mere new names for old places. The Land itself had had
a host of names since his own time—Babylonia, Meso-
potamia, Iraq, and more. Why had it needed all those
names? He had no idea. New men made up new names:
that seemed to be the way of the world. This Africa, this
Asia—America, China, Russia. A little man named
Herodotos, a Greek, had tried to explain it all to him
once—the shape of the world and the names of the
places in it, sketching a map for him on an old bit of
parchment—and much later a stolid fellow named Mer-
cator had done the same, and once after that he had
spoken of such matters with an Englishman called Cook;
but the things they told him all conflicted with one
another and he could make no sense out of any of it. It
was too much to ask, making sense of these things.

Those myriad nations that had arisen after his time, those empires that had arisen and fallen and been forgotten, all those lost dynasties, the captains and the kings—he had tried from time to time to master the sequence of them, but it was no use. Once in his former life he had sought to make himself the master of all knowledge, yes. His appetites had been boundless: for knowledge, for wealth, for power, for women, for life itself. Now all that seemed only the merest folly to him. That jumble of confused and confusing places, all those great realms and far-off kingdoms, were in another world: what could they matter to him now?

"Asia?" he said. "Africa?" Gilgamesh shrugged. "Prester John?" He prowled the turbulent cluttered recesses of his memory. "Ah. There's a Prester John, I think, lives in New Hell. A dark-skinned man, a friend of that gaudy old liar Sir John Mandeville." It was coming back now. "Yes, I've seen them together many times, in that dirty squalid tavern where Mandeville's always to be found. The two of them telling outlandish stories back and forth, each a bigger fraud than the other."

"A different Prester John," said Lovecraft.

"That one is Susenyos the Ethiop, I think," Howard said. "A former African tyrant, and lover of the Jesuits, now far gone in whiskey. He's one of many. There are seven, nine, a dozen Prester Johns in Hell, to my certain knowledge. And maybe more."

Gilgamesh contemplated that notion blankly. Fire was running up and down his injured arm now.

Lovecraft was saying, "—not a true name, but merely a title, and a corrupt one at that. There never was a *real* Prester John, only various rulers in various distant places, whom it pleased the tale-spinners of Europe to speak of as Prester John, the Christian emperor, the great mysterious unknown monarch of a fabulous realm. And here in Hell there are many who choose to wear the name. There's power in it, do you see?"

"Power and majesty!" Howard cried. "And poetry, by God!"

"So this Prester John whom we are to visit," said Gilgamesh, "he is not in fact Prester John?"

"Yeh-lu Ta-shih's his name," said Howard. "Chinese. Manchurian, actually, twelfth century A.D. First emperor of the realm of Kara-Khitai, with his capital at Samarkand. Ruled over a bunch of Mongols and Turks, mainly, and they called him Gur Khan, which means 'supreme ruler,' and somehow that turned into 'John' by the time it got to Europe. And they said he was a Christian priest, too, *Presbyter Joannes*, 'Prester John.' " Howard laughed. "Damned silly bastards. He was no more a Christian than you were. A Buddhist, he was, a bloody shamanistic Buddhist."

"Then why—"

"Myth and confusion!" Howard said. "The great human nonsense factory at work! And wouldn't you know it, but when he got to Hell this Yeh-lu Ta-shih founded himself another empire right away in the same sort of territory he'd lived in back there, and when Richard Burton came out this way and told him about Prester John and how Europeans long ago had spoken of him by that name and ascribed all sorts of fabulous accomplishments to him he said, 'Yes, yes, I am Prester John indeed.' And so he styles himself that way now, he and nine or ten others, most of them Ethiopians like that friend of your friend Mandeville."

"They are no friends of mine," said Gilgamesh stiffly. He leaned back and massaged his aching arm. Outside the Land Rover the landscape was changing now: more hilly, with ill-favored fat-trunked little trees jutting at peculiar angles from the purple soil. Here and there in the distance his keen eyes made out scattered groups of black tents on the hillsides, and herds of the little Hell-horses grazing near them. Gilgamesh wished now that he hadn't let himself be inveigled into this expedition. What need had he of Prester John? One of these upstart New Dead potentates, one of the innumerable little princelings who had set up minor dominions for themselves out here in the vast measureless wastelands of

the Outback—and reigning under a false name, at that—
one more shoddy scoundrel, one more puffed-up little
nobody swollen with unearned pride—

Well, and what difference did it make? He would
sojourn a while in the land of this Prester John, and
then he would move on, alone, apart from others, mourn-
ing as always his lost Enkidu. There seemed no escaping that doom that lay upon him, that bitter solitude,
whether he reigned in splendor in Uruk or wandered in
the wastes of Hell.

"Their Excellencies P.E. Lovecraft and Howard E.
Robert," cried the major-domo grandly though inaccu-
rately, striking three times on the black marble floor of
Prester John's throne-chamber with his gold-tipped staff
of pale green jade. "Envoys Plenipotentiary of His
Britannic Majesty King Henry VIII of the Kingdom of
New Holy Diabolic England."

Lovecraft and Howard took a couple of steps forward.
Yeh-lu Ta-shih nodded curtly and waved one elegant
hand, resplendent with inch-long fingernails, in casual
acknowledgment. The envoys plenipotentiary did not
seem to hold much interest for him, nor, apparently,
did whatever it was that had caused His Britannic Majesty King Henry to send them here.

The emperor's cool imperious glance turned toward
Gilgamesh, who was struggling to hold himself erect.
He was beginning to feel feverish and dizzy and he
wondered when anyone would notice that there was an
oozing hole in his arm. Even he had limits to his endurance, after all, though he usually tried to conceal that
fact. He didn't know how much longer he could hold
out. There were times when behaving like a hero was a
heroic pain in the ass, and this was one of them.

"—and his Late Highness Gilgamesh of Uruk, son of
Lugalbanda, great king, king of Uruk, king of kings,
lord of the Land of the Two Rivers by merit of Enlil and
An," boomed the major-domo in the same splendid way,
looking down only once at the card he held in his hand.

"Great king?" said Yeh-lu Ta-shih, fixing Gilgamesh with one of the most intensely penetrating stares the Sumerian could remember ever having received. "King of kings? Those are very lofty titles, Gilgamesh of Uruk."

"A mere formula," Gilgamesh replied, "which I thought appropriate when being presented at your court. In fact I am king of nothing at all now."

"Ah," said Yeh-lu Ta-shih. "King of Nothing-at-all."

And so are you, my lord Prester John. Gilgamesh did not let himself say it, though the words bubbled toward the roof of his mouth and begged to be uttered. *And so are all the self-appointed lords and masters of the many realms of Hell.*

The slender amber-hued man on the throne leaned forward. "And where then, I pray, is Nothing-at-all?"

Some of the courtiers began to snicker. But Prester John looked to be altogether in earnest, though it was impossible to be completely certain of that. He was plainly a formidable man, Gilgamesh had quickly come to see: sly, shrewd, self-contained, with a tough and sinewy intelligence. Not at all the vain little cock-of-the-walk Gilgamesh had expected to find in this bleak and remote corner of Hell. However small and obscure his principality might be, Prester John ruled it, obviously, with a firm grasp. The grandeur of the glittering palace that his scruffy subjects had built for him here on the edge of nowhere, and the solidity of the small but substantial city surrounding it, testified to that. Gilgamesh knew something about the building of cities and palaces. Prester John's capital bore the mark of the steady toil of centuries.

The long stare was unrelenting. Gilgamesh, fighting back the blazing pain in his arm, met the emperor's gaze with an equally earnest one of his own and said:

"Nothing-at-all? It is a land that never was, and will always be, my lord. Its boundaries are nowhere and its capital city is everywhere, nor do any of us ever leave it."

"Ah. Ah. Indeed. Nicely put. You are Old Dead, are you?"

"Very old, my lord."

"Older than Ch'in Shih Huang Ti? Older than the Lords of Shang and Hsia?"

Gilgamesh turned in puzzlement toward Lovecraft, who told him in a half-whisper, "Ancient kings of China. Your time was even earlier."

Shrugging, Gilgamesh replied, "They are not known to me, my lord, but you hear what the Britannic ambassador says. He is a man of learning: it must be so. I will tell you that I am older than Caesar by far, older than Agamemnon and the Supreme Commander Rameses, older even than Sargon. By a great deal."

Yeh-lu Ta-shih considered that a moment. Then he made another of his little gestures of dismissal, as though brushing aside the whole concept of relative ages in Hell. With a dry laugh he said, "So you are very old, King Gilgamesh. I congratulate you. And yet the Ice-Hunter folk would tell us that you and I and Rameses and Sargon all arrived here only yesterday; and to the Hairy Men, the Ice-Hunters themselves are mere newcomers. And so on and so on. There's no beginning to it, is there? Any more than there's an end."

Without waiting for an answer he asked Gilgamesh, "How did you come by that gory wound, great king of Nothing-at-all?"

At least he's noticed it, Gilgamesh thought.

"A misunderstanding, my lord. It may be that your border patrol is a little overzealous at times."

One of the courtiers leaned toward the emperor and murmured something. Prester John's serene brow grew furrowed. He lifted a flawlessly contoured eyebrow ever so slightly.

"Killed nine of them, did you?"

"They attacked us before we had the opportunity of showing our diplomatic credentials," Lovecraft put in quickly. "It was entirely a matter of self-defense, my lord Prester John."

"I wouldn't doubt it." The emperor seemed to contemplate for a moment, but only for a moment, the skirmish that had cost the lives of nine of his horsemen; and then quite visibly he dismissed that matter too from the center of his attention. "Well, now, my lords ambassador—"

Abruptly Gilgamesh swayed, tottered, started to fall. He checked himself just barely in time, seizing a massive porphyry column and clinging to it until he felt more steady. Beads of sweat trickled down his forehead into his eyes. He began to shiver. The huge stone column seemed to be expanding and contracting. Waves of vertigo were rippling through him and he was seeing double, suddenly. Everything was blurring and multiplying. He drew his breath in deeply, again, again, forcing himself to hold on. He wondered if Prester John was playing some kind of game with him, trying to see how long his strength could last. Well, if he had to, Gilgamesh swore, he would stand here forever in front of Prester John without showing a hint of weakness.

But now Yeh-lu Ta-shih was at last willing to extend compassion. With a glance toward one of his pages the emperor said, "Summon my physician, and tell him to bring his tools and his potions. That wound should have been dressed an hour ago."

"Thank you, my lord," Gilgamesh muttered, trying to keep the irony from his tone.

The doctor appeared almost at once, as though he had been waiting in an antechamber. Another of Prester John's little games, perhaps? He was a burly, broad-shouldered, bushy-haired man of more than middle years, with a manner about him that was brisk and bustling but nevertheless warm, concerned, reassuring. Drawing Gilgamesh down beside him on a low divan covered with the gray-green hide of some scaly Hell-dragon, he peered into the wound, muttered something unintelligible to himself in a guttural language unknown to the Sumerian, and pressed his thick fingers around the edges of the torn flesh until fresh blood flowed. Gilgamesh hissed sharply but did not flinch.

"*Ach, mein lieber freund,* I must hurt you again, but it is for your own good. *Verstehen sie?*"

The doctor's fingers dug in more deeply. He was spreading the wound, swabbing it, cleansing it with some clear fluid that stung like a hot iron. The pain was so intense that there was almost a kind of pleasure in it: it was a purifying kind of pain, a purging of the soul.

Prester John said, "How bad is it, Dr. Schweitzer?"

"*Gott sei dank,* it is deep but clean. He will heal without damage."

He continued to probe and cleanse, murmuring softly to Gilgamesh as he worked: "*Bitte. Bitte. Einen augenblick, mein freund.*" To Prester John he said, "This man is made of steel. No nerves at all, immense resistance to pain. We have one of the great heroes here, *nicht wahr?* You are Roland, are you? Achilles, perhaps?"

"Gilgamesh is his name," said Yeh-lu Ta-shih.

The doctor's eyes grew bright. "Gilgamesh! Gilgamesh of Sumer? *Wunderbar! Wunderbar!* The very man. The seeker after life. *Ach,* we must talk, my friend, you and I, when you are feeling better." From his medical kit he now produced a frightful-looking hypodermic syringe. Gilgamesh watched as though from a vast distance, as though that throbbing swollen arm belonged to someone else. "*Ja, Ja,* certainly we must talk, of life, of death, of philosophy, *mein freund,* of *philosophy!* There is so very much for us to discuss!" He slipped the needle beneath Gilgamesh's skin. "There. *Genug.* Sit. Rest. The healing now begins."

Robert Howard had never seen anything like it. It could have been something straight from the pages of one of his Conan stories. The big ox had taken an arrow right through the fat part of his arm, and he had simply yanked it out and gone right on fighting. Then, afterward, he had behaved as if the wound were nothing more than a scratch, all that time while they were driving hour after hour toward Prester John's city and then undergoing lengthy interrogation by the court officials and then standing through this whole endless ceremony at court—God almighty, what a display of endurance! True, Gilgamesh had finally gone a little wobbly and had actually seemed on the verge of passing out. But any ordinary mortal would have conked out long ago. Heroes really *were* different. They were another breed altogether. Look at him now, sitting there casually while that old German medic swabs him out and stitches him up in that slapdash cavalier way, and not a whimper out of him. Not a whimper!

Suddenly Howard found himself wanting to go over there to Gilgamesh, to comfort him, to let him lean his head back against him while the doctor worked him over, to wipe the sweat from his brow—

Yes, to comfort him in an open, rugged, manly way—

No. No. No. No.

There it was again, the horror, the unspeakable thing, the hideous crawling Hell-borne impulse rising out of the cesspools of his soul—

Howard fought it back. Blotted it out, hid it from view. Denied that it had ever entered his mind.

To Lovecraft he said, "That's some doctor! Took his medical degree at the Chicago slaughterhouses, I reckon!"

"Don't you know who he is, Bob?"

"Some old Dutchman who wandered in here during a sandstorm and never bothered to leave."

"Does the name of Dr. Schweitzer mean nothing to you?"

Howard gave Lovecraft a blank look. "Guess I never heard it much in Texas."

"Oh, Bob, Bob, why must you always pretend to be such a cowboy? Can you tell me you've never heard of Schweitzer? *Albert* Schweitzer? The great philosopher, theologian, musician—there never was a greater interpreter of Bach, and don't tell me you don't know Bach either—"

"She-it, H.P., you talking about that old country doctor there?"

"Who founded the leprosy clinic in Africa, at Lambarene, yes. Who devoted his life to helping the sick, under the most primitive conditions, in the most remote forests of—"

"Hold on, H.P. That can't be so."

"That one man could achieve so much? I assure you, Bob, he was quite well known in our time—perhaps not in Texas, I suppose, but nevertheless—"

"No. Not that he could do all that. But that he's here. In Hell. If that old geezer's everything you say, then he's a goddamned *saint*. Unless he beat his wife when no one was looking, or something like that. What's a saint doing in Hell, H.P.?"

"What are *we* doing in Hell?" Lovecraft asked.

Howard reddened and looked away. "Well, I suppose, there were things in our lives—things that might be considered sins, in the strictest sense—"

"No one understands the rules of Hell, Bob," said Lovecraft gently. "Sin may have nothing to do with it. Gandhi is here, do you realize that? Confucius. Were *they* sinners? Was Moses? Abraham? We've tried to impose our own pitiful shallow beliefs, our pathetic grade-school notions of punishment for bad behavior, on this incredibly bizarre place where we find ourselves. By what right? We don't begin to comprehend what Hell really is. All we know is that it's full of heroic villains and villainous heroes—and people like you and me—and it seems that Albert Schweitzer is here, too. A great mystery. But perhaps someday—"

"Shh," Howard said. "Prester John's talking to us."

"My lords ambassador—"

Hastily they turned toward him. "Your majesty?" Howard said.

"This mission that has brought you here: your king wants an alliance, I suppose? What for? Against whom? Quarreling with some pope again, is he?"

"With his daughter, I'm afraid," said Howard.

Prester John looked bored. He toyed with his emerald scepter. "Mary, you mean?"

"Elizabeth, your majesty," Lovecraft said.

"Your king's a most quarrelsome man. I'd have thought there were enough popes in Hell to keep him busy, though, and no need to contend with his daughters."

"They are the most contentious women in Hell," Lovecraft said. "Blood of his blood, after all, and each of them a queen with a noisy, brawling kingdom of her own. Elizabeth, my lord, is sending a pack of her explorers to the Outback, and King Henry doesn't like the idea."

"Indeed," said Yeh-lu Ta-shih, suddenly interested again. "And neither do I. She has no business in the Outback. It's not her territory. The rest of Hell should be big enough for Elizabeth. What is she looking for here?"

"The sorcerer John Dee has told her that the way out of Hell is to be found in these parts."

"There is no way out of Hell."

Lovecraft smiled. "I'm not any judge of that, your majesty. Queen Elizabeth, in any event, has given credence to the notion. Her Walter Raleigh directs the expedition, and the geographer Hakluyt is with him, and a force of five hundred soldiers. They move diagonally across the Outback just to the south of your domain, following some chart that Dr. Dee has obtained for them. He had it from Cagliostro, they say, who bought it from Hadrian when Hadrian was still supreme commander of Hell's legions. It is allegedly an official Satanic document."

Prester John did not appear to be impressed. "Let us say, for argument's sake, that there *is* an exit from Hell. Why would Queen Elizabeth desire to leave? Hell's not so bad. It has its minor discomforts, yes, but one learns to cope with them. Does she think she'd be able to reign in Heaven as she does here—assuming there's a Heaven at all, which is distinctly not proven?"

"Elizabeth has no real interest in leaving Hell herself, majesty," Howard said. "What King Henry fears is that if she does find the way out, she'll claim it for her own and set up a colony around it, and charge a fee for passing through the gate. No matter where it takes you, the king reckons there'll be millions of people willing to risk it, and Elizabeth will wind up cornering all the money in Hell. He can't abide that notion, d'ye see? He thinks she's already too smart and aggressive by half, and he hates the idea that she might get even more powerful. There's something mixed into it having to do with Queen Elizabeth's mother, too—that was Anne Boleyn, Henry's second wife. She was a wild and wanton one, and he cut her head off for adultery, and now he thinks that Anne's behind Elizabeth's maneuvers, trying to get even with him by—"

"Spare me these details," said Ye-luh Ta-shih with some irritation. "What does Henry expect me to do?"

"Send troops to turn the Raleigh expedition back before it can find anything useful to Elizabeth."

"And in what way do I gain from this?"

"If the exit from Hell's on your frontier, your majesty, do you really want a bunch of Elizabethan Englishmen setting up a colony next door to you?"

"There is no exit from Hell," Prester John said complacently once again.

"But if they set up a colony anyway?"

Prester John was silent a moment. "I see," he said finally.

"In return for your aid," Howard said, "we're empowered to offer you a trade treaty on highly favorable terms."

"Ah."

"And a guarantee of military protection in the event of the invasion of your realm by a hostile power."

"If King Henry's armies are so mighty, why does he not deal with the Raleigh expedition himself?"

"There was no time to outfit and dispatch an army across such a great distance," said Lovecraft. "Eliza-

God. We are here. We have our tasks. That is enough for us to know."

"I felt that way once," said Gilgamesh. "When I was king in Uruk, and finally came to understand that I must die, that there was no hiding from that. What is the purpose, then, I asked myself? And I told myself: The gods have put us here to perform our tasks, and that is the purpose. And so I lived thereafter and so I died." Gilgamesh's face darkened. "But here—here—"

"Here, too, we have our tasks," Schweitzer said.

"You do, perhaps. For me there is only the task of passing the time. I had a friend to bear the burden with me, once—"

"Enkidu."

Gilgamesh seized the doctor's sturdy wrist with sudden fierce intensity. "You know of Enkidu?"

"From the poem, yes. The poem is very famous."

"Ah. Ah. The poem. But the actual man—"

"I know nothing of him, *nein*."

"He is of my stature, very large. His beard is thick, his hair is shaggy, his shoulders are wider even than mine. We journeyed everywhere together. But then we quarreled, and he went from me in anger, saying, 'Never cross my path again.' Saying, 'I have no love for you, Gilgamesh.' Saying, 'If we meet again I will have your life.' And I have heard nothing of him since."

Schweitzer turned and stared closely at Gilgamesh. "How is this possible? All the world knows the love of Enkidu for Gilgamesh!"

Gilgamesh called for yet another flagon. This conversation was awakening an ache within his breast, an ache that made the pain that his wound had caused seem like nothing more than an itch. Nor would the drink soothe it; but he would drink all the same.

He took a deep draught and said somberly, "We quarreled. There were hot words between us. He said he had no love for me any longer."

"This cannot be true."

Gilgamesh shrugged and made no reply.

"You wish to find him again?" Schweitzer asked.

"I desire nothing else."

"Do you know where he is?"

"Hell is larger even than the world. He could be anywhere."

"You will find him."

"If you knew how I have searched for him—"

"You will find him. That I know."

Gilgamesh shook his head. "If Hell is a place of torment, then this is mine, that I will never find him again. Or if I do, that he will spurn me. Or raise his hand against me."

"This is not so," said Schweitzer. "I think he longs for you even as you do for him."

"Then why does he keep himself from me?"

"This is Hell," said Schweitzer gently. "You are being tested, my friend, but no test lasts forever. Not even in Hell. Not even in Hell. Even though you are in Hell, have faith in the Lord: You will have your Enkidu soon enough, *um Himmels Willen*." Smiling, Schweitzer said, "The emperor is calling you. Go to him. I think he has something to tell you that you will want to hear."

Prester John said, "You are a warrior, are you not?"

"I was," replied Gilgamesh indifferently.

"A general? A leader of men?"

"All that is far behind me," Gilgamesh said. "This is the life after life. Now I go my own way and I take on no tasks for others. Hell has plenty of generals."

"I am told that you were a leader among leaders. I am told that you fought like the god of war. When you took the field, whole nations laid down their arms and knelt before you."

Gilgamesh waited, saying nothing.

"You miss the glory of the battlefield, don't you, Gilgamesh?"

"Do I?"

"What if I were to offer you the command of my army?"

"Why would you do that? What am I to you? What is your nation to me?"

"In Hell we take whatever citizenship we wish. What would you say, if I offered you the command?"

"I would tell you that you are making a great mistake."

"It isn't a trivial army. Ten thousand men. Adequate air support. Tactical nukes. The strongest firepower in the Outback."

"You misunderstand," said Gilgamesh. "Warfare doesn't interest me. I know nothing of modern weapons and don't care to learn. You have the wrong man, Prester John. If you need a general, send for Wellington. Send for Marlborough. Rommel. Tiglath-Pileser."

"Or for Enkidu?"

The unexpected name hit Gilgamesh like a battering ram. At the sound of it his face grew hot and his entire body trembled convulsively.

"What do you know about Enkidu?"

Prester John held up one superbly manicured hand. "Allow me the privilege of asking the questions, great king."

"You spoke the name of Enkidu. What do you know about Enkidu?"

"First let us discuss other matters which are of—"

"Enkidu," said Gilgamesh implacably. "Why did you mention his name?"

"I know that he was your friend—"

"*Is.*"

"Very well, *is* your friend. And a man of great valor and strength. Who happens to be a guest at this very moment at the court of the great enemy of my realm. And who, so I understand it, is preparing just now to make war against me."

"*What?*" Gilgamesh stared. "Enkidu is in the service of Queen Elizabeth?"

"I don't recall having said that."

"Is it not Queen Elizabeth who even now has sent an army to encroach on your domain?"

Yeh-lu Ta-shih laughed. "Raleigh and his five hundred fools? That expedition's an absurdity. I'll take care of them in an afternoon. I mean another enemy altogether. Tell me this: do you know of Mao Tse-tung?"

"These princes of the New Dead—there are so many names—"

"A Chinese, a man of Han. Emperor of the Marxist Dynasty, long after my time. Crafty, stubborn, tough. More than a little crazy. He runs something called the Celestial People's Republic, just north of here. What he tells his subjects is that we can turn Hell into Heaven by collectivizing it."

"Collectivizing?" said Gilgamesh uncomprehendingly.

"To make all the peasants into kings, and the kings into peasants. As I say: more than a little crazy. But he has his hordes of loyal followers, and they do whatever he says. He means to conquer all the Outback, beginning right here. And after that, all of Hell will be subjected to his lunatic ideas. I fear that Elizabeth's in league with him—that this nonsense of looking for a way out of Hell is only a ruse, that in fact her Raleigh is spying out my weaknesses for her so that she can sell the information to Mao."

"But if this Mao is the enemy of all kings, why would Elizabeth ally herself with—"

"Obviously they mean to use each other. Elizabeth aiding Mao to overthrow me, Mao aiding Elizabeth to push her father from his throne. And then afterward, who knows? But I mean to strike before either of them can harm me."

"What about Enkidu?" Gilgamesh said. "Tell me about Enkidu."

Prester John opened a scroll of computer printout. Skimming through it, he read, "The Old Dead warrior Enkidu of Sumer—Sumer, that's your nation, isn't it? —arrived at court of Mao Tse-tung on such-and-such a date—ostensible purpose of visit, Outback hunting expedition—accompanied by American spy posing as journalist and hunter, one E. Hemingway—secret meeting with Kublai Khan, Minister of War for the Celestial

People's Republic—now training Communist troops in preparation for invasion of New Kara-Khitai—" The emperor looked up. "Is this of interest to you, Gilgamesh?"

"What is it you want from me?"

"This man is your famous friend. You know his mind as you do your own. Defend us from him and I'll give you anything you desire."

"What I desire," said Gilgamesh, "is nothing more than the friendship of Enkidu."

"Then I'll give you Enkidu on a silver platter. Take the field for me against Mao's troops. Help me anticipate whatever strategies your Enkidu has been teaching them. We'll wipe the Marxist bastards out and capture their generals, and then Enkidu will be yours. I can't guarantee that he'll want to be your friend again, but he'll be yours. What do you say, Gilgamesh? What do you say?"

Across the gray plains of Hell from horizon to horizon sprawled the legions of Prester John. Scarlet-and-yellow banners fluttered against the somber sky. At the center of the formation stood a wedge of horseborne archers in leather armor; on each flank was a detachment of heavy infantry; the emperor's fleet of tanks was in the vanguard, rolling unhurriedly forward over the rough, broken terrain. A phalanx of transatmospheric weapons platforms provided air cover far overhead.

A cloud of dust in the distance gave evidence of the oncoming army of the Celestial People's Republic.

"By all the demons of Stygia, did you ever see such a cockeyed sight?" Robert Howard cried. He and Lovecraft had a choice view of the action from their place in the imperial command post, a splendid pagoda protected by a glowing force-shield. Gilgamesh was there, too, just across the way with Prester John and the officers of the Kara-Khitai high command. The emperor was peering into a bank of television monitors and one of his aides was feverishly tapping out orders on a computer terminal. "Makes no goddamned sense," said Howard. "Horsemen, tanks, weapons platforms, all mixing it up at the same time—is that how these wild sons of bitches fight a war?"

Lovecraft touched his forefinger to his lips. "Don't shout so, Bob. Do you want Prester John to hear you? We're his guests, remember. And King Henry's ambassadors."

"Well, if he hears me, he hears me. Look at that crazy mess! Doesn't Prester John realize that he's got a twentieth-century Bolshevik Chinaman coming to attack him with twentieth-century weapons? What good are mounted horsemen, for God's sake? A cavalry charge into the face of heavy artillery? Bows and arrows against howitzers?" Howard guffawed. "Nuclear-tipped arrows, is that the trick?"

Softly Lovecraft said, "For all we know, that's what they are."

"You know that can't be, H.P. I'm surprised at you, a man with your scientific background. I know all this nuke stuff is after our time, but surely you've kept up with the theory. Critical mass at the tip of an arrow? No, H.P., you know as well as I do that it just can't work. And even if it could—"

In exasperation Lovecraft waved to him to be silent. He pointed across the room to the main monitor in front of Prester John. The florid face of a heavyset man with a thick white beard had appeared on the screen.

"Isn't that Hemingway?" Lovecraft asked.

"Who?"

"Ernest Hemingway. The writer. *A Farewell to Arms. The Sun Also Rises.*"

"Never could stand his stuff," said Howard. "Sick crap about a bunch of drunken weaklings. You sure that's him?"

"Weaklings, Bob?" said Lovecraft in astonishment.

"I read only the one book, about those Americans in Europe who go to the bullfights and get drunk and fool around with each other's women, and that was all of

Mr. Hemingway that I cared to experience. I tell you, H.P., it disgusted me. And the way it was written! All those short little sentences—no magic, no poetry, H.P.—"

"Let's talk about it some other time, Bob."

"No vision of heroism—no awareness of the higher passions that ennoble and—"

"Bob—please—"

"A fixation on the sordid, the slimy, the depraved—"

"You're being absurd, Bob. You're completely misinterpreting his philosophy of life. If you had simply taken the trouble to read *A Farewell to Arms*—" Lovecraft shook his head angrily. "This is no time for a literary discussion. Look—look there." He nodded toward the far side of the room. "One of the emperor's aides is calling over. Something's going on."

Indeed there had been a development of some sort. Yeh-lu Ta-shih seemed to be conferring with four or five aides at once. Gilgamesh, red-faced, agitated, was striding swiftly back and forth in front of the computer bank. Hemingway's face was still on the screen and he too looked agitated.

Hastily Howard and Lovecraft crossed the room. The emperor turned to them. "There's been a request for a parley in the field," Prester John said. "Kublai Khan is on his way over. Dr. Schweitzer will serve as my negotiator. The man Hemingway's going to be an impartial observer—*their* impartial observer. I need an impartial observer, too. Will you two go down there too, as diplomats from a neutral power, to keep an eye on things?"

"An honor to serve," said Howard grandly.

"And for what purpose, my lord, has the parley been called?" Lovecraft asked.

Yeh-lu Ta-shih gestured toward the screen. "Hemingway has had the notion that we can settle this thing by single combat—Gilgamesh versus Enkidu. Save on ammunition, spare the Undertaker a devil of a lot of toil. But there's a disagreement over the details." Delicately he smothered a yawn. "Perhaps it can all be worked out by lunchtime."

* * *

It was an oddly assorted group. Mao Tse-tung's chief
negotiator was the plump, magnificently dressed Kublai
Khan, whose dark sly eyes gave evidence of much cun-
ning and force. He had been an emperor in his own
right in his former life, but evidently had preferred less
taxing responsibilities here. Next to him was Hemingway,
big and heavy, with a deep voice and an easy, almost
arrogant manner. Mao had also sent four small men in
identical blue uniforms with red stars on their breasts—
"Party types," someone murmured—and, strangely, a
Hairy Man, big-browed and chinless, one of those creatures out of deepest antiquity. He too wore the Communist emblem on his uniform.

And there was one more to the group—the massive,
deep-chested man of dark brow and fierce and smoul-
dering eyes, who stood off by himself at the far side—

Gilgamesh could barely bring himself to look at him.
He too stood apart from the group a little way, savoring
the keen edge of the wind that blew across the field of
battle. He longed to rush toward Enkidu, to throw his
arms around him, to sweep away in one jubilant embrace all the bitterness that had separated them—

If only it could be as simple as that!

The voices of Mao's negotiators and the five that Prester
John had sent—Schweitzer, Lovecraft, Howard, and a
pair of Kara-Khitai officers—drifted to Gilgamesh above
the howling of the wind.

Hemingway seemed to be doing most of the talking.
"Writers, are you? Mr. Howard, Mr. Lovecraft? I regret
I haven't had the pleasure of encountering your work."

"Fantasy, it was," said Lovecraft. "Fables. Visions."

"That so? You publish in *Argosy*? The *Post*?"

"Five to *Argosy*, but they were westerns," Howard
said. "Mainly we wrote for *Weird Tales*. And H.P., a few
in *Astounding Stories*."

"*Weird Tales*," Hemingway said. "*Astounding Stories*."
A shadow of distaste flickered across his face. "Mmm.
Don't think I knew those magazines. But you wrote

well, did you, gentlemen? You set down what you truly felt, the real thing, and you stated it purely? Of course you did. I know you did. You were honest writers or you'd never have gone to Hell. That goes almost without saying." He laughed, rubbed his hands in glee, effusively threw his arms around the shoulders of Howard and Lovecraft. Howard seemed alarmed by that and Lovecraft looked as though he wanted to sink into the ground. "Well, gentlemen," Hemingway boomed, "what shall we do here? We have a little problem. The one hero wishes to fight with bare hands, the other with— what did he call it?—a disruptor pistol? You would know more about that than I do: something out of *Astounding Stories*, is how it sounds to me. But we can't have this, can we? Bare hands against fantastic future science? There is a good way to fight and that is equal to equal, and all other ways are the bad ways."

"Let him come to me with his fists," Gilgamesh called from the distance. "As we fought the first time, in the Market-of-the-Land, when my path crossed his in Uruk."

"He is afraid to use the new weapons," Enkidu replied.

"*Afraid?*"

"I brought a shotgun to him, a fine 12-gauge weapon, a gift to my brother Gilgamesh. He shrank from it as though I had given him a venomous serpent."

"Lies!" roared Gilgamesh. "I had no fear of it! I despised it because it was cowardly!"

"He fears anything which is new," said Enkidu. "I never thought Gilgamesh of Uruk would know fear, but he fears the unfamiliar. He called me a coward, because I would hunt with a shotgun. But I think he was the coward. And now he fears to fight me with the unfamiliar. He knows that I'll slay him. He fears death even here, do you know that? Death has always been his great terror. Why is that? Because it is an insult to his pride? I think that is it. Too proud to die—too proud to accept the decree of the gods—"

"I will break you with my hands alone!" Gilgamesh bellowed.

"Give us disruptors," said Enkidu. "Let us see if he dares to touch such a weapon."

"A coward's weapon!"

"Again you call me a coward? You, Gilgamesh, you are the one who quivers in fear—"

"Gentlemen! Gentlemen!"

"You fear my strength, Enkidu!"

"You fear my skill. You with your pathetic old sword, your pitiful bow—"

"Is this the Enkidu I loved, mocking me so?"

"You were the first to mock, when you threw back the shotgun into my hands, spurning my gift, calling me a coward—"

"The weapon, I said, was cowardly. Not you, Enkidu."

"It was the same thing."

"*Bitte, bitte,*" said Schweitzer. "This is not the way!"

And again from Hemingway: "Gentlemen, please!"

They took no notice.

"I meant—"

"You said—"

"Shame—"

"Fear—"

"Three times over a coward!"

"Five times five a traitor!"

"False friend!"

"Vain braggart!"

"Gentlemen, I have to ask you—"

But Hemingway's voice, loud and firm though it was, was altogether drowned out by the roar of rage that came from the throat of Gilgamesh. Dizzying throbs of anger pounded in his breast, his throat, his temples. He could take no more. This was how it had begun the first time, when Enkidu had come to him with that shotgun and he had given it back and they had fallen into dispute. At first merely a disagreement, and then a hot debate, and then a quarrel, and then the hurling of bitter accusations. And then such words of anger as had never passed between them before, they who had been closer than brothers.

That time they hadn't come to blows. Enkidu had simply stalked away, declaring that their friendship was at an end. But now—hearing all the same words again, stymied by this quarrel even over the very method by which they were to fight—Gilgamesh could no longer restrain himself. Overmastered by fury and frustration, he rushed forward.

Enkidu, eyes gleaming, was ready for him.

Hemingway attempted to come between them. Big as he was, he was like a child next to Gilgamesh and Enkidu, and they swatted him to one side without effort. With a jolt that made the ground itself reverberate, Gilgamesh went crashing into Enkidu and laid hold of him with both hands.

Enkidu laughed. "So you have your way after all, King Gilgamesh! Bare hands it is!"

"It is the only way," said Gilgamesh.

At last. At last. There was no wrestler in this world or the other who could contend with Gilgamesh of Uruk. I will break him, Gilgamesh thought, as he broke our friendship. I will snap his spine. I will crush his chest.

As once they had done long ago, they fought like maddened bulls. They stared eye to eye as they contended. They grunted; they bellowed, they roared. Gilgamesh shouted out defiance in the language of Uruk and in any other language he could think of; and Enkidu muttered and stormed at Gilgamesh in the language of the beasts that once he had spoken when he was a wild man, the harsh growling of the lion of the plains.

Gilgamesh yearned to have Enkidu's life. He loved this man more dearly than life itself, and yet he prayed that it would be given him to break Enkidu's back, to hear the sharp snapping sound of his spine, to toss him aside like a worn-out cloak. So strong was his love that it had turned to the brightest of hatreds. I will send him to the Undertaker once again, Gilgamesh thought. I will hurl him from Hell.

But though he struggled as he had never struggled in combat before, Gilgamesh was unable to budge Enkidu.

Veins bulged in his forehead; the sutures that held his wound burst and blood flowed down his arm; and still he strained to throw Enkidu to the ground, and still Enkidu held his place. And matched him, strength for strength, and kept him at bay. They stood locked that way a long moment, staring into each other's eyes, locked in unbreakable stalemate.

Then after a long while Enkidu said, as once he had said long ago, "Ah, Gilgamesh! There is not another one like you in all the world! Glory to the mother who bore you!"

It was like the breaking of a dam, and a rush of life-giving waters tumbling out over the summer-parched fields of the Land.

And from Gilgamesh in that moment of release and relief came twice-spoken words also:

"There is one other who is like me. But only one."

"No, for Enlil has given you the kingship."

"But you are my brother," said Gilgamesh, and they laughed and let go of each other and stepped back, as if seeing each other for the first time, and laughed again.

"This is great foolishness, this fighting between us," Enkidu cried.

"Very great foolishness indeed, brother."

"What need have you of shotguns and disruptors?"

"And what do I care if you choose to play with such toys?"

"Indeed, brother."

"Indeed!"

Gilgamesh looked away. They were all staring—the four party men, Lovecraft, Howard, the Hairy Man, Kublai Khan, Hemingway—all astonished, mouths drooping open. Only Schweitzer was beaming. The doctor came up to them and said quietly, "You have not injured each other? No. *Gut. Gut.* Then leave here, the two of you, together. Now. What do you care for Prester John and his wars, or for Mao and his? This is no business of yours. Go. Now."

Enkidu grinned. "What do you say, brother? Shall we go off hunting together?"

"To the end of the Outback, and back again. You and I, and no one else."

"And we will hunt only with our bows and spears?"

Gilgamesh shrugged. "With disruptors, if that is how you would have it. With cannons. With nuke grenades. Ah, Enkidu, Enkidu—!"

"Gilgamesh!"

"Go," Schweitzer whispered. "Now. Leave this place and never look back. *Auf Wiedersehen! Gluckliche Reise! Gottes Name*, go now!"

Watching them take their leave, seeing them trudge off together into the swirling winds of the Outback, Robert Howard felt a sudden sharp pang of regret and loss. How beautiful they had been, those two heroes, those two giants, as they strained and struggled! And then that sudden magic moment when the folly of their quarrel came home to them, when they were enemies no longer and brothers once more—

And now they were gone, and here he stood amidst these others, these strangers—

He had wanted to be Gilgamesh's brother, or perhaps— he barely comprehended it—something more than a brother. But that could never have been. And, knowing that it could never have been, knowing that that man who seemed so much like his Conan was lost to him forever, Howard felt tears beginning to surge within him.

"Bob?" Lovecraft said. "Bob, are you all right?"

She-it, Howard thought. *A man don't cry. Especially in front of other men.*

He turned away, into the wind, so Lovecraft could not see his face.

"Bob? Bob?"

She-it, Howard thought again. And he let the tears come.

MARKING TIME

C. J. Cherryh

Sycophants flitted up and down the neo-Roman corridors, polished the terrazzo, dusted the statuary, and opened and closed doors with their accustomed zeal, but the emperor Augustus listened to the echoes and felt a little chill, a sense of desertion and siege simultaneously. The desertions were from within, the siege from without, though not the least enemy appeared on the lawn or the manicured and rolling expanse of turf beyond the tennis courts, which led toward woods on the one side, and New Hell itself; and toward the equally manicured and immaculate lawn of mad Tiberius toward the bay: not a sycophant would have *dared* shirk its duty in that lunatic establishment, and not so much as a stray scrap of paper blew their way from that ill-omened quarter.

Wherefore Augustus sighed and felt all the more uneasy, sitting in his office and waiting for the phone to ring ... waiting, hour upon wretched hour, for the calls which came too infrequently and (one hoped) secretly.

Mostly he wished for Julius, who was elsewhere and at considerable hazard—Julius, who was off taking chances with his life, and who had taken with him

Kleopatra, and Antonius (madness!); along with Mouse
and Mettius Curtius and Scaevola; and Machiavelli, that
prognosticating raven, with his tricks and his conniv-
ances: and Hatshepsut, the Egyptian; all of which
absences made the house vulnerable and all of which
goings-on made all their lives less certain.

In fact they had become a house of men, a masculine
domain grown grim and, save the ministerings of the
sycophants, untidy. At the moment, in fact, there was a
half-consumed pizza and an empty wineglass among
the papers that lay like a snow-blanket across the huge
desk, for the sycophants did not dare enter this room to
fetch it out. There were all too many places in the house
lately the sycophants did not go: and the debris rose
higher. But the phone calls kept coming, which assured
the emperor at least that there was still hope in their
affairs. Visitors still came to the house, Horatius primarily, up from the Armory with things too sensitive or
too complex for the simple code of banalities they used.

There was, amid the snowstorm on the desk, a letter
from Administration that wanted answering, one of the
routine surveys—dangerous to let that go longer. There
was a letter from Rameses. In Egyptian. *That* small
finesse gave the emperor chills down the back. Either
Hatshepsut (easily) or Kleopatra (with great difficulty)
could have read it. Both were absent. So were a number
of tanks and other equipment out of Pentagram records,
along with Julius Caesar and two cohorts of the 10th.
And the Supreme Commander sent letters in Egyptian,
damn him, which obviously wanted answering, and Augustus had no idea what to do with them.

About the Administration survey he could do something. Reluctantly. Damned things. How many bathrooms had the villa? Who damn well cared? How many
telephones? That was always a touchy one. The villa
had lines it was not supposed to have. Certain ones
were special lines the Pentagram knew about. Certain
ones were ordinary. Certain ones were ones the phone
company believed were military and the Pentagram

believed were phone company property: they each ran their surveys separately, *not*, thank the gods, coordinated. So did the phone company. And Infernal Revenue. Hell was a maze of bureaus—*all those secretaries*. Julius had said, of that towering skyscraper which stood in view of the window, heart and nerve center of New Hell itself, a great edifice which had its top lost in the roiling red clouds which answered to daylight in this place: the whole thing was bureaus and secretaries and offices checking on other offices and people looking for telephones and bathrooms.

"Where's the damn paper?" Augustus wondered; and a sycophant tenuously whisked into existence, escaping at once as Augustus flung a paperweight right through its substance. *"Fool!"* They were forbidden this desk, above all else in the house. The emperor himself would tidy this room when the emperor himself felt like it.

He lifted papers, he shifted them, he rescued the wine glass before it tipped. And lifted the pizza plate.

"Damn."

It was there.

Someone knocked at the door. *"Princeps,"* a known voice said. A Roman voice. Which reminded him of the time. He looked into the drawer where he kept a wristwatch.

Damn, damn. He wiped his hair into order, shook pizza crumbs off his toga, snatched plate and glass off the desk, drank up the wine, and set the plate and glass into the file drawer.

A second knock. *"Auguste?"*

"T'audivi, Horati. Admitte'm, admitte'm, di nos iuvent."

The door cracked open, widened, and Horatius came in, all khaki and business: Horatius Cocles, Horatius One-eye, with a black patch over his right eye and a scar that went down that cheek, and rakishly up over the other brow, above a hawkish nose and the bright, keen sight of the left side. One could not imagine that man in a toga. Horatius in a tunic was as close to it as he got, when he was on some formality—one of Hell's

legitimate heroes, near old as Rome itself. But right
now it was escort duty, and meant to look like one of
the regular trips from the armory: the important piece
was the man behind him, who *could* have been Roman,
but who was not.

"Bonaparte," Augustus said; and the man shambled
in, in fatigues which fit and still managed to look slept-in,
decidedly not the case.

"Augustus." Napoleon Bonaparte gave a little bow
and pressed his lips to a thin line and folded his arms.
There were other khaki-clad men in the hall: they *were*
soldiers of the 10th.

Augustus snapped his fingers. "The wine, the wine,
pro di, do my guests wait? *Mane sis, Horati, tu quoque.*"

Horatius nodded, and shut the door, standing in front
of it with an irrepressibly grim look. The wine arrived,
materializing on the table, and the sycophant burbled
and left, valuing its existence.

"No, no," Augustus said, preventing Horatius with a
wave of his hand, and took up the bottle and the cork-
screw himself. The things baffled him. Three attempts
to start it and he simply took a pen and rammed the
damned cork down the bottle, smiled cheerfully at the
Emperor of a later age and a hero of Rome, and poured
them all a glass, cork be hanged. "There." He lifted his
glass as Bonaparte offered him the courtesy and re-
frained from courtesies of his own, the carpet in this
office having suffered enough. He *did* keep up with things.
"There, there, let's not be formal, do sit down, Bonaparte, *Horati*, thank you very much. I do apologize for
the running about and the little subterfuges. You're
very patient."

Bonaparte plucked at the knee of his khaki trousers,
the wineglass in his other hand. "*M'sieur*, this makes
me very anxious. So does a letter under my door in the
night."

"Very patient. I do thank you." Augustus sipped at
his wine and sighed. "How much have you told him,
Horati?"

"Nothing," Horatius said.

"Well, well," Augustus said.

"It's the Cong, is it?" Bonaparte shifted uncomfortably and crossed his legs, gestured back toward the Park, where the Viet Cong practiced a confused warfare. "Look, they're not particularly *bothering* anything at the moment, not on my side. Live and let live, I say."

"It's not the Cong," Horatius said.

"Julius," said Augustus, "is out on exercises. Very secret. You have to understand how very much we wish that weren't happening right now. Rameses—you do know Rameses."

"I know him. Not well. I'm out of the Pentagram. I'm afraid I don't keep up with the changes in administration any longer, just not my interest anymore."

"Of course, of course you don't keep up with the old neighborhood anymore. But Julius always talks of you with such respect."

"Mutual, I assure you. But—"

"Now, for instance, he would urge me—*Augustulle*, he would say—he always calls me that, Julius does, a joke, you understand—*Augustulle*. I really think you could rely on Bonaparte, a very good head on his shoulders, a very first-rate general—"

"Retired," Bonaparte said firmly.

"Retired. Of course." Augustus put on a sympathetic frown, and walked round his desk and sat down, elbows amongst the papers. "But do they know it in the Pentagram? You do know about Rameses."

"What about Rameses?"

"There's a little tension, a very little tension, unfortunate factionalism. I would never want to impugn the Supreme Commander, but you know there have been these most incredible mixups in records. You just don't know, absolutely don't know what they may do next over there. Supply is a mess, isn't it, *Horati*? They've reactivated certain commissions, calling up inactive units. Really, Bonaparte, I am very concerned that *you* may be getting a notice in the not so distant future—"

"Is this a specific warning, *m'sieur?*"

"Not specific, not at all specific, only that I do respect your desire for the quiet life. Julius being—absent, Hadrianus being convalescent . . . certain parties have taken that for an opportunity, a very specific and rare opportunity. They will move, do you understand. They will cut off certain ones who might be friends of ours. I would never accuse the Supreme Commander. But it is your *life* I fear for, Bonaparte, as well as your tranquility. Do you see? You persist in living unguarded, you take no precautions. At the least, they can snatch you up, a mere reactivation of your commission—"

"So you bring me *here?*"

"We do so many things. You won't be traced. If you were, we have means to cover that. I could even say—we can take care of your papers. Bonaparte, I mean, the Pentagram is such a maze of records. And it never hurts to have friends who can assist you."

Bonaparte took another healthy gulp of wine, and stared out from under his brows. "Is this a proposition, *m'sieur*, or a threat?"

"The threat is not from us. The proposition is. I doubt you will get one from the other side. Please believe me."

The last of the wine went down. Bonaparte set the glass down, got up and paced to the window, stood there with his hands folded behind him, one tapping a rhythm against the other. The Hall of Injustice was the view. Administration.

Bonaparte turned around with a dour look. "What *is* the proposition, *m'sieur?*"

"Your friendship, Bonaparte. And your retirement. In fact, we have common interests. You want to avoid being called up—certainly you want to avoid being murdered in your bed; and we have the information that can protect you. In turn, we need the information that might escape our nets."

"A spy, sir."

"An observer and a friend. All to your advantage. Your position protected—and all the advantage of inside sources; we only need someone who moves—ah, in *other* circles. And quite frankly we want to preserve you alive, in the case it does come to some untidier confrontation. Certainly we don't want you on their side or removed from all considerations, gods know where. Don't you *know* what your luck would be if you went through Reassignments right now? I really wouldn't care to risk it. We're trying to be careful with all our friends."

"And if you lose your gamble? I've served my turn at exiles."

"And are you content to leave it all to *their* good will . . . when ours is so inexpensive?"

"Damn. Damn. What *kind* of observers?"

"Why, nothing yet. Unless— You don't read Egyptian, do you?"

"Not I."

"Nor know any."

"No."

"Pity. I wonder if any of your contacts know an Egyptian colonel—over at Assurbanipal's court."

"I'm to find out, am I?"

"Surely you have old friends, retired officers, the Club, isn't it so? I mean, a little reestablishment of old ties—social affairs. It's very useful to us that you stay retired. Mutual interest, you see."

"I see. Yes." Bonaparte slouched back to the chair, hands in pockets. "A deal, *m'sieur*."

"Excellent. And your associate?"

"Who?"

"Wellington. Haven't you both retired?"

Bonaparte took the hands out of his pockets and stared.

"Mutual interests there too," Augustus said. "Wouldn't you say?"

"But who is he?" Brutus asked, lifting the shade ever so little at the stairwell window, and the sycophant at his elbow whispered: *Napoleon*.

"A friend of my father's?" Brutus wondered. "Is he Old Dead?"

Yes-yes-yes, the air said, and: *No-no-no, New.*

Brutus stared. New Dead were a novelty in Augustus's house. Not unknown, but a great novelty. Many were very tall. This one was not. This departing visitor was, at least, not Viet Cong, nor, he supposed, anyone associated with them, and perhaps he was one of that group of soldiers who somehow kept an eye to things about the house and grounds and made him think that his father Julius was somehow watching over them all at distance.

He had had a confusing arrival in Hell, had Junius Brutus—riding down a country lane on a summer's day, he had blinked and come to—

He did not like to recall that part of it—the old man, the knives, the bewildering gray fog and white glare, out of which he had landed in Augustus' villa and discovered Rome had changed a great deal, and people had walked on the moon, and the netherworld was a place where machines flew and buildings towered into the clouds.

Most of all he had found his natural father, and it had gone *right* this time. Julius Caesar had hugged him and called him son right along with Octavianus Augustus, who had been Julius' adopted son and heir—

But what had happened that Julius had had other children, and the mysterious Caesarion who was off with the Dissidents, an unnatural rebel—what had come about in those years? *Don't you remember?* someone had asked him. *Don't you remember?*

He did not delve into that. He was seventeen. His father was off with the army, the Viet Cong who had attacked them once were skulking about the park again, and Marcus Junius Brutus existed in an agony of worry. He stood now watching from the lower hall till Horatius and the stranger Bonaparte and the other soldiers had gotten into the jeep and gone off out of the driveway, then he turned and went up the stairs, a spatter of tennis shoes on the terrazzo: T-shirts and jeans were what the sycophants provided him, which he was doubtful of at first, and he still tripped a bit over his own feet, but such clothes were Modern, and Julius had taken to modern things, so Brutus took to them with a vengeance. He studied. He tried to do everything that would please Julius when he asked, on his return, what his newest son had been up to.

Up the stairs and down the hall to the end where Dante had his rooms—he knocked ever so gingerly, and knocked again.

"Who?" the voice came through the door. "Who is it?" And perhaps, inside, a sycophant answered; for: "*Scelerato!*" the voice raged. "Out, out of here!" As the door opened and Dante Alighieri stared at him all exhausted-looking and with his long hair frizzed and disordered. "Busy," Dante said. "I'm busy, doesn't anyone care?"

"Dante, there was a New Dead here. Napoleon Bonaparte. Is he a friend?"

Dante took in his breath and leaned in the doorway, his pale, large-knuckled hand gripping the frame. "Buonaparte, you say?" His eyes were large. "With whom?"

"With Augustus, I think. Horatius brought him. The sycophants said he was a friend."

"Buonaparte," Dante murmured, and wandered into the maze of books and papers that was his room. The Machine glowed there, its monitor screen alight, dominating a littered desk. The heavy velvet curtain was drawn, making the room far too dark for comfort. Dante ran a hand through his hair, faced about again. "With Augustus." Dante often repeated things. He was a wizard of sorts, a *magus* and a *grammaticus*; and continually communing with his machines as he did, he seemed to find talking with actual people a confusion to him. But he would talk, when there was something like this afoot; and no one *else* would tell a boy anything.

"What is it?" Brutus asked. "Is he dangerous?"

"Dangerous," Dante said, and raked his hand through

his hair a second time. "The whole situation is *dangerous*, young man."

"Is he a friend?"

"Of Julius', once, yes. But resigned, *resigned*, you understand, nothing could get him back here. How did he look?"

"Worried."

"Augustus sent for him. Augustus has sent for him or he has come to Augustus."

"Is there something wrong out there?" Brutus went and looked at the arcane numbers on the screen in hopes of reading something, anything, of that tenuous connection with the Armory. "Is my father all right?"

"I don't like this," Dante said, and paced and wrung his hands. "Oh, damn, *damn*."

"What are you talking about? *Magister*, what have I told you?"

"Where is Sargon?"

"I haven't seen him. Not since—since—" He felt a little chill, realizing it. "Yesterday. *Magister Dantille*, where is he?"

"I'm asking you."

"I don't know—but—but a lot of people have come and gone—"

"A snake," Dante said, wiping his hair back with both hands. "A snake with huge coils—" Sometimes Dante declaimed poetry. Sometimes he looked frighteningly mad. He did now, his hair fallen wildly about his face, his eyes large and white around the edges. "We can't see them all, it's far too large, large as the hills. Buonaparte is here. And he would never come here."

"Enemies, you mean." Brutus grasped after meanings like a suppliant after a sibyl's utterances. "You mean it's enemies, *old* enemies."

"Old enemies, yes. And new. Go, go, out, I'm busy here, very busy—"

"But who?" Brutus asked, being shoved at the door. He dared not affront the man. "What enemies? The Cong?" That they had come slinking back to the Park seemed a sinister thing, full of omen. "What is my father doing?"

"Saving us all. Like the emperor. Saving us all. Don't spy. It isn't polite."

Brutus found himself outside the door. And the door shut. The lock snicked.

Inside, Dante Alighieri took another harried wipe of his hair. He was trembling. The boy was part of it. The boy was *their* piece, and did not know it. That was the terrible thing. One was so tempted to forget that, and see only the boy.

He went back to his console, sat down, and called up the latest reports. Nothing informative. Julius kept in contact, that was all. Mettius Curtius and his communications tests bleeped and blipped at appropriate intervals and, once, reported liches.

Augustus was moving on his own initiative. Dangerously. Strategy was Julius' forte, never Augustus'; and the very worst of Dante's nightmares was actuality. Augustus was taking matters into his own hands, *having* to move, without any of the assistance he was accustomed to rely on, except only Sargon and Horatius and the remaining cohorts of the 10th. There were other legions to call on. But to move them would cause ripples.

And Augustus always came to Dante when he wanted something done with the records—would not understand, did not want to hear, how repeated delvings into Pentagram computers were more and more difficult, how they must not do this recklessly: Julius would understand. Machiavelli would understand. Augustus refused to understand, and sought miracles to save them from consequences.

Dante was running out of magic numbers.

There were places in Hell which were hell indeed, and which oppressed the soul. This was one such, a gray and black street in the concrete canyons, under the glare of electric lights, brick and peeling signs, a blink-

ing scrawl of red and green neon that afflicted the eye
without relieving the gray and the dark at all. *Oasis*, the
letters said, but the palm tree was half dead and the *i*
was flickering like a dying fire. Canned music wailed
out of that den, a spill like the clientele that strayed
beyond the door and hung about there, red and green
like the blinking sign, and at the same time colorless.
They were the usual images: glisten of seldom-shaven
faces dyed red in the light, 20th century khaki, the
sullen glint of chainmail and ringmail and metal studs
on leather. It was a bar at the bottom of an alley in New
Hell, in the very armpit of New Hell, as it happened,
down in that section where all the light was neon or
sodium, and the gutters ran with unhealthy streams of
something in which Sargon had no wish to wet his
sandals.

The Lion of Akkad was incognito tonight, playing the
Assyrian, which he had passed for before—plain soldier's
kilt, plain leather belt, a cloak and the proverbial dagger. The ringlets of his hair and beard were fuzzed and
unkempt, he reeked of spilled wine and garlic and a
whore's bed, and wandered a little in his steps, but the
drunken lads outside who gave many a visitor a jostling
did not move when he went past. They only stared from
calculating eyes and underwent an uncomfortable uncer-
tainty—Old Dead were small, and this one was, but not
wiry as some were: a short-legged bull of a man, with
the profile of a god and a bearded scowl that said
Middle Eastern, like many another that hung out in this
place.

None of them were precisely civilians in this place
off-limits to every regular soldier in Hell. The dress here
was all bits and pieces of uniforms of this and that
army, armor composed of bits and borrowings. There
was a gentleman in naval not-quite uniform, with an
unkempt black beard and a cutlass scar that left one
side of his face a white-eyed wreck, a couple of beard-
scarred, khaki-clad Africans who looked up from their
table in a furtive pass of dark eyes; a man in the uni-

form of the British raj with a rope scar around his neck; turned round again—a clutch of Hittites huddled over their beers. Music blared out of a rattling speaker.

Sargon went up to the bar and got a beer—American and cold, not to his taste, but it fought a fair battle with the garlic. He hunched his shoulders and watched the reflections in the mirror as he drank. No Romans, for which he praised the doubtful gods. No Akkadians or Sumerians either, for which he praised them doubly: they generally avoided this quarter—liked the taverns, not the hard-light bars. So he went to this place, drank up enough beer to make him want a trip to the back, and staggered on to the restroom—it was a pit—and out again, to lean against the wall with the glassy stare of a man who was contemplating sliding down it, there not too far from the table with the Hittites. A few moments more. A deep breath or two. Then a heave of his shoulders and a rolling walk toward the Africans. He reeled instead against one of the Hittites, leaned on the man's chairback and shoulder and gripped that shoulder with a strength that would persuade any sensible man to take an apology. "Sorry. Sorry, Hey—" Looking across the table and leaning on it then. "I know you?"

Dark eyes looked up at him. "No," the man said shortly. And backs stiffened all round as Sargon dragged an empty chair out, sat down, and hunched it close to the table with a resounding belch. "Too damn many New Dead, too damn many—*Hey!*" he shouted toward the bar. *"Beer."* He nudged the man next to him, a rock-hard man. "Hittite, huh?"

"This isn't your table," the man opposite said.

"Hey, buy you a drink." Sargon made a loose gesture round. "Damn watery beer, damn rotten beer, damn New Dead, real tired, I tell you—" Another belch. "Tired of this." He leaned an elbow on the table, "Undertaker's damn jokes. Tenth time. Tenth time, dammit—"

It was very quiet at the table. Not hostility now. They were mercs ages old in Hell. And the Trip left a man a little crazy first off. Multiple Trips made a man crazier.

"Damn New Dead," he muttered again. "I was at Babylon. Died at Babylon. You ever been to Babylon?"

"No," one said carefully. "Hey, who are you with now?"

Get the guy back to here and now, pry him out of the past. Careful. Like handling a ticking bomb.

"I'm not with anybody. *Not with any damn body!*" He slammed his fist on the table, one, two, and three, and glared through tangled hair. "Not any damn body." He thought of tragedies in his own life and let his mouth wobble; drunk, it was not hard. "Not going to go back there. Damn New Dead." The beer was coming. A round of it. He watched as the bartender set it down, and named the tab. He felt round himself. "Damn. Damn." He grew agitated and pulled off his thumb-ring with main force. "Tha's gold. Gold. All I got. All I got left."

"Take it," one of the Hittites said to the barman. "Call it a pawn."

"How do I know it's—?"

"Take it," the man said harshly, while Sargon picked up his mug and took a drink.

"No money," Sargon said. "Was an officer, once. Damn New Dead treat you like dirt. Give you watery beer and stupid orders. *I knew the damn snipers was out there, dammit. They give us this fool modern with all his tricks, and he led us right into it, right into it—*"

"You looking for something better?"

Sargon snuffled and wiped his eyes, his nose, took another deep drink of beer and gusted out a shaky breath. "I was a good officer. Damn New Dead don't think we know anything."

"You want to talk to a man?"

Another drink. Sargon wiped the froth off his mustache. Sniffed again. "Somebody's hiring? Damn New Dead?"

"No."

"Where?"

"You don't ask where."

"Who, then?"

"You don't ask that either. Hear me?"

Another drink. "Yeah. Well. Hell."

"You want to walk out of here? Take a right. We'll follow you."

Sargon took the beer down and stood up, scraping the chair back. Fool, a voice told him. Should have left it. Half.

But he stayed on his feet and staggered out.

Past the lot of hangers about the door and on down the street, into the gray and the dark, his ears picking up the sounds of someone else coming behind him.

The First Citizen reckoned it worth this risk.

Sargon reckoned it worth it, too, or he would not be where he was, shambling drunk and stinking down this pesthole of a street where such assignations were made.

He hoped to all the gods that Horatius was on the job.

"Quis es?" Augustus wrapped a sheet about himself and stumbled out of bed.

Dante, Dante, Dante, a sycophant whispered, identifying the knocker at his bedroom door. The lights went on. A robe drifted across the room, and he let fall the sheet (which whisked ghostlike back to the bed across the room) and shrugged on the robe, raking his hand distractedly through his hair. Dante knocking at his door at this hour—was trouble, trouble with Julius, trouble at the armory, trouble elsewhere, gods knew—

"Porta'," he muttered, waving his other hand. *"Dis t'auferat, portam."* As a veritable cloud of sycophants rushed the aforenamed door and opened it on a disheveled and night-robed Italian. *"Abite!"* Augustus snarled, and sycophants rushed out, like a ghostly wind, disturbing Dante's robe and making him clutch it about him.

"Signore," Dante said, and wished with a gesture to pass the door, which he did quickly as Augustus stepped back. *"Signore,* there's b-been a c-call—I must protest, *signore,* th-this u-u-use of the equ-qu-quipment. . . . Your majesty has to underst-st-stand—that l-l-line—"

"Horatius," Augustus said.

"Exactly s-s-so, *signore*, wh-wh-which is what I absolutely—absolutely have to protest, this imp-prudent—use—*use*—of the—"

"What did he say?"

"He's l-l-lost s-sight of Sargon, *signore*. He called from somewhere—I have no id-d-dea. There was m-m-music—".

"*Pro di*. What did he say?"

"That. He hung up. S-*signore*, one c-cannot k-keep on with this—this *reckless!* use of the lines—"

Augustus went to his desk, sat down and scribbled, furiously, a note for Curtius, out with Julius. And another for the armory.

"*Signore*, I have said—"

"Get the night guard. Have him courier it. Tell him to watch himself."

"B-but—"

There was movement in the hall. The boy Brutus was there, looking disturbed, his hair wild from sleep.

"Hush," Augustus said. "Go do it." He went to the door, and leaned there as Dante edged out it. "What is this?"

"My father—" Brutus said.

"Your father," Augustus said, with his grimmest and most official face. "If *our* mutual father were here, son, *I* wouldn't be roused out of my sleep, *I* wouldn't be standing here answering questions. Absolutely nothing to do with your father. Go back to sleep. Let me to mine."

The boy's face was pale and worried-looking. As well it should be. The lad was no fool. But he was a stranger in Hell, so he avowed and so the records showed. And he was respectful. "Yes, sir," Brutus said, and turned and went away.

Augustus gazed after him, gnawing at his lip. *Mithridates*, he thought. *Mithridates sent you, boy. Or Sulla's well-hidden in Hell since we sent him off the last time. Egyptians and conspiracy and Mithridates, the power behind that fool Rameses. Fifty thousand Roman civilians the butcher murdered to start his damnable career, and so, so cleverly he's gotten himself a catspaw in that damned Egyptian, not being the top man, never sitting up where he's a target.*

But try after try unseats him. Hadrian learned it. Hadrian—

"Dante!"

The emperor Augustus went running barefoot down the hall, down the stairs, to overtake the harried poet.

The Hittites followed. They had promised. They delivered. Sargon ambled along with a little wobble to this side and that, a little course correction down the foul little street, and they caught up with him, behind and to either side. That was all right. Steer them this way and that and round the corner and that was fine too: drunk as they were, Horatius and a few of the boys could take them. Wrap them up and take them to a quiet spot and just ask them questions a while. That was the way they had planned it. Sargon the bait, and lads from the legion as the muscle.

Soon now. Any minute now. Down the alley. The Hittites were friendly but they did not push him. The shellshocked drunk he claimed to be was a dangerous man. They only walked along with him a ways and muttered comments on the state of their stomachs and their skulls: he went along with that and muttered the same; and knew that they were working up to a laying on of hands.

"Damn New Dead," he mumbled again, drunk as they were, and threw off the hand when it landed on his shoulder, but they steered him round the corner and the whole street was a blur and a confusion of lights. Hittite arms were about him. They reeked of sweat and oil and drink and whatever godsawful food they ate. "You don't have to deal with them," they told him, someone did; and they staggered together, shoving a passer-by, and reeling on together. Someone had brought a bottle. It went the round. It was raw whiskey. "Have some," that someone said, and Sargon tipped it up to his mouth and sipped it and passed it on, with Hittite arms about him. "Died in Babylon." It was important to his story. He was having trouble finding the threads of it. He craned his neck as they passed a corner; he blinked and tried to read what bar·that was, and to figure where they were going, but New Hell was a maze and this part of it was worse than most. *Dammit, Horatius, where? When? Where are you, huh?* "Where're we going, where're we going?"

"Come on," they said, and he walked willy-nilly. It was still where he had intended to be, staggering along in the drunken company of mercs who knew what he wanted to know, who knew faces and names he wanted to know, who could lead to other names. But it was feeling more and more like a screwup. Horatius was holding back. There was something wrong. Witness, maybe. Too much hazard. So it was over to the backup plan. Go along with it now. Get himself inside, to the recruiters who were spilling money into the dissident cause, siphoning talent out of this sink, talent that never served without pay; it was do what he could, get the hell out as fast as he could. . . .

Only he had drunk that last round of beer, and he did not know the streets; it was Niccolo's kind of operation, this. And he devoutly wished it were Niccolo in this situation, as his band of Hittite pirates steered him round a corner and toward an alley and a door open on that alley.

Mephistopheles Bar & Grill, the neon said; and they took him down into that doorway, through a room with tables and a few slumberous patrons, and back through a curtain.

"Hey," he said; he thought that the drunk he was playing would object at this mystery: he set his feet as they took him through the hall. "Where's this?" In a narrow, shadowy hall. They staggered with him to the wall and his gut tightened up as he backed into a clutter of hanging cloaks; garlic and beer fumed into his face, comradely hands held his shoulders, a Hittite stared into his face close as a lover.

"You don't need to know," the Hittite said, and patted him on the cheek. "Pawn your ring—" Belch. "You just sign up with the captain and you got no troubles, no troubles at all." Second belch. "Got real high friends. Real money. You take the Trip, you come back again, they got this man in Reassigments—"

"The hell you say."

Belch. A pat and a paw at the shoulder. "—gets you back right proper, he does. *Our* guys come back. Always come back. They don't lose us."

Pentagram. My gods.

"Come on," another Hittite said. "Piku, shut it up." A shove, an arm about Sargon's shoulders. "Come on, friend."

Down the hall, around the corner, a staggering course, himself glued to a Hittite's sweaty side, arms about shoulders.

Guards up ahead. Men with pistols. Paramilitary types. They were out of the Tigris for sure. But not his century or the last fifty-odd centuries he had trafficked with descendants of his empire in Hell.

"Who's this?" one asked, bringing his Colt up. "What's this?"

"This is—" the Hittite said, and clapped him on the shoulder and looked at him nose to nose. "What's your name?"

"Uballit," Sargon muttered, face to face. And to the guard, grandly, with a wave of his hand: " 'M signing up."

"You're all drunk."

"These're m' friends." Sargon draped himself over the Hittite and gazed ardently into his face. "What's your name?"

"Dudu," the other said. And hiccuped. They propped each other up. Everyone laughed. And the door got opened, the guns moved, and one of the guards went inside the room while the other one stood there scowling at the drunken horseplay.

Then the first came out again. "Bring him in," that guard said.

Sargon took a breath and went. And near lost it again, inside that room, with guards at his back and an Assyrian officer staring at him from the other side of the desk. His excellency Col. Kadashman-Enlil.

Old acquaintance.

"Oh, shit," he said, and turned to leave. Like any confused drunk.

They had the door blocked, of course. Like any security guards who thought the guns were enough.

He took them out, one and two, before they expected the move, and dived through the gawking lot of Hittites, who were there to soak up the Assyrian's gunfire when it came through the door.

He was through the hall and around the corner in the front room when the surviving Hittites came round that corner and through the curtain. Right into a chop to the throat and a kick that threw a man down howling. And *that* woke the room up.

"Damn!" he yelled, and charged through it to the front door as the bystanders got up and rushed for him, themselves in the way of gunfire from behind. There were shots and howls and shrieks.

He hit the street running, kept the damned cloak despite the drag; it confused aim from behind. Sandals cracked against the pavement and sandal straps strained as he took the corner and ran like hell diagonally across the street, right behind one passing car and right in front of another that swerved and honked. Damn noisy bastard.

Up another sidestreet. Loungers stared with dead and sullen eyes: not their trouble. Maybe his pursuers were not either. He hoped. And kept running. Short legs. Gods, if it was some damned long-legged New Dead on his track he was in real trouble. Damned 20th century giants. He sucked air and put another spurt into it as he took a corner and headed through the loungers about a bar and a restaurant, another skewed course through traffic.

There was a pain in his side. His legs burned and his lungs ached. Run and run and run. A gang of youths loomed ahead of him and got themselves prudently back against the building, hooting catcalls and curses after him, but knowing trouble when it came barreling through them with more trouble in its wake. He heard another chorus of shouting and reckoned that his pursuers were back there.

He dived into the street, dodged cars, cars dodged him; he went for an alley and ran another half block. Doubled back this time, and across the street, more blowing of horns and squeal of brakes. A bar blared music and spilled patrons out onto the walk: he ran through them, knocking a woman flat and a man sideways. Curses followed him, howled into the night. So did more tangible pursuit, another rage of voices and running steps.

He took an alley and doubled back, limping now, bent over the pain in his side as he ran, looking over his shoulder. He hit the previous street and walked it, looking for a cab, for anything, wary of eyes that might recognize him and seeing step-sitters staring in the flat, all-seeing way of their kind. A horse cab trotted by with a prostitute and a client. A phone booth on a corner showed itself graffiti-sprayed and vandalized.

No way to get help. No way except to keep walking until the pain in his side let him run again and try to get out of the area. Lose himself among the millions and the concrete canyons. Find a place to clean up, get a cab, get back home.

It was a screw-up for sure, royal and painted red for half of Hell to notice. Damn Kadashman-Enlil, damn conniving bastard, one of Assurbanipal's nest of vipers and clear as a whore at a wedding. It was a Pentagram operation, covert as it needed to be. And covert no longer. He knew and they knew he knew. Damn Hittites. Never should have picked Hittites.

He walked and gasped and panted, shouldered his sweaty way through passers-by and street people. The far side of the street was a solid row of bars and all-night pawnshops where, gods knew, they took anything in trade. Might get a phone over there. Might lose something else.

He crossed another street, feeling safer now, breathing easier, saw the subway light around the corner and crossed a deserted street to dive down that rabbit hole, down littered steps, a clumsy, exhausted vault of the turnstile, and down more steps to the dimly lit arch and the platform around the corner.

"Hey, man," a young voice hailed him at his left, in that lazy way of punks immemorial. That was what the world came to. They used to rob caravans and now they lounged against subway tunnel walls and wore metal studs and black leather. Six, seven of them.

And it was likely one of them had a gun.

Publius Aelius Hadrianus Caesar blinked and blinked again at the sound that disturbed his night; and lay in his bed in a moil of uncertainties til the sycophant (there were so few of them lately, and so few the aides that remained on staff) told him there were visitors.

"Who?" he asked it.

Romans, it said. *You aides are refusing to let them in. The visitors insist.*

This sycophant almost had a voice. Almost he knew it. It had been with him so long. He was abjectly grateful. He feared the others as he feared the aides. He had so many enemies. Like Caesar. Like Rameses. Like Augustus and Tiberius and Tigellinus and Lawrence and gods knew, the Parthians and the Germans and the Egyptians who smiled like crocodiles and supplanted him. His staff had deserted him. His servants had fled. His lover had vanished—whether they had killed him he had no idea. He asked few questions in his misery.

He did not want the answers—he, Hadrian, once supreme commander over the legions of Hell. When a man fell this far, he had no friends.

It was not the Undertaker he feared, though that was horrible. It was existence. It was living, knowing that everyone around him was shifting, seeking some new loyalty, that the staff that stayed with him was likely Rameses' staff, or worse, Mithridates' or Tigellinus'. That the servants spied on him. The sycophants deserted him. Only the one stayed, the one so near to reality, the one who for centuries had pinned its reality to his and, poor creature, so close to its goal, too close to start over, knew that it served a declining influence. It alone had reason to be loyal. No one else. If there were Romans they had come to harm him, though what form that harm might be when Reassignments seemed so doggedly determined to return him to New Hell, he could not imagine. Kill him again and again and again? And each time Reassignments would put him back. They surely knew that.

But this Roman kindred had come to him and his traitor staff had determined to block them, because they wanted him alive and in their hands. Two sets of his enemies fought over the corpse, that was what. He lay here in bed, weak and hallucinating of crocodiles, and his enemies tore at his flesh and bartered away the scraps of his souls, such as he had left.

He could not decide what to do. He could not decide anything any more. He did not want to decide. But he hated the traitors with a personal spite. And that alone brought him out of bed, brought him staggering to the door and wrapping about him togalike the sheet the lone sycophant had brought for his dignity.

He clung to the rail and walked the few steps down to the hall and to the door of his apartment, where by the entry desk he saw two of his staff arguing with someone on the intercom at the door.

"Open the door," he said, and his staffers turned around, whey-faced and furtive. "Open it," he said in his old voice of command, such as he could muster. They had drugged him. He knew that they had. All the room swam. He staggered forward and reeled against the wall where two gilt swords and a funerary shield made a display. Ripped a sword down and staggered their way. *"Open it."*

The lock clicked. The door swung open. It was the sycophant which obeyed him, not his fish-mouthed aides.

Beyond that door, framed in the tasteful, civilized apartment corridor, Atilius Regulus stood in city-dress khakis, backed by half a dozen of the legion in the same. There were Uzis in their hands. Hadrian stared at them and the aides stared and melted away out of the line of fire.

Hadrian made a small desperate gesture. "Welcome," he said in Greek, it was so ingrained in him; and saw them frown in offense, though they understood that tongue. He knew that Regulus did. An old Roman; a name for honor; but it was a bloody-minded kind. Tears suffused Hadrian's eyes, a profound longing for these countrymen who despised him and had come to do him more hurt; but with them it was at least a personal hate. *"Salvete,"* he said. "Come in. Or do you do your business from that doorway?"

"Octavianus sends you his affections," Regulus said, clipped and measured. Augustus. The *emperor* Augustus, he meant. This was a Republican Roman: no titles, no bending of the head, no respecting of majesty in that stare. Not even for the majesty he served. *Affections.* Hadrian did not miss the irony in the voice or in Regulus' basilisk stare and sphinxish smile. "Majesty. He asks after your health.".

"How will it be?" Hadrian asked. His voice was faint, but it was assuredly the sphinx who had come to catechize him, assuredly the ancient, ritual riddling game. He gave it smile for smile, weary though he was. "You will have to tell me, *Atili.*"

Regulus waved his hand. The legionnaires moved inside and shut the door. One imediately started through the staff desk. Another picked up the phone.

"Here," an aide objected. And fell quickly silent as he received too much of their attention. All the aides were silent. The legionnaire began unscrewing the receiver of the entry hall phone. Another, beyond the arch, took a small detector the sweep of the living room, with particular attention to the van Gogh.

Hadrian watched, dully. Turned his eyes then back to Regulus. "What does he want?"

"Your well-being," Regulus said in soft and modulated tones. "Majesty."

"Oh, go away," Sargon said wearily, to the rabbits foot-decorated pack. Green and pink rabbits feet. Gods. Mouthing obscenities. Demanding money. "You damn fools."

The gun turned up. The fool was going to wave it about. Sargon let them move in on him, let them shove him back toward the wall of the platform. His right hand beneath the cloak had his dagger. He rammed it up and put it right under a leather jacket, ducked low and drove with legs and shoulder, carrying that one and two others right off the platform and onto the tracks. The gun went off. And the fool missed, but the bullet ricocheted and sent chips of tile flying like shrapnel. Sargon just continued the sweep as the one punk freed his blade and brought it around into the leather jacket with the gun, grabbed the gun hand with his left and squeezed the wrist, which sent the pistol tumbling: jerked him again, kneed him, and slammed the knife under his jaw when the fool lost his wind and his self-defense. That left two. Who were headed up the stairs. Fast.

Sargon wiped the blade and picked up the gun—stared, as down the platform a wino blinked at the whole thing and picked up himself and his bottle and began to shamble into retreat.

Sargon smiled a wolfish smile and beckoned. The

man shook his head and backed off. But he did not look to be fleet of foot.

"Quite, quite," Augustus said, and scribbled an answer to the message that the courier brought, quite a tidy little stack of papers they had garnered from the uptown apartment where Hadrian kept his diminished state. *"Caius Julius Caesar Octavianus Augustus to his esteemed colleague Publius Aelius Haedrianus Caesar,"* he wrote, *"SVBEV.*

"How concerned we have been to hear of your misfortunes.

"In these trying times we of course consider it an act of public as well as private piety to support a kinsman in afflictions suffered in his long service to the state, which the gods reward.

"Knowing your generosity, which in no wise has failed in consideration of your kinsmen and friends, we do this not without the confidence that our pious acts may be reciprocated in some proper hour whether in your fondness for us or in your good will toward our affairs.

"Rely on Atilius as on myself."

It was not an alliance he formed gladly. It was one which might be abrogated at convenience—whether at Julius' whim or his own, or the annoyance of Rameses II. It was always useful to have throwaways in a negotiation, if there was to be a negotiation.

But his dear successor would know that. And wish to be indispensable.

That far had Hadrian fallen.

He did what he could, did Octavianus Augustus, and thinking of Julius still felt that avuncular presence at his shoulder, which made him conscious of his too-large ears, his freckles, his schoolboy stoop: in Julius' absence he did what he could, and put his personal seal to yet another damning message.

"This will be destroyed once read," he told the courier; and the youth, who had died in Julius' service once, in Africa, nodded gravely and tucked it away.

Sargon was missing and Horatius hours out of touch. He imagined that presence at his shoulder, darkened with that frown that presaged calamities, presaged a spate of legion-Latin and a direct order to *do* something, *anticipate* the enemy, and be *first* for once, damn you, nephew.

Augustus feared the enemy hardly more than that cold, despairing shake of Julius' head, with which he regarded fools. He was damned if he did the wrong thing, damned if he did not do enough, and damned if he sat still: Tiberius was tottering toward the enemy, the dissidents were getting professional help, and he worked like a scenery shifter at a play, putting a pot here, a tree there—*here, good people, is the army, here the threat; here the presence of Caesar, imminently to return and confound his enemies; do not mistake it. Our enemies will regret any hasty move.* . . .

The fact was that he did not *know* where Julius was. Not any longer. Affairs were under his direction now. Entirely under his direction. And the enemy was moving faster than he liked.

The street was quiet now, in the hour just before the dawn. Horatius slouched in the seat behind the wheel with his hat tilted low over his face and his chin sunk into the collar of his coat, watching as he had watched—not the ideal occupation for a one-eyed man; the sidewalk was his blind side and the eyepatch and his Roman profile and scarred face were all detriments to this kind of work. The emperor usually put him where he wanted a really conspicuous spy—to divert attention off another one of far less theatrical appearance; it was his *job* to be obvious.

Only now—now with the household a shell of itself and under siege from inside and out, now with young Galba screwing it up and letting traffic cut him off, he took his post himself. No second screw-up. Galba was back at the downtown station—still likely snuffling and vowing he would slit his wrists—which would land him where they were all too afraid the Akkadian had gone: Horatius had remarked as much, at which Galba had gone redder in the face and plunged his face in his hands in uttermost despair.

Heroes. Gods save us. He recognized the pattern, the overwhelming compulsion to take responsibility. Same thing that had stood him out on a bridge they were cutting out from under him. But he had lived through that one. Died in another battle, of a sword cut on his blind side. Never saw the damn thing coming. Made a man feel foolish. Wish he hadn't done that, hadn't made that move, had a chance to try it over.

Like the poor kid whose job it was to tag Sargon, who had just misgauged the traffic.

Heroes out here at the moment they did not need. Just somebody sitting at the last-ditch pickup point, car parked among other cars, man at the wheel dozing under his hat. With one slitted eye traveling continually over the deserted street and from mirror to mirror to mirror as he rested there. With a Beretta 92 in the well between the seats, a shell in the chamber. In case they were cracked wide open and the authorities, or the enemy, or gods knew what else got onto it.

Walkers were very few at this hour, an occasional pair of them, the scruffy sort; a cluster of them walking along loud and drunk, that made Horatius finger the gun and think about trouble. Long quiet after. Then one old man in a ragged overcoat who staggered this way and that with a paper-bagged bottle clutched up against his chest.

Who staggered right up to the car and thumped into the fender and bent down to stare through the windshield into the muzzle of an automatic.

Damn! Horatius checked his finger on the trigger, gulped a breath, and shoved himself up in the seat and flipped the power-lock on the passenger side. "Damn," he said aloud as Sargon opened the door and flung himself in. Horatius turned the key and the engine caught. "Damn." Putting it in gear. "Trying to get yourself shot?"

"Where the hell were you?"

"Where were *you?*" He threw it in forward and nosed out into the empty street, pulled a right at Mammon and gathered a sedate if brisk speed as Sargon slouched down into the seat. "Are you all right?"

"An Assyrian's doing the recruiting," Sargon said in a low voice.

Horatius gave him a short, sharp look.

"He saw me," Sargon said. "He might have recognized me. Name's Kadashman-Enlil. One of Mithridates' own pet rats. I walked right into it. Dammit, where were you?"

"Too late and you were out of sight. Traffic. You moved too damn fast." Horatius took a corner onto de Sade Boulevard and shifted. Pulled a vent and got a little air into the car. "Was it noisy?"

"Damn noisy. Nothing they'll complain about. Officially. Gods." Sargon's voice went weak and strangled. He started unbuttoning the shirt. "It's got fleas."

"For godssake, keep covered, you want to look peculiar?" He cracked a window. Air blasted through the car and relieved the worst of it. "Damn, an Assyrian. You know him personally?"

"Long time back. With Assurbanipal. Pentagram money, that's what it is, flowing right into rebel fingers. Mercs in with the rebels, the Pentagram planting merc officers *they've* paid for, got a man in Reassignments—damn *fool* dissidents, they've swallowed snake eggs, that's what they've done, taken 'em whole right into their gut—oh, *ba'al and scorpions!*" Sargon scratched furiously in his hair.

"Or they always *were* snakes," Horatius said glumly.

Sargon came in at dawn. In military khaki. That was not unusual, but the hour was. Brutus watched from the stairs, how the king of Akkad slipped in; and he guessed that Sargon had no wish to talk to a boy just now. A woman, he imagined. The kind of mystery that men pursued and he had only longed after in his life.

In fact it was a long time before Sargon showed himself in the main wing of the house: he was swimming, the sycophants said, and steaming, and swimming again, and when Brutus, chafing in idleness, thought to go downstairs to ask the king for his lessons.

The Lion wants to be alone, a sycophant whispered; and added, for sycophants always had to fear displeasure: *Please.*

Brutus sighed, and slouched down the stairs, small dispirited skips of rubber-shod feet. He could take the whole stairs on his heels. Most everyone would think it impudent. It was hard to be his father's son, and to have to live up to that.

He hoped for Augustus, at least. But: *Hush, hush,* a sycophant said, before he could touch the office door. *The emperor is having a nap.*

He went and sat on the steps, elbows on knees, and hands between ankles, and sighed again, and a third time.

Hell for him was mostly waiting.

TABLE WITH A VIEW

Nancy Asire

Napoleon sat on his front step, sighed quietly, and tapped the envelope on his knee. To his left, the sound of cutting shears drifted across his front yard. Wellington was trimming the hedge. Again. It made no difference that he was cutting on Napoleon's side of the shrub row. Neatness was neatness. Napoleon stared across the bushes at Wellington. *How can I draw him into an attack on* my *weeds?* Non-Participants rarely rated sycophants.

But no, first things first. The envelope fluttered spitefully before a small breeze. Napoleon shook his head, stood, and reached into the rear pocket of his jeans. Flipping open his well-worn leather billfold, he stared at his driver's license. The expiration date was exactly as he remembered it: next month. Yet the letter he had received from the Hall of Injustice said his license had expired two weeks ago. He put the billfold back in his pocket.

Dammit. Augustus said I wouldn't have to worry about things like this.

Napoleon grimaced. Altered records or not, there was no hope for it this time. And he dared not drive. So it was The Bus, or—

"Wellington!"

The Iron Duke paused in his bush clipping, straightened, and flicked a few leaves from his uniform.

Napoleon arose and sauntered very casually down his driveway and then across it to the hedge where Wellington stood waiting. "Are you doing anything this morning?"

"Other than what you see, no." Wellington rubbed the end of his long nose and sneezed. "Bloody leaves! What do you need?"

"Management says my driver's license expired. It hasn't, but—well, could you give me a lift to the Hall of Injustice?"

Wellington frowned. "I don't like that place."

"Who does? You can stay in the car."

"Well—"

Guilt time. "After all we've been through together . . . ?"

Wellington paused for a moment. "When?"

"Today. Now. I'll be in there for hours as it is."

"You don't expect me to wait all that time for you to—"

"Here speaks the man who broke the Guard at Waterloo?"

Wellington sighed.

There were—of course—no parking places close to the Hall of Injustice, and Wellington ended up pulling into a spot a quarter mile from the entrance. Napoleon got out, slammed the car door, and set off across the parking lot.

Wellington watched him go and shook his head. Napoleon was a decent enough chap, a good neighbor and all that—but the way he dressed! Faded jeans, a blue work-shirt, and those God-awful sneakers. . . . He leaned back in the seat, turned a bit sideways so he could cross his knees, and looked across the parking lot at the Freshly Welcomed who stood blinking at the front doors of Hell.

Napoleon had been standing in line now for just over an hour and there was one person left ahead of him—

the same one who had been there when he arrived. Not many drove I.C. vehicles in Hell; many of the famous Old Dead preferred to ride horses or use carriages, and few moderns rated them, except when on the Devil's business.

He looked around the room, suddenly, for no immediate reason, uneasy. *What was it someone had said? Just because you're paranoid doesn't mean that you're not being followed. A* mal mot *if ever there was one.*

Finally the fellow abandoned all hope, muttering curses under his breath. Napoleon watched him go and stepped up to the counter, hoping that he would have better luck.

He carefully spread the Official Notice of Expiration on the counter top and pulled his billfold from his hip pocket. Flipping it open, he took out his license and laid it beside the letter.

"There seems to be a mistake here," he began with studied politeness. "My license is still good for another month."

The clerk—an old, old woman, whose glasses threatened to fall from the end of her nose—stared at the letter and then at the driver's license. She shoved the glasses back up, and peered across the counter.

"It's a software bug in the main computer," she confided, then sniffed primly. Clearly she did not approve of bugs of any kind.

Software bug? Napoleon frowned. *What else? Either that or someone* wants *me here.*

The clerk pulled a form from a drawer and slipped it into an old Royal typewriter. Placing Napoleon's driver's license next to it, she started pecking at the keyboard. "Now, is your name correct? Napoleon Bonaparte?"

Napoleon sighed. "Yes, that's right." This was going to take forever.

Tap, tap, tap. One-fingered typists were a horror to watch. "All right. Hair-brown. Eyes—grey-blue." Tap, tap, tap. "Height—"

Napoleon tried to see into the typewriter but the

counter top was too high to lean across. "Five foot even," he said.

Tap, tap, tap, tap. "Your address is still the same?"
"Yes."

"Out by the Country Club? That's not a bad neighborhood." Tap, tap. She paused, shoved her glasses back up her nose, and stared at the form. Satisfied, she pulled it back out of the typewriter and extended it and Napoleon's driver's license back to him. "Now take this form and your license down there." A quick gesture to the end of the room.

Napoleon forced a smile, slipped the envelope and letter into his shirt pocket, and turned away.

Two men and three women sat in a partitioned section of the large room. Four of them already had people with them at their desks and were busy keying information into their terminals. He shrugged, glanced at his watch again, thought briefly of Wellington in the parking lot, and headed over to the empty desk.

The woman sat with her back to him, arranging papers in an overflowing out box. He sat down in the chair beside her desk and waited, idly watching the fluorescent light play across the woman's blond hair. She finished her task and turned around. Napoleon's heart leapt to his throat and his mouth went dry. "Marie?" he whispered, not believing what his eyes told him was true. "O God above! Marie! You *can't* be here!"

Marie's heart stopped, fluttered briefly, and began again to beat. It was *he*. Short, broad-shouldered, olive-skinned; though he was thinner and younger than when first they had met, still she would have known him anywhere. Even, indeed, here, though only his eyes had not regained the aspect of youth. Deep-set they were, and compelling—windows into a world of infinite possibilities, each of which she wanted only to explore.

Tears blurred her vision as memory engulfed her. Warsaw, Poland—New Year's Day, 1807. The first time they had seen each other. A chance meeting by a snowy roadside, and they had fallen in love. The Emperor Napoleon and the Countess Walewska had begun an affair that would only be ended by his final exile—an affair which had produced a son whose descendants were still living.

"Mon dieu en ciel!" Napoleon glanced around, but no one seemed to be interested in his blasphemy. *Who's responsible for this? The Management? Augustus trying to be nice?*

He looked back at Marie, afraid she might disappear. She was exactly as he remembered her—tiny, a bit shorter than his own height, golden blond hair and wide blue eyes. Younger than when last they had been together, but not younger than he remembered. He drew a deep breath. "Not you. Not here."

"C'est moi."

"Vraiment."

She reached out and took the form and driver's license from his hand. "I've got to look busy," she said, her voice trembling. She turned from him and keyed up a menu.

"But—" He shook his head helplessly. "I can't believe it. Why haven't we met? You died before I did."

She lowered her voice and her eyes. "I can't say."

Napoleon bowed his head. "A fiat of Administration?"

She nodded helplessly. Perhaps it was a Torment.

Well, at least the glitch with the software was explained.

His throat tightened. "How long have you been here?" he asked at last.

"Several months." She punched in a command and began typing.

The next question was agony. "And how much longer have you got left to stay."

A small tear trickled down her cheek. "I don't know. They said I'd . . . be told."

Napoleon cursed softly. "Where are you staying?"

"I've got a small apartment close to the Hall."

His heart jumped. "They don't care where you live?"

She shook her head.

"Marie." He reached out and gently touched her arm. "Please. Come home with me."

She stopped typing and covered her eyes with both hands. "Don't, don't ask. They'll just separate us when it hurts most."

This can't be happening! Not here. Not Marie— He moved his chair closer. "Let's make the most of what time we've been given."

"Oh, Napoleon," she laughed, looking up from her hands, her eyes full of tears. "That's what we always used to say."

"When's your shift over?"

She glanced up at the large clock on the wall. "Four-thirty."

"I'll be here."

"But that's nearly three hours from now." She squared her shoulders and started typing again.

He closed his eyes. Wellington—the parking lot. They could refight Blenheim. Wellington could never resist that.

"It doesn't matter. We'll get your things from your apartment and go on out to the house. Marie. I've never stopped loving you."

She caught her breath, punched the store key, and turned to him, her cheeks flushed. "And I've never stopped loving you." She glanced sidelong and switched back to English. "I've keyed in the proper information and you should be getting your new license in the mail. You didn't drive, did you?"

He took his license from her and flicked his gaze to one side—the woman to his left had finished her job and was watching. "No. A friend brought me—my next-door neighbor, Wellington."

Marie put one hand to her mouth. "Wellington? Your neighbor? How very . . . ironic."

"And fitting. He's not so bad. Anyway, I'm glad he moved in. But I left him in the parking lot and I better get back out there before he dies of boredom."

* * *

Two Wimpy Burgers, three orders of fries, one chocolate sundae, and the battle of Blenheim later, Wellington drove back to the Hall of Injustice. Napoleon watched the traffic as they drove, primed to yell "Right side of the street!" when Wellington gravitated in true British stubbornness to the left. He glanced at his watch—4:28.

"Now you're sure she'll be waiting for us?" Wellington asked.

"She'll be there." Napoleon stomped on the floor-board in a braking reflex. "Jesus, Wellington! Watch that bus!"

Wellington swerved in and out of the rush hour traffic. "I am watching it. You certainly are jumpy today. My driving can't be *that* bad."

"It's not your driving."

"Aha! It's your little Polish Countess." Wellington's long narrow face broke into a grin. "Wait until Josephine hears about this!"

Napoleon waved a hand. "She had a chance to move in with me. I was too boring."

"You? Boring? Huh!"

Napoleon looked ahead. *O Lord. Am I making a mistake? I can trust Marie. But what if she is a plant and doesn't know it?* He rubbed the back of his neck. *Of course she was a plant. The only question was whose. But, very frankly, right at this moment it hardly mattered. As long as they let her stay with him. Augustus never said this would be an easy job. And maybe Marie's string led back to his finger. A quick glance at Wellington. And how am I going to tell him what I've got us involved in? He'll have to know sooner or later.*

The driveway to the Hall of Injustice was at the next corner. Napoleon looked through the traffic. There— standing by the front doors—

"Marie," he whispered. He gestured Wellington on.

Wellington grinned again. "Buy me a cigar, and I'll promise to look the other way on the drive home."

Napoleon sighed and pulled the covers up to his chin. The house was quiet and his bedroom was only dimly lit by the daylight outside. Closing his eyes in utter contentment, he tightened his embrace and drew Marie even closer. *Today—think only of today. The future hasn't come yet.*

"Napoleon?"

He opened his eyes and looked at her face so close to his own. He laughed quietly and kissed her again. She hadn't changed, his beloved Marie. It was as if they had parted yesterday. It was like gaining back a part of himself he thought he had lost forever.

A distant explosion rumbled out of the park. Marie started in his arms, her quick intake of breath loud in the silence.

"Viet Cong," Napoleon explained. "In the park across the street. They're usually harmless."

"But I thought you told me Caesar and the National Guard had destroyed them."

"That's another thing about Hell. They keep coming back. Everybody keeps coming back. Now that Hadrian's out and Rameses is Supreme Commander, Lord knows." Reluctantly he disentangled himself and glanced at the wind-up clock on the bedside table—7:30. "Wellington and I had planned on going down to the club for dinner at 8:00. Shall we go? Or . . ."

Marie laughed. "We have to spend *some* time on other things."

Hellview Golf and Country Club sat across the creek and behind Napoleon's house. The entire neighborhood was surrounded, front and back, by untenanted land. The golf course stretched south along the rear of the row of houses and, with Decentral Park to the north on the other side of the street, offered a fair amount of privacy. Usually the only problem with the golf course was an occasional errant golf ball that turned mowing into an exciting event.

Wellington glanced sideways as he turned the car down the long driveway into the club. The Countess Walewska was dressed in a pale blue pantsuit, looking fresh and beautiful. Even Napoleon had consented to dress up a bit, exchanging his sneakers for boots and trading his faded jeans for a new pair and a freshly ironed shirt. Wellington rubbed his nose to hide his smile. Perhaps Marie would be a good influence on Napoleon after all.

The parking lot was full, but there was a place close to the door. In Hell, such luck was cause for paranoia, but Wellington pulled into it, turned off the ignition, and got out. As Napoleon helped Marie out of the car, Wellington put on his hat, reached into the back seat for his sword, and closed the door.

He stood for a moment, looking off at the polo grounds. A game was just ending and he recognized Attila's stocky figure atop a black pony. Marie and Napoleon laughed at something and he turned around. *You lucky little Corsican, you. If only I might find the Duchess of Richmond here serving tea.*

The dining room was full, so Napoleon put his name on the waiting list and led the way into the bar. He stood squinting in the dim light, Marie at his side and Wellington slightly behind. The first person he recognized sat alone at a table on the far side of the bar, black eye-patch looking all the more sinister in the shadows. Horatius! Not that the Romans from across the park never came to the club. But since his meeting with Augustus, it seemed that no matter which way he turned, he saw Romans.

A quiet, secluded table just large enough for three stood empty across the barroom from Horatius. Napoleon pointed to it, motioned for Marie to go first, and followed her across the room.

Pulling out a chair for Marie, Napoleon gestured Wellington to the one that would put the Iron Duke's back to the one-eyed Roman. He kept his face carefully bland. *I've got to tell Wellington. But I don't dare say anything here.*

A group of short, wild-haired men swaggered into the

bar. The polo teams. Napoleon stared at them, seeking familiar faces.

Attila came through the door last. "Drinks for everybody!" he bellowed, a wide grin on his flat face.

Napoleon glanced at Marie. "Attila," he murmured. "Once a week there's a match—Huns vs. Mongols. Looks like Attila's team won tonight."

"At least we'll get free drinks because of it," Wellington said, leaning back in his chair and flicking at invisible dust motes on his snow-white trousers. He lifted a disapproving eyebrow. "Still, one might wish that those barbarians wouldn't be quite so . . . barbarous."

Napoleon grinned slightly, then turned to Marie, but was interrupted.

"Napoleon!" A rough, loud voice carried over the noise.

"Merde!" Napoleon glanced across the crowded room. "Atilla's seen us."

"O Lord," Wellington murmured. "And I suppose he hasn't showered after the game, either, or the last several before that, for that matter."

The short, stocky figure of the Scourge of God and captain of the Hun polo team bulled its way across the room.

"And Wellington!" Attila paused by the table, his drink tilting in one hand, and slapped Wellington's shoulder in greeting. "Holy horse-turds! It's good to see you!" He pulled over a chair, uninvited, and sat down. "And who's the good-looking lady?"

"Countess Marie Walewska." Napoleon made the introductions. "You won tonight, Attila?"

"Blew their asses right off the field! It was *glorious!*" Narrow slanted eyes capped a wide grin. "You missed a good one."

Wellington had finished brushing off the shoulder Attila had slapped. "Busy," he said. "Sorry."

Attila was a member of the National Guard, and sometimes intimately involved in the struggle with the dissidents. Napoleon watched him closely as he said, offhandedly, "You've missed a few matches yourself lately, haven't you?"

Attila laughed uproariously. "Best damned thing that's happened in a long time. With those bitch wives of mine—" He leaned across the table and lowered his voice: "Long life to the dissidents, that's what I say."

Wellington rolled his eyes ceilingward. "Lord, Attila, you must enjoy the Undertaker's jokes."

The warrior-king was incapable of admitting to fear, but the entity under discussion was no laughing matter, not even to Attila the Hun. Attila sobered.

Napoleon motioned for silence as a barmaid came to their table ready to take their orders. "Wine?" he asked, looking from Wellington to Marie and receiving their nods: "Chablis?" More nods.

The barmaid scribbled and turned away.

"You know, Napoleon," Attila said, his voice amazingly near a conversational level, "the way things are going, you and Wellington may get called up to the Army again."

Napoleon's heart froze. *"Quoi?"*

"Well, old Rameses is dead set on cleaning things up. He's been on a tear lately. Downright pissed. Talks about wiping out the dissidents for good."

Wellington raised an eyebrow. "They'd come back again. Like the Cong to the park. Good thing there's Romans to this side, I say. Caesar and his lads. What does *he* have to say about it, I'd like to know."

"Don't ask me," Attila said, lifting one hand. "I haven't seen him either."

"Antony was driving up and down like some bat out of—excuse me—Hell," Wellington added.

Attila lifted both hands and assumed what was, for him, an innocent expression. "I know nothing . . . I see nothing . . . I hear nothing!"

Wellington snorted. "The devil you do. Come on, Attila. Out with it."

The noise in the bar had grown even louder as the polo teams were by now into their third round of drinks.

Attila glanced over his shoulder, then looked back. "Don't ask."

The barmaid returned with three glasses of wine. Distributing them, she turned to Attila. "On your bill, too?"

"Damned right, toots!" Attila grinned, reached out to pinch, but the barmaid, only recently a sycophant and very conscious of her new-found dignity, such as it was, sidled away.

Napoleon rubbed his chin. He and Caesar were on good speaking terms, but periodic parties and infrequent dinners at the club were about as far as their socializing went. Augustus had said that Caesar was out on "maneuvers." Strange, Caesar had not mentioned it the last time he had come to the club. Attila's veiled hints, coupled with Augustus' warnings, set faint alarm bells ringing.

A sudden wave of silence spread across the bar. Napoleon glanced at the door and froze. A small bespectacled, ferret-faced man stood there, mouth turned down in a sour frown. Goebbels.

O Lord! Horatius at one end of the bar—Goebbels at the other! "Marie," Napoleon whispered. "Follow my lead and don't ask questions."

Wellington was gesturing frantically to Attila with one hand. "Goebbels," he hissed, then looked down into his glass of wine.

Attila stiffened. Conversation started again in the bar, only it was hushed and lacked the noisy abandon of post-game revelry. Attila stood.

"Nice seeing you again," he said, with a forced grin on his face. "I think I'm going to move this party outside. Starting to smell like a damned meadow-muffin in here," said the man who had once remarked that a good horse was worth more than any of his wives.

"Shower more often and you'd notice it sooner," Wellington murmured as Attila walked away.

Marie made a little shrug. "And I was just about to

ask him what it was that Pope Leo said that turned him from the walls of Rome."

"Oh, *that*," Wellington said. "I'll tell you later."

The polo party began to gravitate toward the tables outside. Attila was back in form again, cursing, laughing, waving a new drink over his head. Napoleon met Wellington's eyes and nodded toward the door.

"We've waited long enough. Our table's got to be ready. See if you can distract Goebbels so I can get Marie out of here."

Wellington nodded and stood: tall, elegantly thin, he walked slowly across the bar, hat under his arm and sword held close to his side with his other hand. He and Goebbels passed each other with a brief nod.

Goebbels had not risen to the bait. Napoleon shrugged, glanced across the room at Horatius, and stood, offering Marie his hand. Better to be on the move than sitting if Goebbels cornered them. Motioning for Marie to precede him, he started off across the room. As he had expected, Goebbels maneuvered in between the tables to face them.

"Ah, General Bonaparte," he said, a thin smile making his face appear even more skull-like. "And how is our resident Emperor this evening? Who's the young lady?"

"My date," Napoleon said lightly, putting his arm around Marie. He had told her earlier that Goebbels worked for the Management, lived next door, and was a general pain in the ass; now he felt her tremble and knew she sensed the danger. *God! Don't let Goebbels think it's anything serious!* "Met her down at the Hall of Injustice and decided to show her a good time." Napoleon lifted one eyebrow and smiled slowly. "If you know what I mean."

Goebbels frowned, straightened his back to ramrod stiffness. "You always were one for the ladies, weren't you?"

Napoleon shrugged. "You know how it is, Joseph. Reputations, earned or unearned, follow us even after death." He turned, kissed Marie's cheek, then glanced back. "If you'll excuse us? We've a table waiting."

He guided Marie around Goebbels' motionless figure, his hand resting casually on her back, just above the place that he fervently hoped Goebbels would assume constituted his entire interest.

The first thing Napoleon and Marie passed as they walked into the dining room was a table full of young Roman officers. He groaned inwardly. Where the Karmic connection lay, he failed to see. Would he find Romans in his bathroom some morning? The five officers wore khaki undress uniforms; he glanced at their left shoulders: each uniform sleeve sported the "X" of the Tenth Legion. *At least they're Caesar's—and Augustus'.*

Wellington sat at a table by the large bay window that framed the polo field. Napoleon guided Marie in that direction, pulled out a chair for her, then took his own.

"What's that sneak doing here?" Wellington asked, motioning with his eyes back to the bar.

"Goebbels? Spying, as usual." He *hoped* it was merely "as usual." Napoleon looked over at Marie and his heart turned over as she smiled. He drew a deep breath and shifted in his chair—dinner had better not last long.

"What I can't understand," Wellington said, his nose buried in the menu, "is what he thinks he's getting away with. Everyone *knows* he's the Management's local fink."

"Maybe he thinks he'll get lucky. Fools do, sometimes." Napoleon reached under the table for Marie's hand and held it tightly. He glanced at her, and her eyes twinkled back at him in the lamplight. Suddenly Napoleon cursed himself for a fool who had gotten lucky—and then gone off to dinner. *An excuse—think of something to get away. Anything—*

"I say," Wellington's voice intruded. "Look at that."

Wellington was pointing off across the polo field. There—at the far end of the field. Napoleon leaned toward the window and saw a distant figure. What the—

"Who is it?" Marie asked.

"I don't know." A chill ran up Napoleon's spine. He glanced at Wellington. "I don't like this."

Wellington set his menu down, his eyes still trained on the field outside the window. "He's not alone."

It was true. Behind the approaching figure Napoleon could now make out several others—then more, and more. They moved ahead slowly, crouching, keeping close to the ground, about thirty of them. He squinted against the slight glare in the window. The lights had been left on around the polo field. A quick glint of imperfectly blackened metal out there caught his attention.

A trip from the armory; a desk full of papers; the refined face of Rome's first Emperor; Augustus' words: *It's your life I fear for—*

"Marie!" Napoleon turned quickly to her. "Stay close." He glanced at Wellington. "Outside. Quick!"

Wellington nodded his understanding and rose.

Napoleon stood, helped Marie to her feet, and followed Wellington out the dining room door into the lobby, leaving a bewildered waiter behind.

"Now what?" Wellington hissed.

Napoleon gestured sharply, dismissing the question. "Where's Attila?"

"Moved his party out to the polo field, I think."

The lobby was crowded. Napoleon looked quickly around and spotted a side door that led out to the opposite end of the parking lot by the field. He jerked his head toward it. "Let's go!"

Disregarding multitudinous stares, they made for the door and stepped outside.

As the door closed, Wellington's face turned grim. "Dissidents?"

"I think so."

"What the bloody—? Why are they coming at the club?"

"I don't know." Napoleon walked faster. "There are a lot of Personages here tonight. I saw several of Caesar's in the lobby when we left. Then there's you and me. If things are deteriorating as fast as Attila hinted, what better way to cripple the enemy than to take out a large number of its officers—and potential officers?"

Wellington said thoughtfully, "D'you think Goebbels is behind this?"

"Possibly. But I'd be willing to bet they'd like to get him, too."

"Ugh. Him? With *us*?"

"What's going on?" Marie asked in a steady voice.

A distant part of Napoleon's heart warmed at her cool-headedness, though his mind paid scant attention. "I'm not sure, but I think a dissident commando team is about to attack the Club," he said absently. He gestured to Wellington. "Let's find Attila."

Starting off at a quick trot, he led the way around the corner of the Club toward the polo field. Attila and his Huns were still there, along with the Mongols.

"Attila!" he called in something very like a shouted whisper.

The short, stocky figure turned, swaying slightly. "I'll be fried! Come to join our party? Damned sight better than snoot city in the bar."

Napoleon reached Attila's side and pointed across the polo grounds at the slowly approaching, crouched-over figures. "Look over there!"

Attila sobered instantly. His eyes all but disappeared as he squinted off through the garish lights. "By the Sky!" he swore. "An attack on the Club?"

"I'd bet on it. Are you and the rest too drunk to ride?"

"Us? Too drunk to ride?" He spun around to face the raucous polo teams and gestured sharply at the barely discernible commandoes. "Get to your horses, you dungheads! Ride! This is going to be even more fun than the polo game!"

"Wellington," Napoleon turned and gestured at the

Club. "There's an electrical switch back there at the
corner of the building—"

"Cut the lights to the polo field, eh?"

"Yes, at the appropriate moment. You've got the long
legs." Napoleon grinned. "Go for it!"

Wellington grinned back and ran off. Hissing curses,
Attila and his Huns sprinted toward their horses, the
Mongols close behind.

"But, Napoleon," said Marie. "What about the dissidents' guns?"

"You're right," Napoleon agreed. "We'd better get
over there, out of the way." He gestured toward the line
of trees separating the field from the parking lot. Because
he knew Huns and Mongols were *always* armed to the
teeth, he'd missed the real point of Marie's question. He
trotted off toward the trees, holding Marie's hand. Glancing over his shoulder, he could see that the ragged line
of dissidents had reached the center of the polo field.
Light glinted from the angles of their weapons. Napoleon caught a tree with one hand and tugged Marie
closer to him with the other, swinging to a halt behind
at least the appearance of shelter.

The lights went out, leaving the dissidents blind when
the glare about them was replaced by the crepuscular
sickliness that passed for night in New Hell.

And speaking of Hell, where was Attila?

Suddenly horses brushed past the screen of trees behind which he stood with Marie, more and more horses,
hooves thudding on the polo ground like so many cannons being shotted home. Save for that, the charge was
silent—for the moment. Attila grinned like a madman
at the head of the combined polo teams. He was guiding
his pony with his knees so that he could wave a sword
overhead with one hand and swing his polo mallet with
the other.

Several of the dissidents had ducked when the lights
went out, expecting a burst of shots from the country
club to follow. They were focused in the wrong direc-

tion until one of their number looked behind him and screamed.

A score of bloodthirsty horsemen from the plains of Central Asia screamed back.

At least two of the dissidents managed to open fire before the charge burst over them. A horse went up on its hind legs, spraying blood from its nostrils—and then collapsed in a thrashing heap, its throat slashed by its solicitous rider before he vaulted from his saddle.

For the rest, the battle was entirely one-sided.

Unlike ordinary horses, the polo ponies had no tendency to shy away from contact. Dissidents who escaped mallets and the swords of watered steel were slammed down and trampled to pulp by living half-ton missiles.

Anybody on foot was fair game—including the Mongol whose horse had been shot. He ducked the swipe of one of his comrades, then vaulted onto the saddle behind his attacker. Overloaded but still eager the pony lurched back into the fray with a sword now flickering to either side.

A terrified dissident screeched and fired his automatic rifle straight in the air as two Huns rode down on him from opposite directions. The nearer horsemen swept past, his sword continuing its arc after the head leaped from the dissident's shoulders. The mallet of the second Hun caught the head before it hit the ground and sent it flying over the trees as Wellington came pounding up and took cover.

Napoleon winced, afraid to look at Marie. Wellington was muttering and dabbing at his blood-spattered forehead with a lace handkerchief.

One of the dissidents was trotting toward the trees, stumbling because he was trying to look behind him as he ran. A rider broke from the skirmish, yipping his horse toward the escapee. It was Attila, his sword visible only as wavering flecks of brightness glinting through a smear of drying blood. The dissident, panting and frightened, turned and raised his rifle to port as if to physically ward off the shadow thundering down on him.

Napoleon took a deep breath. "Excuse me," he muttered, snatching the purse from Marie's hand. Whirling the purse on the end of its chain strap, he stepped out from the trees and let fly just as the dissident, who had remembered what his rifle was for, was raising it to his shoulder. The swarthy commando yelped as the purse clipped him over the ear, and his first shots blasted high. Before he could recover, the King of the Huns had caught him on the opposite side of his head with a full forehand sweep of his polo mallet.

Attila skidded his mount to a stiff-legged halt, all four hooves braced on the dissident's body. "Yai-HAH!" he shouted, waving his mallet above his head. *"Goal!"*

Even as he shouted out his victory cry, he and his pony spun and galloped back toward the fast-dissolving melee. "After them, you bowlegged sons of the steppe," he roared. "Whoever brings me the most heads, heads the team next week!"

Attila's voice had remarkable carrying power; the remaining handful of dissidents ran even faster toward the so-distant brush. Whooping joyfully, swords and mallets raised on high, the laughing horsemen thundered after.

The hum of excited conversation spilled out into the lobby as Napoleon and Marie followed Wellington back into the dining room. A number of people had gathered by the large window overlooking the polo field, but Goebbels and the Romans were not among them—doubtless off to make reports. Napoleon sighed quietly. The crowd in front of the window looked like it was not going to move. So much for a meal with a view.

The maitre d' came across the room. "A table? For three?"

Napoleon glanced around, saw a table off to one side, more dimly lit than the others. He nodded in its direction. "Over there, please."

Once seated, Napoleon leaned back in his chair and sighed quietly. With any luck, no one would have noticed the part he and Wellington had played. Only the Romans. O, *bon dieu!* And Goebbels.

Wellington looked at the menu. "Ummm. I'll take the Beef Wellington."

Napoleon laughed and said, "Only you—"

"What do you mean, 'only you'?"

"Who else would order something named after him?"

Wellington replied complacently, "Anyone who had something decent named after them. . . . Besides, they named it after me because I was fond of it." Then he smirked. "*You* could always have a pastry, or some booze."

"*Touché!*" Napoleon turned to Marie. "And you, *amore?*"

A commotion came from the lobby—yells, laughter, cheers. Napoleon glanced toward the doorway and his heart sank.

"Napoleon!" There was no disguising Attila's voice. "Wellington!"

"O my God!" Wellington looked hastily around. "Is there no escape?"

"Coward," Napoleon muttered. "I was thinking about the curtains."

"There you are!" Attila's stocky figure seemed to fill the dining room doors. Still carrying his sword, somebody else's blood running down his left arm, the Hun stalked across the room, thoroughly commanding the attention of all the diners present. His mustached face bore a bruise over his right eye, but he seemed otherwise unharmed. "By the Sky!" he grinned, stopping by the table. "What a rout! Talk about kicking ass! Yai-Hiii!"

By now a crowd had started to gather. Wellington pulled his neck down into his tall uniform collar, his ears flaming red. Napoleon kept his head bowed, pretending to study the menu.

"What happened, Attila?" someone asked.

"Dissidents!" Attila basked in the attention. "Wellington and Napoleon spotted them and warned me. Haiya! What a way to end a polo match."

Napoleon glanced sidelong at Wellington, who, turtle-like, was drawing deeper down into his collar.

"It's a fine mess you've gotten us into this time."

Wellington blinked, his head rising. "Me? Who made the suggestion to go outside?"

"I wouldn't have suggested it if *you* hadn't brought the commandoes to my attention!"

Attila beamed down at Napoleon and Wellington. "Modest, aren't they?" he asked of the growing crowd.

"And the dissidents?" another person asked.

Attila roared a laugh. "The Undertaker's going to be busy tonight!" Evident through the bay window, various decomposing lumps flared brightly, smoldered, and were gone. He turned to the crowd. "You'd all have been eating bullets by now if I hadn't been warned!" He warmed to his theme.

"It was one of the best damned fights I've been in for weeks! We mounted up—"

"Wellington." Napoleon leaned over and lowered his voice to a whisper as Attila launched into his tale. "Shall we go?"

"Lead on. I'm right behind."

Napoleon turned to Marie and gestured with his head toward the door. "Ladies first. Let's get out of here before they miss us."

Napoleon stood at the front doors of the club and took a deep breath. He glanced at Marie, took her hand, and followed Wellington to the car.

Napoleon paused on his side of the car as Wellington unlocked the door for him and Marie. "Let's make it quick, Wellington. The sooner we're out of here, the better."

"Eh?" Wellington was halfway around the car.

"The Authorities."

Wellington lifted an eyebrow. "Like flies to honey."

His eyes narrowed, focusing behind Napoleon's right shoulder; then he smiled and waved.

"Who was that?" Napoleon asked across the car roof, helping Marie into the front seat.

"Oh, just Horatius. Been into his spirits from the looks of him. Napoleon? Are you all right?"

"Fine. Wonderful." Napoleon resisted the urge to turn around. *If I see another Roman before the night's out, I'll run amok.* He glanced at Wellington. *Tell him now, before things really get— No. Not in front of Marie. It'll have to keep.* He slid into the seat next to her and slammed the door.

"To Wimpy's?" Wellington asked, starting the car and backing out into the parking lot.

"It's either that or McBats."

"To Wimpy's." Wellington turned out of the driveway leading to the Club and set off down the street.

They had driven only halfway down the block when three cars packed tight with Authorities roared by them through the night.

Napoleon sighed. Whoever had Marie thought they had him: Dissidents, Authorities, Administration, Romans, it didn't matter. As soon as they made themselves known, he had a chance.

He turned to her. In the soft glow of the auto's console, her eyes shone. "Marie . . ."

She faced him, and found his expression both warm and somber. Tears came into her eyes.

"Marie, I would—I will—do anything for you."

She could not find the courage to tell him that she was just a Temp.

THERE ARE NO FIGHTER PILOTS DOWN IN HELL

Martin Caidin

A great fist smashed the airplane violently upward, wings askew, ramming Jake Corwin's upper teeth into his lower lip. Jake cursed through the bloody haze of crashing reversals of positive and negative g-forces pooling blood in his eyes and brain. No way could he control the Duke in this insane storm. He tried to keep the wings approximately level, to control his attitude and to hell with everything else. His positive thoughts vanished as a savage blow wrenched control from him and tumbled the machine in a crazy cartwheel. He felt a rib crack as his body pummeled the armrest. He ignored the pain. He was but an instant away from losing a wing, and only by the greenish glare of lightning reflecting from the soaring cloud mountains was he able to again level out and keep his speed down.

For the first time in his life Jake felt he'd met his match in this storm that was battering man and machine in such fury. He'd flown through monsoons and blizzards and sandstorms where everything from ice to howling dust had pumiced and trashed his airplane, and he'd never doubted coming out in one piece. But he'd never stumbled into anything like this killer cumulus, an unprecedented monster riding the heavens like a maniacal juggernaut. Jake had been flying all his life.

According to those who'd survived battles with him in the skies, he was as pragmatic as they came, no matter how extraordinary his skills and his wild *elan*. To Jake a storm was a storm was a storm. He'd plunged into the great battlements seventy thousand feet high, knowing you could never predict the gibbering nightmare that might await you, and after expected violence he'd been spit out of the storm in a final touch of contempt, his aircraft dead of all power and flung aside like some broken plastic toy. Jake was long familiar with cockpits stained from his own blood torn from eyeballs and capillaries, with his internal organs spasming from pain, with bones bending and sometimes breaking. Yet Jake would always laugh with the wonder and the fury of it all and he'd never failed to marvel of his intimacy with energies boiling upward from the planet to brush the edges of space.

Jake knew no pilot could ever *beat* a thunderstorm. You *survived* them. For more than fifty years Jake had been accepting the gauntlet. He'd been flying since he was twelve years old, when he stolen away in the wet morning grass of his father's Oklahoma farm strip. He'd climbed furtively into the cockpit of the Stearman and with loving care primed the engine and the moment the big radial engine caught he was taxiing, praying to the oil pressure gauge to move into the green before his father caught him. He'd barely made it and he turned at the end of the grass strip and poured the coal to 450 horses and with his boyish hands white-knuckled on the controls he sailed into the skies.

By the time Pearl Harbor entered the national lexicon Jake's father had both tanned his hide and taught him to *really* fly. The Japs had barely begun their Pacific rampage when Jake, just turned eighteen, signed up. Not many aspiring flight cadets had 3,000 hours in their logbook. Jake Corwin, Oklahoma farm boy with the wide grin and the straw-colored hair, quickly became an officer and a pilot, a by-God real-enough *fighter* pilot. And like his peers, none of whom could touch

Jake's mastery at the controls, he learned to drink and to wench and to sing bawdy songs. His favorite quickly became the raucous "There Are No Fighter Pilots Down In Hell." Jake agreed with the punster who'd written the lyrics—

> There are no fighter pilots down in Hell,
> There are no fighter pilots down in Hell.
> The place is full of queers.
> Navigators, bombardiers,
> But there are no fighter pilots down in Hell.

Besides, Jake was the best damn fighter pilot in the world. That was *always* a truism. All fighter pilots knew this to be so about themselves. If they didn't believe it, if they didn't *know* it, then they weren't fighter pilots. Jake liked that. He liked the utter and absolute honesty of being the best fighter pilot there ever was. You could only lie about what you were *on the ground*. Sure as God made little green apples you couldn't lie to your airplane because it would kill you. And you couldn't lie to your enemies because *they* would kill you.

So the true honest-to-God fighter pilot is a man with an unblemished soul. When he's in the skies he is purity to the absolute. Jake loved it. No quarter given; none asked. He served his country by killing the enemies of his people and no man can do better than *that*. And if ever a man was dedicated purely to sustaining the honor of his profession it was Jake Corwin. He fought for what was right and he never harbored hatred or animosity for his enemies because Jake *never had any enemies*. They were opponents with the same killing implements as Jake carried into battle. That made every fight a fair fight. Jake Corwin absolutely reeked with honor.

Jake went through air combat in the second world war like a runaway bulldozer through wheat, both utterly methodical and as free-spirited as any nymph of the skies. Every time he took off he willingly put his ass on the line. He also put a lot of German and Italian asses under six feet of sod, and after he'd racked up thirty kills in Europe he went off to the far Pacific to teach the Japanese about God, Mom and Apple Pie. By war's end Jake didn't really know how many planes he'd shot down. True to his purity of self as a fighter pilot he didn't care about the scoreboard. His fellow pilots allowed as there was no way he had less than sixty or seventy kills in the air.

A few years passed and Evil Communism flared about the globe, and Jake got twelve more confirmed in the Korean potboiler. He loved his Sabre sweptwing jet fighter, with which he chewed the agile MiG-15's to metallic ribbons. With Korea behind him the Air Force gave him a false identity and loaned him to the Israelis for their 1956 clash with the Arabs. He flew French Mirage fighters with the Star of David and he slashed his way brutally through the best Russia could build, flown by less-than-adept Arab pilots. Add nineteen more to the scoreboard.

Jake flew a few more potboiler wars in Africa. By his standards of honor and purity it was strictly garbage time. But at least he was back in the locomotives he had flown before—the heavy P-47 Thunderbolts from World War II, still as rugged a machine as anyone ever built. Smarter than ever now about survival, Jake surrounded himself with a crackerjack ground crew and his engine always ran sweet and his guns never jammed and he had eager rookies always watching his ass for a bounce out of the sun, and by the time he returned to the States he'd racked up another fifty kills or so. He had thirty or forty more kills than the redoubtable Baron Manfred von Richthofen in his blazing red Fokker Triplane from the first world war. Jake told adoring newsmen on his return to the Good Old U.S.A. who insisted on comparing his style to that of the Bloody Baron that the only reason Richthofen ever got eighty-two kills was because he'd never met up with Jake Corwin in the air. Everyone except the Germans agreed with Corwin, who was by now a legend in his own time.

The Germans didn't agree, but they'd lost two world wars in a row and no one gave a shit about what *they* thought.

Finally there was Vietnam and Jake was back in the Big Iron, with afterburners and machmeters and Vulcan cannon and missiles, but it was still guts and glory and skill that made the difference and he went on tiger hunts and scratched eight MiG-21 supersonic fighters from the fetid air of Asia.

They never shot down Jake Corwin. But they'd shot him up a dozen times or more. He'd been punched and slashed with bullets and pieces of cannon shells and rockets and he'd been burned with hot oil and hydraulic fluid. His body was a scarred mess. But heroes don't care and Jake Corwin was a Hero.

Then the years ground down on him and Jake hung up his uniform. What he loved most was flying and he stayed with it. They made a wonderful movie about his life, and even if Jake knew it was really a Reader's Digest stinker he made a bundle of money from it, so he bought himself a pressurized Beech Duke and modified it with huge turboprop engines and long-range wings and he went off to look at the world he'd saved for honor and purity. His soul was unblemished. He was 63 years old and maybe 20 years from finally hanging up his flying gloves and tattered silk scarf.

None of this, of course, occupied his thoughts as he swept into the mighty storm high over the Pacific Ocean on his leg from San Francisco to Hawaii, en route to Australia. Jake allowed to himself that he might not make Australia, or Hawaii, or even back to San Fran. But with that thought of impending doom went the typical Corwin gratitude that he was alone and no one else would share this final flight.

He survived the most violent winds, hail, and rain he had ever known and believed the worst of the storm behind him. *Then* the lightning bolt came out of the heavens, a mile wide and in seeming slow motion, a gushing flood of naked electrons hissing and blinding and he knew nothing made by mortal man could withstand that fury. He braced for the sledgehammer blow even as he marveled at how slowly the lightning fell out of the sky, and then the bolt was there with him. It didn't strike the Duke; it enveloped man and machine with pure atomic fire, and even as Jake was blinded by the electrical maelstrom he finally *heard* the explosion and he spun off into blackness.

Instinct kept his hands locked to the controls. Explosion or not, he was damned well going to keep flying to the last instant, his last breath, and he forced open his eyes into an appalling redness all about him, a sky of ugly red stink and filthy clouds and he was drenched in sweat and his instruments were mad, his mag compass cracked wide open and spraying out alcohol, his gyros screaming and useless but to hell with it, he was flying by instinct and that meant he still had control, and as he talked and shouted to himself he righted the Duke along that ugly red horizon. One part of his brain told him that he was dead or mad or he was sane and the world about him was mad because there was no more row of giant thunderstorms and it wasn't raining and there wasn't any ocean. He looked down beneath the red sky, staring at ash-laden mountains with glowing lava gouging their slopes, and smoke blanketing the upper ridges. Below him, much closer, were dense forests mixed with naked escarpments and a hellish scene of tens of thousands of tiny figures, men caught in the teeth of a withering artillery barrage, being ripped to pieces. Jake winced with the savage pinpoint glare of bursting shells and the familiar outward-rushing concentric rings of blast pressure. He dropped lower and his body tightened as he saw the winged shapes slicing out of that awful red sky and tearing at men, the great wings flapping—

Flapping? He dove earthward in the shaking, vibrating Duke; he paid his own near-disaster no attention, his eyes locked on a winged shape expanding swiftly as he closed and he made out the leathery shape and barbed

tail and great outstretched talons and his finger by
instinct caressed the gun tit that wasn't there. Yet Jake
flung the Duke in a mad rush at the shape before him.
The best fighter pilot in the world had a final look at
rows of huge spikelike teeth and blazing red eyes and
then he collided with the dragon or whatever the hell it
was and blood burst from his nose with the impact. He
fought for renewed control as the Duke fell. He barely
got the wings level as an open field loomed before him
and he chopped power, dropped full flaps, slammed the
props forward, decided to leave the gear up and he
killed the switches and bashed into the ground. The
Duke slewed wildly and went into a wide slow turn as
pieces tore away and the ship caromed to destruction.
It stopped in a geyser of ashes and red dust. Flames
licked upward from both engines and Jake threw off his
harness, found his exit blocked by a jammed door, turned
and slammed both feet into the escape window. It broke
free and he went out through flames that singed his face
as he tumbled away from the mushrooming blaze. He
came up running, counted to ten, threw himself flat,
heard the explosion and the WHOOMP! of air passing
over his body.

He climbed slowly to his feet, taking one thought at a
time as he stared at the roiling red sky and ashes about
him. The battle over which he'd flown was far off in the
distance, but he saw a few of the ugly red shapes in the
distance, flapping leisurely and he knew the flailing
stick figures in their teeth were human beings.

He started walking to the nearest hill. Now that he
had a better grip on his thoughts, what he saw about
him—except for those leathery flying things—wasn't
much different from what he'd experienced before. He'd
been on Okinawa during one of the more violent battles
and *that* sky was roiling red and the world full of ashes
and tens of thousands of men were being torn to pieces.
Jake remembered tearing up German armored columns
in France and how smoke and dust hid most of the
world, and at sunset the sky was savage red. Well, now,

that made him feel better. Things were pretty close to a
wartime normal, anyway. He looked more carefully about
him. The ground showed signs of grass and brush but
they were red or blue; so what? He'd seen blue, brown,
grey, black, red, and white plants in many a botanical
garden. Anyway, Jake was going for the high ground.
Always go for the high ground. Get the best look around.
He glanced up as the air sweetened with thickening
growth about him and he breathed deeply and almost
at the same moment he saw the beautiful alabaster skin—
and supple fingers slid between his moving legs and
upward along his thigh to gently clasp his balls.

Jake stopped dead in his tracks. He was very fond of
his balls but the sudden whole-body rigidity wasn't of
his own doing. *He couldn't move.* Except for his eyes. He
fought to move just his head but couldn't. Neither could
he speak. He saw just enough before him and down to
know a stunning naked female body was doing things to
his body. Jet black hair, impossibly red lips, full upthrusting breasts, fiery red pubic hair, and those slender fingers now unzipping his khaki flight suit—

Khaki flight suit? It couldn't be! He was wearing jeans
and boots and a leather shirt and—he hadn't worn a
khaki flight suit since 1945 when he flew a P-38 against
the Japanese! But he was wearing it *now*, and he felt
the zipper tab moving upward from his crotch and that
silken hand reaching inside. Then he moved in a sudden
release from complete rigidity. He could move, but he
didn't dare. Not with those long nails gripping his nuts,
he didn't. This thing was crazy. . . . He lifted his left
hand to look at his watch. G.I. issue, dulled from the
Pacific sun and salt, his wrist and arm hard and mus-
cled and the skin smooth— He stopped himself short.
What had happened to that deep scar he'd gotten from
a MiG cannon shell in Korea? The skin was unblemished. He felt incredibly light, powerful, and he *knew*,
somehow, that he wasn't Jake Corwin, 63-year-old retired colonel, but Jake Corwin, Captain, USAAF, *and he*

was 22 years old. Physically, but not mentally. Between the ears he was still heir to all his experience and savvy.

Don't think. Go with your instincts, Corwin, or you'll go mad. The cool inner voice had always done him well before and now he followed instinct and balled his right hand into a fist and he smashed a straight right against the forehead of the beautiful naked girl with her gleaming, shining, bright red lips poised at his crotch. Her head twisted violently and he howled as her nails raked his scrotum as the force of his blow hurled her away and aside. As she half-fell he kicked her mightily with a G.I. boot in the stomach and heard air smash out of her lungs as she tumbled ass-end over teakettle, breasts wildly askew as she thumped against the ground.

She lay in a crumpled heap, then lifted her head and showed a dazzling smile with pearly teeth and spoke in a voice of crystal music. "That's no way to greet the Welcome Woman," she told him, pouting coyly as she spoke.

Jake ran forward, aimed again at her stomach with that boot and even as his foot went toward her she shimmered and her voice became a strangled croak. Jake spun awkwardly, staring down at a scab-encrusted filthy creature with pendulous breasts and scraggly pubis with something *writhing* in it and a mouthful of broken yellow and black teeth. Flies buzzed about open lip sores and cockroaches fed at huge boils along her body.

He knew now he *was* crazy, this was all a nightmare, but he felt the blood trickling from his scrotum where her nails raked him when he'd clobbered her. He knew, somehow he just *knew*, he'd done the only right thing . . .

She cackled and pointed a bony finger from the shimmering form, and he snarled and got ready to kick in her head this time when the ugly face went flaccid and dissolved to a putrid slime and the rest of her dissolved into bubbling mud and then only fetid smoke remained.

Jake Corwin said, "Je-suz Khee-rihst," and gingerly closed his crotch zipper.

"Please," a deep voice answered, "not down *here*, if you don't mind." Jake spun around with the .45 Colt leaping from its holster into his hand and his thumb snapping back the hammer. He held the piece dead-on to a German officer in a starched uniform, wearing a monocle, who raised an impeccable gloved hand and gestured with his riding crop. "No need for *that*, old fellow. I'm on *your* side."

The .45 held steady. "Who the hell *are* you?"

The portly German smiled, his lips wide and glistening, every inch of him a perfectly manicured dandy. He wore a diamond-studded iron cross about his neck, his boots gleamed, his riding breeches—

"Holy shit," Jake breathed. "Its Fat Herman. But you're dead!"

"I hope you'll find a better name than that," Herman Goering sniffed. "After all, I am, I *was*, Reichsmarshall of the Luftwaffe; the man who was head of all German fighting forces in the air is deserving of more respect, wouldn't you say?"

"But you're *dead*. You've been dead forty years!"

"True," admitted Goering. "But then, so is everybody else down here. Except his Satanic Highness, of course, and *he's* immortal." Goering laughed. "But there are times when even he wishes he wasn't!"

"That means I'm dead, or crazy, or both," Jake said slowly. "Or none of the above. I don't know. But I know you're dead, since you poisoned yourself after the Munich war crimes trials when the war ended."

"Suicide is preferrable to a hangman's knot, my smartass young friend. Or so I thought then."

"If I'm in hell I must be dead," Jake repeated.

"Most assuredly," Goering said with a flowery gesture, inhaling a white powder that appeared magically on his gloved wrist. "You're dead!"

"Then ... if I'm dead, how can I *hurt*?" Jake winced as he thought of those long nails furrowing about his scrotum. *My poor gonads.*

"You don't stop feeling pain in *hell*, old chap. In fact,

it gets worse. The pain is unremitting, deeper, more savage, burning, searing—" He sucked in air as beads of perspiration sprang to his upper lip and he flushed with excitement.

"Shut up," Jake said. "You're a crock, Fat Man. It doesn't hurt any more."

Goering flapped a wrist at him. "Oh, you're just saying that to upset me."

"That broad nailed me in the nuts. The pain was wild. But it doesn't hurt any more." Jake repeated.

"If you say so," Goering lisped.

"Who, or *what*, was she, anyway?"

"The Welcome Woman, of course. The harlot supreme."

"She said that also. But who is the Welcome Woman?"

Goering smiled. "An offshoot of a quaint American custom. The Welcome Wagon. She greets all newcomers with very personal attention." Goering opened a vial, inhaled deeply, rocked on his feet and smiled hugely at Corwin. "You know, you really are a remarkable specimen."

"Answer the question!"

"Oh, I am, *I am*. You don't understand. I'm not being personal. Not *that* way." A wrist floated by and hung limply. "How you managed to resist her, I mean. She is always the most alluring female that ever existed. Until you're well underway . . . then her real self starts oozing out. We all see her differently, you know, you sweet thing, you. *And*, if you'd zockoed her in the canyon like she wanted, right now you'd have a half-dozen diseases and only a trip to the Undertaker could cure you." His eyes widened. "But you didn't! You're *clean!* Clean and lovely in your very first body, with the essence of the upperworld still fresh on you. Oh, my!" Goering drooled onto his immaculate tunic.

"Why doesn't it hurt any more?" Jake pressed.

"Oh, I know you're a brave soldier, and your mother must be proud of you," Goering snickered, "but really, Kapitan Corwin, we both know better, don't we?" He winked at Jake. "Once she gets her nails in you, *that's it*.

You'll hurt, um, down *there*, forever. For eternity."
Goering licked away the drool. "But *I* could make it
better for you. It's a wonder what a kiss will do. In the
right place, of course."

Jake turned his back to Goering, unzipped his flight
suit, reached down and gingerly hoisted a handful of
testicles. *No blood, no nail marks, no pain.* A wild idea
began sprouting in his head.

"I say, old man, you're frightfully selfish, you know,"
he heard Goering whimper behind him. "Are you whack-
ing off all by your lonesome?"

Jake tucked everything in and turned back, a thin
smile on his face. "No, just checking."

The wrist pinioned a loose hand at Corwin. "I know
just how you must feel. Our little lady is *very* bad. You'll
have to live with it just as long as you're dead, you
splendid thing, you. You really should have me kiss it,
you know. It will never be better until you die again."

"Yeah, yeah, I know," Jake said, becoming swiftly
tired of Germany's Fart Factory. "We said the same
thing when we were kids. A bottle of pus and a scab
sandwich, please."

"Oh, that's mahvelous!"

"What the hell happened to your British accent?"

"Boston will do for the moment."

Corwin sighed. He knew he must bring things to a
boil. He winced with his own rotten choice of words.
But he was falling in all too quickly with this madness.
He needed to *think*. Could he really be in Hell? He
didn't need to be hit over the head with a hammer to
see the truth. After all, he'd only been struck by the
biggest lightning bolt in history, whipped through time,
rejuvenated in his younger body, had all his clothes
switched, survived that blast of lightning, and then survived a midair collision with a dragon, for God's sake,
and here he was talking with the solidified ghost of
Herman Goering, supreme commander of Germany's
air force for Adolf Hitler!

"Is Hitler down here?" he asked Goering.

Fatso Herman raised his eyes for a moment. "He's not up *there*. Of course he's down here, that paper-hanging bitch. You wouldn't recognize him though." The Reichsmarshall shuddered delicately.

Corwin ignored the flesh mountain before him. That bolt of lightning. He'd been dragged down through—through *what*? A time vortex? Spacewarp? Twist in time's fabric? *Where* the hell was Hell? Jake was about as good an amateur astrophysicist as they came, and next to flying his most intense occupation had been the study of relativistic physics. But nothing had even remotely prepared him for *this*. He'd been transported here, and that explanation must suffice for now. But that savage battlefield over which he'd flown, and banging into that dragon, and then that Welcome Wagon broad, and Goering—

"Herman, tell me something."

"Anything, sweetie."

"You said I'd never heal."

Of a sudden Goering blurred; now the fat bastard even *looked* British. "Ah, but you were lucky, sir! You resisted her wiles. You did not dip the wick, wash the willow, gallop the—"

"How come I resisted her?"

Goering's mouth froze in a thick-lipped O. "That's *right*. You *did*. Why, I don't know, old bean. In fact, I've never known anyone to do that before."

"Which makes me wonder if I'm dead. And if I am, what am I doing down *here*?"

"Oh, *that*. Nobody really expects to be down here. Except perhaps Hemingway, and that pig, Mussolini—"

"But I *didn't die*."

"You really don't remember your final moments?"

"No, because I didn't have any."

"You're *such* a stubborn little boy!"

"You make me want to throw up."

"I'll lick it from your boots, dear fellow," Goering said happily.

Jake ignored the blissful anticipation. "You showed

up here just after I crashed, as if you were expecting me, right?"

"Of course."

"How'd you know that I'd be here? And how'd you know where to find me?"

"Silly. It was posted on the squadron bulletin board, of course. I was recovery officer today; I get only the special cases, you know, and we simply checked your spacetime coordinates." Goering laughed wetly. "We didn't expect you to have a midair with Lothar."

"That the dragon? A *real* dragon?"

Goering sprayed perfume down his trousers. "Just in case there's an unexpected liaison," he simpered. "Why, of course Lothar was real. As sure as His Satanic Holiness made little red apples, that wasn't a Stuka, you know."

"I killed it?"

"Deader than Hitler's wickstick. And *that's* dead."

"How can something in Hell die?"

"Oh, you die here again and again, you know. Lothar disappointed the Master. He'll be recreated as a legless cat whose private parts will be eaten by rats every day of its miserable existence to come."

"Why, damnit!"

"Satan is a rotten loser."

"How could he have lost anything? It was an accident!"

"Well—"

Jake stared. "You son of a bitch!"

"You couldn't have known my mother, pumpkin."

"I was *supposed* to hit that thing?"

"You were supposed to *lose* the fight."

"There wasn't any fight."

"That's what pissed off His Majesty. Lothar wimped out."

Corwin had enough. He could keep asking questions for years and there'd be years of questions in waiting. He had a hunch that was a real part of Hell. So he went straight to the point. "How do we get back to your field?"

Goering motioned for Jake to follow as he started over the hill. "Tante Ju."

"Tante what?"

Goering pointed down the other side of the hill. "There." Corwin gaped at the three-engined corrugated bomber on the grass field below them.

"How the hell did *that* get here?"

"The same way as everything else. Corporeal read-justment, I suspect." Goering pushed out a petulant lip. "I'm a technical man. A pilot. A leader of men! I'm not an answer machine. His Ultimate Personality keeps me here to maintain his fleet of combat machines. We've got fighters and bombers here from some very good wars, you know."

They arrived at the bomber. "Why?" Corwin asked.

"There *are* dissidents, you know. Right now it's that filthy Cuban upstart, Che Gaucamole or whatever his stupid name is. He simply won't take his medicine. The dear, stubborn fool. He's got a hot revolution under way. Lucifer is determined to end it very soon, I'll tell you *that*."

Corwin shrugged. They climbed aboard the ancient machine. Two Russians and an orangutan in a Brazil-ian Air Force uniform made up their crew. Jake ignored them. He'd concluded that was the secret to sanity down here. Massive ignoring. Goering fired up the engines and took off from their parking spot. It was a short flight and soon they circled a huge grass meadow filled with airplanes of many wars and times. Jake stared and pointed. "Over there! All those fighters? How come they're not flying? I saw all those bombers taking off."

"No one flies the fighters, Jake, love!"

"Why?" He had come to hate the damned word.

"You of all people should know *that*! Because there are no fighter pilots down in Hell!"

"*You* were a fighter pilot in the first world war!" Jake shouted back.

"Suicide cancels out all benefits, m'lad!"

They slid to a smooth landing. A jeep raced under the

nose and skidded beneath the right engine. Jake stared
in horror as the huge propeller sliced up the two men in
the front seat of the jeep, splitting their skulls, chests,
cutting downward through their torsos and hurling skin,
brains, bones and intestines back along the cockpit and
fuselage of the Ju-52. Goering slammed on the brakes
and skidded to a halt. He killed the engines and silence
returned.

"I do wish those idiots would be more careful," he
whined. "We waste so much time cleaning up the gore
and brains."

"This happenes, uh, often?" Jake asked.

"All the time! Every time we land," Goering laughed.

"Hell of a way to die," Jake muttered.

"Of course, you buttercup. This *is* Hell, remember?"

I must be in an old movie rerun, Jake Corwin told
himself. *Somehow I got flattened in spacetime and I'm
alive on a celluloid reel.* He leaned back in the comfortable cushioned old swivel chair in Hades Base Ops,
sipped a shot of Jamaican Pimento Liqueur and inhaled
deeply of the marvelous Cuban cigar he brought to his
lips. Nah; he didn't really believe that. Too much here
was happening on a sustained basis, and deep down
you knew when you could bust out of a dream. He'd
been doing some very heavy thinking, and a lot more
concluding, and to his amazement he was starting to
like what was emerging from his self study.

First, you couldn't get cigars like these— the perfect
Uppman—anywhere in the U.S. in 1986. They were
strictly the Havana-Moscow connection, and he sur-
mised wryly that those two places had a lot of one-way
traffic down here. Second, he'd examined his body in as
much detail as he could. He was damned well only 22
years old, physiologically, at least. He didn't have a
single dental filling in his mouth and his vision had
returned to that marvelous 20-10 that gave him such a
one-up position against his adversaries. His muscles
rippled, he felt terrific, and he was as horny as a three-

legged goat on a slippery mountainside. He had good reason to temper his feelings: the Welcome Woman could have nailed him forever. She could become any one female, he reckoned, which made the Officers Club on the base safe enough with its three female bartenders. But every time one of those busty, panting beauties managed to raise his interest and a few other things, she vanished. Snap of the fingers and the broad was *gone*. He figured The Boss was behind that. Trying to rattle his cage. Let the horned bastard keep right on trying. Jake had made up his mind he wasn't falling into that trap.

Third: I should never have gone to Hell. It was that simple. He refused to complicate the conclusion. *I'm not dead and that's that. Either someone fucked up and kicked me here by mistake or I'm here for a reason I don't yet understand. And it looks more and more like there's a very specific reason.* That conclusion was reached in several ways. Whatever powers brought him here had transmuted his body back to the best physical shape he'd ever had. His best fighting trim. His 1945 body. He'd been uncomfortable about that until he discovered Napoleon here in his prime. Patton roared through the field perimeter in a tank convoy, standing out of the lead Sherman and bellowing orders like a madman. Even his damned dog was with him. Jake had recognized so many historical figures, each in their prime age, that he accepted the situation as one of the prime moving forces of Hell. He'd even come to accept *that*.

Goering was a sore thumb stuck in the eye of his rationale, but he figured, what the hell, the fat reichsmarshall had his own cross to bear. *Oops; got to watch that*, Jake chided himself gently. But it was true. One moment he saw Goering in *his* best shape, as the fighter pilot in World War One who'd taken over Richthofen's command when the Baron got zapped. Then he seemed to shimmer and when the eye-stabbing blurs were gone Jake would be staring at a grossly corpulent, diseased, half-crippled obscenity. *That* was the Goering Jake remembered best from history.

The same Goering who'd killed himself with a poison capsule after the Nuremburg war crimes trials. That whole situation had been a bit tougher to dissect and understand. But the truth was becoming more and more evident. Of all the military figures down in Hell, Fat Goering was the *only* fighter pilot. Other than Jake, of course. And Goering had been emphatic over that statement that there were no fighter pilots down in Hell. *He* was here because of his own transgression. Goering had commited suicide, a crime of such enormous insult to the only true gift of life—free will—that in his own words, "That cancels out all benefits," and by that Jake judged the benefits cancelled meant the way upstairs was now closed to Fat Herman forever.

Well, to Hell with Goering and his problems and, for that matter, with anyone else already here. For whatever reasons they were supposed to be here. They made up the nifty balance of souls between Here and There, or Whatever. They all had one thing in common and that excluded Jake.

They were *dead*.

Jake wasn't. Dead, that is. He didn't know how he knew it, but he *knew*. His conviction gave him tremendous strength, and as long as he remained unshaken in his faith about himself not even Satan could rattle his cage. There were some strange rules down here, but understanding them would come soon enough.

So Jake sipped pimento liqueur and luxuriated in pure Havana leaf.

Besides, things were getting interesting here. *He had a mission.* Not some nonsensical crap between the ears, but a *real* mission. In a fighter! Everyone else knew about it before he did. No one had told him to check the bulletin board outside Base Ops, but the orders were there, charred into parchment stolen right from the Vatican. Captain Jake Corwin, USAAF, was to intercept an enemy fighter over the confluence of the Ghoul and

Misery Rivers. Two P.M. that same afternoon. Jake didn't like the posted orders. Too much was missing. He went in search of Fat Herman.

Goering was coming through the door of the Ladies Room in Base Ops. He looked like Mae West at the height of her worst, in a grease-stained silk dress that had barely survived a circus fire. Heavy rouge and smeared lipstick didn't help, even if Goering aped Dustin Hoffman at his best as he staggered on spike heels. Goering had topped it off with huge falsies, a moth-eaten fur boa and a huge feathered hat. He waved a bejeweled and fingernail-polished hand at Jake.

"Yoo hoo! *There* you are, you sweet boy. You've seen your orders? Aren't they *wonderful?*" Jake reeled from a blast of ghastly perfume, toilet water, underarm deodorant and aftershave lotion, all of which somehow served only to emphasize the real smell of Fat Herman.

"What kind of crap are those orders?" Jake threw back. "There's no altitude for the intercept."

"His Satanic Worship is sometimes less than efficient," Goering admitted. "So busy, you know, darling. But—"

"That's a crock of shit. *He* knows it and you know it." Jake enjoyed his first touch of long-distance devil's tail-tweaking. And sure enough, he grinned to himself, *someone* far off was listening. An angry breeze danced outside Base Ops. Glowing coals drifted through the door. Corwin looked at the door and held up his right hand, middle finger extended stiffly. The ground trembled. Goering turned visibly pale even beneath all the guck on his face. He swayed.

"Don't do that," he said in a strangled whisper. "We'll pay for it a thousand years!"

A siren howled before Jake answered. Goering sighed with relief. "It's time," he told Jake.

Thank God, Jake said to himself, and learned that even such thoughts could brighten the glowing coals piled against the doorway. Jake didn't care. Oh, that marvelous spring in his step! That terrific catlike agility and coordination! He knew he was heading for one hell of a fight and he was absolutely in his own private heaven. With the thought the ground split slightly to spew smoke from the piddling crevice.

They turned the corner of the ops building. Jake stopped, staring. *Everything had changed.* Every plane but one on the flight line had vanished. No bombers anywhere. One fighter.

"Isn't she beautiful," Goering gushed.

Jake stared at a battered, holed, paint-peeling, deep-bellied Republic P-47N Thunderbolt from the second world war. The famed, massive, rugged Thunderbolt. He'd flown these in the Pacific. The single-engined monster with better than 2,300 horsepower. It was huge and impossibly heavy compared to other fighters, but it was also a magnificent machine. Something nagged at Jake. He looked beyond the Thunderbolt, across the grassy field, and found what he suspected might be there.

The other fighter. Barely visible a mile away in tall grass. Jake pointed. "What is it?"

Goering's sad attempt at nymphing vanished as some steel from yesteryear stiffened his backbone. "One of *our* finest. Focke-Wulf 190."

"What model?" Jake's questions were crisp and hard.

"Why, E Fourteen."

Jake ran through the data in his head. The FW-190E14 was a special model with multiple-stage engine blowers. Fat-bladed prop for better climb and turning. He remembered now. Made to counter American escort fighters protecting the bomber streams over Germany. A specialized machine for dogfighting. Jake *knew* it was pristine just as much as the Thunderbolt—the venerable Jug, as its pilots called it—was weary.

"There's no intercept, is there, Fat Man." It was more statement than question.

Goering paled, shifted uncomfortably. He scuffed a diamond-encrusted toe in the ash. "Well—"

"You mean Satan *cheats*?" A volcano erupted miles away.

"Don't even *think* that," Goering gasped. "His Majesty doesn't—"

"The fact that he *thinks* he has to cheat ... why, the old bastard is afraid of a fair fight!" Jake said with glee. It had all become clear now.

Goering had dropped to one silk-stockinged knee. "Please," he whimpered.

"He's afraid of *losing*," Jake said with a surge of understanding as certain floodgates in his mind were released. *"He's afraid of losing!"* he shouted at the top of his lungs.

The blood-red sun barely visible through the roiling red clouds darkened. Leathery birds fell in droves above the field. Ash swirled, the air rumbled, demons howled.

"Cut the shit!" Jake yelled. Instantly everything was as before. He knew now why he was here. This was a setup, *a jousting match*. And it had been laid out from Above.

The song! Of course; *the song!*

There are no fighter pilots down in hell ... Queers, navigators, and bombardiers up the ass, but no fighter pilots. Except for one Jake Corwin. *Watch it, he warned himself. This may be a jousting match but its for real. He beats you in a dogfight and this is where you end up, Jake, old buddy.*

Jake grabbed the ratty boa about Goering's powdered neck, wound it twice around his throat and yanked. Arms flailing, purse spilling hologrammed porno on the ashy ground, Goering stumbled and tripped along behind Corwin. Jake jerked him up tight before the Thunderbolt.

"Let's get things straight," Jake said, very cool, all professional now. "No intercept, right?"

"*Guk*," Goering said, the boa digging into his throat and nodding furiously.

"It's the old one-on-one adversary rules, right?"

"*Glak*." Nod, nod.

"Directly over the field at three thousand feet, head-on one to the other, each breaks right, no holds barred from then on?"

"*Smork*." Goering flailed for breath and Jake released his grip. Fat Man was on his knees, falsies down to his belly, tears from choking running his mascara.

"Your lipstick is smeared," Jake spat. "Answer me, asshole. I want your Boss to acknowledge."

The voice sounded in his mind, absolutely clear, deep and powerful. "Acknowledged, Jake Corwin."

Jake didn't bother looking around. "Nice touch," he said in his own mind, already anticipating complete telepathic ability on the part of Lucifer.

"Thank you."

"Never mind the horseshit, mister—" Jake broke the thought. "What *do* I call you?"

"Your Worship, Your Eminence, anyone of those adoring phrases will do nicely."

"You're getting to sound like your trained pig, here," Jake thought with a laugh.

A vision of glowing horns and twitching barbed tail floated into his mind. "You're here for a fair fight, Jake."

"Okay," Jake mused telepathically. "So why don't we both knock off the horseshit and keep this on a professional level?"

"Are you stalling for time, Jake?"

"Listen, your Asshole Worship, this isn't a fair fight. You've rigged the odds."

He had a vision of a clawed hand held against a heartless heart. "*Me?*"

"You." Jake had been doing a lot of thinking. "We pick our own fighters, don't we?"

There was the briefest hesitation, a sulphurous sigh and a python-like acknowledgment. "Yesss."

"Then how come I get a wreck of an airplane?"

"You love the Thunderbolt, Jake. You got eleven kills in it."

"You're cute. You know that? Real cute," Jake sent. "Okay, I'll take the Jug."

"Good boy," the words came with an almost-visible smile.

"But not this pig."

"All right. I'll give you another one."

"*Hold it!* Not the N model. I want the M. You know, M for Mary, for Madonna, for—"

"Enough! All right, you have the right to select."

A brilliant glare gushed from the flight line. The battered old Thunderbolt shimmered, wavered in view, and then the glare vanished. No more junkpile. In its place was a gleaming P-47M model. Jake felt *much* better. He clamped down on his thoughts.

"Upstairs at three thousand in twenty minutes," he thought fiercely. "You come out of the north and I come up from the south."

"As you wish, Jake Corwin."

"No favors!" Jake snapped a mental whip. "Them's the one-on-one rules of all *real* fighter pilots."

Hot wind floated by. "All right," came the petulant touch in Jake's mind.

"One last thing."

"Yes?"

"I want your Satanic word."

"You're becoming quite impossible. What is it?"

"I haven't started yet," Jake told his distant adversary. "When we finish this nose-to-nose talk, you get the hell out of my mind *and you stay out*."

"I do not need to agree with *anything*, Corwin!"

"Yes, you do," Jake chortled, "because you agreed to all these terms before I ever got here, right?"

Lucifer ignored the barb. "Anything else?"

"A parting thought."

Jake had a mental image of huge teeth closing about his neck. He ignored it. It was replaced with a final query from the Top Office in Hell. "What is it, Corwin? You no longer amuse me."

"*Amuse* you?" Jake laughed. "I'm going to cream your ass, mister!" Before Satan could respond Jake closed it off. "Now, *get out!*"

Compared to what filled his mind an instant before, all was now mental cool waters. Jake had visions of

snow, icebergs, running brooks, tall cool drinks. This
was more like it. He yanked hard on the boa and
slammed Fatass Goering into the choking ash. That was
even more like it. He went to the gleaming P-47M and
nodded with self-satisfaction. M from N changed all the
odds of the dogfight. He started to do his walkaround of
the fighter, but changed his mind. Everything had to be
on a fair and equal keel. Everything with this machine
would be perfect. Again Jake had that strange feeling
that what he thought was *right*. A one-on-one dogfight,
if nothing else, had to go by the rules—or it wasn't the
jousting match any more.

The huge Pratt & Whitney engine ran honey-smooth,
belting out better than 2,300 horses, hauling the Thunderbolt skyward with ease. Jake took her to seven thousand feet, uncomfortably close to the glowering cloud
banks above what formed a solid deck to obscure the
sun, or whatever it was casting its hellish glow downward through the ashy cloudstuff. He ignored it. He was
here to fight, not muse over soiled meteorology. At seven
grand he inflated his g-suit to full pressure, cinched his
harness a last time and without further thought slammed
the stick hard over to the left as he shoved in hard full
rudder. A hellish red horizon whirled crazily but under
perfect control as Jake tested his own responses and felt
out the big machine. He whipped through a tight loop,
banged through a half-snap at the top and aileron-rolled
in a diving pursuit curve out of the high arc. The Thunderbolt responded like the thoroughbred she was.

Then Jake was ready. Almost time. He eased off the
throttle and dropped the nose, swinging in a wide turn
toward the southern perimeter of the field, where he'd
turn tightly and then come straight at Satan in the
Focke-Wulf.

*The old bastard was pretty smart. He nearly outfoxed me
with the P-47N. That* model had been designed for long-
range Pacific warfare. It weighed thousands of pounds
more than the standard Thunderbolt. It could fly four

hours, fight, and have enough fuel left to fly home another four hours. It would stay in the air so long it even had an autopilot so its human pilot could relax in long overwater missions.

It was also so heavy *it was a dead duck in a dogfight*. Weight meant your rate of climb was screwed up, your acceleration was lousy, and you couldn't turn to save your own ass. The N model was strictly to go the distance, come down like the lead sled it was to hit the enemy, and get out of there as fast as it could go. Not even Jake Corwin, against a really top pilot in the Focke-Wulf, had a decent chance in a one-on-one scrap.

But *this* baby, he grinned, was something else. They hadn't built many of the P-47M models, and few people knew the plane even existed. It was never built to dogfight. Compared to the standard Thunderbolt, the M was a greyhound. They were built to chase down and destroy the German V-1 pilotless jet bombs hurled against England in 1944 and 1945. They were stripped of armor plate, long-range tanks, two of their eight .50 caliber machine guns, and anything else not needed strictly for speed. What they ended up with was also a superb dogfighting machine, two *tons* lighter than the ordinary Jug. The M could hit 490 mph on the straightaway, and that was fifty mph better than the FW-190E14 could handle. And with all that weight gone, with water injection for bursts of speed, and a huge paddle-bladed prop, she was a real killer.

Jake set up his last turn. He wondered who would be flying the Focke-Wulf with the wide wings and powerful supercharger. It wouldn't be Lucifer. Not in mind and skill, anyway. Lucifer would adopt the body and mind of one of the greatest fighter pilots who'd ever lived. He could arrange that just for this battle. Again there was that eerie *knowing* that Jake felt, that this fact he'd just run through his mind was real.

Jake bet his life that he'd be up against one of the best from the first world war. Most likely it would be Oswald Boelcke, who whelped Manfred von Richthofen, who was the best fighter pilot over the Western Front until he was killed in a collision with one of his own students. Of course! That meant that Boelcke, supreme ace that he was, *had never been defeated.*

It also meant that he'd be thinking in terms of jousting in the old fabric machines of that war. And what was the one element of performance denied to all German fighter pilots when Boelcke died? *Speed.* They lacked speed. They whirled like dervishes, but they were agonizingly slow. Jake made up his mind. Satan-Boelcke would come at him balls to the wall, throttle jammed to the stop, propeller blades clawing at the air.

Which is just what Satan expected Jake to do. Maybe he wasn't such an asshole after all! Jake took a deep breath. Of course! The clever son of a bitch figured Jake wouldn't accept the battered old P-47N but would opt for a *faster* model. Which was why he was in the M and—

Knock off the shit, Jake told himself. He came out of his last turn, leveled the wings exactly at 3,000 feet, and went straight for the tiny dot he knew was the FW-190 coming at him from out of the north. And then Jake did a dumb thing. He eased off on the power and the big Thunderbolt began to slow in its rush at Jake's foe. Boelcke for a moment would have to consider *why* the two fighters didn't meet over almost airfield center. He'd known the P-47M was faster than the German ship, and *that* quickly he would understand what Jake had done.

But Jake would be ahead of Boelcke in that train of thought and as the two fighters loomed toward a head-on collision and each pilot broke to the right, Jake was already into a clawing turn to his left, standing on left rudder, the throttle slammed all the way in now for power for the turn, fuel injection hurling an extra four hundred horsepower to the prop; and Jake had both hands on the stick, pulling for all he was worth. The Thunderbolt shuddered on the thin edge of the power stall, trembling through every inch, and Jake himself

airplane was, that the Chirri was a fine machine for its day but was hopelessly outclassed by the Mosca.

And all you assholes are supposed to think exactly that. Including your Host.

His fighter wasn't a CR.32 Chirri. It *looked* almost exactly like the CR.32 but it was a CR.*42*. Outwardly there was hardly any difference. Beneath the engine cowl there were 275 more horses, and in a lightweight biplane fighter that meant *everything*. It improved the turning ability of the Chirri so much they were two different airplanes. The Mosca had four machine guns compared to the CR.42's two weapons. But like that concealing engine cowling looks and numbers were terribly deceiving. The Mosca's guns were 7.62-mm with a high rate of fire *but very short range*. The Chirri had two 12.7-mm machine guns with a slower rate of fire than those of the Russian fighter, but with nearly three times *the effective firing range*.

And there was another difference, completely concealed from view. The 42 model was structurally twice as strong as its predecessor, and that also would play a critical role in the battle to come. Jake took enough time to light a fresh Uppman and then hit the starter button.

Sweat rolled into Jake Corwin's eyes, trying to blind him with burning salt. He could hardly see his instrument panel, but it didn't matter that much. He wasn't flying by instruments, but by his ass, which he was coming perilously close to losing. He'd underestimated this Pyushkin son of a bitch. The Russian had been turned loose by Satan to fly, fight, and kill his adversary, and to Pushykin all he knew was that a familiar opponent was out there to be shot down. Vladimar Pyushkin had fourteen kills to his credit along the Manchurian border in fights with the Japanese, and he had seventeen more in Spain, and he was a brilliant flyer. A natural, a man at home in the skies, one of Russia's finest.

He had held off Jake Corwin from the moment they sped at one another, almost collided in their stubbornness to give way, and then each broke right. But Pyushkin didn't turn. Not right away. He hauled back on the stick, already at full power, and a thousand horses threw the Mosca into the deep red sky as if it were a rubber ball. Then he came over on his back. Now he had the high bounce position and he made the most of it, coming down in a slewing pursuit curve that let him pick and choose the first firing pass. He closed to pointblank range and threw a rainstorm of bullets at the Chirri. He didn't try for accuracy in the turn, but walked his rudder back and forth so that his hail of redhot lead *must* score some hits. He was amazed that he'd missed . . .

But he hadn't. Jake took a slug in his thigh on that first pass. The Russian had him nailed beautifully and the only way out was to jerk back on the stick, plunge through the Russian fire, and go for broke in a crazy tumbling maneuver that would take him straight up, kill all his speed, and force the Russian to race past at high speed so he must make a wide turn to come back. Jake jerked the stick back and to the right and stamped right rudder and then banged the stick hard over to the left. The Chirri went berserk and whirled crazily, then threw tail over propeller, bashing Jake about in the cockpit but gaining him a precious escape.

For the next twenty minutes they went at one another like two fencing masters. Each used the special advantages of his plane with superb skill. When the Russian got close Jake could only use all his experience and skill to ward off the fierce attacks of Pyushkin, dodging and twisting to keep bullets out of his back. Then they would change positions and separate. The Chirri lacked the speed to close on the Mosca, forcing Jake to use tricks he had never before used in combat. Now the twin 12.7-mm machine guns came into their own for him. Every time Pyushkin maneuvered to set up another attack, Jake was able to lead his path of flight and hose the Mosca with a deadly burst.

But it wasn't enough to gain him the final advantage. Pyushkin proved able to slip through the long-range bursts of fire with minimum damage, and when he closed in on the Chirri he again had the upper hand. Jake could almost hear Satanic laughter.

Finally he was up against it. He was almost out of fuel and the Mosca had much more time remaining in its tanks. If they kept up this head-to-head stalemate, *Satan must win.* Time was on his side. Soon the Chirri would run out of fuel, the engine would quit and even a high-speed glider was a clay pigeon against a powerful and maneuverable fighter with plenty of juice in its tanks. If he was going to come out of this one alive, Jake thought with quiet desperation, it was now or never.

He skidded beneath another firing pass of the Mosca, almost hearing the hail of bullets through and about the Chirri. Then Pyushkin was past him and Jake shot his wad. Full left rudder, stick over to the left, full power, then full forward on the stick into the start of a tumble, kick opposite rudder, reverse the stick and head straight down out of a whirling snap. The Chirri dove with everything it had. Immediately Pyushkin was on him like a hornet. To the Russian's surprise he couldn't catch up with the clumsy biplane fighter, and Pyushkin *knew* he should be able to outdive the CR.32.

Jake took the CR.42 down with everything it had. He had jumped the gun with his dervish maneuver and sudden dive; it took the Russian time to assess the situation and come after him. And biplane or not, the CR.42 could run away from the Mosca in an all-out power dive.

Pyushkin felt cheated (but only for a moment as Satan increased his control over the Russian's mind). *The other man was running from the battle!* How could he gain a decisive win this way? It was not possible. Far ahead of him the Chirri slowed suddenly, close to the ground, and Pyushkin saw it bounce on the grass airfield.

Of a sudden there was no more Pyushkin. Satan whipped his ass back to Limbo where he kept many a fighter pilot "on ice" for the day of reckoning when he'd banish that triple-damned song and bring all those hot jocks under his fiery fingernails. Now Satan was in the cockpit and on his own and enjoying the moment tremendously. He saw the Chirri fighter with that yellow shit Corwin at the controls rolling on the grass, wings rocking as Corwin fought a crosswind trying to upend his wings on one side. The Chirri bounced and swerved out of control, and Satan pounded the throttle to its stop, wind screaming past the vibrating Mosca. The Chirri appeared in his gunsight. Satan was playing this one strictly by the rulebook. Everything was fair and square. Not a stitch out of the Contract From Above was awry. And now he was going to cut Jake Corwin to pieces. That the American upstart was imprisoned in his helpless machine made it all the better.

Far below, Jake Corwin shot a glance over his left shoulder. There was the Mosca, trailing a thin line of black exhaust smoke as Satan closed in for the kill. *Just a little closer, Jake said aloud to himself, just a little closer, rhino-head . . .*

"*Now!*" Jake shouted to himself and he rammed the throttle forward, tromped on left rudder *and brake*, reversed his ailerons and popped the stick forward a notch. The Chirri bounded ahead, swerved wildly to the left on one wheel and as it spun around it lunged forward into the hot wind that always blew across the field. Jake kept up the turning motion to give Satan fits with his sighting. By now Jake had flying speed but it wasn't right, not yet. Almost, just a little more, just a little more, and he kept his eyes glued to the wings of the diving Mosca and then he saw the bright flashes of the machine guns in the wings and instantly Jake hauled back on the stick, the Chirri jumped into the air and bullets tore up the ground beneath in blazing spurts of ash, but the Chirri was gone, it was flying and the nose was coming up to point just ahead of the diving Mosca. Satan realized what was happening barely a second too late. He tried to turn but his speed was too great for a fast maneuver, and the Mosca was locked in the grip of aerodynamic forces and his howling dive, and even as it happened he knew Jake Corwin was taking his own sweet time, that he had the Mosca stuck on a giant spiderweb of speed and centrifugal force in the sky, and the heavy machine gun bullets reached out from the Chirri and smashed the engine of the Mosca and shattered the oil tank and split the fuel lines and continued upward to blow the head completely away from the body of Satan, horns and all.

Headband of pure crimson, flowing robes of burgundy, lips scarlet, his paps smeared with brilliant ochre, deep red rubies on seven of his fingers, Herman Goering, totally in love with the myths and sexual prowess of Lawrence of Arabia, swept into the outer office of Hell's skyscraper headquarters. Huge rats nibbled at the toes squishing from his sandals, and leeches dropped from the ceiling to suck on blood-gorged earlobes and neck. Goering paid them scant attention. In the near presence of the Angelic Host he was a blubbering mixture of obeisance and awed servant, scared out of his mind as to what displeasure might suddenly amuse his Satanic Majesty.

Lucifer, he knew, was in a rotten mood. Easy to tell from the rumblings of earthquakes and the activity quotient of the nearest volcanos, belching horrible fumes and gushing lava. Even the dragons moved warily through the highest of all lairs in Hell, for Lucifer in his anger was as quick to rend them wing from talon as he was head from torso of his human slaves. But not now.

Satan had an air-hammering headache, a skull splitting from hastily assembled parts and pieces by his chief morticians. Satan knew he might rue the day when he left himself vulnerable to human pain and dismemberment, but he'd never counted on a stream of fifty-caliber slugs tearing *his* head from *his* body, and having to suffer his own worst torment while they searched the area with a Geiger counter to find every last missing scrap. The ride home in that clattering bucket of a stupid hellicopter was no better. Nor was the landing at Angelic Helliport, where the clumsy oaf of a pilot set down with a scrotum-smashing impact. He made a mental note (corporeal, since his own mental capabilities were at that moment scattered across the airfield) to strip the wings from Icarus. Stupid Greek fool; he should have stuck to his wax and feathers. Satan swore to himself Icarus needed at least a thousand more plunges from high altitude to teach the Mediterranean idiot a lesson. And where the hell was Achilles, anyway? Satan made a note to make someone in Assignments very sorry that Hell's finest chopper pilot was somewhere in lower bumfuck just when he was required *here*.

He'd dispatched a Dragon Express to his airfield to have Goering bring Jake Corwin to him. He hated the thought. One look at that pubescent young American, his loins filled with unsoiled seminal juices bursting to be set free in pulsing gushers, would have Marilyn a-twitter for a week. Her spelling and typing would be shitty that whole time. But, Satan moaned through his still-knitting skull, he had given his word to Corwin for a face-to-face. And in this situation, with those On High watching every move, Satan was bound to honor his own promises, grimly false they might be to anyone else.

Goering-*cum*-Lawrence swept into Satan's private chambers with a blubbery flourish. "Sire!" he cried. "I am your humble and obedient servant, your awe-struck worshipper, your slave—"

"So what else is new, pisspot," Satan said with a grumble that terrified the mob waiting in the outer chambers for an appearance. "And who in Hell are you supposed to be *now*?"

Jake watched with amusement as Goering groveled. Lucifer flicked a finger and Goering was unable to speak. He drooled and sniveled and salivated but without words.

He stared, horrified, at the power behind the finger. Satan lost his feeling of pleasure as quickly as it came. He tapped a glowing hoof on the lava floor beneath his desk and lesser devils appeared at once. Satan pointed a bony finger at the drooling Goering-Lawrence. "We're low on soap. Melt him down again. *Slowly* this time."

They dragged Goering away, leaving behind only a trail of slime and excrement. Satan waited for the Charwoman to appear: Josef Stalin in a potato sack and a babushka with a bucket in one hand and an ash-spewing mop in the other. "Clean it up," Lucifer growled, and Jake watched Stalin, strangely eager, extend a blue tongue, drop to all fours, and lap up the trail of the fat Nazi. His sort were not usually let into this level of Hell even for Special Effects, and he didn't want to go back any sooner than he had to.

"Very impressive," Jake told Lucifer when they were alone. "You make and break the rules as you please, I see." Jake settled into a deeply cushioned easy chair. It was alive; *it was human*. It was also comfortable. "If they bother you, bang the left armrest," Satan said amiably. "It's equal to a sharp stick in the eye or a really good shot in the nuts."

"Thanks." Jake withdrew another Uppman cigar and held it in his teeth. Before he could light a match Satan flicked another finger and a small intense flame hovered in midair at the end of the cigar, lighting it without effort on Jake's part. "Neat," Jake said. "What's next? Parlor tricks? Yuri Geller time? You bend bodies, maybe?"

So much for spooking Corwin with Fates Worse Than, and one of his own more gruesome aspects. "Let's dispense with that," said Lucifer. "I have a ding-wally of a headache."

"I'll bet," Jake grinned. He gestured with the cigar. "You, ah, don't mind if I smoke, do you? Anti-smoking rules back home, you know. People are paranoid about smoking in public."

"I know. I helped pass those rules. More of them will

smoke in bed now, and my share of the loot goes up. No, I don't mind if you smoke. There aren't any rules against smoking here. In fact, there aren't any rules here. For example," Satan added with a smirk, "if *I* decide your cigar won't smoke, it just won't."

"Horsecock," Jake said, and blew a cloud of pure Havana into Lucifer's face. Despite himself the Devil breathed deeply and made sounds of pleasure. So did his Familiar, perched atop his shoulder. He materialized slowly, a savage little shit of fiery eyes and huge teeth, green warts and bedraggled ears. He breathed in the smoke from the Uppman and then shook himself in a spasm of delight so great he almost swooned. He lurched and fell to one side, his claws reaching out for support but instead slashing at Satan's ear and tearing away chunks of flesh.

Jake flicked a cigar ash expertly in a bank shot off the barbed tip of the Devil's tail lashing the air. "See?" he said. "It's all in knowing how to lead your target. Besides," he said as he returned to their original subject, "not even *you* can put out a fire in Hell."

"I said there are no rules here!" Satan thundered. The air vibrated like an enormous gong struck by an equally enormous hammer.

Corwin laughed. "Checkmate! You've *already* established the absolute rule: if there aren't any rules here, *that's the rule.* Lucifer, I know you're unbelievably powerful, but not even *you* can work magic. You may twist time and warp space and tie dimensions into knots, and I readily acknowledge all your powers, but you can't make something out of nothing. Not you, not God, not me, not nobody. And nobody can't exist or *we* wouldn't be here. So with all your majestic powers, even you work within the rules. Let's knock off all this crap and get down to cases, shall we?"

"You haven't done enough damage already?" Satan thrust back at him. "Do you realize how many people I've got working day and night now in my press relations office to maintain my image? Do you think I can endure tarnished horns and dulled hooves forever? Corwin, you don't realize what a workload it takes to keep up appearances."

Corwin inhaled deeply. "Do you have a cold beer handy? No buffalo piss, please."

"How about a hot toddy?"

Corwin nodded. Satan's tail described an intricate maneuver in midair and a tall drink materialized in its last coil. He held it before him, dipped a finger in the liquid to bring it to a boil. The tail stretched across to Corwin and he took the drink. "Let it rest a few moments, Corwin. It needs to breathe to get down to the right temperature. Now, let us get down to cases, as you say in your crude language."

"Shoot."

"Please. Find another phrase, if you don't mind." Satan winced from a stab of pain.

"I whupped your butt again today. What next?"

"You won fair and square. I didn't make up *those* rules." Satan flicked a thumb to indicate above him. "*They* did. By the by," he added suddenly, "what's your gimmick? How did you beat not just me, but Boelcke and Pyushkin?"

"Outflew them, I guess," Corwin said with a shrug.

"Actually, you got in their way. They were men of honor. You're not. Unless someone holds your feet to the cold, I suppose."

"What in Hell's name has honor to do with it!"

"Keeps the heart pure and the mind clear."

"Heavenly horseshit, my young friend. There's no such thing as honor, Jake. It doesn't exist."

"Of course it does. It's as real as you are."

Burning ashes materialized in the room and fell slowly to the floor. Steel sparks fizzed from Satan's eyes. The Familiar shuddered.

"Don't push, Jake."

"Up yours. *You're not real.* Not in my world, anyway. But you exist. Obviously. I suppose Hell lies in some temporal nowhere and that's the key to it. It's nowhere. Like getting to a place over the rainbow."

The Familiar grinned horribly at Jake's words and Satan's tail pirouetted. "A nice touch, that. Thank you, Jake."

"You're welcome. But all that's the same as honor. You can't be nowhere, unless you're not somewhere. Honor's the same thing."

Satan sighed. His tail flicked out to remove the ash from the Uppman cigar and he brought back the flat barb. His Familiar expertly whipped it into his mouth and chomped happily.

Jake had an idea. He drew deeply on the cigar to build another ash, then flicked the still-hot grey matter away from him.

Before it struck the lava under foot and hoove, the devilish creature hurtled from his Master's shoulder to snab the ash in midair. There was a *snap!* and a gulping sound and a sibilant hiss of pleasure. "Neat," Jake said with true admiration. "Diving pursuit curve, you led the target perfectly and you broke away and up like a true pro." The nasty thing smiled at him, a horrible grimace of shit-yellow fangs and garbagy breath.

"Get back to honor. You amuse me, Corwin."

"Okay," Corwin said amiably. "Honor keeps the planets in their orbits, the galaxies wheeling in harmony. Honor is what makes me me and you you. Without honor you'd be out of a job so fast this place would be an ice-skating rink by morning. Honor is the stuff from which dreams and nightmares are made."

"Very erudite," Satan murmured. "You sound like you came straight from the Catholic Church." He smirked. "Of course, *they're* my best customers. But back to you, friend Jake. You used many words. Now prove what you said about honor."

"That's the curse and the wonder of it, Luci, old buddy. It's not *my* job to prove honor. I'm just a li'l old fighter jock and you're the top man—sorry, top dog; damn, I really *am* sorry—the Supreme Commander here.

El Commandante, King Tut, you know what I mean, right? Well, being the All of Everything I guess the monkey's on your back. Jake glanced at the Familiar. "No offense," and turned back to his Host. "Being the Supreme Intelligence here, *you*, sir, *disprove* it."

Satan snarled a threat of eternal physical dismembering and indescribable agonies. But Jake only smiled. Any threat of that nature lacked the real punch of swift verbal response.

"I do not need to disprove *anything*," Lucifer grated.

"Are you pleading the Fifth?" Jake shot back.

Satan's jaw dropped and his Familiar took the moment to perform his main task, using claws and barbed tail to clean Devilish Molars. Sometimes the Familiar hated his condemnation to Hell as an animated toothpick for Satan, but even this was infinitely better than his incarceration in Heaven as a Prime Example.

Satan shook himself. "*I'm* not pleading anything," he told Jake. "I called you here to make you an offer."

Jake let one eyebrow raise. "Oh. You clear it with Upstairs?"

"That won't be necessary."

"Oh, you Devil you. I bet you tell that to all the mortals down here."

"You're the *only* mortal down here!" Lucifer thundered. "Do you want to listen to my damned offer or not!"

"Mind rephrasing that, Luci? Somehow my considering any 'damned' offer strikes me as pretty stupid."

"Done," Satan said briskly. "Now, you're interested?"

"Hell, I'm your guest."

"So you are." Satan paused a moment. "According to the rules from," he raised his eyes and then looked back at Corwin, "*them*, you've won fair and square two out of two. You've proved to Heaven, Hell *and* the land of mortals that you're the best fighter pilot in the world and then some beyond that."

"True," Jake admitted.

"Which means I have to send you back." Satan sighed. "With all your body parts intact."

Jake leaned forward. "You're crapping me again, mister. No way would I go through all this horseshit without *some* return on the nickel, right? You're holding out on me."

"Well, there *are* certain dispensations."

"Which are?"

"You pick the age at which you return."

"But with all my memories intact?"

"Yes."

"No tricks?"

"My hands and tail are tied."

"I just say, hey, let's do it and I'm out of here?"

"Almost."

"Spill it, Luci."

"I still have certain powers, Jake."

'Tell me, *tell me*."

"If you go back now you remember everything and you're just coming out of that storm where we nailed you."

"That's all?"

"You're a man of honor, Jake Corwin. You'll know that you kept the status quo. There won't be any fighter pilots down in Hell."

"Okay."

"Want to hear the rest?"

"Shoot."

"Like I said, you can also pick any physiological age for your return, with all the memories to right now, but—"

"But what?"

"You're got to beat me a third time."

"Three out of three, huh? Not as good as arm wrestling."

"Spare me your homilies, Jake. You want to deal or go back an old man, you decide."

"Not so fast, buster. I have another question I want you to answer.

"You *want*, Jake?" A horn glowed.

"OK, OK, we'll do it your way. You want to suck ego, you got it. But I'd appreciate an answer."

"That's better." Satan snapped his fingers and a freshly charcoaled but still-twitching rabbit appeared in mid-air. He speared it with his tail and popped it into his fangs. "I do love bunny fricassee," he burped.

Jake ignored the scene. "I've gotten a pretty good idea of why I'm here," he began, but I'm lacking particulars, and—"

Satan belched as he leaned forward. His brow furrowed and his horns twisted with his evident amazement. "You mean you've been kicking the shit out of me *and you don't even know why?*" He was a stunning picture of hellish amazement.

Jake shook his head. He'd stumbled onto something but he played it close to the vest. "No, I don't," he said truthfully.

Satan went into an animated frenzy of waving arms and barbed tail. "It's that triple-damned prayer!" he shouted. "You stinking fighter pilots—"

"What the hell are you talking about?" Jake shouted back.

"The *prayer*." Satan ground down on his teeth. "Of course to you goody two-shoes it's not a prayer, it's that stinking miserable song."

"Song?" Jake echoed. Then it hit him. *Of course!* The song they sang religiously through the war: "There Are No Fighter Pilots Down In Hell."

"It's not a song!" shouted Satan. "That damned thing was written by a Hindu pilot flying with the British in Malaya. It was a trick from the beginning. It's a Hindu chant, a guru's filthy twisting of reality against me. Tens of thousands of fighter pilots all over the world, all nationalities, all languages, all praying. Before every flight, during every flight, in battle, after battle, when they were eating, drinking, or getting laid, they were always praying. Jake, did it ever occur to you that you have a lousy voice? That you can't carry a tune? You're not singing; you're *chanting*."

Satan fell back into his living chair. "I've got more fighter pilots in Limbo than I can count, but I can't break them loose." His voice fell to whining. "Jake, Jake, I need fighter pilots! I need them like crazy. I need them so badly against these rotten dissidents that I—*me*, of all the demons—asked for special dispensation from up—you know, up *there*," and his finger stabbed upward.

"You know what they told me? They told me they'd send down one pilot, and if I could beat him fair and square I could have all of them. And would you cooperate? Oh no, not Goody Two-Shoes Jake Corwin. *You* had to whip my Satanic ass!"

"Never mind the sob-sister routine," Jake snapped.

"You better believe it, you shitty little mortal you."

"And if I lose, you get me, plus I give you all those fighter pilots hanging out in Limbo."

"That's the way the contract reads, Jake."

"And if I whip you again?"

"I've already told you."

"It's not enough, Jake said harshly. "If I win—and I'm going to win—*I* get control of all those fighter jocks in Limbo."

"Never!"

"Then stick it, buster. I'm ready to leave. Send me back."

"But I *need* those pilots!"

"Then stick to the deal, you flaming shit!"

Satan glowed from inner fires. Finally, he nodded.

A contract appeared out of thin air. He shoved it forward.

"Put your thumbmark on this parchmant, Jake."

Jake leaned forward, rested his thumb on the Vatican paper. He felt icy cold and his thumbprint was etched in fire on the deed. Satan did the same with the barb of his tail.

"By the way, you have any particular planes in mind?" Jake asked.

"Of course!" Satan boomed with a huge smile. "I'll fly the Mustang. You, Jake, get the P-40. A real bucket of lard, as you and your boys called it. While you have the opportunity, Jake Corwin, I suggest *you* kiss *your* ass goodbye."

"Oh, shit," Jake said, but he didn't protest.

Hemingway wiped the bar clean for the tenth time in as many minutes. He kept his eyes on the door of the O Club at Hades Field. Hemingway nudged the man to his right. "He's coming."

Teddy Roosevelt raised himself higher to see over the bar. "I want to talk to that son of a bitch before the Old Man waxes his ass for good."

Hemingway showed surprise. "You? When did you get interested in a dogfight?"

"Fuck the dogfight, you literary asshole," Teddy growled at him. "I want to know how he keeps his cigars lit down here. I haven't had a decent smoke since San Juan, and I—"

"Can it, will you?" Hemingway broke in. "I've heard that story, what, ten thousand times?"

"Twelve thousand," Roosevelt smirked.

"And I've written the book four hundred and seventy nine times," Hemingway groaned. "But the triple-damned manuscript always gets lost at the printer. I hate this."

"You're *supposed* to hate it," Roosevelt said through his drooping moustache. "Don't you guys with all the fancy words ever learn anything? This is Hell!"

"I really need you to remind me," Hemingway sighed.

The former American President showed a faceful of large yellow teeth, like a rabbit with his molars gone mad. "The trick, Hem, is to develop a—"

"Forget it," Hemingway groaned. "Hey! He's here." They saw Jake Corwin entering the club.

"Jake!" Hemingway called. "Over here!"

Corwin leaned against the bar. "You two seen anything of Fatso Herman?"

"The Nazi pig?" Hemingway asked.

"Yeah. Last time I was with him, the Big Man had him dragged out of his office. It was a mess."

"He's back," Hemingway said. He reached down within the bar and came up with a large carton he dropped heavily on the bar. "This came for you earlier. A present from headquarters."

"What is it?" asked Corwin.

"Soap," Roosevelt chortled. "Two hundred and ten bars. Its Goering Green. Really sick."

"That's terrific," Jake said drily.

"Never mind him," Hemingway pushed. "I want to write a book about your dogfight jousting with the Big Man."

"Nobody will ever read it," Roosevelt jeered.

"Shut your fucking socio-political mouth," Hemingway snapped.

Roosevelt jerked a thumb at Hemingway. "On earth or in Hell, these eggsucking liberals can't stand criticism."

Corwin decided to stay out of their exchange and turned to Hemingway. "What kind of book?"

"I've written about bullfighters, fishermen, mercenaries, soldiers of fortune—"

"Do an autobiography," Roosevelt chuckled. "Then you'll have a book on an asshole."

"—but never one on the best damn fighter pilot in the world."

"Why?" Jake pressed.

"Because it's never been done! And this is the ultimate joust!" Hemingway shouted.

"And you're the ultimate jerkoff," Roosevelt sneered.

Corwin started walking to a table. "No thanks, Hem. I don't have the time. I got a fight to fight."

"You fucking commoner! He'll tear your balls off!" Hemingway shouted.

"Sure," Roosevelt quipped. "*His*, maybe. Not yours, right? You lost 'em when you shoved that shotgun in your mouth. Fucking coward."

They fell down behind the bar, kicking, punching and fighting fiercely. No one else in the club paid attention to them. Instead they sat or stood in small groups,

watching Corwin. Bomber pilots, bombardiers, navigators, gunners, engineers; crewmen of every kind. Somehow, Corwin wasn't an outsider any more even if he
was one of those insanely egocentric fighter pilots.

A large man with white hair, bundled into a Royal
Air Force sheepskin-and-leather jacket, clumping heav-
ily in sheepskin boots, came to Corwin's table. "Mind if
I talk a moment, sir?" he asked.

Corwin waved him to a chair, studied the man with
open interest. "You're twenty years older than me,"
Jake observed. "You're obviously an oldtime veteran
and you fly—"

"Lancasters. I flew a hundred and three missions over
Germany up there," he lifted his eyes upward and then
down, "and I've flown two thousand and some down
here. But I didn't come here to talk about myself. I'm
speaking," he said heavily, "for myself and the others.
All of them. We wanted to say 'thank you.' "

Jake was completely taken aback. "But . . . but, *why*?"

"You have no idea?"

"None!"

"One thing is for sure, Captain. You don't fit the mold
of insufferable braggarts. You know, the best damn
fighter pilot in—"

"Oh, but I am," Jake said quickly.

"Yes, but you have *never said it*. You don't brag, it
would seem. Just the plain truth."

"Why the thanks?" Jake pressed.

"You've given us hope. We all watched those two dog-
fights. Incredible, really. Especially when we thought
you'd lost, yesterday. The whole time you were always
on top of the situation."

Jake thought of the slug he'd taken in his thigh and
his dwindling fuel supply. "I'm not so sure of that," he
said warily.

"And tomorrow? What about tomorrow?" the RAF
pilot asked.

"What about it?"

"We hear he's given you a real doggie of a machine,

while he's got *the* fighter for himself. The latest Mustang."

"You hear right."

"He's convinced he'll take you, you know."

Jake shrugged. "Doesn't matter. He won't."

Eyebrows went up. "You're that confident?"

"It's not a matter of confidence, Wing Commander," Jake told him. "It's a matter of what's going to happen. That's all. I'll whip his ass."

"In a *P-40*?"

"I don't care if it's a garbage truck."

The RAF pilot rose to his feet, a smile twitching at the side of his lips. "I'll pay for this, you know," he said, "but it's worth it."

"What's that?"

"Give the old sod a couple of bursts for us, will you?"

Jake hesitated before answering. Then he nodded, rose to his feet and gripped the other man's hand. "Consider it done, Wing Commander." The RAF pilot walked away heavily.

Hemingway and Roosevelt were at the table almost immediately. Hemingway grinned through a split lip and a swollen eye. "He'll have to get rid of you now, bucko!"

"Who?"

"Lucifer, that's who!" Roosevelt shouted. "You've got the lost souls in Hell rooting for you! And *He* can't stand that! Do one for us, lad . . . tear his fucking heart out!"

Roosevelt turned and rushed for the door and disappeared around the side of the building. Jake stared after him. "He left because he didn't want you to see him," Hemingway said sadly.

"See what?" Jake asked, honestly baffled.

"Tonight. Satan will quite literally tear *his* heart out of his chest. They do it to him every night, and then cook his heart in front of him. Not until then does he die. The pain is indescribable. I never thought I'd see anything so important to him that he would risk even greater punishment." Hemingway gripped Jake's hand. "God bless you!" he cried.

The lightning bolt that tore through the ceiling of the club nailed him first in the balls, and then spilled his intestines, charred and smoking, at his feet. Hemingway screamed but he couldn't move as tiny shards of lightning raced up and down *within* his body. Corwin had enough. He left with Hemingway's howls of agony echoing behind him.

He was grateful all this had happened. He was starting to believe he'd be in a fair fight tomorrow. Bullshit!

Seat belt and shoulder harness secured, inertial lock free, rudder pedals proper distance, all friction knobs right setting, throttle and mixture set, prop control set for start, hit the primer and shove some juice in the Allison engine, fingers across the switches, she's alive, kick the energizer, engage the starter, move the mixture forward from cutoff to running, watch the prop, she's turning nicely. Jake felt the shivering rumble of the P-40N Warhawk coming alive and quickly he took the measure of its innards. Oil temp and oil pressure, electrical systems on line, gyros and vacuums and the engine coolant light. A fast check of the armament, the gunsight and the six fifties, three in each wing. The gauges moved where they were supposed to move and Jake eased on power and released brakes and felt the P-40 trundle over the grassy surface. He turned into the wind for the extra cooling, checked the mags at 55 rpm drop each, rechecked his trim settings, decided no flaps, cranked the canopy forward. Jake looked through the side of the plexiglas. Across the field he saw the silvery blur of the Mustang's huge propeller, the all-red fighter waiting for him to become airborne. He knew Satan himself was flying today. No figurehead from history for him to assume. And he would let the P-40 take off first, a final gesture of contempt because he'd catch up with Jake at altitude with ease.

There was more than ease at stake here. Again Jake

rued the verbal exchange old Lucifer had used to sucker
him in. Chagrin hung heavy on Jake's shoulders. Fool!
He had Satan boxed. All Jake needed to do was hang up
his leather helmet one more time. He'd have protected
every real fighter pilot forever. All Jake needed to do
was return to his own time and place in time. He would
have these terrific memories and "There Are No Fighter
Pilots Down In Hell" would have remained the all-time
international anthem for *all* fighter pilots. But Jake got
greedy, reaching out for more, sucked in by that over-
powering lure of reliving all his adult life and having so
incredible a brain vault of knowledge.

*You lose this one, asshole, and Hell will be overflowing
with fighter pilots. . . .*

He reviewed swiftly all the elements of the Mustang
under Satan's powerful and talented hands and hooves.
By any stretch of the imagination Captain Jake Corwin,
USAAF, was barely a hair short of being a dead duck.
Even the design of the P-40 was already ancient, a
hand-me-down from the antique P-36 altered by little
more than an in-line engine. If you listed all the performance characteristics of the Mustang against those of
the Warhawk, then the joy of Curtiss-Wright was a
garbage truck, a plodder against the sleek laminar-flow
wings of the 'stang.

Yet there were other elements to be added to the list
and they transcended speed, power, climb and all those
goodies fighter pilots love. First, the Mustang had far
greater range than the P-40, but who the Hell cared?
We're not going anywhere, sweetheart, Jake said to himself in a message intended for the Supreme Commander.
*We're staying right over this field and all that range ain't
worth a crap.*

The Mustang could fly and fight at 40,000 feet. Above
16,000 feet the Warhawk was a gasping plodder, which
was to be expected from an engine that never had a
supercharger. If ever they fought at altitude Jake would
be dead meat on the table. *But we're not fighting at
altitude, Beezlebub old buddy, because the cloud deck, the*

*ceiling here in Hell is only 8,000 feet above the ground,
and you can stick that supercharger you got right up your
royal Satanic ass for all the good it's going to do you.*

The Mustang was a hundred miles an hour faster
than the Warhawk. *So what? This isn't a race ...*

The Mustang can climb twice as fast as the Warhawk.
Right. Got to watch that. It's one hell of an advantage ...

But most important of all were the pilots. Satan knew
what he had in that P-51 *and so did Jake.* If Jake fought
the battle against the best of the Mustang he wouldn't
stand a chance. Therein lay his strategy.

Never fight the other man's (or Devil's) fight.

Jake pushed forward on the throttle and held in right
rudder to compensate for yaw, and the Allison surged to
52 inches manifold pressure and the prop spun out at
3,300 rpm and with surprising agility the P-40N was off
the ground and climbing. Jake held her low, brought up
the gear, watched the speed build up. He banked steeply
and saw the Mustang racing across the field. When it
crossed the perimeter he knew Satan was going for a
quick upthrusting kill. Jake grinned.

In a few moments the Big Man of Hades was going to
run smack into an astonishing truth. If Jake had the
choice of fighters for today's Final Battle, considering
the nature of the fight and its rules, *he would have
chosen the very airplane he was flying*—the P-40N! His
Warhawk was an absolute joy to fly, a magnificent
flying machine that in terms of pilot feel was smoother,
faster, and lighter on the controls than the vaunted
Mustang. It left Jake totally free to fly-fight. In that
Mustang, Satan *must* pay much more attention to simply flying his airplane, giving Jake a subtle but vital
edge.

Jake came back on the stick, still hanging in his turn
to keep an eye on the Mustang. Satan flat-hatted it out
across the pumiced ground and then abruptly hauled
the Mustang up into a beautiful, wicked climb, an arrow released by catapult that would bring him up and
beneath the P-40, yet with tremendous speed. In this

one swift maneuver he could gut the Warhawk and it was Bye Bye Birdie for Corwin.

Satan half-rolled to get into firing position and—*the P-40 had vanished!* Satan looked everywhere but his was the only machine in the sky. "Filthy mortal!" he shouted to himself as he cursed the Rule that allowed him only a mortal's-eye view of the action. "I'm the only one who can make an airplane disappear!"

Jake hadn't done any such thing, except visually. It was child's play to figure Satan's move, and Jake had hit full power, half-rolled back to wings level and pulled full back on the stick to bring the P-40 into a tremendous loop. He locked his eyes on the instruments as the P-40, on its back and soaring up and over, penetrated the red thick clouds now so close above. The world was a blinding red everywhere, ghostly, funeral red, but Jake didn't care as he held his eyes steady on the gauges, flying the P-40 through the loop strictly by instruments and under perfect control.

But Satan would be barreling right into that same cloud deck without expecting it, because he'd be going bananas looking for the P-40 that wasn't there, and when he got deep into the shit he'd find the Mustang stalling out and he'd be frantically scanning his gauges trying to make out shit from breakfast. The Mustang doesn't like that kind of flying. It's an unforgiving machine. It whipped out right from beneath Satan's hands and hooves and whirled into an uncontrolled spin.

Jake came out of the clouds, half-rolled slowly and found what he was looking for—the thin exhaust trail of a Merlin engine under full power and going straight up into the cloud deck. He swung into a wide turn, rechecked his machine guns, and steepened the turn, waiting, waiting—

The Mustang came out of the clouds inverted, spinning wildly and rocking as it fell, and no doubt Satan had endowed himself with the skills of one hell of a pilot because he was already recovering. But when you're recovering and you've got the greatest damn fighter pilot in the world *or* Hell up there with you, you are up to your neck in slime.

Jake cut neatly around, pointed the long nose of the P-40 just below the line of flight the Mustang *must* take as it fell, the wings slowly regaining lift, and then fired a series of short bursts. The Mustang *fell* into his machine gun blast and Jake saw hits flashing all over the Satanic fighter. Pieces chopped off and back from the Mustang. Satan did the only thing that would save his demonic ass; he went to full power, slewed the 'Stang out of the spin and went straight down. The Mustang accelerates faster than the Warhawk and by a whisker Satan eluded the second burst of gunfire from that—oh, he hated to admit it!—Hellish Warhawk.

Satan went right down to the pumiced rock below. His chagrin and anger radiated out in all directions and all the grass on the field below burned with a thick oily smoke, an unexpected Dante's Inferno through which the fighters flashed as they sped closer to the ground. Satan had speed now and he whipped into the boiling smoke columns and Jake lost him. He couldn't tell which way Satan was turning in that smoke but he would have bet a box of Uppmans that the son of a bitch had the ability to *see* in the smoke of his own making. The situation probably wasn't even covered by the Rules!

Jake turned to the right, which was just what Satan wanted, for the Mustang was whipping around in a cruel turn with wings vertical to the ground. It was a beautiful maneuver and it nailed Jake and he took a burst through his wing that shook the P-40 like a rat in a terrier's jaws. Satan kept up his speed, and Jake knew he had trouble this time because he could never match the 'Stang in balls-to-the-wall flying.

Never fight the other man's fight. And what Satan didn't know was that the P-40 could turn inside the Mustang all day long in any kind of dogfight you want to mention. It was a thousand pounds lighter, it had a tremendously effective high-lift wing, and it turned much tighter than North America's pride and joy. So Jake didn't go after the P-51. He hung it in slow and tight, the Mustang racing around him like a dog gone berserk, tongue hanging out and going like hell but just burning up gasoline. Jake knew Satan must come in after him and he suckered him in, keeping his speed down, and sure as Hell, there he was, the huge prop flashing silver and hurtling onto the P-40's tail.

Jake looked in his rear-view mirror and kept the Mustang constantly in sight as Satan kept punching around hard for his moment to open fire. And then he was just about in position, the P-40 snared in his web, and in that bare second of difference, Jake pulled out the stops and gave Mr. Beezlebub a grand flying lesson.

Jake slammed the throttle full forward, stomped full left rudder, banged the stick hard over to the left and then back into his gut, all in a single blur of movement. He had to grasp the stick in both hands and his g-suit was on full and Jake yelled like mad to keep his blood pressure as high as he could and instantly the horizon snapped to vertical, the wings trembled with incipient stall; Jake caressed the stick forward a hair. The P-40 had virtually stopped flying and the Mustang had overrun his own firing position, and as Jake pointed the P-40 at empty space the Mustang flew smack into his sights and he squeezed off a long burst.

Fifty caliber slugs smashed the tail trim, chopped away a chunk of right wing, put three holes in a propeller blade and shattered the left hoof of Satan. Lucifer gritted his fangs and ordered the pain to stop so he could keep flying. Fly he did, rocking from side to side and hurling the fighter into a fast shallow climb safe from the P-40's guns.

Satan figured that Jake wouldn't figure him to repeat an earlier maneuver that didn't work. He dove through the smoke clouds below and set it up carefully and with the Mustang vibrating from tremendous speed, he hauled up into a near-vertical climb. Jake laughed. It was a trick he'd seen many a Messerschmitt Me-109F pilot try on him. Satan would climb until the 'Stang hung on its prop and then he'd kick rudder back and forth while the P-40 was right above him and shoot it to shit. The only escape for Jake was full power and break away to force the Mustang into a climbing pursuit curve.

Jake didn't take the only escape. It was time to end this once and for all. Instead of slamming in full power he cut throttle and brought in flaps, the P-40 grumbling with the sudden drag, but dropping its speed and gaining enormous lift. Jake cut tight left. Satan watched the maneuver and altered his climb angle slightly to keep his advantage.

Jake advanced power, held rudder pressure, brought the stick back farther. The P-40 walked into a tighter and tighter turn, that marvelous high-lift wing hanging in there and absolutely grabbing sky as it turned tightly.

The Mustang was all over the place. Satan couldn't believe what he was seeing, the old clunker P-40 turning like a damned Zero. Satan expected a wider radius of turn and had his guns all set to fire, but the P-40 never flew into his sights. Angry, frustrated, Satan tried to force the Mustang to hold its steep climb. Jake laughed aloud. Even the Mustang has to run out of piss and power, and it bled off speed dangerously. Jake hauled up flaps, hit full power, dove with full left rudder, and now the too-slow Mustang was below him, the controls moving violently but ineffectually, like a bird going berserk with its pinions and feathers and feet but getting nowhere.

Satan had run out of steam, he had no power reserve, he was wobbling on his tail, nose pointed almost straight up and his airspeed was whipping away like a sentence of death, and of a sudden Jake was fed up with it, and as the Mustang fell into a tail slide, Satan struggling desperately to bring the nose around and down through a hammerhead, Jake was on him with killing fury.

He dove to pointblank range and, as the Mustang fell around and through the stall, Jake was there waiting for him, and he held down the gun tit and six fifty-caliber machine guns tore the cockpit of the Mustang to shattering wreckage. The canopy dissolved and a thousand pounds of blazing lead hammered into the cockpit, exploding Satan's skull, smashing his shoulders, pulping his spinal column and turning the cockpit into incadescent gore.

A primal scream tore through Hades, bringing all and everything to a frightened, whimpering halt.

The Ultimate Edict took effect.

There are no fighter pilots down in Hell.

Jake Corwin vanished.

Where he had been a pilotless P-40 dove straight into the ground and exploded.

"Where am I?"

You're between Heaven and Hell, Jake.

"I thought that was on Earth." He *felt* the warm chuckle in his mind. Like the voice.

No. Not there. That's a Testing Ground, you know. We use the Mark Four planets like your Earth through most of this Galactic Sector. But this isn't the time for vector analysis, Jake.

"I'll buy that. I can't see or feel, but I feel good. Are you God?"

Most people would say that. I'm afraid I'm not worthy of that High Office.

"Who are you?"

A guide, Jake. Your guide.

"To where?"

Why, we're going to leave that up to you, Jake. You did a wonderful job Down Below. That was really magnificent flying. All your fighter pilot friends, from all Earth nations and Time, are quite safe now.

"Thank you."

Select where you'd like to go. The universe is yours, Jake. Literally.

"You mean, like reincarnation?"

In a way, only better. Pick anyplace, anywhere, anyone from your memories or your dreams. You've earned it.

"Gee, I really don't know . . ."

Take your Time. There's no rush or Time where you are.

"Well, I've got this crazy dream, and there are all these guys waiting in Limbo."

Jake hesitated in his thoughts.

"That deal goes through, doesn't it? I mean, that if Satan crapped out the pilots come with me?"

That was the deal. It stands.

"Life is boring without a challenge, you know?"

Yes.

"And it's not too difficult to see where we'll be in the future. I mean, we've discovered life forms on a few planets, and ever since the CETI program picked up those signals from Alpha Centauri ... well, it means we'll be having visitors on Earth before too long."

That's reasonable, Jake.

"The way I look at it, the Universe is a pretty bad neighborhood at three o'clock in the morning, and while there may be angels, there really ain't no Easter Bunny."

We know, Jake.

"So *all* our people, all the people of earth, are going to need someone, some team, to defend them."

That's the way it usually is, Jake. You know, we help those who help themselves.

"Sounds fair to me. Ok, I got it. My request—"

Go ahead, Jake.

"I'm a fighter pilot. So are the rest of the guys—my guys—in Limbo. We've always been ready to put our lives on the line. We believe in people, in whatever it is that makes up the human race. And as fighter pilots we've got to be able to defend them."

Stay a fighter pilot, Jake, not a politician. Keep it 'tight,' as you would say.

"Yessir. Sorry.

"I guess it should be about the year Two Thousand and Three. That's enough time to design and build the new ships, and to train the guys in their new tactics and systems. We'll call it—well, we'll get to the names later. But I'd like our main bases to be in Tycho, Ptolemais, a few craters like that—"

You're sure that's what you want, Jake?
"Hell no!" Jake laughed. "But it's my best shot."
Good-bye, Jake. You're a good man.
"Good-bye. I—"
The line went dead.

Captain James Corwin, Earth Strike Team One, Base
Tycho, raised his arm, glanced left and right, then
pumped his gloved fist up and down. He already had
his head hard against the cushion rest behind him. The
railgun hummed with a sound that rattled his bones
and shook his teeth, and then he was hurtling down the
long track on the lunar surface, impelled by a huge
electro-magnetic charge. Without a sound, without a
spark of flame, Jake sailed with tremendous speed away
from the lunar surface. To each side were rows of
Lockheed Apex fighters, all ready to ignite their theo-
implosion engines.

"Charge your weapons," Jake radioed to his fighting
team."

Lights charged across his control board. Everyone
was ready. A voice came into his helmet.

"Captain Corwin, we confirm contact. You have a
Main Battle Fleet at six. A.U., cubic vector Nine, Delta,
Zulu. You're in perfect position to strike the Alpha
forces."

"That's affirmed, Control," Jake said calmly. He and
his men were ready to engage the enemy. It would be a
savage and terrible fight, and the lives of billions of
people depended upon its outcome.

He wondered what it would be like when he boarded
the enemy Alpha flagship. How incredible, the way things
turned out: Who could ever have imagined the domi-
nant Alpha life-form would have horns and a tail . . .

'CAUSE I SERVED MY TIME IN HELL

David Drake

"How did you come to be here?" asked the Mandarin coolly as Slick attached the wires to the detonator and the Moor played his flute.

"There...." said Slick, drawing out the word into two syllables as he eased down the clip of the little hand-held generator.

He looked up and smiled, wiping his forehead with the back of his hand. The gangly American's hair was curly and brown with sweat boiled from him by the light of Paradise. When dry it had auburn highlights that suited Slick's fair, freckled complexion. "Can't trust blasting caps," he said. " *Specially* not here."

Not all the freckles were what they seemed at a quick glance: some of them left long blood-smears on the back of Slick's hand. He glanced at the blood and faked a smile as he brushed the hand clean against the trousers of his jungle fatigues. The markings on his forehead were unchanged.

The Moor rolled his eyes and grinned broadly around the mouthpiece of his flute, which was fashioned from a human thighbone. An hour before, the trio had stumbled into the depression in which they intended to lie in

---

ambush. A lich with skin like parchment squatted there as if waiting for them. The Moor had, with his usual moronic unconcern, decapitated the creature. For the next instants, the Mandarin looked around in feigned indifference, ready to snatch up his robes and run if more liches rose from the light-blasted grasslands. Slick crouched down, thumbing the selector arrow of his M16 back to automatic—a different response prepared for the same anticipated stimulus.

But the Moor had sheathed his sword, a heavy-bladed yataghan sharpened on the inner curve, and prodded with his fingers in the lich's dissolving body to find the flute the creature carried instead of a weapon. After they—he and Slick—had set the four directional mines to crisscross the trail with their blasts, the Moor began to play a surprisingly good rendition of "El Capitan."

The lilting, satirical tune bothered the Mandarin ... but of course the hulking brute was too stupid to mean anything by it.

"I asked you a question," repeated the Mandarin as Slick squatted down. "How did you come to be here?"

Slick smiled, perhaps a little uneasily, and carefully put down the detonating clacker. A sharp squeeze on its handle would set off the nearest claymore twenty-five yards away, and the chain of det cord connecting that mine to the other three would blow them in near simultaneity. The sixteen thousand jagged steel beads blasted from the claymores would shred every living thing in their interwoven paths.

"Well," said the American, stopping his hand before he wiped blood across it again, "we had orders to report to you. To close an escape route some rebel bigwig might try."

"Mithridates," nodded the Mandarin, "but that isn't what I meant. How did you come *here*?" His slim hand and the brocaded sleeve of his silk robe swept in an arc that demanded notice of more than the immediate terrain.

Which was, of course, hellishly bleak. The shallow

depression in which the trio waited was deep enough to hide them (if they squatted) from anyone on the nearby trail, but it was no shield against the blazing, burning light of Paradise. The grass was waist high, sere, and glass-edged.

They had hiked the last mile to the ambush site so that the clop and whine of the helicopter which inserted the team would not pinpoint it for the rebels—if the rebels were anywhere around.

The grass had nicked the Mandarin's hands, despite his care, and sawn through the toes of his light slippers. Slick had rolled down the sleeves of his fatigue shirt, but the rifle he ported in front of him had ensured that his hands and wrists would be covered with grass cuts. Those scratches had dried, unlike the speckles on his face.

The Moor's gauzy pantaloons had been reduced to gay-colored shreds. His skin was unmarked even though his arms were bare, and his chest was covered only by crossed bandoliers of ammunition for his 40-mm grenade launcher.

The Moor had been in the lead during the march. Despite the weight of the pack with the radio, the claymores, and most of the team's water, he had been fresh enough to deal with the lich before either of his fellows realized what was happening.

"*Stop* that," the Mandarin snapped as the Moor's mocking tune filled Slick's silence.

"Whatcha gonna do, boss?" murmured the man in jungle fatigues. "Condemn us to Hell?"

But good nature and the habit of discipline reasserted itself before the Mandarin thought of a way to deal with the insubordination. Slick wiped his forehead, grimaced tiredly, and said, "Guess you'd say I bent over at the wrong time. I was ridin' loader on the Captain's tank when the dinks popped us. Usually I'd've been up on the turret, workin' the co-ax we'd moved up to my hatch ... but Captain, he fired the main gun and I ducked down inside to load another round a' canister."

Deliberately, the man who had been an American soldier touched one of the false freckles on his face and held up the smear on his index finger for the Mandarin to see. " 'Bout that time," Slick continued, "some dink put a B-41 rocket into the side a' the turret. Blast went through one side and most ways out the other. I splashed."

He cleaned his fingertip on the gritty soil while still meeting the Mandarin's eyes. "I guess," he added, "somebody figures I'll forget that if they don't remind me."

The Moor had set the flute down in brief obedience. Now he began to play with it again, blowing on the wrong end. It was incredible that someone with his grinning, vacant face could have teased a recognizable tune from the instrument.

"I killed Peterkin," the Moor said, answering by apparent chance the question which Slick had dodged or misunderstood a few moments before. His voice was guttural, but it filled the declivity as thoroughly as did the blaze of Paradise above. "He was a fool. He bothered her when she wanted me."

The Moor smiled at the Mandarin, then at the flute. His dark fingers flexed, crushing the instrument into shards of bone still fresh enough to be yellow in the damning, brilliant light. "Of course she wanted me. He was only a marionette. And he was a fool."

"Women'll get you into trouble, all right," said Slick as he unbuttoned the big lower side pocket of his trousers; but he was offering only words to the conversation, without the sort of emotional loading to suggest that they held a personal memory for him. He took a pistol from the pocket.

"When d'you figure they'll come by?" Slick added, catching the Mandarin's eye but waggling his free hand back toward the waiting mines.

From where the Mandarin stood, the nearby trail was only an undulation in the grass and the claymores were completely hidden. Slick had placed flares a little farther beyond the trail, also. Individual wires led to the team's hiding place so that a quick pull would release the ignition striker of the flare to which that wire was connected.

"I was informed," said the Mandarin, as if oblivious both of the question and the pistol Slick was beginning to polish with a handkerchief, "that you could set the claymores to go off without us being present. With tripwires." He looked sharply down at the American.

"Got the wrong guy," Slick whispered, his lips the only part of his body that moved as he stared blankly at the gun in his hands. Finally he began to polish the black enamel surface again. In something closer to his normal voice, he said, "You want an automatic ambush, you fix it yourself. And—" he raised his eyes, a blue as pale as winter skies "—you watch me pack the fuck outa here when you start. Roger?"

The Moor drew a deck of cards from his backpack. "She's a ballerina," he said, and his thick lips curved in an even broader version of the smile that was habitually on them. He held the cards out to Slick. "We play?"

The Mandarin squatted down, fluffing his blue robe with his hands so that it pooled around him instead of being caught in the scissors of his shanks. "The operation against the suspected hideout," he said coolly, "will begin after nightfall." The dragon embroidered on his breast in gold wire and scarlet rippled as its wearer breathed. "It is of course possible that Mithridates will move earlier, from suspicion or for other reasons of his own."

"Yeah, sure, man," Slick said, taking the cards from the Moor. He slipped the pistol back into his side pocket so that he could shuffle the deck. "You wanna play, man?" he asked, glancing over at the Mandarin. Though the American's voice had regained its placidity, his face was sallow enough that the speckles of blood stood out.

"No," said the Mandarin without emotion. "The—weapon you carry in your pocket. There is no magazine in it."

"Naw," agreed Slick, smiling with his natural diffidence as he began to deal the four hands of honeymoon bridge. The Moor flattened patches of grass with his dark, powerful fingers so that the cards could lie face down. "Bought it fer two hundred bucks from one a' the interpreters. That was in Cambodia. Some off-brand French ammo, .32 sorta but not like our .32. Figured it'd make a nice souvenir—don't it look nice?—even if I couldn't find the ammo."

He looked up from his cards. "Which I didn't. But there wasn't a whole lotta time neither."

"You brought it with you?" asked the Mandarin in puzzlement as Slick resumed dealing. "To here?" He had devoted his life—a very long life—to knowledge, and he neither could nor desired to change that habit now.

"Well. I guess it *was* here," the American muttered, uneasy again. "I dunno, prob'ly isn't the same one, just . . . well, seemed like I oughta keep it even though it's not good for nothin'. *Nothing's* good for nothin' here, right?" He met the Mandarin's eyes again.

"One heart," said the Moor. His eyes, dark as mud-wallows and as empty of intelligence, were fixed on the Mandarin.

"Oh," Slick said, picking up both of his hands of cards. "Yeah. Two clubs."

"Don't the cards change as you play?" the Mandarin asked, slewing his interest from the emotionally loaded to what he thought would be neutral. All information had the same value, until he had gathered enough—and the right sort—to weave himself a ladder of knowledge out of this place.

Knowledge had made him immortal. Almost.

"Three no trump," said the Moor.

"Play 'em out, then," responded the American with a shrug. He looked at the Mandarin. "Us two, we been together a while. They did, you know, when we started. Nothin' stays the same here. But it passed the time just the same—" he led a jack from his dummy, then cast off low when the Moor played an ace "—and pretty much now, what you see is what you get."

The Moor led a jack.

"After all," said Slick, "It don't *mean* nothin' ..." and the Moor's attempted finesse fell to the queen.

"Yes ..." whispered the Mandarin. "That is so."

He stood and turned, lifting his head until the brim of his padded circular cap cut the blaze of Paradise in a line just beneath his eyesockets. Even he could not bear that direct splendor.

"I am one of the world's greatest in wisdom," the Mandarin said, loudly enough that his immediate companions could hear him. "I was. I would not die, and I could not be killed so long as I willed it."

The Moor whuffled and laid down the hand with the lead. It was all hearts, the only hearts remaining unplayed. Slick gathered up the deck to reshuffle.

"I went into a tavern," the Mandarin continued, to his subordinates or to God. "A dive. It was dangerous, but not to me."

"In China, this was?" Slick asked as his partner shrugged off a cut.

"In Köln," said the Mandarin. "But it could have been anywhere. I lived in the world. The whole world was mine."

For a moment, the only sound was the whisper of the cards. Then the Mandarin went on in a voice as sweetly arrogant as a muted trombone. "There was a woman. I wanted her. I went into the back, and the men who were her confederates set upon me with knives."

The Mandarin faced around again. Paradise flung his shadow, bulky with robes and shoulder cape, across the cardplayers. Slick was watching him, listening; and the Moor, though he rolled his eyes and made his lips squirm into shapes that were scarcely human, seemed to be listening also.

"They hanged me then," the Mandarin said, "and still I laughed at them until they ran away. But the woman

. . . the woman cut me down and took me in her arms. And I forgot everything but how much I wanted her."

He smiled so tightly that the down-curled tips of his moustache did not appear to move. "So the wounds began to bleed, and I forgot about her as well as about life."

"I guess," said Slick, who started the motion of dealing a card but paused again to look up at the Mandarin. "I guess that's one way t' learn t' stay outa dives."

"No," said the Mandarin. "I learned not to care about anything. A little too late."

"Don't mean nothin'," said the Moor in a nearly perfect imitation of his American partner.

Slick began to deal. "Yeah," he said softly, "but you know . . . I think maybe, you know, you oughta care. Some things. . . ."

A drop of the blood that would not dry on his forehead fell onto the deck of cards and splashed.

Slick deliberately wiped the droplet away on his pants leg, then started to thumb the card out to resume dealing. His hands paused as they touched one another on the deck. Then he set the cards down on his crossed ankles and, speaking toward them, said, "They don't have t' remind me, you know. I'm not gonna forget."

The Moor was as motionless as a tailor's dummy. The Mandarin waited in equal silence, meeting Slick's eyes when they were raised to him.

"I used t' set automatic ambushes, you know?" the American said. "A tripwire and a couple claymores. Somebody come di-di-boppin' down the trail after curfew and bam! he's there fer us in the morning. Got an honest t' fuck VC paymaster the one time, carryin' about a quarter million pi."

He licked his lips, pausing for breath and the correct words. "So okay, I was good at it. We set 'em up at night, and then we go out before dawn and take 'em in. No sweat. Only—" he breathed deeply, raggedly, "—the one morning, one a' the tanks in my platoon wouldn't crank and we fucked around with it. Not long, fifteen minutes. We still got to all the AAs before dawn."

Slick wiped his forehead and attempted a rueful smile. "Thing is, a kid was trying to beat curfew by maybe fifteen mikes too. Driven' his buffs to the water. Killed half a dozen buffs, too. Kid didn't look so bad, but his face, you know, that had stopped some pellets."

Slick looked down at his bloody hand. "He was seven, his mother told us. Didn't look that old, but dinks're little people. And I guess it was a little too late for me t' learn not to set automatic ambushes, too."

"Deal the cards," said the Moor.

"There is a way out of here," said the Mandarin, but he said it to himself. His voice was lower even than the mocking slither of the cards.

The others ignored the Mandarin to play out their empty hands. As Slick had said, the two of them had "been together a while—" which was more likely a measure of incident than of mere time. The Mandarin, their temporary leader by the writ of faceless authority, was a factor to be accepted like the saw-toothed grass and the baleful purity of Paradise as it slipped eastward to set.

The Mandarin wrestled the heavy two-way radio from the Moor's pack. Slick looked up, willing to help but too uninterested to interfere. The unit was set to receive, and even with the volume low there should have been a hiss of static instead of silence from the speaker.

"Dead," said the Moor with guttural brightness, leading the queen of spades, which Slick promptly covered with the ace.

The volume slide did not bring the speaker to life.

"When were these batteries last changed?" asked the Mandarin coldly as he unlatched the battery compartment.

"Just before we left," Slick replied without concern at the threat implied in the question. He began to reshuffle the deck, although light was failing: "Loaded magazines and changed batteries . . . but you know, you can't trust 'em here."

The Mandarin had to pry the four cells from the housing. Their steel cases were covered more with corrosion than by the original olive-drab enamel, and caustic fluid bubbled greasily over the electrodes. The Mandarin threw them down with needless vehemence.

"Dead," repeated the Moor.

"There's two more sets in the pack," the American offered, "but hardware, it don't do what it ought to here."

He smiled mildly, engagingly, as the Mandarin ripped open the boxes of waxed cardboard holding fresh batteries. "You never could trust it, I guess," Slick continued, "but here it seems like worse, you know, even than Nam?"

The batteries from the sealed boxes had corroded worse than those in the radio. The Mandarin set them and the unit itself down with an air of regal unconcern.

"Well," said Slick. "This far back in the boonies, I dunno that was gonna be much use anyways. Figure we stand our watch, then in the mornin' we hump back t' the landing zone and wait for the bird."

"*If*," said the Mandarin, "we haven't made contact."

"I guess ten pounds a' C-4 goin' bang in the claymores oughta send a pretty good signal t' the support platoon," the American replied mildly. "But it don't seem like much really happens when you're expectin' it."

It had become hellishly dark more suddenly than a tropic sunset. The Mandarin heard the aluminum breech of the grenade launcher open and close as the Moor checked his load by feel.

"Yeah, guess it's about that time," said the American, sighing. The selector of his automatic rifle clicked minusculely to its third detent, full auto.

The trio waited in the darkness that was never friendly, textured by faint screams which could have been the wind and could have been the souls of others damned as they were.

Slick was motionless. Somnolent, the Mandarin would have said, except that the American's eyes gleamed in the skyglow which was too faint to limn figures. By contrast, the Moor was as restive as a hunting shrew. He drew and resheathed his long knife, toyed with the grenade cartridges in his bandoliers, and even snuffled at the air like a beast.

But the Moor was as silent as his partner. Though he had seemingly the attention span of a kitten, he displayed also the instinct that kept a carnivore in ambush from giving itself away to potential victims.

The Mandarin let his mind slip within itself, trying to recapture the sense of self knowledge and self control that had been his throughout his adult life—until the moments of his death. He had not felt that unity of self since death, since finding himself in this *Hell*, which he would have described as a puerile fantasy during the ages when he believed implicitly in his own immortality.

But if the goal eluded him—if he knew at some level that it would elude him during an eternity that was as real as the "immortality" which preceded it had been false—then it served the Mandarin as cards had served his subordinates. It passed the time.

He had expected the first warning of movement to be a subtle thing, caught by the beast senses of the Moor or by Slick's battle-trained instincts. Instead, there was a jingle of harness and a yipping cry that carried, as it was meant to do, across the grasslands. Moments later came the echoing whine of a two-stroke diesel laboring on the rocky trail which debouched onto the plain where the ambush waited.

Mithridates was not skulking away. He was abandoning his former encampment in a motor vehicle escorted by horsemen.

"Well, fuckin' A." Slick muttered under his breath. There was no longer need for dead silence since the rebels' approach was too open to admit of scouts inching forward on their bellies to cut the throats of the ambush party. "You didn't tell me it'd be an armored personnel carrier, buddy. I'd've angled the claymores up a little bit if I'd figured that."

As the veteran spoke, his left hand closed unerringly over the clacker that would detonate the mines.

"How was I to know?" hissed the Mandarin, furious at the implied rebuke by an inferior and suddenly terrified at what was about to happen.

Death *here* meant the Undertaker's slab, pain and degradation beyond anything he had experienced in the most esoteric of his researches during life. The Mandarin had steeped himself in a mercuric elixir that leached the vital force from each of his cells in order to armor them against change and the death which resulted from change. The agony of that process would be pleasure by contrast to the Undertaker's hideous technique.

The Moor hunched down at the edge of the depression which hid them. His yataghan was sheathed and even the dull, anodized barrel of the grenade launcher was hidden beneath his body. His eyeballs rolled and shone with unholy glee as he awaited a signal from the American.

Nothing in the Mandarin's experience had prepared him for the firefight that jangled closer on caterpillar treads. He had expected to set the mines and lurk no closer to the site than was necessary to gather information about the results—at some safe time in the future.

When *that* plan foundered on Slick's refusal to set an automatic ambush, the Mandarin's mind still failed to accept the reality of being twenty-five yards from the claymores and their intended victims. He simply had no data from which to construct an image of the on-rushing events.

The hands with which Slick had shuffled and dealt the cards now held his weapons with equally practiced skill. The pistol grip of the M16 was in his right hand, muzzle horizontal, ready to trigger a burst if need arose too suddenly for him to drop the clacker first. The little detonator, the only real hope of the team's success or even survival, was held firmly but without panic in his left.

Because he had to see his target in order to be sure it had entered the killing zone, Slick raised his eyes to a level with the grass heads. His companions watched him, pools of darkness in darkness.

One of the outriders passed within twenty feet of the men in ambush. The Mandarin hunched over the gold embroidery on his breast and followed the rebel with his eyes. He was afraid that the motion of turning his head to search for other enemies would call down the attention of this nearest man.

The rebel wore a fur cap with a spike at the peak of it. Brass ornaments or even tiny bells dangled across the chest of his pony, and the stock of an automatic rifle slung muzzle-down stood in vague silhouette beside his head. He paused, twisting back in his saddle to yip at his fellows. Then he lifted his handi-talkie radio from its belt holster and made a singsong report which was answered by a burst of static and a word of curt acceptance.

The outrider pressed the pony forward with his knees, reholstering the radio.

The boxy, uncouth form of the armored personnel carrier rattled its way out of the rocky defile from which the horsemen had preceded it. A single headlamp, slitted and covered with a yellow filter, sufficed to guide the driver at the speed a horse would walk in darkness. Grassblades reflected and channeled the light, becoming for a moment sulphurous tubes that stood out against the night.

Then the treads caught the grass and ground it to tattered ruin, dead beyond cavil in a waste where death usually counterfeited life.

"Roger, baby . . ." whispered Slick, and his left hand moved only enough to assure him that it was there, that its muscles would work when he called on them.

There were men riding on the top of the armored

vehicle, their figures merged into an irregular mass that contrasted with the squared lines of the metal supporting them. One of them might be—should be—Mithridates. Pellets from the claymores would churn the rebel leader and his fellows into cat meat, dying in agony to form again in agony on the Undertaker's slab—and back in Satan's hands.

Slick squeezed. The clacker made the angry snapping whirr that sent a jolt of electricity into the detonator of the nearest claymore.

Nothing else happened.

"Fuckin' A, buddy," Slick murmured, but he did not say it as if he were angry or even surprised. Things didn't do what they ought to, here.

The Moor rolled to a kneeling position, aware—though the Mandarin was not—of what was about to happen. Slick clamped shut the clacker again, vainly again, and dropped it to seize the wires that ran to the three flares set on the far side of the trail.

He jerked them in turn: nothing from the first wire; nothing from the second—nothing from the third, while the armored vehicle turned to negotiate the jog in the trail that marked the end of the killing zone. The left tread dug in while the right, declutched, clanged its track blocks and freewheeled in temporarily unloaded condition.

The first flare ignited after all, a spurt of yellow wrapped in gray smoke—surging abruptly into a blaze of magnesium as white and intense as anything short of Paradise.

The flare went off almost under the feet of an outrider's pony. Its whinny was almost a scream. The rider, who managed to shoot at the flare as his mount bolted, was both skillful and unfortunate: one of the rebels on the armored vehicle cut man and pony down with a pintle-mounted machine gun.

The figures on the back of the vehicle were silhouetted by the flare as their eyes and guns searched the wrong side of the trail. The one in the center, who had snaky locks and a double chin for the instant that he turned, had been Mithridates VI of Pontus when he lived as king on Earth. The three-shot burst from Slick's rifle sent the king sprawling, his blood a cloud through which the magnesium blazed.

Then the M16 jammed, and the grenade which the Moor fired with a hollow *thunk!* bounced from the vehicle like a tennis ball instead of going off.

"*Di-di lam!*" Slick shouted to his fellows as he and the Moor both ducked away—the latter shoving another grenade cartridge into his stubby weapon while the American jerked vainly at the cocking piece of his M16. The casing had ruptured, wedging part of itself in the chamber mouth while the remainder molded to the bolt like a brass lichen.

Rebels switched on the searchlight mounted behind the driver's hatch of the APC. The diesel roared to power the dazzling beam that swept above the men in ambush. Slick and the Moor, poised to *run fast* as the American had shouted, froze as rigidly as the Mandarin whose instinct in chaos had been to draw within himself. The darkness which should have hidden flight now melted in a blue-white glare.

The intensity of the searchlight beam provided momentary cover. The outriders were themselves blinded, and the flattened ambush team was beneath the line of fire of the vehicle's automatic weapons. Those guns blasted the night with red tracers, following the sweep of the light and crossing it with vicious, microsecond shadows.

The rebels had no precise target—Slick's burst had been too short and too unexpected. As the light quartered away from the depression, the Moor rose and chunked another grenade at the APC. The fat, wobbling projectile was in perfect silhouette at the instant it struck the searchlight. The beam jerked as the grenade smacked the shatterproof lens at an angle before caroming off into the darkness. Shouts of warning and direction were chopped and fragmented by the roar of automatic weapons.

The Moor slid out of the sheltering depression like an eel in a breeding marsh. He was headed for the APC, not toward escape.

A bullet cracked past the Mandarin's face. It was a tracer fired at random by one of the outriders, a minute green flare whose smoke trail burned the back of the Mandarin's mouth. He lunged away from the machine guns and fell flat because Slick, foreseeing his leader's panic, had grabbed a handful of the heavy silk robe.

The searchlight swept back across them. Had the Mandarin bolted from the depression as he intended, the shots raving overhead would have chopped him down in half a step.

The Moor leaped up beneath the slab sides of the APC. His yataghan curved and flashed with blue-white splendor as it caught the side-scatter of the beam.

"But—" thought/said the Mandarin, who expected the knife to glance from the polycarbonate lens-cover the way the grenade had done.

Sparks roared like a tiger slaying. The filament went yellow, red, and black so suddenly that eyes were still blinded by the dazzling brilliance of an instant before. The heavy steel blade had cut the power cord instead of attacking the armored lens.

"*Now!*" cried Slick, slapping the Mandarin's buttocks as if he were a hog to be urged through a gate.

The Moor was a shadow against the dying trip flare. Men on the APC were shouting, but there were no aimed shots from the vehicle—perhaps because of the sparks which snaked like wave fronts over the aluminum sides.

The claymores went off, lightning on a daisy chain of det cord.

The explosions were hollow but so loud that they filled the world like nearby thunder. The armored vehicle jumped as its flanks torqued and tore with metallic screams, but the diesel continued to wheeze undamaged. No one on the vehicle's deck was still alive.

The backblast of the nearest mine caught the Moor and flung his body, legless, to the depression ten yards away.

The white flash of the claymores had given one of the outriders a target. He shot twice and, yipping for his fellows, rode toward his memory.

"Help me!" Slick cried as he slipped his left arm beneath the shoulders of the groaning Moor.

"*Leave him!*" screamed the Mandarin, terrified alike to wait for the vengeful horseman or to flee alone. "He's not *human*. He's a marionette!"

The Moor's throat gurgled with laughter or unintelligible words. His tattered thighs were dribbling something too heavy for sawdust but not blood or any other residue of life.

"Fuck *you*!" the American shouted, lurching to his feet despite the weight of the burden he was willing to support alone. "He's human as me!"

The outrider fired from point-blank range, but his pony shied at the lip of the shallow depression and threw the burst high. The horseman wheeled his mount, guiding it with his knees while his hands steadied his automatic rifle.

Slick had drawn the pistol he may have forgotten was unloaded. He fired at the horseman, who cried out, dropping the rifle to grasp his pony's mane. The American shot again and the rebel tumbled forward, his spiked cap slipping off and bouncing to the ground a moment before he did.

Hardware doesn't do what it ought to—here.

The Mandarin caught the pony's reins and boosted himself into the saddle with a remembered skill. Racing hooves thudded in the near distance. A splutter from the flare glittered on the edge of a sword being waved high.

"Help us!" cried Slick as the Mandarin kicked his skittish mount into a gallop toward enveloping darkness.

A horseman yipped, and a long burst of automatic fire echoed another pistol shot.

The fool could have run. Even on foot, he and the Mandarin could have evaded the startled horsemen until dawn brought helicopters and the support platoon to mop up the rebels.

There were more shots, none of them directed at the Mandarin. Someone—something—cried out in a voice too loud to be human.

The night blazed, forcing the Mandarin's eyes away as he tried to glance behind him. It threw his distorted shadow across the plains of Hell in capering obscenity.

He wasn't sure what was happening.

But it looked very much as though the darkness had cracked to let the light of Paradise pour through.

MONDAY MORNING

by C. J. Cherryh

Mithridates walked gingerly down the polished hall, in that restricted area of Pentagram corridors which gave protected access to inmost offices. Cleanliness and order and quiet were a balm to the king of Pontus: he had had a hot bath, soothing massage, and his hair was ringleted and banded with gold about the brow, his tunic and breeches glittered with silver and bronze medallions. In fact he looked tolerably well for a man lately dead, but one felt it in the joints, in the creak of stiff ribs and soreness of the gut, and in the lingering stink of cold and formaldehyde, a combination of sense and smell of that peculiarly nightmarish sort that persisted past perfumes and oils and the ordinary office smells which cut through it without dispelling it. It was the odor of humility, the chill of the grave, and the memory of defeat.

More than that it was the smell of a Roman agent in the works, and Mithridates had an abiding, burning hatred of the breed.

It had the smell of a Pentagram leak, *something* having poured out a chink somewhere, and he was on the hunt for it this morning like a hound to the track—albeit a slow-moving one and a stiff and a cursed sore one.

Dying *hurt*, dammit. And when it was a damned screw-up it hurt doubly. The stuff started coming in, and by the time they had it pegged that it was *not* an attack by dissidents who had stumbled onto the base of operations ... that it was, in fact, friendly fire, there had been no damned choice but to tough it through.

Now, there was the small matter of courtesies, a *necessary* courtesy; and when he had passed the guards with a sullenly returned salute and a glower for whatever thoughts passed behind their eyes ... Egyptians of Ptah Regiment, gold-belted and kilted and watching him with dark, long eyes behind his back. He felt the stares as he passed—Egyptian guards, at doors which opened onto a carpeted foyer, and the splendid mahogany doors beyond, with the brass insignia of the vulture and the snake—

Modest, considering the occupant. There were more guards. There were damned fools who insisted on ablutions and passed him through a room of reeking incense that made his stomach heave.

And behind that last door, a bald, stoop-shouldered man in khaki; a man of elegant, Egyptian profile, who wore a pair of wire-rimmed glasses perched on his arched nose, who looked up from his reading with a blink of slightly magnified eyes. "Eh. Oh. Indeed. Back again."

"Back, yes." The rage in Mithridates seethed up to the surface and threatened to break out in shouting. He drew instead a quiet, a very quiet breath, and smiled as if he were strangling. One *needed* this man, this delver into books, this womanizer, this ... *fool:* Rameses II, who gave them the might of Egypt.

"It was a great misfortune. We are making inquiries."

We are making inquiries, we are making inquiries. Mithridates caught his breath and clenched his hands. "We were targeted, do you understand?"

"We understand it was a very extensive mistake. We do *not* understand how this arose. We do not understand why you did not use the radio to advise these attackers to cease. They *were* our forces, were they not?

Friendly fire. *We do not understand why we are subject to these mistakes, king of Pontus!"*

Because you are an ass, king of Egypt.

But aloud: "Because we have traitors among us, because we have damned traitors and we do not make examples, Pharaoh."

"Why did you not use the radio?"

"Because—" Infinite patience. A tilt of the head, metallic precision to the voice. "Because, Pharaoh, light of the Two Lands—we were blown. How were we to explain to our own forces *why* we had a base in dissident territory, or what I was doing there? Or should we prolong the skirmish, let the fire draw other attention, and bring down the whole damned countryside? Eliminating our witnesses or getting ourselves out of there, light of Egypt: those were the choices, and they were damned well set when they opened up. They had position on us."

Pharaoh slid the wire-rimmed glasses down and peered over them. "But how did they find you, king of Pontus? How did this happen?"

"I am investigating." All but a whisper. "Believe me, Pharaoh, I will find out. We will bring them through Reassignments."

As you did Maccabee—

"Tsssss. Not without its value."

"Not with full value either, as we understand it. We do not know Hadrian's whereabouts, Kadashman-Enlil is in our displeasure, our severe displeasure—"

"Look to Tigellinus and his staff! I warn you, Pharaoh, I have warned you that *there* are our leaks. Confide in Stalin if you must, but Romans are poison. Romans have relatives, information spreads from household to household like plague, and Tigellinus' patron is a lunatic with ties to Julius Caesar. I warn you. I do earnestly warn you."

Pharaoh blinked, replaced the glasses, and stared at him with the minutest alarm, not of common sense, to be sure, but because Mithridates was rarely so blunt with him; and he was offended.

"Light of the Two Lands," Mithridates said, out of breath, for breath seemed thin in him this morning, and his voice hoarse and strained of a sudden, the words difficult as he tried *not* to say things that would make this man hard to manage . . . this man more interested in his papers than in the real events those papers represented. "I am going to my office. I am going to inquire into this."

"We will want a report." In a brittle, precise tone. Pharaoh adjusted the glasses. "We are not convinced of this strategy. We do not trust these elements. We were faced with a rabble ill-officered and ill-equipped. So we give the dissidents both superior officers and more modern equipment? This seems to us a curious economy, king of Pontus."

"It worked for Stalin." Mithridates found a convenient chair back and clenched his hands upon it, leaning there to keep his balance as vertigo and rage chased each other round and round in his brain. "First, Luminance, you infiltrate, then you divert, then you control their movements and their policies. Except we have lost our field office, Luminance Arising, which is a damned great nuisance, but not a fatal one, except to the one responsible for this, when I find him, and when I find out whose staff blundered, Pharaoh, I assure you I will be back to you."

"We distrust temper. We distrust precipitate acts and staff quarrels. Most of all we dislike commotion, king of Pontus. We truly abhor it. This is precisely what we warned you, that rabble in our pay, for whatever reason, will generate disorders in our organization—"

"This was friendly fire, dammit. This was our own damned *orderly* forces."

"Nevertheless. Disorder is generated by the very existence of rebels. Confusion and chaos. Sloppy accounting." Rameses picked up a sheaf of papers and waved it. "We have no notion where funds are going. We have equipment unaccounted for. All for Stalin's clandestine operations and this buying of the very rebels we fight. We do not trust accounting like this!"

The air grew thinner and thinner and the red rage more difficult to master. One had to remember the value of this man, who had infinite skill in putting a wall of forms and bureaucracy between themselves and Administration, who was successful in his maddening, meticulous way, at diverting and soothing and screening in ways bureaucracies trusted and went to like pigs to swill. It was Rameses who stroked Administration and kept them well-disposed.

"I will provide you a list," Mithradates said.

At which point the red phone rang, and made a silence in the room.

Rameses picked up the receiver. He listened a time with a frown making a seam between his brows and the corners of his mouth turning down further and further.

"Yes," Rameses said. And: "Yes." And: "Thank you." Precisely. From a man to whom *thank you* was a foreign idea, professionally practiced. "Quite. We are very glad." Rameses was never *I*, even in bed, one suspected . . . *damn him, damn him, what is it?*

Rameses set the receiver in its cradle. "So. Well."

"Caesar is back."

"Back?" Mithridates' voice cracked, as it was not wont to do. Air failed him for the moment. His heart sped and lurched against the counsel of his body, which lagged behind the rage and the will to do something, anything. "Back where? Doing what?"

"A routine equipment check-in, as it seems. It will not be advisable to move now; let us have no precipitate actions. We will scrutinize his list and his reports, of course, but bear in mind, bear in mind, king of Pontus, we do not invade administrative levels, we do not wish to take rash actions or place ourselves in absolute positions, king of Pontus, in places without retreat. We do not know who may have backed him in this venture, and until we know, we do not pull threads at random. Do not raise your voice with us, we are not at fault."

"Of course not." Mithridates drew in a lungful of incense-tainted air, and brought himself to shuddering calm. "Of course not, Luminance." He gave a precise, courteous nod. He managed even to edge backwards to the door, in that way Pharaoh found courteous, and to go out without slamming it.

He wanted weapons in hand. He wanted the field. He wanted Caesar in his sights. Wanted, as a Roman emperor had expressed it, the whole lot of his enemies with a single neck so that he could lop it. Repeatedly.

In Hell there was no end to enemies. They came back. A man who hated could never get rid of his hate, or those he hated. But he could take from them what they loved; he could work revenge without end; he could, if he were willing, consume an eternity in that revenge.

He was a dedicated man. A man with a cause. The kind of man the Pentagram never let to the top; but the kind that would not be prevented, either, because to him everything was expendable, except his hate and his vengeance. In that much he was pure and without taint; that he truly believed in something, and counted it holy.

GRAVEYARD SHIFT

Janet Morris

Someone had scrawled, "I'd rather be living," in red paint or blood beside the double doors of New Hell's Administration building.

Inside, the Undertaker was very busy—too busy, in fact, to note the special instructions on the toe tag of the corpse named Nichols that one of the morticians was reviving.

The tag said: *Hold for Achilles' pick-up*, but the mortician on Nichols' case had only rudimentary Greek and a smuggling operation under way. The very next corpse on the mortician's docket was a White Death mule; its body cavity had been evacuated and filled with heroin. The "China White," ten kilos in weight, would make the mortician rich.

Consequently, he was in a hurry to finish with the body before him; he scribbled *Nichols, Achilles* on the credentials card he held, then slipped the attached chain around Nichols' neck and wheeled the gurney into the freight elevator which would take its load of revivifed corpses upstairs to Reassignments. Then he returned to his station and the object of his preoccupation: enough drugs to buy him a waterview villa on the best side of

Decentral Park, and bribes for all the bureaucrats who'd have to sign off on his relocation application.

You had to use your initiative to succeed in New Hell, where the drug trade was one sure way to the Top—if nobody caught you at it. And J. Edgar Hoover was a master of deception, a student who'd learned his lessons well in life—an expert on international trafficking, policing, politicking, and criminality of every sort.

Humming, he bent over the carrier corpse that Mao had sent him, just one more 'body bag' in an endless stream of them. Narco-terrorism might fund the Dissidents, but it was the operators and outland movers like Mao who got rich from it.

And like J. Edgar. Still humming the *Battle Hymn of the Republic*, the mortician picked up his scalpel and began to cut, oblivious to the way the flesh under his hand shrank and quivered. They might die on the battle plain of Troy or on the slopes of Kilimanjaro or in the town-and-country warfare of the Dissidents, but they never truly separated from their bodies.

The dead felt every anguish of their destruction, their decomposition, and their rebirth. It was the Devil's way of reminding them that, no matter the rumors of angelic talent scouts or temporal Judges or tunnels leading to Heaven or temporaries flitting back and forth to Purgatory, there was no way out of Hell.

There was only the Undertaker and his staff, a cold slab and time . . . time to regret, time to recant, time to die and die again.

As his scalpel slipped through the flesh surrounding the glassine bags of China White, J. Edgar began singing aloud: ". . . He was trampling out the vintage where the grapes of wrath are stored . . ."

The Oasis was one of New Hell's most pestilential bars. Entering in grimy, tattered disguise, the angel called Altos seemed to hold his breath while he paused at the head of the stairs, as if he expected all carousing to stop, all heads to turn his way, and all voices to be raised against him.

Then he shuffled down the three stairs and past a contingent of American Marines who'd died in Beirut and waited here for any luckless Arab or Persian who happened their way.

One of the Marines half rose, noticed the pale eyes of the angel, and sat back down, muttering.

Tamara Burke saw her companion stiffen and then relax. The man opposite her at a corner table watched everything with a gaze as cold and sharp as glass. But that glass was fogged with confusion and fly-specked with regret. His name was Welch and he'd lost part of his memory, among other things, on a sojourn with Julius Caesar's party through tunnels to a deeper Hell and back.

"That's the angel, y'know," said Welch out of the corner of his mouth, his diction whiskey-sloppy. "Headed straight for Caesarion and those mercs."

"I know," said Tamara Burke, putting out a pale and shapely hand to touch Welch on his knotted forearm.

The contrast of limb against limb held her attention for a moment: her arm was tiny, dusted with almost invisible blond hairs, giving it the look of votive alabaster when placed against his—so much stronger, so much coarser with its deep tan and darker, thicker hair. Welch was one of the Devil's Children, as was she. And yet no infernal aid had been forthcoming for Welch, this agent in distress. No R&R had been decreed, no attempt made by the Agency or any other agency to mitigate his plight. "It's all right, Welch. It's not our problem—not the angel or the Roman brat," she continued, hoping to bring her companion's gaze and focus back to her and away from the angel sliding into a seat at Caesarion's table.

"Are you sure?" Welch did turn to her, and the torment in his face shimmered clearly through the drink for an instant before it subsided, replaced by that soulless look of a drunkard in Hell.

The Devil's Children—Hell's most secret society. What they both were, what they both did . . . the errands of Authority, on demand, without question. Tamara could have been as drunk as Welch—she had good reason. Her last assignment, the retrieval of Hadrian from the Dissidents, had gotten her an express trip to the Undertaker's table, minus her head. But the eyes in that head had seen Che Guevara's lovesick confusion when he'd witnessed her murder, before she'd seen nothing at all for far too long. . . .

They were both putatively between assignments— Welch because he couldn't remember enough details of his last outing to finish his report and she because Yuri Andropov didn't like her and was trying to transfer her to the Insecurity Service or the Infernal Bureau of Investigation.

So it was disciplinary, that the two were standing down, idle and temporarily without the perks and clout of their class.

Otherwise, Welch was right: they'd have inserted themselves into the party containing Caesarion, who was keeping bad company *before* the angel joined them, and at the very least dragged the little brat home by the ear. For grins. To assert Authority. To keep the supposedly "undercover" angel in his place. Because any movements of the Dissidents were their business, and the provenance of the mercs who signed on to Dissident actions for pay was the question of the hour, and because proof that the mercs' paymaster was Mithridates, Tigellinus, or anyone else from the Pentagram would be worth its weight in perks.

But mostly because players had to know the other players, and the graveyard shift had to be worked.

Welch had said that, in better days: "The graveyard shift is lonely, but it must be worked." In much better days.

The way Welch was coming apart scared Tamara— she wanted to stop it not from altruism, not to show the higher-ups how you ought to treat a loyal actor, but because she wasn't any better (none of them were) than he, and if he went to pieces, they all would, sooner or later.

Sooner or later, in the zero-sum game they played, with Eternity as the first round.

His hand slid under hers and somehow their palms touched and their fingers intertwined. Very unprofessional. Very uncool. But it made Tamara feel much better as they watched while the angel and the son of Julius Caesar and a bunch of radical mercs got up, paid their bill, then thrust their way through the crowd and out the door, whispering together conspiratorially.

Well, Tamara thought, if we're tasked to locate Caesarion, we know where to find him. And she shivered, remembering Che's base camp where she'd so recently died.

And shivered again because Welch was still holding her hand, in public, and his grip was increasingly tight.

She repeated, "Not our business;" added, "not yet." And when he didn't respond beyond further tightening his hold: "Let's go to my place. Something for ourselves, to make us feel better...."

Then paused, because she had no idea whether Welch had sexual problems. So many here did. Welch's old file data wasn't relevant anymore: his jacket hadn't had a single negative notation in it when last she'd seen it— before it became clear he couldn't (or wouldn't) turn in a final report on his most recent mission, just mutter in Attic Greek about the Trojan War.

Now he said, in English: "Feel better? We can do that right here." He let her go and held up two fingers, signaling the bar for refills.

She would have left him then, because he was scaring the hell out of her, except that her job was to stick on him like glue until he either wrote his after-action report and it could be substantiated or she knew the reason why he wouldn't.

Couldn't. If that were so.

If it weren't, Welch was in something subversive up to his oh-so-well-educated neck and that was the scariest thing of all. If he was shamming, it was the best job of it Tamara Burke had ever seen. But some of the data he *had* submitted had been contradicted by other eyewitnesses. And she needed to find out why. For all their sakes.

But most especially for her own. Not just because she needed to get on the right side of Andropov, not because she cared so terribly much if she was transferred to the IBI. Anything that could compromise Welch could rip the Devil's Children apart. They could lose everything— their privileged status, clearances and all; their integrity; their faith in one another . . . their jobs.

And the work meant everything: Hell was forever.

It was night, not that the term had terribly much meaning in New Hell, where darkness could last five minutes or contain any number of twenty-four-hour spans, be pitch black or (more usually) blood-black with a glowering Paradise like pus centering the infected sky.

Machiavelli slipped through the night like a part of it, dressed like a sentient shadow, into the Admin building via the Hall of Records and up to Reassignments, where he had no right to be.

Caesar was up to his old tricks, now that he was back. This errand that Caesar demanded of Machiavelli, who had served the Roman better and longer than most, was too dangerous. . . .

But certain treacheries had been unearthed, during the Trojan Campaigns, as everyone who was in the know now called them. And Caesar did not forget.

He had said to Niccolo, "I want Welch. Put out an APB if you have to. Get him assigned here. And forget your vendetta . . . for now."

It had been a three-beat pause, before the 'for now.' Which meant that Caesar was very serious indeed. Caesar would brook no insubordination in this matter, no fortuitous error.

It had happened, this conversation, when Caesarion had slipped surveillance. Caesar wanted Welch . . .

wanted the expert of his choice to handle the matter of this black-sheep son. Caesar could have left Caesarion to Niccolo. Should have. It was an insult and one delivered with studied intent.

Because of what had happened on the battle plain of Ilion . . . in ancient Troy or whatever simula crum of it they'd stumbled into, Julius, Cleopatra, Hatshepsut, Alexander of Macedon and the rest. And Caesar held his grudges forever.

So it had been necessary to force little Dante to twiddle the Pentagram computers, then those in the Admin building itself. Dantille, quaking with fear, could refuse Machiavelli nothing. Obedient minions were a must in Machiavelli's profession.

But it still rankled that history's master spy must be reduced to the status of a personnel clerk. Or would have, if Machiavelli had time now to worry about things more peripheral to his survival than not being caught with his hand in the silicon cookie jar.

The Reassignments computer was perhaps the most sensitive in New Hell. Everyone's fate rested in its banks. One could snatch a man out of bed and soundest sleep and cause him to find himself snoozing in the belly of a whale or the jaws of a hungry crocodile . . . or between the Dissidents' tents. Even that could be done. Enemies could be dealt with, from here.

Slipping through dimly lit hallways where half-burned-out fluorescents buzzed angrily and flickered so that headache stabbed the back of a man's brain, Machiavelli repeated to himself the entry codes Dante had begged him to memorize.

"One slip," the terrified little man had said, his long nostrils flaring and every hair and pore black against the whiteness of his face, "and you will bring Mephistophelian wrath down upon us in proportions such as Man has never dreamt . . ."

And more of the same, for Dante was rewriting some piece of prose and couldn't manage to say anything concisely, these days. . . .

Machiavelli had occasionally had audiences with the Devil. He kept this datum, along with many others, to himself. He had connections all up and down the hierarchy. But not even those could protect him if he were caught meddling with the Reassignments computer.

Nothing could.

Dark halls. Quiet, fitful mutters of computers talking to one another. Whirrs and starts of media reels on mainframes.

And then a glass door: AUTHORIZED PERSONNEL ONLY, under which someone had scrawled with blood-red lipstick, "Abandon all hope, ye who enter here."

As if there were any other way.

Beyond the glass were functionaries, their heads bent to terminals, a dozen or more even on the graveyard shift.

Machiavelli heard a sound behind him like the scraping of feet and turned. The corridor was empty. At its other end was an elevator of the sort that let one out wherever Reassignments decreed—the same (or one of the multitude of portals to the same) dimensional gate/elevator that brought souls to Hell in the first place. Its doors were contentedly closed.

Machiavelli had come another way. He would leave as he had come, via back stairs with pilfered keys. But even the glimpse made his hackles rise. Fear of Reassignments superseded most other fears among those who lived in the villas and had made a sort of life here which was bearable.

It was equaled only by the fear of the Undertaker's table: some from Caesar's family—or his extended family, his soldiers and his progenitors and descendants—had never returned to the villa from the Undertaker. Where they were, only Reassignments knew. And Reassignments wasn't saying.

Machiavelli squared his shoulders, commanded his feet to their most authoritative gait, and pushed open the door.

No one even looked up. Inside, before the unmanned

reception desk, he waited for someone to come. But no one did. His gut spasmed in the bright light as he realized that he'd made a mistake.

Act as if you know where you're going, Niccolo. What else had Dante said? Ah, he remembered, and threaded his way past work stations until he found a group of cubbyholes against one far, white wall, all the while with muscles jumping in his back and phantom stares boring into him.

The third cubbyhole, the one he wanted, and blessing his luck . . . sitting down, booting up, typing in a code word and another, to get him by the flag on the file he wanted.

The data came up: *028495 . . . welch, r . . . n/a; inc.*

Welch, not available; incomplete?

What it meant, Machiavelli couldn't imagine. He gnawed a knuckle and then began, very carefully and slowly, to delete the notations and insert those that would reassign Welch to Caesar's villa, while his heart thundered in his ears and his hands shook.

Nichols rolled off his slab in a flurry of red sheets and red johnny, cursing the gurney which threatened to roll out from under him when he most needed its support, and began bawling for an attendant.

You had to know how to handle these Admin types. Sycophants flitted toward him, wraiths in the light, barely visible but for the clipboards and field gear and weapons they carried.

It used to spook him something fierce, waking up here in the recovery room and seeing M-1s and backpack nukes and what-have-you floating toward him borne in transparent hands.

By now, Nichols had been here too many times to let it bother him. Pragmatism was his religion. He got the job done and, often as not, came home the hard way.

His hitch as Welch's aide de camp had been no exception.

He snatched the clipboard floating before him and

snarled under his breath, "Get me steak and eggs, a Bloody Mary, and a pass to Reassignments. *Move!*"

Sycophants mewled and scurried, a platoon of see-through buck privates who'd hold his coat and clean his gun and get him anything he asked for, up to and including a ground-effect tank with his monogram on the turret, if his requisition was approved by Authority.

Not out of fear: Nichols' sycophants didn't scare easy.

Whatever the sycophants were, they loved just the kind of abuse Nichols, whenever he came out of another death cranky and mean, was prone to dish out.

Night-action coveralls and swat-team black webbing glided toward him. Probably meant New Hell was in a dark phase—or wherever he was going would be.

He didn't care. He'd been handed more kinds of battle dress since he'd come here than he cared to count. The flak vest was a pain in the ass, heavy and hot, but he shrugged into it and scanned a second clipboard held by iridescent hands that told him to go to Reassignments and pick up his briefing book.

No rest for the wicked, you bet.

Clomping down the hall ten minutes later in Airborne jump boots (that matched the 101st tattoo on his arm, the only souvenir from life and afterlife that was dependably resurrected with him), he was whistling.

Damn, leave it to Welch to find soemthing for him right out of a resurrection bay. The guy didn't know from R&R. Relief percolated slowly through Nichols' stubborn, armor-plated psyche: there had been rumors that if you died on the battle plain of Troy you couldn't make it back to base. "Base," for Nichols, was the Admin building, Undertaker's table and all. He usually saved up bad jokes to share with Old Sewer-Breath, who customarily saw to Nichols' corpse himself. This time it had been a couple of Rock Hudsons, but he hadn't needed them. . . .

A figure came skulking out of Reassignments, a little rat-faced guy in black that Nichols remembered all too well. The rest was reflex, autonomic, little more than a test run of his reconstituted body's efficiency.

A blur of motion later, Nichols was holding Machiavelli by the throat against the wall, the slight Italian's feet an inch off the corridor's white tile. The rage Nichols felt, pounding in his temples and making his voice scratchy, was more than a dry run for his adrenals—he'd had to give this piece of Wop slime up to a "political" solution during his last mission. But as far as Nichols was concerned, it wasn't over.

As far as Nichols was concerned, it would never be over between him and Machiavelli. Nichols' head had ended up on a pike for "political" reasons that had way too much to do with the greasy little snitch he was holding for it ever to be over.

He leaned close to Machiavelli, white with fear and as pop-eyed as a trout flopping on a deck, and said, "How you doin', little man? Glad to see me? You better have your shit together, buddy, as to what you're doing here and why, or I'm going to pop you straight back to Slab A, on general principals."

Machiavelli's face was now purpling and Nichols had to let him down far enough for his feet to touch the tile before Machiavelli could get air enough to answer. "Nichols . . . I thought . . . You're supposd to be with Achill—"

"Never mind where I'm supposed to be, pencil-ass. I'm policing this corridor and you'd better have some serious need to be here. C'mon. Spill. Or get ready to greet the Undertaker."

"Welch . . ." Machiavelli paused, gasped a quaking breath and began again. "I am here on Caesar's business. An APB is out on your friend Welch." A weak counterattack, a flicker of pride and resentment—and memories of the sort of debriefing Nichols had given Machiavelli in Troy: "If you know his whereabouts, Authority should be informed forthwith. He's urgently summoned." Machiavelli's hands came up, inside Nichols' arms, to push Nichols away.

Uncertain because the reaction wasn't the one he'd expected, Nichols released his hold.

Machiavelli straightened his shoulders, then his garments, irritably. "An APB, I say again. Your superior," the word was laced with derision, "must report to the villa immediately. Do tell him when—"

"Why's that, rat-face?"

"Caesarion," said Machiavelli with all his court gentility returned. "Caesar wants him found. Perhaps we will meet again, yes? When your superior reports for duty under our command."

Caution overwhelmed Nichols momentarily. *Our* command. Then the implication became clear. "I've fragged COs better'n you for less than you did to me, buddy," he replied, the sheer murder-lust in his voice masking his qualms well enough. "I got all the time in the world to ream your ass, after I check with Welch. So let's just look forward to it, okay?"

He stepped back far enough for Machiavelli to move past him without either of them having to say anything more, and pushed through the Reassignments doors with his neck burning and his muscles stiff. The thing he hated most about Hell was the number of movers and shakers and slimebags he had to put up with because you just couldn't tell the goddamn players without a scorecard and the Devil made up new rules as the game went along.

But the thing with Machiavelli was too personal to wait forever. Inside Reassignments, a warrior-bishop who'd creamed lots of Frogs in his time summoned Nichols familiarly to his cubicle.

Some things, at least, hadn't changed.

When Nichols hit the streets an hour later by his black chronometer's digital reckoning, he'd confirmed Machiavelli's story that there was an APB out on Welch, but not the reason for it. Nichols' Reassignments officer either didn't know or wouldn't tell. And he'd found out that he was on hold until Achilles showed up, at which time he was to receive a sealed orders packet.

He wasn't real thrilled at the inference—that he'd be under Achilles' command for at least one mission. He didn't like the Old Dead, and he didn't like Achilles. The short, red-haired bastard was as arrogant as they came, and twice as foolhardy as anybody who'd been in Hell for centuries had any right to be.

But orders were orders. And no orders were no orders. Until he got some, he was going to find some sour mash and get as drunk as he could for as long as he could. He was useful enough to Authority that his kidneys and liver were almost always in good working order. And if he happened on Welch, he'd find out what the fuck was going on ... the man he'd known wasn't one to withhold information. Welch was a stone pro. Something had glitched up somewhere.

And if it turned out that Welch was playing some game of his own, that he knew about the APB and being seconded to Caesar's service and was hiding out, Nichols was prepared to do whatever was necessary to help his former commander ... his friend. Even if it meant smuggling Welch out with him in the inevitable helicopter Achilles would have with him, because that was what Achilles was: Hell's premier chopper pilot.

You know a guy, you know where he drinks.

The Oasis was full of ex-military types from a hundred nations, some of which had names Nichols couldn't even pronounce, let alone spell.

But he could spell M-A-R-I-N-E-S, and when he saw the Beirut contingent near the door, the twitchiness in his shoulders began to ease.

Home was where you could find enough of your own type to know what the game and the rules would be for the next little while. The Oasis was primarily a New Dead bar, though some of the short hairy guys from B.C. were scattered about—those who had made the adjustment, like Achilles, and knew the butt from the business end of a firearm.

Finding Welch in that crowd wasn't going to be hard—just ask around, Nichols knew. The Ivy League former intelligence officer called Welch was easygoing, a passable shot, and everybody's best hope when the intrigue got thick as shit in a sewer. He did a lot of free consulting for soldiers who needed backgrounding on new assignments—even when the company you were assigned to was from so far back in history you'd flunked it in high school. Welch was real bright, and never held it over anybody's head. The Oasis crowd loved him like a weekend pass.

A bottle of Old No. 7 bought and paid for at the bar, Nichols started on his reconnaissance, looking for a friendly face to ply for info, when he stopped in midstep and stared fiercely at a shadowed, corner table.

Welch in the flesh. With a bimbo. Cursing himself for the luckiest sonofabitch in New Hell, Nichols ambled over to the table, plunked down his bottle, and said, "Hiya, sir. Let's lose the skirt. We gotta talk," before he realized just how drunk Welch was.

Elbows splayed on the table, Welch peered up at him. "Skirt? Yeah, yeah. Tanya . . . Nichols. Siddown, Nichols. Nichols was my ADC in . . . in . . . shit." Welch shook his head slowly from side to side.

Nichols' focus sharpened. The woman was pretty in an aristocratic way, blond and thin, not anywhere near as drunk as her companion, and there was a slight frown between her eyes when she glanced from Welch to him.

She said in slightly accented English, "Ah, from the Trojan Campaign, then. Good. Do sit, Mister Nichols."

He almost told her he wasn't anybody's 'Mister,' but he sat instead and fingered the bottle he'd brought nervously. "I gotta talk to him alone, lady. It's urgent."

"We are in the same business, Mister Nichols. Don't worry," as if that was going to solve everything.

Welch leaned forward and said, "Hey, Nichols, you remember anything about—where we were an' all?"

And something inside Nichols hurt, quite suddenly and distinctly, as he looked into Welch's glassy eyes and realized that what he'd been told in Reassignments was true—or that Welch wanted him to believe it was. Ignoring Tanya—Welch was still Welch and had more sense than to get this drunk around a woman he couldn't trust—Nichols said, "Look sir, I'm here now. We'll get all this straightened out. But they want you over at Caesar's—I got it straight from Reassignments. So if you don't want the Angels to come and drag you over there, we'd better get outta sight until—"

The woman was already rising. "I know where to hide him. And you. Where you can talk safely. Come, bring him."

There was something about her, this blond bitch with the commanding airs and the cool voice, that made Nichols hop to. And that bothered him so much that, with Welch's arm slung over his shoulders, he paused long enough to add, "Hey, lady, bring the bottle. I paid for it." And: "What did you say your name was?"

"I didn't. Tamara Burke."

"The hell you say." Tamara Burke, Che Guevara's nemesis. The honey pot of all time. If Welch wasn't in trouble before he'd hooked up with her, he sure was now.

Going to her place, yet. Where it was safe. But that was what Welch seemed to want, and Nichols couldn't think of a better place. Although he did think, all that long way through the darkest streets of Hell, that if he got caught helping Welch go AWOL, he was going to regret it a long time on the Undertaker's table.

Welch realized the shit was about to hit the fan before Nichols or Tanya did—as soon as he saw the bare-breasted woman lounging under the apartment building's awning. The woman had only one nipple, and if you couldn't recognize Mata Hari by her jackboots or her riding crop or carnal knowledge, you could trust the missing nipple: an American general had bitten it off in life and, no matter how many times she visited the Undertaker, she could never get it back.

Welch knew her from a dozen operations and a score

of intimate encounters; knew her well enough that he'd have recognized her if she was swathed in purdah. And because he did know her, he understood what her lack of disguise was meant to telegraph: Fallen Angels on the rooftops with sniper rifles and light-intensifying scopes; more of Satan's shock troops in adjacent doorways and parked cars on the ill-lit streets—in short, *Surrender now, don't make us bring you in the hard way.*

Mata Hari's presence was a courtesy call, a flag on the action about to commence, a perk due one of the Devil's Children who'd seen better days. First Tanya, now Mata Hari. . . . Shit, Authority was throwing everything at him but the kitchen sink.

It should have made Welch feel better, but it made him feel worse. Useless. Outmoded. Down a quart. Used up. He prided himself on his memory, and it was shot full of holes. And he was drunk enough to be truculent. The last thing he wanted was to be shunted off to Caesar and that crowd of inbred ancients again. That was where all the trouble had started . . . whatever it had been.

All of this must have run through his mind in the space of one deep breath, because Tanya was still walking beside him on the left and, on his right, Nichols hadn't yet grabbed for his weapons (with which Nichols, as always, was well supplied).

About the time Welch was scanning rooftops and coming to a stubborn halt, Mata Hari—Gertrud Margarete Zelle—sashayed a few steps forward and said cattily, "Guten abend, girls," and Nichols got the message.

A pistol butt was thrust his way and Welch took it, while the blur that was Nichols in a combat situation continued to deploy assets: The M-11 snapped out of its holster on Nichols' hip and Tanya was suddenly a living shield, Nichols' free arm around her throat as he wrestled her in front of him.

A chorus of *snicks* from rooftops, scattered cars and doorways was the only response from the Fallen Angels under Mata Hari's command.

In the silence, over Tanya's harsh breathing, all that could be heard was the *tap, tap* of Mata Hari's riding crop against her jodhpur-clad thigh and Nichols' whisper: "Any way you want to play it, sir."

Welch answered by thumbing the safety off the cocked and locked, laser-sighted 9mm Nichols had just thrust at him. He escalated matters one additional step by potentiating the laser-guide so that its red dot appeared (wavering and then dead steady as Welch braced his shooting wrist with his other hand), on Mata Hari's single remaining nipple.

"To what do we owe the pleasure, Gertie?" Welch said, sounding more sober than he was.

Mata Hari hated to be called Gertie. She looked down at her laser-targeted breast and then at Welch, frowning. She stamped one spit-polished bootheel and half a dozen helmeted shock troops separated themselves from the shadows, looking like linebackers from some pro football team whose uniform was unrelievedly black.

"Sir?" Nichols whispered urgently. "We gonna rock 'n' roll or not?"

This because of the full auto weapons in evidence on Mata Hari's side of the argument.

Tanya hadn't said a word, Welch realized, not even to protest being choke-held in front of Nichols like an Achaean shield. . . .

Something stirred in his data-punched memory, some phantom vision of a man no taller than the shield in front of him, a man with a crested helmet and a chiton. . . . He pushed it all away. It was nothing, a phantom from a Greek hyhton, Diomedes and the birds on some piece of museum-quality clay he'd seen somewhere, from his real life in modern Athens, from studies at Harvard, from . . . from the goddamned battle plain of Ilion!

"*Sir?*" demanded Nichols urgently, wanting only to be unleashed, quivering so that Welch could feel it, standing so close, like a Rott or a Doberman or any other good piece of equipment tuned up and ready to go.

Something inside Welch desperately wanted to say, "Yeah," and squeeze one off from his own weapon, precipitating a fire fight and an express trip back through the system, so that he could wake up on the Undertaker's table and see if his memory of recent events improved.

He'd lost an eye in life, but he never needed his glass one when he took the Trip—he came through with everything a human body ought to have, unlike Mata Hari. And to Welch's way of thinking, memory was something he had to have. So maybe it would be worth it to. . . .

No. It wouldn't. Not for Tanya, who'd just come out of there and who was toughing this mess out with all she had . . . unless she was a part of this setup.

And certainly not for Nichols, not at any price. Welch had gotten Nichols killed the last time, sacrificed because Welch's understanding of Roman justice wasn't what it should have been. He'd . . .

Remembered! Not everything, but some of it. . . . He grinned at Mata Hari and the grin widened, and became a chuckle, through which he managed to get out, "Okay, okay Gertie, I surrender," before he doubled over in a paroxysm of laughter that brought him, teary-eyed, to his knees on the sidewalk.

Nichols freed Tanya with a disgusted shove and knelt down there beside him, under the watchful eyes of the Fallen Angels, trying to help him, confusion like a pall over the commando's face. But to Nichol's queries, all Welch could manage was, "Don't mean nothin'," and then, when the storm of laughter had passed, leaving him weak and still drunk, he let Nichols help him to his feet and the two of them faced the pair of women and what turned out to be nearly two dozen Angels for backup.

"You will come with us now?" Mata Hari's eyes

gleamed in the half-light. Her hand was on her milky, unviolated breast. "To Caesar's?"

"Yeah, yeah," Welch said, still leaning on Nichols for support. "Both of us, though." And then he thought about what he was asking of Nichols, and what he was beginning to remember, and about the two women before him. So he added, "As soon as the four of us—you, me, Tanya, and Nichols—get back downstairs from Tanya's apartment. Nichols told me they wanted me over at Caesar's, but I promised him a little R&R . . . *you* know, there's the hard way and the easy way, Gertie."

So he'd pulled it out, Welch thought as weapons were holstered and grumbling shock troops stepped back. Gone on record that Nichols wasn't part of any perceived problem. Got the ball of command back in his own court.

It wasn't really that much of a risk he'd taken. It had to do with knowing your enemy. And he knew Mata Hari. She always did things the easy way. The real bone of contention, with her, was who ended up on top.

Feeling much better, Welch followed Tamara Burke's pert little ass up the stairs. He was about to see to it that Nichols had the time of his afterlife, courtesy of Mata Hari, one of the best pros in the business.

It wouldn't make up for getting Nichols wasted in Ilion, but it was a damned good start.

Nichols couldn't believe the mess he was in some hours later, about the time the sky began to lighten, while Caesar and Welch took turns chewing each other out about slights and command breakdowns and Caesarion and insubordinations real and imagined. Beyond Caesar's office window, a Huey put down in the courtyard.

Whatever Welch wanted wasn't going to matter squat, not to Caesar or to Authority, like whatever Nichols wanted wasn't going to matter.

Tamara Burke was playing stenographer in the office while Caesar and Welch hashed it out enough to put

together an after-action report that would get Welch off
the hook and on to new business.

Nichols felt good about that. Welch was as fine an
officer as served in Hell. However Nichols felt about
officers in general, you had to have a couple guys up the
spout who had your best interests at heart, if only because they owed you.

Welch wanted Nichols. Watching Achilles swing down
out of the chopper with a briefcase under his arm, it
was as clear to Nichols as his memory of Mata Hari's
disfigured breast that Welch wasn't going to get him.

Welch wasn't going to get much else he was asking
for either, Nichols was willing to bet. The Old Dead had
been here so much longer, they plain had more strings
to pull.

Nichols slipped out of the columned, gilt-edged lair of
the Roman brass unnoticed.

Might as well make it easy on everybody. It wasn't
that easy to sneak around in jump boots on marble
floors, though: Tamara Burke came following after.

"Thought you was takin' notes," Nichols said gruffly.
He didn't like her sort of woman, and he didn't like
talking to women in general, with the exception of the
sort of talk he and Mata Hari had had. (He'd promised
never to call her "Gert" or "Gertie" and received her
phone number in return.)

"I was," said the woman who'd set up Che Guevara's
execution for either the CIA or KGB, Nichols had never
learned which.

So maybe she was the enemy, still. Nothing she'd
done where Welch was concerned proved otherwise.
She swung in file beside him, as if they were old
acquaintances.

He said, after two corridors and too much silence,
"Look, lady, go back to work. That's what I'm doin'."

She only shot him a doe-eyed look that made him rub
angrily at the back of his neck.

And then there was Achilles, taking the stairs two at a
time because he was so short-legged the stairs were a

problem and pushing things was always Achilles' response to problems. The short guy with the long red hair was a chronic overachiever, the kind that got you killed.

In Hell, where that wasn't a one-time occurrence, Nichols regularly avoided guys like Achilles as if they had crabs. But there was no way around it, this time. He had his orders.

Achilles saw them, put one hand on his flight-suited hip above a non-regulation disruptor in a quick-draw holster, and said, "Right. Burke? Somebody filled you in, I hope."

A horrible suspicion began gnawing at Nichols' gut.

Then the blond woman replied, "Just a little while ago," and Nichols remembered how she'd had her head together with one of Mata Hari's big, armor-plated boys on the way over here. "Something about a cache of heroin being found in the Mortuary and J. Edgar Hoover having confessed that he's been running it in here in collusion with Mao, right?"

"Very good," said the little antiquated shrimp of a ladies' man, preening. From under his arm he took a red-bordered folder and handed it to her. "Your copy, Madame. We can read up in the chopper. And yours, Nichols," Achilles added, acknowledging him directly for the first time.

Nichols took the folder and slit it with a fingernail, leafing through the typescript, shaking his head.

Achilles was still talking. ". . . think I've anticipated all your weaponry needs, Nichols, but if there's anything special, we can stop by the armory."

At the mention of the armory, Nichols looked up from his paperwork. Achilles was grinning broadly.

Nothing Nichols saw in his orders seemed remotely humorous. He wished fervently that Welch could have swung it, kept Nichols on as his ADC.

"What I need, buddy, they ain't got in that armory. Says here that while we're tryin' to stop the whole fucking drug trade out of the Triangle, we're supposed to find this Gilga . . . Gilgam. . . ."

"Gilgamesh," Tamara Burke said helpfully, pronouncing the name slowly. "And Enkidu."

"You're kidding," Nichols couldn't help saying when he heard the second name pronounced.

"We don't name 'em," said Achilles, long, vicious eyes narrowing, "we just separate 'em. That's what our orders say: 'Gilgamesh and Enkidu are to be separated.' It's their punishment, or some such."

"And how are we going to do that?" Nichols demanded with real irritation. The two men in question were evidently friends. No pictures of them were included in the briefing material. The only helpful data from Reassignments was that they'd be with a certain caravan on a certain date at a certain location. Part of the mission definition was to return the two men for reassignment.

Nichols had had too much experience with orders of this sort from Authority to think there would be anything straightforward about the mission in question. And he didn't want Tamara Burke along to complicate matters with Achilles, as any woman's proximity did wherever the chopper pilot was.

Achilles shrugged, his eyes on the woman, full of suggestions that were going to make life miserable for everybody involved. Over Achilles' shoulder, at the foot of the stairs, Nichols glimpsed Machiavelli staring up at them, a gloating smirk on his rat's face.

So Nichols asked again: "I said, how are we going to find these guys in a caravan full of strangers without any kind of solid description? This whole thing stinks." He slapped his orders against his palm.

"It's a drug-running caravan, isn't it?" Achilles snapped. "They're part of our mission parameters too, aren't they? Far as I'm concerned, we kill 'em all and let the Devil sort 'em out."

"Damn," Welch had said, watching out Caesar's window while Achilles' chopper, with Tanya and Nichols aboard, lifted into the bloody sky.

"Damnzione," an unctuous voice had agreed from behind him, and Welch had turned to find Machiavelli there, all velvet and olive oil smile.

The smile had ripped through the encrustations on another part of Welch's memory and he'd found himself fingering Nichols' 9mm gift at his hip as he said, "Your doing, right? Strings pulled in Reassignments. Tanya to muck things up. Nichols because you Italian bastards can't ever let anything go ... because of vendetta." *Because we beat so many secrets out of you, you limp-wristed word merchant, in the com truck on the hill of Troy that night. Because you can't stand to lose and this thing's going to go on forever because I won't let you win at the Children's expense.*

No reply came from the smiling lips of the founder of deception, the man who'd made science out of instinct, who'd taken all objective notions of right and wrong and turned them on their collective head, leaving only history to come down on the side of any winner as right, any loser as wrong, in the games of nations. If you could put all his dead under Machiavelli's feet, their corpses would have made a pyramid that reached up to Paradise.

But now Welch knew, from a glimpse through glinting eyes into what passed for Machiavelli's soul, how he'd ended up here, seconded to Caesar for a babysitting job any skydiving wimp from Insecurity could have done better.

And anger made him turn on Caesar, who was at the root of Machiavelli's maneuvering—or who should have been. Welch had said, "This isn't about Caesarion at all, is it, Julius? It's about Machiavelli's ass—starting with him murdering Judah Maccabee and double-crossing—"

"It is," Julius Caesar interrupted, "most especially about Caesarion." Caesar rose to his full five-feet-ten-inches, where he could look Welch nearly in the eye. He pulled on his long nose and his dark eyes narrowed. Off to one side, Machiavelli fairly faded into the woodwork.

Hours later, readying his chute to air drop out of an old C-130 into the woods near Che Guevara's camp,

Welch was still haunted by the anguish hiding in Caesar's face as the Roman had told him, "Augustus will kill Caesarion if he finds him. Then, no matter what strings you think Niccolo can pull, we may lose him forever. . . . Brutus was—is—an eighteen-year-old boy. Do you understand what that means? We just got him back. We don't know from where. He doesn't remember anything. You, of all men, ought to sympathize with that."

The revelation had stopped Welch cold for three heartbeats. Then professionalism had taken over. Maybe he didn't recall everything he should of the Trojan Campaign, but he had years of life and afterlife to call on. He'd turned on a mental dime and said, "Fine. I'll take Brutus with me—I need somebody Caesarion can relate to, somebody he'll trust. Another one of your sons ought to do the trick."

And Julius Caesar had gone white as a ghost while Machiavelli sought the window, turning his back on the proceedings hurriedly, as if afraid his expression might betray him.

Welch had a sharp intuition, a definite perception that he was digging his way into a snakepit he wasn't briefed to handle. There was something odd, perhaps advantageous, about Caesar's reaction, he was almost certain.

The Roman's next words confirmed it: "He . . . Brutus doesn't know Caesarion; they've never met here. Anyone but Brutus, Welch. Anything but that." Pleading, or as close to it as a Roman could come who'd refused to take the title emperor but who was emperor over all Romans in Hell, Julius took a step toward Welch, hand out, seeming suddenly to bear the weight of all his thousands of years here.

Welch's reply stopped the Roman in his tracks. "No deal. No conditions—on your side. I get you your juvenile delinquent, Caesarion, and you get off my case. Undo whatever your snake here has done; return me to my command structure. I don't want anything more to do with you or yours once I've brought the kid in. And I want carte blanche to do it—I know how you types tweak the motor pool and the armory. I want . . ."

He'd begun the list of equipment and logistical support that had gotten him here, in the C-130, ready to jump out into thin air, count off seconds of free fall, and pull his rip cord so that the sky-red chute deployed and he could get the hell on with it.

Jumps. He wished he'd had Nichols with him. Nichols didn't mind jumps. Once, together in a situation like this, Welch had asked Nichols how you got used to it, and when. "You don't," Nichols had replied.

Welch hadn't, that was for sure. He flexed and jumped and his stomach lagged about three seconds behind all that long fall down through palpable air and ruddy mist, until he pulled his cord and a hand jerked him to a full stop in midair.

Then he floated, thinking about gravity wells and physics and how his body didn't mind the jerking and swaying anywhere near as much as freefall.

The ground always comes up deceptively fast, as if you'd been thrown toward it. Hard as you hit, it's never unwelcome, even if you break a bone, because its solid ground and if man was meant to float, he'd breathe vacuum and swim between the stars.

This time, Welch didn't break anything. The concussion made the soles of his feet sting as if he'd stepped into a convoy of army ants and his knees twinge as if somebody were making him two inches shorter the hard way, but he rolled with it.

When he came to a stop and shrugged out of his harness, he lay there for a moment before he gathered up the billows of his chute, just glad to be breathing with lungs that hadn't been pummeled to jelly.

He was too old for this shit. He was too valuable to waste. He'd made Caesar a promise and gotten one in return, though.

He sat up, got his chute in order, and watched the sky, out of which young Brutus was descending.

You wanted that kind of leverage, dealing with Julius and his oligarchic buddies. Caesar had wanted assurances that Welch wouldn't fill Brutus in on what the kid had forgotten, wouldn't try to jog his memory or suborn his sympathies.

As if Welch gave a damn. He'd given more of a damn about what Machiavelli had as much as admitted he'd done—gotten Tanya assigned to Achilles for the duration, gotten Nichols, Achilles, and the woman involved in outland drug wars.

Vendetta. All right, Welch had thought as pieces of the puzzle began to snap together, any number could play. The Children had their own resources. To use them, Welch had to accomplish this mission for Caesar so that he could get his decks cleared, reestablish his credibility, and be ready for any assignment Authority wanted to throw at him.

Machiavelli would keep. His kind always did.

He watched the scab-red dot that was Brutus fall from the sky. Fall too fast. Caesar's favorite son? Welch's classics education fell far short of what was necessary to scope relationships changed by thousands of years in Hell.

But if the kid didn't pull his cord soon, or engage his emergency procedures, it wasn't going to matter what Brutus meant to the larger scheme of things. Not for a while, it wouldn't.

Splat! and back to Slab A, as Nichols would have said.

Squinting at the rufous sky, sitting on his chute to keep it from billowing, Welch got out his field phone and began trying to contact Brutus.

Just as he finished yelling at the kid to pull his "damned cord, over!" Brutus' chute deployed and the boy began swinging back and forth like a yo-yo in an amateur's hands.

And he was both of those: the boy was nearly a blank slate, stuck in some temporal glitch where what grown men thought of him was all that mattered. He read as clearly as any raw recruit of good family to Welch, who'd handled dozens of Brutus' type in life and after: spoiled rich kids looking for something real, anything real, to validate their existence.

This sortie into Che's territory ought to do the trick.

Welch looked away from the slow-falling jumper, down at the field phone he held, courtesy of Machiavelli's connections. It was an advanced model, and it went places it had no right to go, like into the very bowels of Authority's command structure, where its LCD displays could be trusted to mirror whatever data was being sent or received by the Hall of Injustice's mainframe. Or from Reassignments'.

Damned thing was worth its weight in passes to Purgatory, and not just because Welch was about to use it to request an emergency pickup (now that the C-130 was out of sight) by a particular craft with lots of specific requirements.

He was dead sure he was going to get it, too, with Brutus along as his insurance policy.

The kid was almost on the ground. Welch patched into Brutus' com circuit: "Get ready to flex your knees. Don't stiffen up. Roll with . . ."

Boy hit ground, hard enough that Welch got up to see if there was anything left worth tying up.

There was and he did: Brutus tied to a tree with a gag in his mouth was a lot safer than Brutus opening that mouth at the wrong moment and getting Welch into more trouble with the Dissidents than he could handle, alone.

The boy, dazed, hardly struggled. Welch snapped a homing beacon, the size of a pack of matches, on "send" and stuffed it in the kid's pocket, while big brown eyes liquid with betrayal implored him not to do this.

"Don't worry, kid, we'll work up some heroic story for your daddy. I just can't risk you doing something stupid. Caesarion's already *done* something stupid, so he won't be arguing."

As Caesar had said, Caesarion didn't know Brutus from Adam. Checking Brutus' beacon, on which the

extraction team would home in, Welch patted the youngster on the shoulder and swung off toward the wooded
ravine leading to Che's camp.

He looked back once, at the boy tied to the tree at the
edge of the small clearing. Damn fine job, so far; damn
fine.

It wasn't Welch's kind of operation, hadn't been for a
long time—jumping and hiking and armed to the teeth.
But he could still handle it. It was nice to know that.

Infiltration was another story. If he didn't, in his
professional judgment, consider the threat posed by fac-
tions within the Pentragram more serious than that
posed by the Dissidents whom they seemed to be fund-
ing, Welch would have been digging himself in among
Che's people for a long stay.

But the hostile threat indices told him that the Pentagram treachery was what he ought to be tracking. And
Welch had a stubborn streak in him, one that had gotten him killed in life because he couldn't go to ground—
consider himself neutralized, impotent—just because his
name and address were published in *CounterSpy* as an
enemy of the revolution.

Walking insouciantly into Che's camp—into the sen-
tries guarding its perimeter, more precisely—wasn't the
easiest thing he'd ever done. The muscles along his
spine crawled and ticked and his tongue and throat got
so dry they felt as if he'd been chewing cactus.

Sticks cracked. Leaves rustled. Pines whispered. And
the pulse in Welch's ears was twice as loud as any of
that.

When a figure separated itself from the trees and
barred his path, he flinched before the sentry said, "Halt!"

"No sweat," Welch responded, slowly bringing his
hands up to his shoulders, fingers spread, trying to see
the sentry's face under its rusty dapples of camouflage
paint.

The sentry came close, finger trembling on his plasma
rifle (Where the *hell* did Che get this stuff, when Welch
couldn't have requisitioned one of those to stop an as-

sassination plot aimed at Old Nick himself?), held its muzzle under Welch's chin as he frisked him with trembling hands, and then knelt down to examine the loot he'd taken off Welch's well-prepared and unresisting person.

The field phone got most of the attention. It was supposed to. It was supposed to get Welch an audience with Che himself. But the look in the sentry's eyes said maybe it wouldn't.

The kid was so obviously considering shooting Welch out of hand so that he could claim the spoils that Welch said, "Look, anybody's got a right to defect, so I heard. If I'm wrong, you can keep the stuff and I'll just go back the way I came. But maybe your boss would like to chat with me. Maybe I'm worth more than what you see there. After all, I did get out of New Hell with all of that."

Dim wits started fitfully, coughed like a recalcitrant diesel on a cold morning, and churned slowly. Then the sentry said, "I guess," and began stuffing Welch's 9mm and extra clips and night goggles and survival knife and various black boxes into his fatigues' pockets. Finally, the sentry slung the field phone over his shoulder. "After you, hot stuff."

Welch was glad to oblige him and careful not to slip or make any unexpected moves.

Hands laced at the crown of his head, he negotiated three checkpoints with the sentry's gun barrel cool against the side of his throat before they made Che's base camp.

There Welch paused in disbelief at the extent of the place, hidden under cammo netting. As big as a small town, the Dissident camp was ringed with pilfered hardware, jeeps and trucks and tanks and artillery, and awash with women and children.

There was no way anybody with Pentagram resources could have failed to find this place unless Pentagram resources were turned to making sure nobody did.

So it was all clear as a bell, now. And as soon as

somebody hit the right dummy button on one of those
black boxes or tried to fuck with the field phone, conditions here were going to change drastically. Tac air was
biddable, and Welch had pulled every string of his own
he could ever remember collecting.

Now all he had to do was get out of here with Caesarion
before somebody accidentally sent the "go" signal by
screwing around with Welch's equipment—before all
hell broke loose, or before somebody found Brutus and
turned off the homing device. In which case, by his own
order, Welch was to be considered expendable.

He always liked to give that order himself, before
somebody else did: it made him feel less the fool.

Hell was full of fools, and the worst of those were
right here, clustering around him.

He saw faces he knew from history books among
those he didn't—Confucious, Homer, Madame Curie, Judah Maccabee ...

Maccabee! Luck wasn't something Welch expected,
but it was staring him in the eye, nodding twice, and
shouldering through the crowd.

"I know this man," said Maccabee in Israelite-accented
English. "I will vouch for him."

And Maccabee did, deftly extracting Welch from the
nervous sentry, getting his gear back, and taking him to
"see Che."

Outside the rebel leader's tent, Maccabee said under
his breath, "So? You are a rebel now?"

"There aren't going to *be* any rebels by morning, at
least not here."

They knew each other. They'd fought together. Maccabee simply nodded. Someone passed by, peering at
them curiously. Both men waited.

Then Maccabee said, even more quietly in the open
air, raking his dark curls with a hand. "You didn't come
to warn me, not all this way. What do you want here?"

"Caesarion. I'll explain why later. Want to help?"

'I prefer it to the Undertaker, yes. Where do you want
him, and when?"

Welch explained quickly, and saw Maccabee frown. "Problems?"

"When are there not? It's the one called Just Al, a blond man who brought Caesarion—"

"Not a man," Welch said absently. "Bring him too."

"And you? How will you get out?"

"It's what I do, remember? If I can't help you with the boy, do what I said. You're on the right side of the Agency, remember. I know it doesn't suit your ethics, but it'll keep you alive."

"I wasn't here because of ideological—"

"Alexander, right?" The missing friend. It was always something like that, with the better men. Personal struggles. Personal pride. Personal redemption. Authority could keep them out of Heaven but it couldn't keep them from behaving like men, not animals. For Welch's money, it was more than enough. He clapped Maccabee on the shoulder: "Go on, let's blow this place."

It was a double entendre lost on the Hasmonaean commando, but Maccabee went, first sticking his head in between the flaps of Che's tent and securing Welch his audience.

The tent was full of shadows and the handsome face of Guevara was full of worse. Rumor had it that Tamara Burke's last visit here had done Che's mind more damage than her AK had his body. Slugs could be dug out; bones, eventually, healed. Love was another thing, and the wounds of betrayal bled forever, the lifeblood of Hell itself.

The lassitude of the rebel commander made conversation difficult, but answered Welch's most pressing questions: underlings had allowed this camp to grow so large, so cumbersone, so indefensible. Che was too smart for the kind of mistakes Welch had seen: for large quantities of civilian personnel, for women and children and possessions and immobility. The perfector of modern terrorism hadn't forgotten his own rules. He just didn't care any more.

And that bothered Welch. It could happen to him.

Humanity was caring, fighting against ridiculous odds—against death in life, against everything in afterlife.

Guevara only said, with a sigh, "Another gringo? What makes you so special?"

Welch thought, *Because I'm going to fry your ass, buddy, and from the look of you, I'll be doing you a favor. You've been waiting for someone like me for a long time now.* He said, "I've got some new equipment, that's all. They thought you should see it. I thought I had to sign up here, tell you my story, get your okay to stay."

It played, Hell's demons, it played. Guevara waved a hand at him as if the effort tired him beyond expression. "Go make what you can of your time, gringo. Don't expect me to validate you. Or invalidate you. Go."

You didn't give a guy you were about to incinerate a pep talk; you didn't engage in philosophical discussion with the enemy, except for the express purpose of extracting information. Welch got up, his questions not worth the risk he'd take by asking them, and then stopped at the tent flap and said, over his shoulder: "Mithridates sent me; when you're feeling better we'll talk about it."

It was a shot in the dark, a wild card, a thing he'd never have done if he hadn't so recently begun to wonder if he was losing his grip—if there hadn't been holes in his memory, the most important single attribute of the entity named Welch who'd been through the system so many times that his integrity was something totally separate from his Hell-revivified body.

"Tell Mithridates," said Guevara, coming up on one elbow, "that it will take more than arms and willing, walking corpses, this time. It will take proof of a way out of Hell."

Bingo. One point for intelligence collection. You poor bastard, if you had two working brain cells to rub together, you'd know you had your "proof" right in this camp. The fucking angel is washing your dishes and peel-

ing your potatoes. But you blew it, feeling sorry for yourself. Some guys really do deserve to be here.

Welch got out of there, before he said something he'd regret.

Letting the flap drop, he straightened up and saw the angel watching him, Caesarion at his side like a puppy. The angel was blond and this was the closest Welch had ever been to one. He fancied he could feel all sorts of things—peace, love, patience, compassion—emanating from the pale flesh of the messenger of God. Then he looked closer at Altos' companion, at the pimply, dark-haired youth with Caesar's stubborn chin, telling himself that if, out of everyone unjustly sent to Hell, the angel was concerning himself with this historical nonentity, it wasn't any better Up There than it was Down Here.

Anyway, here was where the action was. Welch could testify to that. He flicked a look at his wristwatch, pushed down on the stem to start the clock on fire and brimstone, and broke the silence, saying, "Come on, you two, I've got something to show you beyond those trees over there."

"Judah told us," said the angel in a voice like your father had.

"Just Al," rasped Caesarion in his spoilt-brat tone, "where are we going?"

"Nowhere, if you open your mouth again," said Welch before the angel could reply. "Come on, Judah knows what to do." Judah Maccabee should have had them out of camp by now; this was their patched-together fallback.

It would have to do. He hoped, walking as nonchalantly as he could manage with the angel and this Roman kid back the way he'd come, that Maccabee made it out.

They were looking at nineteen . . . no, eighteen minutes to firestorm, and Welch still had to get his charge through the camp, down the path, and beyond the trees to where Brutus, the living extraction beacon, ought to be waiting. He hitched his field phone up on his shoulder and hoped the sentry who'd captured him wasn't going to give him any more trouble. Of course, putting a 9mm through that slow brain wouldn't be murder, it would just be jumping the gun, so to speak—sending the sentry back to Slab A a little quicker than the rest of these.

When they'd cut across the camp and negotiated the path, Caesarion began to whine: "Where are we going, Just Al? Who *is* this guy?"

Welch slowed his pace until the kid and Altos were ahead of him, in case he had to knock the boy out or use his pistol. If he had to, he'd forward Caesarion to Caesar via the Undertaker instead of air mail. He was pumped full of adrenalin and wishing he had Nichols at his back and waiting for something to go wrong.

About the time they made the clearing, Welch could hear aircraft in the high sky, up above the clouds. Pretty soon there'd be other things to hear: whistling rockets and bomb impacts and napalm eating up the forest with its roar. He wanted to be airborne before that happened, and what he was listening for so that he took increasingly shallow breaths wasn't the sound of airplane props.

It was the sound of chopper blades.

Maccabee waved from the far side of the clearing, where he'd untied Brutus.

Caesarion saw the other boy and stopped dead in his tracks. "Just Al, what is this? Where are we going?" He crossed his fatigue-clad arms and his face reddened, two symmetrical blotches on either cheek.

Welch, still behind them, caught up so that he heard the angel say sadly, "Your lot, my son. For now. I'm sorry, but I must leave you."

"Leave me? You mean leave the Dissidents? But why? We were—"

"Leave you in Agent Welch's capable hands. You are not ready. Another time, perhaps."

The sadness in Altos' tone weighed on Welch as if a

truck had rolled over onto him. Then the angel regarded him with eyes as blue as the Med and Welch
realized that Altos knew him—exactly and precisely,
who and what he was. *Leave you in Agent Welch's capa-*
ble hands, Altos had said to Caesarion.

The implications were staggering. Welch said only,
"Look, get out of here, or we'll find out where your kind
goes when they get head-shot. Don't say anything else. I
don't want to hear it." It wouldn't be a pass out of here,
if Caesarion was to be left with him. "I'm dropping the
kid at Caesar's," he added as he grabbed with offhanded
precision for Caesarion's arm, twisted it around, and
prepared to frog-march the protesting youth across the
clearing to where a chopper, finally, was beginning to
put down out of low-hanging mists.

"As you wish," said the angel with the awful eyes,
who brushed past him, back toward the camp where a
scouring air strike was about to commence. "God bless,"
Altos added, the words tossed off as he strode away.

"Where the fuck you going, guy?" Welch called out,
though he shouldn't have. "Don't you know what's going
to happen there in . . . seven minutes?" That was what
his watch said: seven minutes.

The angel didn't stop, but he answered: "Of course I
do. But those poor souls need me."

And then there was no more time for suicidal visitors
with special perks, there was only time enough to hus-
tle Caesarion across the clearing, clap Maccabee on the
back, and struggle into the chopper against the gale of
its churning blades.

"You," said Achilles sourly as they came aboard and
Nichols secured the sliding door. "I shoulda' known
when they put me on emergency call."

Welch barely heard him: he and Nichols were hug-
ging each other and Welch was trying to explain that,
once he remembered what he was supposed to be doing
and got the alcohol out of his brain, he'd found some
strings to pull that Machiavelli'd never thought of.

Even in Hell, where there was a will, there was a way.

They flew a beeline back to New Hell, not because Welch had any qualms about the blazing camp and the carnage in his wake, but because it didn't matter if he saw the Dissident camp destroyed.

He was on the floor of the chopper with Nichols and Tanya, anyhow, talking about the drug interdiction to come and what kind of game they could run on Mao.

It was the work that mattered, and in Hell there was plenty of that.

COMPUTER BOOKS, TOO

We also publish the Pournelle Users Guide Series of computer books—reasonably priced guides to computing that are written, edited, selected or approved by Jerry Pournelle himself! Titles include The Guidebook for Winning Adventurers, Free Software!, Artificial Intelligence, and more. We are offering the Pournelle Users Guidebooks at the same great savings—buy at least two books, pay only half the total! Prices from $6.95 to $9.95.

AND THE BEST IN
SCIENCE FICTION SOFTWARE

Want quality software at a righteous price? How about TWO FOR THE PRICE OF ONE? We have games of all types, including BERSERKER RAIDS and WINGS OUT OF SHADOW, by SF superstar Fred Saberhagen, as well as fascinating utilities. Software for IBM, Apple, Commodore, Atari, and Tandy. Remember, just total the suggested retail prices of books and software, and send us a check for half that amount. No strings, no kidding!

If you know what you want, make your book selections from the following list and send it with a check or money order made out to Baen Publishing Enterprises at:

Baen Books
Book Club, Dept. B
260 5th Ave, Suite 3–S
New York, NY 10001
Tel. (212) 532-4111

Or, send three 22-cent stamps or one dollar for the whole Baen catalog. Either way, what a deal!

We'll take it from there. Please allow 72 hours for turn-around, and two to five weeks for the Post Office to do its thing.

ISBN #	Title # Author	Publ. List Price
55979-6	ACT OF GOD, Kotani and Roberts	2.95
55945-1	ACTIVE MEASURES, David Drake & Janet Morris	3.95
55970-2	THE ADOLESCENCE OF P-1, Thomas J. Ryan	2.95
55998-2	AFTER THE FLAMES, Silverberg & Spinrad	2.95
55967-2	AFTER WAR, Janet Morris	2.95
55934-6	ALIEN STARS, C.J. Cherryh, Joe Haldeman & Timothy Zahn, edited by Elizabeth Mitchell	2.95
55978-8	AT ANY PRICE, David Drake	3.50
65565-5	THE BABYLON GATE, Edward A. Byers	2.95
65586-8	THE BEST OF ROBERT SILVERBERG, Robert Silverberg	2.95
55977-X	BETWEEN THE STROKES OF NIGHT, Charles Sheffield	3.50
55984-2	BEYOND THE VEIL, Janet Morris	15.95
65544-2	BEYOND WIZARDWALL, Janet Morris	15.95
55973-7	BORROWED TIME, Alan Hruska	2.95
65563-9	A CHOICE OF DESTINIES, Melissa Scott	2.95
55960-5	COBRA, Timothy Zahn	2.95
55551-5	COBRA STRIKE!, Timothy Zahn	3.50
65578-7	A COMING OF AGE, Timothy Zahn	3.50
55969-9	THE CONTINENT OF LIES, James Morrow	2.95
55917-6	CUGEL'S SAGA, Jack Vance	3.50
65552-3	DEATHWISH WORLD, Reynolds and Ing	3.50
55995-8	THE DEVIL'S GAME, Poul Anderson	2.95
55974-5	DIASPORAH, W. R. Yates	2.95
65581-7	DINOSAUR BEACH, Keith Laumer	2.95
65579-5	THE DOOMSDAY EFFECT, Thomas Wren	2.95
65557-4	THE DREAM PALACE, Brynne Stephens	2.95
65564-7	THE DYING EARTH, Jack Vance	2.95
55988-5	FANGLITH, John Dalmas	2.95
55947-8	THE FALL OF WINTER, Jack C. Haldeman II	2.95
55975-3	FAR FRONTIERS, Volume III	2.95
65548-5	FAR FRONTIERS, Volume IV	2.95
65572-8	FAR FRONTIERS, Volume V	2.95
55900-1	FIRE TIME, Poul Anderson	2.95
65567-1	THE FIRST FAMILY, Patrick Tilley	3.50
55952-4	FIVE-TWELFTHS OF HEAVEN, Melissa Scott	2.95
55937-0	FLIGHT OF THE DRAGONFLY, Robert L. Forward	3.50
55986-9	THE FORTY-MINUTE WAR, Janet Morris	3.50
55971-0	FORWARD, Gordon R. Dickson	2.95
65550-7	THE FRANKENSTEIN PAPERS, Fred Saberhagen	3.50
55899-4	FRONTERA, Lewis Shiner	2.95
55918-4	THE GAME BEYOND, Melissa Scott	2.95
55959-1	THE GAME OF EMPIRE, Poul Anderson	3.50
65561-2	THE GATES OF HELL, Janet Morris	14.95
65566-3	GLADIATOR-AT-LAW, Pohl and Kornbluth	2.95
55904-4	THE GOLDEN PEOPLE, Fred Saberhagen	3.50
55555-8	HEROES IN HELL, Janet Morris	3.50
65571-X	HIGH JUSTICE, Jerry Pournelle	2.95

ISBN #	Title # Author	Publ. List Price
55930-3	HOTHOUSE, Brian Aldiss	2.95
55905-2	HOUR OF THE HORDE, Gordon R. Dickson	2.95
65547-7	THE IDENTITY MATRIX, Jack Chalker	2.95
65569-8	I, MARTHA ADAMS, Pauline Glen Winslow	3.95
55994-X	INVADERS, Gordon R. Dickson	2.95
55993-1	IN THE FACE OF MY ENEMY, Joe Delaney	2.95
65570-1	JOE MAUSER, MERCENARY, Reynolds and Banks	2.95
55931-1	KILLER, David Drake & Karl Edward Wagner	2.95
55996-6	KILLER STATION, Martin Caidin	3.50
65559-0	THE LAST DREAM, Gordon R. Dickson	2.95
55981-8	THE LIFESHIP, Dickson and Harrison	2.95
55980-X	THE LONG FORGETTING, Edward A. Byers	2.95
55992-3	THE LONG MYND, Edward Hughes	2.95
55997-4	MASTER OF SPACE AND TIME, Rudy Rucker	2.95
65573-6	MEDUSA, Janet and Chris Morris	3.50
65582-0	THE MESSIAH STONE, Martin Caidin	3.95
65580-9	MINDSPAN, Gordon R. Dickson	2.95
65553-1	THE ODYSSEUS SOLUTION, Banks and Lambe	2.95
55926-5	THE OTHER TIME, Mack Reynolds with Dean Ing	2.95
55965-6	THE PEACE WAR, Vernor Vinge	3.50
55982-6	PLAGUE OF DEMONS, Keith Laumer	2.75
55966-4	A PRINCESS OF CHAMELN, Cherry Wilder	2.95
65568-X	RANKS OF BRONZE, David Drake	3.50
65577-9	REBELS IN HELL, Janet Morris, et. al.	3.50
55990-7	RETIEF OF THE CDT, Keith Laumer	2.95
65556-6	RETIEF AND THE PANGALACTIC PAGEANT OF PULCHRITUDE, Keith Laumer	2.95
65575-2	RETIEF AND THE WARLORDS, Keith Laumer	2.95
55902-8	THE RETURN OF RETIEF, Keith Laumer	2.95
55991-5	RHIALTO THE MARVELLOUS, Jack Vance	3.50
65545-0	ROGUE BOLO, Keith Laumer	2.95
65554-X	SANDKINGS, George R.R. Martin	2.95
65546-9	SATURNALIA, Grant Callin	2.95
55989-3	SEARCH THE SKY, Pohl and Kornbluth	2.95
55914-1	SEVEN CONQUESTS, Poul Anderson	2.95
65574-4	SHARDS OF HONOR, Lois McMaster Bujold	2.95
55951-6	THE SHATTERED WORLD, Michael Reaves	3.50
	THE SILISTRA SERIES	
55915-X	RETURNING CREATION, Janet Morris	2.95
55919-2	THE GOLDEN SWORD, Janet Morris	2.95
55932-X	WIND FROM THE ABYSS, Janet Morris	2.95
55936-2	THE CARNELIAN THRONE, Janet Morris	2.95
65549-3	THE SINFUL ONES, Fritz Leiber	2.95
65558-2	THE STARCHILD TRILOGY, Pohl and Williamson	3.95
55999-0	STARSWARM, Brian Aldiss	2.95
55927-3	SURVIVAL!, Gordon R. Dickson	2.75
55938-9	THE TORCH OF HONOR, Roger Macbride Allen	2.95

SCIENCE FICTION AND FANTASY (continued)

ISBN #	Title # Author	Publ. List Price
55942-7	TROJAN ORBIT, Mack Reynolds with Dean Ing	2.95
55985-0	TUF VOYAGING, George R.R. Martin	15.95
55916-8	VALENTINA, Joseph H. Delaney & Marc Steigler	3.50
65898-6	WEB OF DARKENSS, Marion Zimmer Bradley	3.50
55925-7	WITH MERCY TOWARD NONE, Glen Cook	2.95
65576-0	WOLFBANE, Pohl and Kornbluth	2.95
55962-1	WOLFLING, Gordon R. Dickson	2.95
55987-7	YORATH THE WOLF, Cherry Wilder	2.95
55906-0	THE ZANZIBAR CAT, Joanna Russ	3.50

COMPUTER BOOKS AND GENERAL INTEREST NONFICTION

ISBN #	Title # Author	Publ. List Price
55968-0	ADVENTURES IN MICROLAND, Jerry Pournelle	9.95
55933-8	AI: HOW MACHINES THINK, F. David Peat	8.95
55922-2	THE ESSENTIAL USER'S GUIDE TO THE IBM PC, XT, AND PCjr., Dian Girard	6.95
55940-0	EUREKA FOR THE IBM PC AND PCjr, Tim Knight	7.95
55941-9	THE FUTURE OF FLIGHT, Leik Myrabo with Dean Ing	7.95
55955-9	THE GUIDEBOOK FOR WINNING ADVENTURERS, David & Sandy Small	8.95
55923-0	MUTUAL ASSURED SURVIVAL, Jerry Pournelle and Dean Ing	6.95
55929-X	PROGRAMMING LANGUAGES: FEATURING THE IBM PC, Marc Stiegler & Bob Hansen	9.95
55963-X	THE SERIOUS ASSEMBLER, Charles Crayne & Dian Girard Crayne	8.95
55907-9	THE SMALL BUSINESS COMPUTER TODAY AND TOMORROW, William E. Grieb, Jr.	6.95
55921-4	THE USER'S GUIDE TO CP/M SYSTEMS, Tony Bove & Cheryl Rhodes	8.95
55948-6	THE USER'S GUIDE TO FREE SOFTWARE, Tony Bove & Cheryl Rhodes	9.95
55908-7	THE USER'S GUIDE TO SMALL COMPUTERS, Jerry Pournelle	9.95